THE EDGE OF TRUTH

MICHAEL BRADY BOOK 5

MARK RICHARDS

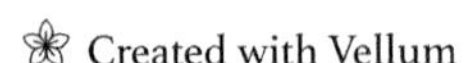
Created with Vellum

AUTHOR'S NOTE

Like all the Michael Brady books, *The Edge of Truth* is set in and around Whitby, on the North Yorkshire Coast.

As I'm British and the book is set in the UK, I've used British English. The dialogue is realistic for the characters, which means they occasionally swear.

As this is a work of fiction names, characters, organisations, some places, events and incidents are either products of the author's imagination or used fictionally. All the characters in this book are fictitious. Any resemblance to actual persons, living or dead, is purely coincidental.

www.markrichards.co.uk

1

RUNSWICK BAY:

SUNDAY NIGHT, SEPTEMBER 2016

The push that sent Diane Macdonald over the cliff edge was surprisingly gentle.

Almost apologetic...

"COME *ON*, Reggie. Let's go home. It's getting cold."

She pulled the zip of her jacket up, thought for the thousandth time that a holiday home in France would have been a far better idea and waited for the cocker spaniel to catch up.

"There, that wasn't so difficult was it?"

The dog looked at her expectantly. "Have a word with yourself, Reggie. You don't get a biscuit just for turning up. Maybe when we're home. And come on, the wind's getting stronger. And it's starting to rain."

She glanced to her left. The sea a long way out. "The first spring tide of the autumn, Reggie. Only in England would that make any sense. And it'll be a proper high tide at two in the morning."

She looked up. A retired couple walking towards her.

The man shook his head. “Every time,” he said. “It always starts to rain when you’re furthest from the van.” Diane smiled. Didn’t have time to reply before they were past her. Started to walk more quickly. “Is this it for the cliff top, Reggie? A week of rain and it’ll be a sea of mud. Back to the beach next time we come over. Rolling in a dead fish. Your favourite.”

Someone else coming towards her now. A man. Mid-forties? Younger? It was hard to tell with his collar turned up. His woollen hat pulled down low...

“Good evening,” she said, determined to speak first this time.

He looked up. Squinted at her despite the fading light. Spoke in an accent that was halfway between Newcastle and the Scottish lowlands. “Let’s hope so, love.”

A hot shower when she got home. A glass of wine. Turn the fire on. Finish watching *The Night Manager.*

The house to herself. Charlotte safely dropped off at the airport. Graham in Poland for another three days. Or was it Hungary? She’d stopped caring.

“And one job to do tomorrow morning, Reggie. Just the one job.”

‘He was brilliant, Diane. Bloody brilliant. And ruthless. Two-thirds of the fat bastard’s pension. The house in Tuscany. One mention of the *Sunday Mirror* and Roger came to heel like a whipped dog.’

The number was on her desk. First thing tomorrow. Coffee, slice of toast. And phone the solicitor.

‘Make the appointment, Diane. Start the ball rolling.’

“One fucking ‘researcher’ too many, my love,” she said out loud. “At least as far as the judge is concerned.”

She heard a noise. Looked up. A jogger now. “It’s like Piccadilly bloody Circus, Reggie. In the rain as well.”

Maybe she should call this one a runner. Going quickly for someone on the cliff top and two feet from the edge.

One of those fell runners? Away for one last summer weekend with his family?

Suddenly he stopped.

Twenty yards away.

Bent over.

Is there something wrong with him? Don't say he's having a heart attack. What can I remember from that first-aid course? Fifteen years ago. Not a bloody thing.

"Hello?" Diane said from five yards away. "Are you alright?"

The runner didn't speak. Bent even lower, hands on his knees.

Now Diane was next to him. "Are you alright?" she said again.

Still didn't speak. His breath was coming in gasps.

"Are you – "

He suddenly uncoiled.

Straightened up.

Much taller than she was.

Cropped blond hair. A black top.

His right hand darted forward. Grabbed the front of Diane's jacket.

What is this? Rape? On a muddy cliff top? Like hell it is.

Diane tensed. Prepared to fight.

Shouted. "Fuck off! Let go of me! Bastard!"

Instinctively pulled away.

Fell backwards over the leg he'd hooked behind her.

She flung a hand forward. Desperate for something to cling on to.

Felt something.

But it was gone.

And now the hand was pushing her.

'Quite gently,' she found herself thinking. 'Almost apologetic.'

But with enough force to send Diane Macdonald over the edge of the cliff. Her scream lost among the wind and rain, the cry of the gulls.

Reggie stood on the cliff edge and barked furiously.

The man with the black top and cropped blond hair ignored him.

Started running again.

Back the way he'd come.

2

Michael Brady locked the front door of the new house behind him. Looked across Whitby harbour, the early morning sun dancing off the water.

Autumn soon. Cold, crisp, clear mornings –

"Stop looking wistful, Dad."

"I'm not looking wistful, Ash."

"Yes, you are. You're gazing across the harbour and I'm supposed to think you're deep in thought. You're not. You're looking at Dave's. And I know what you're thinking, 'Have I time for a bacon sandwich between dropping Ash at school and getting into work?'"

"The thought hadn't crossed my mind."

"It's your birthday next month, Dad. I'm going to buy you a drone."

"A drone? What – "

"You can sit on the balcony in your pyjamas and fly your drone over to Dave's."

"Right across the harbour? You'd need a licence for that."

"Dad, you are Detective Chief Inspector Brady. If *you* can't get a licence no-one can. So fly your drone to Dave's. He can load it up with your bacon sandwich – "

"And coffee."

"It's a drone, Dad, not a jumbo jet. Dave can load it with your sandwich and you can fly it back."

Brady laughed. "Supposing the seagulls attack it?"

"Come on, Dad, we'll be late. I can't be late on the first day of the new term. There's a summer's worth of gossip to catch up on."

BRADY PULLED into the school lay-by.

"You got everything, sweetheart?"

"Too late if I haven't, Dad. Unless your drone's going to drop it off at morning break."

"First day of your GCSEs. Hope it goes well."

Ash sighed. "All first days are the same, Dad. Timetable. Double Maths last thing Friday afternoon. Disgusting stew for lunch. Welcome back, boys and girls. The prison canteen is open for business."

Brady laughed. Told her to have a good day. Told her he loved her. Watched her walk through the school gates, start talking to one of her friends.

Four more years. Two years of GCSEs. Two years of A-levels. And then I'll be taking her to university. Driving down a motorway with her...

"Did you mean it, Ash? When you said you wanted to study in America?"

'Yeah, I think so. There was a girl who used to be at the school. She came back and gave a talk. She went to Cambridge. Then she went to somewhere called MIT.'

Or to an airport...

Brady reached for his phone. Read the message a second time.

I'll be back on Friday night. I miss you, Michael Brady.

Two emojis. A face blowing a kiss. An emerald green heart.

I miss you too, Siobhan. And I never thought I'd say that again...

He checked the rear-view mirror. Checked it again. Waited for two girls far more interested in their phones than his reversing lights to walk past. Turned the car round. Glanced at the time. Reached forward and pressed *Frankie* on the car's phone display.

"I'm just on my way to Dave's. You want – "

"Yes, boss, I do. But you haven't time."

"Why not?"

"Because I was going to phone you. Because you're going to Runswick Bay. And you'll need your wellingtons."

"What's happened?"

"Two calls, boss. Within five minutes of each other."

"Tell me."

"A Mrs Stokes phones to say she hasn't seen her neighbour for twenty-four hours. And she hasn't heard the dog. And the paper's still in the letterbox. And five minutes later we get another call. Much younger than Mrs Stokes... To say there's a body on the beach."

"Oh shit."

"No, boss. Whatever comes after 'oh shit.' The neighbour she's worried about is Diane Macdonald. Graham Macdonald's wife."

"Graham Macdonald? The MP Graham Macdonald?"

Who grew up in Whitby? Who was in Robin Hood's Bay on Christmas Eve twenty-five years ago?

Brady saw the flashing blue lights. The Astra crushed against the tree. John Clayton lying on the ground...

"*That* Graham Macdonald?"

"*That* Graham Macdonald, boss. Who has a holiday home in Runswick Bay. Whose wife was apparently walking on the cliff. And who is now lying on the rocks at the bottom of the cliff."

"She's dead?"

"Very dead."

"Who found her? The proverbial dog walker?"

"A young couple. And from what they said... Well, you'll see for yourself."

"Where's Macdonald?"

"Hungary, apparently."

"Hungary? What the hell's he doing in Hungary?"

"Some parliamentary mission. Trade, I think..."

Brady knew the answer before he asked the question. "Has anyone told him?"

No. That would be your job Detective Chief Inspector.

An MP's wife. Fuck. And Kershaw will need to know. He'll be all over this like a rash. What did he say last time I spoke to him? 'Whitby's had its excitement for this year.'

I bloody well hope so...

3

Brady picked his way carefully across the rocks.

Very carefully.

Summer holidays when I was a teenager. I'd run across these rocks. Sure footed. Nimble. Agile. Now all I can think about is falling. Hearing the crack from my middle-aged ankle...

Finally reached the end. Stepped onto the beach. Suppressed a sigh of relief.

Looked up.

Saw the body.

The privileges of rank. Or celebrity. Joe Average falls down a cliff, a uniform checks he's dead and we winch him away. An MP's wife – assuming it is an MP's wife – and it's the boss tip-toeing across the rocks. The cavalry standing round the body...

Frankie and Geoff looking down at her.

Jake Cartwright 20 yards away, talking to a teenage couple. And holding a makeshift orange lead. With a chocolate cocker spaniel on the end of it.

Brady glanced at the body, told Frankie he'd be with her in a minute and walked across to Jake and the teenagers.

The girl had a blanket round her shoulders, visibly shivering.

And not from the cold...

"Good morning." Brady glanced down. Couldn't help smiling. "And who's this?"

"His name's Reggie," Jake said. "That's what it says on his dog tag anyway."

The dog was whining quietly. Brady bent down, tilted Reggie's head up. Looked into his brown eyes. Ruffled his head. "Hello, mate, how are you doing? Christ, Jake, he's wet. Has he been in the sea? Here – " He rummaged in his pocket. Found a dog biscuit. "Here, it's all I've got left. Not much of a breakfast for you."

He straightened up. Held his hand out. "Sorry, I've got the bigger version at home. I'm Michael Brady. Detective Chief Inspector. I'm guessing you found the body? And Reggie?"

The girl nodded. Nervously shook hands.

Long dark hair. A yellow and white top. Ripped jeans. Three or four inches of midriff showing.

Bloody hell, she's barely older than Ash.

She shivered, pulled the blanket round herself more tightly.

"Ali Osmond," she said. "And Connor. Connor Murray."

A check shirt over a black T-shirt. Long hair. The beginnings of a beard. Ridiculously good-looking.

"You want to tell me the story?" Brady said.

Ali shivered again. Brady looked at her. Saw his own daughter even more clearly. Took his jacket off. "Here. Put that on. This won't take long. Then we'll get you home."

"We were at a party," Connor said.

"On a Monday night?"

"A friend's. In Runswick. His parents are away."

And what did you tell your mum and dad, Ali? A sleepover at a friend's house?

"We couldn't sleep. So we thought – "

"We'd come out for a walk," Ali said. "See the sunrise. Connor checked the time on his phone. Except we'd missed it. Not by much – "

"What time is sunrise?"

"Quarter past six."

Brady looked at the blanket. Tried not to imagine Ash 'seeing the sunrise' with a teenage Mr Darcy.

He gestured behind him. "You came across the rocks?"

Ali shook her head. "Down the path."

Brady looked at the cliffs. "What path?"

"Just up there? About a hundred metres? There's a path you can walk down. Well, if you're careful. It's a bit slippery right now."

"So you come down the path. Walk over here. Then what?"

Connor shook his head. "We heard a noise. About halfway down. Just – " He gestured at Reggie. "Whining. The noise he's making now. He was stuck. Trying to get down to the beach. I managed to reach him."

"Thank you," Brady said. "Then the three of you were on the beach?"

"Yes. And he ran off. Ran away from us. Then we saw what he was running towards. Just a shape – "

"I thought... At first... We couldn't see much because of the sun. I thought it was a seal that had been washed ashore."

"And then we saw her," Connor said. "And the dog. He was going mad. Ali found the rope by the rocks. Tangled up with a lobster pot. So I made the lead. I thought... Well, I don't know what I thought. I just didn't think it was a good idea if he disturbed the body."

Brady looked at him. Sent a small prayer that Ash's first serious boyfriend would be as responsible as Connor Murray.

"You've done a good job," Brady said. "A really good job. One question. You didn't touch her? Disturb her in any way?"

Ali shook her head. "No way. It's like a horror film isn't it? There's no way we were going to touch her. The dog did. But not us."

"So you phoned?"

Connor nodded. "We didn't think we'd get a signal under the cliffs."

"But you did. Thank you. I'm sorry this happened to you. The best thing you can do now is get yourselves home. Get warm."

Try and come up with a story your parents will believe. But I'll happily give you a character reference.

"I'll sort out a car for you. And we'll need to talk to you again. Official statements and so on."

Connor nodded. Put his arm tentatively round Ali. Looked at Brady. "Who was she? Someone important? It's just... There's a lot of you. And you look worried."

Brady smiled. Shook his head. "I can't tell you. And I'm in charge. So I always look worried. But get yourselves home now. And one other thing. You wouldn't be human if you didn't take photos. But she's got a family. She could be your mum. You're good kids. Keep them to yourselves will you?"

They nodded. Turned to go. "Ali," Brady said. "One other thing. Can I have my jacket back?"

She laughed. Pushed a stray lock of hair back behind her ear.

The same gesture as Ash...

"Sorry. I'd got used to it."

4

She was lying on a rock. Jacket ripped, jeans ripped, right leg bent behind her at an impossible angle. Left hand resting on another rock, the wrist visibly broken. Right arm flung out behind her, only the top half visible as it disappeared into a rock pool. Head resting on a third rock –

Exactly like a pillow...

– turned sharply to one side, hair still wet from the high tide, mouth open, eyes open.

No. One eye open.

One eye missing.

Diane Macdonald didn't have a left eye. A socket. A thin trickle of blood. Trailing fibres of flesh.

Cartilage? Sinew? Ligament? What the hell holds your eye in place?

"This is one you'll see at three in the morning, boss."

Brady nodded. "What don't I see at three in the morning, Frankie? She'll need to queue up though. Becky Kennedy, Billy and Sandra Garrity... There's plenty in front of her. We're sure are we?"

Geoff nodded. "I met her, Mike. Wife took me along to a Macmillan charity do. Shook hands, talked for a couple of minutes. Even without – " He gestured at the missing eye. "Even with that it's still Diane Macdonald."

"Are we back in Gina Foster territory, boss? Is that why we're all here?"

Brady looked up at the cliff. "Statistically she fell, Frankie. Unlikely, but a lot more likely than anything else. And those two teenagers said it was slippery."

"Only since yesterday, Mike."

Brady looked at the pathologist. "What are you saying, Geoff."

"I'm saying she's been here longer than last night. I'll confirm it for you but my guess is she's been here since Sunday night."

"You're saying she's been here for thirty-six hours? Her dog's here, Geoff." Brady shook his head. "Someone would have heard him barking."

"Maybe not, boss. It started raining Sunday night. Didn't stop 'til Monday night. There's a fair chance no-one walked on the cliffs yesterday. And even if they did – poor little dog can't bark all day."

"Bloody hell, no wonder he's wet."

Brady looked around. Couldn't see anything. Did the only logical thing.

Took his jacket off. Handed it to Frankie. Took his jumper off. "Jake! Here. And bring your mate... Here." He handed Jake Cartwright his jumper. "Rub him down with that. Then wrap it round him. Keep him warm."

"Boss, it's your – "

"Just do it, Jake. Rub him down. Keep him warm."

Brady put his jacket back on. Zipped it up. Felt the wind off the sea. Shivered. Caught Frankie looking at him. "It was a present from Grace," he said. "I didn't have the courage to tell her I didn't like it. Where were we? An MP's wife. So the answer's 'yes,' Frankie. I want the answers before Kershaw asks the questions. Geoff, what do you think? Apart from Sunday night."

The pathologist shook his head. "Not the way I'd choose to go, Mike."

Brady looked at the cliff a second time. Nodded. "She must have been rolling, Geoff. Trying to grab hold of something – "

"Assuming she's conscious."

"Will you be able to tell? Scratches on her hands? If she's conscious she'll grab at anything."

"Maybe. But I hope for her sake she wasn't conscious, Mike. Because if she was conscious she had hope. 'I can survive this. I won't die.' And then she goes over the edge. Twenty feet. Twenty-five. Straight onto the rocks."

"And the dog follows her as far as he can. Then he gets stuck."

"And he stays with her all night. All the next day. There's loyalty. What's he called?"

"Reggie."

Geoff laughed. "Right. Let's hope he doesn't have a twin. Otherwise we're all in trouble."

"Reggie, boss. What are we going to do with him?"

Brady turned round. Jake Cartwright was still holding the dog's lead. Brady's jumper was over Reggie's back, the sleeves tied underneath him.

Brady shook his head. "Three sizes too big... We'll wait for his owner to turn up, Jake. But seeing as he's in Hungary, that's not going to be any time soon. So take him back to the station I suppose. Can I leave that with you? Here." Brady fished in his pocket, handed Jake a five pound note. "Stop on the way. Buy some dog food."

"Supposing he won't leave, boss?"

Would Archie do that? Stay with me if I'd fallen? Refuse to go? Yes, he would.

"Good point. Don't distress him. Geoff, you're going to stay with the body until someone gets here? We're going to need the chopper. In that case, Jake, you and Reggie wait with Geoff. Then take him to the station. Two things. Don't touch his collar. Get it checked for prints back at the station. A hundred to one but so is falling off a cliff. So first job, Jake."

"What's the second one, boss?"

"Buy some poo bags. Just in case. Wouldn't be a good look if one of us got arrested. And Jake – "

"Boss?"

"When you're sure Reggie's warm and dry... Throw the jumper away. It doesn't suit him."

5

"Come on, Frankie. Let's go."

"Where, boss?"

Brady gestured to his right. "If those two can come down it, we can go up, slippery or not. And slowly in my case. But let's have a look from the top. Like I said, I want the answers before Kershaw asks the questions."

BRADY STOOD on the cliff top, Frankie next to him. Tried to get his breathing under control. Failed.

"I used to run up the steps to the churchyard when I was a teenager. Bloody hell..."

"A lot easier going up than coming down..."

"Less risk of injury. Bloody hell..."

"You've just said that, boss."

Brady looked down. Saw Geoff and Jake still standing over the body. "What do you think, Frankie? Straight down. Or..."

Couldn't get an image out of his head.

Those Penny Falls machines in the seafront arcades. Drop

your penny, watch it bounce. Everywhere but where you wanted it.

Diane Macdonald, bouncing down the cliff...

"What do you think, Frankie? She could go over the edge twenty, thirty yards either side of here?"

"You *are* treating this as suspicious, boss."

Brady shook his head. "I'm not. Like I said to you on the beach. Before I had a cardiac arrest climbing the cliff. Accident is more likely. A hundred times more likely. But it's not Mrs Average down there on the rocks. So if there *is* anything, let's find it. Before it rains again. Before half a dozen ramblers stand here drinking tea and admiring the view."

"There's some grass flattened down over here," Frankie said five minutes later.

"There's some grass flattened down over here as well. But what is it, Frankie? Diane Macdonald fighting for her life or someone watching the sunrise? Standing here with their iPhone taking photos? We both know which is more likely." Brady shook his head. "Come on, let's get back. I'll send Dan Keillor out to do a search, But I've a phone call to make."

'HAS ANYONE TOLD HIM?'

No. That would be your job Detective Chief Inspector.

When was the last time I saw him? Five years ago? Six? That drugs conference. A suit straining under the weight of yet another official reception. A big, belligerent face. One that dared you to contradict him. Even more arrogant than he was at eighteen...

"Phone his office at Westminster, Sue. That's as good a starting point as any."

She came back to him ten minutes later. "Boss? I did

that. They told me to phone the British Embassy in Budapest. I did that as well. He's in a meeting apparently. Some trade delegation. Something to do with defence."

Brady nodded. "And they said he was too important to disturb? It never changes, Sue. Just get me through to whoever you were speaking to."

"Inspector Blakey, I have already explained to your secretary – "

"It's Brady. And I need to speak to Graham Macdonald. Or MacDougall as he's probably known to you."

"Really, there's no need to be facetious, Inspector. Could you tell me what it's about?"

"I could, but I don't think that would be appropriate. But whatever he's doing now, this is more important."

"I can assure you that nothing – "

"His – " Brady stopped himself just in time. "Please. I'm phoning from North Yorkshire. Where he has a holiday home."

Surely to God he'll realise something's happened...

"Very well. Let me take your number. He's a *very* busy man. That's the best I can do."

Brady looked at his watch. Nine-thirty. Reached for his pad. Started to make notes.

You're treating it as suspicious. You can't help yourself...

Waited for Graham Macdonald to ring...

...HAD TO WAIT THREE HOURS.

"Detective Chief Inspector Brady." Macdonald had never had a Whitby accent.

Where's his constituency? Hampshire. About as far from North Yorkshire as it's possible to get.

"To what do I owe the pleasure of being dragged away from an important meeting?"

Dragged away? It's taken you three hours...

"Mr Macdonald, I – "

"Call me Graham. We may not be old friends but we go back a few years."

So we do. Right back to you running away as Lizzie Greenbeck lay dying.

"And if it's a problem with the house in Runswick surely my wife can deal with it."

"Graham. There is no simple way to tell you this – "

Exactly the words I said to Clare Bailey. My role in life. Phone people. Tell them someone they love is dead.

" – But I'm really sorry to tell you that your wife is dead."

There was no reply. Brady heard the noise of heels clicking on a wooden floor.

Parquet flooring in the Embassy...

The heels stopped. Retreated. Brady saw the hand signal. *'Not now. I'm busy.'*

"When?"

"We think Sunday night. Although her body wasn't discovered until this morning. I'm truly sorry – "

"How did she die?"

Matter-of-fact. A man who simply wants the information.

"Our assumption is that your wife had a fall while she was walking the dog. Her body was found at the foot of the cliffs."

Another long silence.

Why is this reminding me of Kershaw? I can hear the calculations.

"Thank you, Michael. Thank you for telling me."

The heels were back.

Not stopping this time. Someone standing next to him.

"You'll be flying straight back I assume?"

"What? No, I can't. I have commitments. Obligations. Our delegation doesn't fly back until the weekend."

"Is there anyone else you'd like me to contact for you?"

"No. Our daughter is away. Italy. Something to do with her degree. No, just do what you have to do. I'll be back by Sunday. No, I'll speak to Charlotte."

'Reggie, boss. What are we going to do with him?'

"One other question, Graham. What do you want us to do about Reggie?"

"Reggie?"

"Your dog, Graham."

"The dog? I don't know. Christ Almighty, I'm part of a Government delegation. I can't be worrying about a dog."

"He's here at the station..."

"Well stick him in bloody kennels or something. Phone the dog warden. You must have a bloody procedure. I can't waste time on a dog for God's sake."

Brady put the phone down. Reflected on a man who didn't seem to care about his wife. Or his dog.

6

"Anything exciting happen on the first day of school, Ash?"

His daughter looked up briefly from her phone. "Vicky Dolan," she said.

"Vicky Dolan? Is she the one – "

"Yes, Dad. The one all the middle-aged men can't stop looking at on Parents' Evening."

"What's happened to her?"

"She's not coming back. At least not this term. She's pregnant."

"Pregnant? She's the same age as you."

"Duh, Dad, seeing as she's in my year. Technically she's older. Her birthday's in September. So she's fifteen. Just."

Brady shook his head. "How the hell did she get pregnant?"

"Aren't you supposed to tell me that, Dad? Birds and bees and all that? Good job there's the internet..."

"You know what I mean, Ash. What about your GCSEs? Lessons. Did you get double Maths last thing on Friday?"

"No. We escaped, thank God. No, nothing happened. I have to go again tomorrow, though..."

Brady laughed. "Not for much longer, sweetheart."

"Four years? Four years is an eternity, Dad. It's like... a quarter of my life. Oh, I'm away at the weekend. We're playing hockey somewhere in the Arctic Circle. Near Middlesbrough. I'll probably stay with Jess on Friday seeing as we need to leave before it's even daylight. So I won't be here if Siobhan comes round for – "

Brady's daughter smiled at him. Made an inverted commas sign in the air. " – Spaghetti Bolognese."

Brady hesitated. Wondered if he should risk asking.

"Do you like her, Ash?"

"I'm not dating her, Dad."

"You know what I mean."

"You said that thirty seconds ago, Dad."

Ash, I love you with every breath in my body. But why are you so deliberately bloody obtuse at times?

"Allow me to re-phrase the question, m' lud. Do you like her, seeing as your dad sees her occasionally? *Very* occasionally."

"Yes, she's alright. I don't really know her. She mostly comes round when I'm out, doesn't she? But yeah, she's alright. We haven't really talked."

"Would you like to?"

"Talk? You mean would I like to be formally introduced? That all sounds a bit *Pride and Prejudice*, Dad. And it's a bit late, you've been seeing her since May. Anyway, I'm needed upstairs. A boy's – "

Should I ask her this?

"Ash, before you disappear. Do you know a girl called Ali Osmond? Or a boy called Connor Murray?"

Ash shook her head. "They're not at school if that's what you mean. Sixth form college maybe? Why?"

"No, nothing. They're maybe a couple of years older than you. Sorry, you sound like it's something important. Homework?"

"Way more important than homework, Dad. A boy's asked Jess to go out with him. We need to make a decision."

7

Brady stood outside the neighbours' house.

'Mrs Stokes phoned to say she hasn't seen her neighbour for twenty-four hours. She hasn't heard the dog. The paper's still in the letterbox.'

Glanced to his right. The paper was still in the letterbox.

A well-tended hedge, a drive sloping down to the garage. A pond in the front garden, a solar powered pump waiting patiently for the clouds to part.

Brady looked through a window. Found he could see straight through the house. A dining table, stylish glass doors behind it. A conservatory leading onto the back garden. A settee, coffee table, a running machine standing incongruously in a corner.

He walked down the path. Reached his hand out. The door opened before he could press the bell. Face-to-face with a man in his late 40s. Good-looking. Close-cropped brown hair, a beard. Intense, pale blue eyes. Faded jeans, a dark blue sweatshirt, a grey bodywarmer with a hundred pockets, a black and grey backpack over one shoulder –

The size you take up a mountain...

– What Brady assumed was a camera case over the other.

"Mr Stokes? Michael Brady."

He nodded. Held his hand out. "Cam Stokes. The late Cam Stokes. Very late. And you're going to have to excuse me, Inspector. Detective. Whatever I call you. I need to be in Durham. Time, tide and the ten-seventeen to Edinburgh Waverley wait for no man. Maggie's just finishing in the bathroom. She says wait in the kitchen. Make yourself a coffee."

The slightest hint of a Scottish accent. Someone who moved south at an early age.

"Thank you. Safe trip." Brady smiled. "And remember the speed cameras when you're out of North Yorkshire."

Stokes nodded. "The story of my life." He hesitated.

A man who needs to say something...

"Don't keep her too long, will you? She's tired this morning."

CAM STOKES WALKED across the road to an Audi Q2. Laid the camera case on the passenger seat. Opened a rear door. Threw the mountain backpack inside. Brady stepped into the hall.

No sign of Maggie...

Found himself looking at some of the best wildlife pictures he'd ever seen.

Some very clearly taken around Whitby. Some in what looked like the Scottish Highlands. Half a dozen penguins in Antarctica, somehow looking like a group of men gossiping about football. An iceberg in the background towering over them.

Brady moved on to the next one. A door opened. Maggie appeared.

"He's good isn't he?"

He was right. She does look tired. A woman who's been reading her book at one, watching TV at two and playing solitaire at three.

"They're by your husband?" Brady said. "He's not good. He's... I don't know. I don't know enough about photography. It's landscape, but every picture tells a story."

She laughed. "Rod Stewart? Stop it. You'll make me feel old."

Brady smiled. "You and me both, Mrs Stokes." He nodded at a picture.

"This one. It's..."

"A cormorant."

He laughed. "Thank you. My knowledge of birds is next to nil. Not even that high. I'm walking the dog on the beach, I see something that's not a seagull. I've no idea. The same on the Moors. Hawks, kestrels... I'm clueless. But it's not the bird..."

The cormorant was flying vertically. The sea below it, the outline of a cliff in the background. Jet black, neck and beak extended, its wings spread.

"...It's the symmetry. The precision. It's a bird but it's not a bird. It's got purpose. Focus. This sounds stupid. Your husband's made it look like a stealth bomber. A prototype someone shouldn't have spotted."

She pursed her lips. Looked half quizzical, half amused. "That's very eloquent, Mr Brady. Did you once arrest an art critic?"

Brady laughed. "No. I had a rather more down-to-earth clientele. But I know what I like." He held his hand out. "And my apologies. Now we've covered music and art I should probably introduce myself. Detective Chief Inspector Michael Brady. Thank you for seeing me."

"My pleasure, Inspector. Albeit in unpleasant circumstances."

Mid to late forties. Hair that was just holding on to blonde. A broad, strong face. A wide smile. Brown glasses pushed down so she could peer over the top of them. A well-worn Newcastle University sweatshirt.

A handsome woman. In the old-fashioned sense of the word.

But a face that was lined as well. That had accepted some pain. Some harsh truths.

"Let me make some tea. Or coffee."

Brady followed her down the hall. Checked himself as she stopped and put a hand on the wall. Started walking again. "I thought we'd talk in the kitchen if that's alright with you." She gestured for Brady to sit down at the table. "Which would you prefer?"

"Coffee's fine, Mrs Stokes. Thank you."

"Milk? Sugar? And Maggie, please. I'm not quite ready for Mrs Stokes yet." She raised her eyebrows. Looked resigned. "Or for 'Maggie' in that special tone of voice reserved for the infirm."

She opened a cupboard door. Found the coffee jar. Brady watched her struggle with the lid. Try to hide her frustration.

How long should I wait? 'Reserved for the infirm.' Not long...

"Would you like me to help?"

She nodded, passed him the coffee jar. "Would you mind? It's a new jar. I have arthritis in my hands. Quite what I've done to deserve it at forty-seven I have no idea." She shrugged. "But who said life was fair?"

Brady was about to say there was a gadget for opening

jars. Sensed she knew all about gadgets for opening jars. That it wasn't a bridge she wanted to cross.

"Would you like me to make the coffee?"

"No, no. You're fine. It's just the new jars I struggle with." She smiled. "And books of stamps. Not many people get Christmas cards."

She put the coffee down in front of Brady. Sat down opposite him. Looked straight at him. Pale grey eyes.

Eyes that remind me of Frankie. A woman who wouldn't panic when the wagon train was surrounded. Who'd tell her children to lie down. And then reach for a rifle...

"You reported Diane Macdonald missing."

She nodded. "I did."

"May I ask why?"

"The answer is simple, Inspector. Light. Or the lack of light."

"From the house?"

"I walked out into the garden. I wanted some fresh air before I went to bed. Glanced next door. Diane wasn't a woman who went to bed early. But there were no lights on."

"But you didn't report her missing then?"

"No." She shrugged. "We're all entitled to an early night once in a while. And Diane sometimes suffered from migraines."

"But there was no light the following morning?"

"More importantly there was no noise from Reggie. I waited for a civilised hour – just after eight – and knocked on the door. That was always enough to bring Reggie to the door. He's an excitable little thing. But nothing. And the house 'felt' empty. The knock echoed. I'm sorry, that sounds stupid."

Brady shook his head. "No. I know exactly what you mean."

Darren Kidby's flat. Three knocks echoing round an empty flat. A week later he's confessing to a murder he didn't commit...

"No," Brady said again. "I do know what you mean. So you reported her missing?"

"I did. And events took their course."

Brady nodded. "Procedure, yes. Can I ask you some background questions about Diane?"

She nodded. "Of course. And the first one is do I think she committed suicide..."

Brady smiled. "I wasn't going to be so blunt but, essentially, yes. Was she happy? Did you know of any problems in her life? What was she like as a person?"

Maggie Stokes finished her coffee. Weighed her answer. "I think so to the first one. We were neighbours, not friends. So no to the second one. And what was she like? Intelligent. Slightly unfulfilled maybe? But I'm speculating again."

"The night you reported her missing. There was just you in the house?"

She smiled.

A tired smile...

"There's very frequently just me in the house. Cam travels a lot. He's a cameraman. Cam the cameraman. Our own version of *Happy Families*. And a photographer, obviously."

"The pictures in the hall?"

"The pictures all over the house. Bluntly, Inspector, I can't even have a pee without a bloody moose staring at me."

Brady laughed. "Not in Whitby then?"

"Not in the slightest. I tell him he's too old for Siberia. Canada. The Antarctic. But it's always 'just one more trip.' Northumberland last week. Lindisfarne. Now it's the

Western Isles for a fortnight. Or until the director's satisfied."

"Children?"

She shook her head. "We both wanted to travel. Both had careers we wanted to pursue. So no. Friends, extended family. But no children."

"I have a daughter. She tells me she wants to travel. Backpack round the Far East. Study in America. Be a human rights lawyer."

"Leaving you on your own? I read about your wife. I suspect most of Whitby has read about your wife. I'm sorry."

Brady nodded. Was surprised by how much he liked her. "Thank you. If it's not a rude question, Maggie... What do you do? You sound like someone with a lot of free time."

"Now? I read, mostly. I walk on the cliffs. Down to the beach. But if your real question is 'what *did* I do?' then I was a historian. Women in Medieval England."

Brady smiled. "I have a colleague whose partner – "

Is that the first time I've said it? The first time I've acknowledged that Frankie has a partner?

" – is a historian. A museum curator. Specialising in witchcraft apparently."

She nodded. "Lochie McRae? I know him. And not just witches. Folklore. He's very good. Very knowledgeable. Wasted at the Folk Museum in my opinion. He should be at a university somewhere." She stopped. Shook her head. "That's wrong of me. Strike that from the record, Inspector. Who am I to judge other people?"

"So you're retired now?"

She nodded. "Retired from teaching. Lecturing." She held her hands up. "The unfairness of life. I couldn't work anymore. But my aunt conveniently died. Her only child had died at a young age. So I'm free to pursue my heroine."

"Who's that?"

"Aethelflaed, the – "

"The Lady of the Mercians? I saw her described as Britain's greatest military commander."

Maggie Stokes raised her eyebrows. "I'm impressed. Very few people have heard of her. But they were right. At least in my opinion. The daughter of Alfred the Great. She saw off the Vikings and more or less unified England."

Brady looked at her again. Not a trace of make-up. A square, determined jaw.

I can imagine that, Maggie. The warrior queen in her chariot...

8

"Mike? Come down will you? Whatever you're doing, this is more important."

Brady closed Google, stopped reading about the House of Commons Defence Select Committee –

For this relief much thanks, Geoff...

– and walked down to the underworld. Pushed the door open.

Smelled the familiar mix of chemicals and death. Saw Diane Macdonald's white, naked body on the table.

Geoff Oldroyd bending over it. Holding her right hand.

He looked up. "So what killed her, Mike?"

Brady raised his eyebrows. "I thought you told me, Geoff? I thought that was how it worked?"

"Humour me? What killed her?"

"The fall. One hundred feet down a cliff and it has to be the fall. Except that – "

"Except that I wouldn't be asking the question if it was the fall. No, I wouldn't. She drowned, Mike."

"Drowned? You're saying she survived the fall?"

Geoff nodded. "I'm saying she's got enough broken

bones to keep a dozen orthopaedic surgeons working overtime. But cause of death? Drowning. Her lungs are full of the North Sea."

"So she lay on the rocks..."

Geoff Oldroyd nodded. "Yes. The unfortunate Mrs Macdonald lay on the rocks unable to move – her back's broken – and the tide came in."

"Was she conscious?"

"Hard to say. There's a few scratches on her hands. Drifting in and out of consciousness if you want me to guess. Would she realise she was drowning? Yes, probably."

Brady gestured at her head. At where Diane Macdonald's left eye had been. "Tell me she wasn't alive when that happened."

Geoff nodded. "My guess is no. If only because of the time of day. Seagulls don't see well in the dark. So some time on Monday is more likely. Before our young lovers turned up with their hormones and their blanket."

"But it could have happened while she was alive? That must be a first, even for Whitby."

"Maybe. But it won't be the last. I was at a conference once. Got talking to a guy from the States. Ohio. Up near Lake Erie. He was telling me how much he admired seagulls. 'Very intelligent, Geoff. Highly aggressive. Opportunistic.' Doesn't – "

"Aggressive? Opportunistic? What's Kershaw got to do with it?"

"Very droll, Michael. 'It doesn't matter what environment they're in,' he said. 'Seagulls are always successful.' And then he gave me the details."

"Which you're going to share, on the off-chance I haven't digested my bacon sandwich."

Geoff laughed. “Would I do that to you, Mike? I thought I had you with Becky Kennedy’s bones though.”

“Bloody nearly…”

“So my American pal tells me about a new strategy seagulls have. Been seen in a few different locations. They’re attacking seal pups, especially new-born ones. And they’re eating their eyeballs. Any soft tissue they can find.”

“Diane Macdonald is a long way from a seal pup, Geoff.”

“She is, Mike. But she’s lying on the rocks. Unconscious or semi-conscious. Drifting between the two. Would gulls investigate? Yes, they would. But like I say, I think it happened post-mortem. If only because of the light.”

Brady shook his head. “It’s a hell of a way to go, Geoff. The tide and the seagulls. It’s all a bit *Game of Thrones*.”

Geoff looked up at him. “Prometheus if we’re getting literary? Chained to a rock and had his liver pecked out every day? Not by a seagull, I grant you.”

“Could she just have had a blackout, Geoff? I spoke to her neighbour. She said Diane suffered from migraines.”

“In theory? Maybe. In practice? Anne gets migraines. And she always gets a warning. Flashing lights, something like that. So the last thing she’d do is walk on the cliff.”

Geoff shook his head. Sighed. “Leave me to it, Mike. If there’s anything, I’ll find it. Just thought you should know about the drowning. Give me another couple of hours. Then I’ll bring you up to date. Is that lovely daughter of yours playing hockey after school?”

“She is, Geoff. And then she’s going to her friend’s.”

“Your rock star girlfriend, Mr Brady?”

“She’s in London until Friday.”

“So the planets are in line. I’ll present my report in the Black Horse.”

Brady laughed. "Normal fee?"

"Of course. Except my son tells me I should be drinking IPA. 'More fashionable, Dad.'" Geoff shook his head. Sighed. "And I thought I'd done a decent job of bringing him up..."

9

"You got a minute, Frankie? Come through will you? Close the door. Let's just keep this between ourselves for the time being."

"What's happened, boss?"

"Diane Macdonald. The poor bloody woman didn't die from the fall. She drowned."

Frankie winced. "Are you saying she lay there all night? All through Monday?"

"'Her lungs were full of the North Sea.' Those were Geoff's exact words. So yes, I think I am. Sunset was at seven-forty. Still light but it's fading fast. So let's say she falls somewhere between seven and seven-thirty. High tide was at one-thirty in the morning."

"Six hours..."

Brady nodded. Hesitated. "You said it, Frankie. Are we back in Gina Foster territory? Asking the same question?"

She sighed. Brought her left hand up. Traced a finger along a silver chain round her neck. "I don't know. But you're right. It's the same question. Why do we fall on a path we've walked a hundred times?"

Brady pulled the keyboard towards him. Tapped the query into Google. Read the replies. "Last year," he said. "Dorset woman cheats death. Then... Five years ago. Man has miracle escape. High winds near Scarborough."

"So people do fall off cliff top paths. Just not very often."

"Maybe it's more common... Maybe the miracle escapes get more hits. But the guy at Scarborough was a holiday-maker. Diane Macdonald must've known that path like the back of her hand. Even if the light was fading."

"What do you want to do, boss?"

"For now? Nothing. Have a pint with Geoff after work. He said he needed a couple more hours with her. Let's see what he comes up with."

"Boss..."

"What?"

"The fall or drowning. From our point of view it doesn't matter."

Brady nodded. "No. The end result's the same. But from Diane Macdonald's... I don't know about Gina Foster, Frankie. We're back with Billy Garrity. Someone taking forever to die. And with a bloody seagull tapping its fingers impatiently..."

"WHERE WERE WE, MIKE?"

"Drowning, Geoff. The fall didn't kill her, drowning did. Seagulls and soft tissue. And if you want me to be specific, you were holding her right hand."

Geoff nodded. Sipped his pint of Doom Bar. "She stumbled over the cliff edge. Half fell, half rolled. Then suddenly there's twenty-five feet of sheer cliff, she's over the edge and she lands on the rocks. Multiple, multiple fractures but the cause of death is drowning. That's where I left you."

"And that's the conversation I had with Macdonald this morning."

"He's still in Hungary?"

"He is. I can't believe it, Geoff, but he is. If anything – "

"You don't need to say it, Mike. You and me both. We'd both have been on the first plane back. But maybe this'll make him come back..."

Geoff picked his glass up. Drained half of it. Looked at Brady. Spoke over the background noise of the Black Horse. Conversation. Laughter. Beer hissing into a glass as the barmaid pulled another pint.

"You need to add murder to your list of options, Mike."

Brady didn't speak. Picked his glass up. Sipped his beer.

'Are we back in Gina Foster territory, boss? Is that why we're all here?'

'Statistically she fell, Frankie. Unlikely, but a lot more likely than anything else.'

Or maybe not...

"Why, Geoff?

"When you walked in I was holding her right hand. I was just about to check under her fingernails. I did. I found some skin."

Geoff Oldroyd looked at Brady. "I sent it for analysis. Am I hopeful? Not even remotely. The saltwater will have degraded it. We're not going to get anything."

"It's definitely not hers?"

"Did she scratch herself? No. I've been over the body with a fine-tooth comb. A very hi-tech fine-tooth comb. No, I don't think it's hers."

"So a struggle? She's on the cliff path. Someone pushes her over the edge. Is that what you're saying?"

"She reaches out. Or fights back. Catches him. The cheek, somewhere like that."

Brady nodded. “Her husband’s abroad. So she’s not fighting at home. You’re certain it’ll degrade?”

“It was the first thing I noticed. Her right arm flung out behind her. Half in a rock pool. The tide goes out, leaves the rock pool. So probably from the time she fell. What’s that? Thirty-six hours? So like I say, I’ve sent the sample off. But I’m not expecting anything positive.”

“Time of death?”

“Sunday night or Monday morning. As soon as the tide came in far enough. We’ll need a date, so Monday. High tide.”

Brady nodded. Took another sip of his beer. “This is turning into a mess, Geoff. Maybe it’s murder, maybe it isn’t. Throw her husband into the mix. Kershaw will be on the phone every bloody half hour. What happened to the good old days? Did I ever tell you about George Robertson? Smothered his wife then phoned us up. ‘Forty years wed, Mr Brady, and she never stopped talking. I just wanted some peace.’ I can hear him saying it now.”

“Nostalgia, Mike. You’ll be wanting warm beer next. You got time for another half?”

Brady shook his head. “I’d better get back, Geoff. I need to take Archie on the beach while there’s some light.”

And I need to sit and think...

BRADY MADE HIMSELF A CHEESE SANDWICH, opened the French doors and sat on his balcony. Shivered. Went back inside for a fleece. Remembered the dog biscuits this time.

“Come on, Archie. Let’s see if we can work it out.”

Looked at his watch.

Just gone seven. Around the time Diane Macdonald went off the cliff...

Texted Siobhan. Asked her how it was going in London. Wondered if she'd reply with emojis he could understand.

'She lay on the rocks unable to move – her back's broken – and the tide came in.'

'Prometheus? Chained to a rock and had his liver pecked out every day? Not by a seagull, I grant you.'

Brady reached for his phone. Tapped the name into Google.

Best known for stealing fire from Zeus in the stalk of a fennel and giving it to mortals for their own use.

"So Zeus was pissed off, Archie. Had our boy chained to a rock. An eagle ate his liver every day. Then it grew back overnight. Endless torment. Just like paperwork."

Brady ruffled the dog's head. Gave him another biscuit. Looked at the lights on the pier.

Skin under her fingernails. She's fighting back. But who? Who did Diane Macdonald piss off? Not Zeus. Someone a lot more mortal...

The old car horn sounded on Brady's phone. He glanced down at the message. Siobhan.

I might be back on Friday afternoon. I miss you.

The emerald green heart again.

'I'll be out on Friday night, Dad. So I won't be here if Siobhan comes round for – ' Brady saw Ash make the inverted commas sign in the air. '*– Spaghetti Bolognese.'*

There's more than one way for a woman to get skin under her fingernails, Geoff. Maybe Diane Macdonald wasn't fighting...

10

"Boss, there's someone to see you. Says he wants to speak to whoever's in charge."

"Thanks, Sue. I'm guessing this isn't a photocopier salesman?"

Brady walked down to reception. Shook hands. A tall man with a long, lined face. A goatee beard, grey hair that had once been rock star length but had made a reluctant concession to age. "Keith Adams," he said. "We saw the story on the news. My wife told me to come and see you."

"Thank you. Let's go into an interview room. You want to risk a cup of police tea?"

Adams laughed. "I've stayed in a B&B in Sunderland. You can't frighten me."

"We're in the van," he said. "Motorhome. We call it the van. And we saw the story about Mrs Macdonald."

"You're on holiday in the area?"

Adams shook his head. "We're touring. A hundred years ago I was in a band. Born Too Late."

Pretend you've heard of them...

"We did alright. Not mega money but respectable. Then we got old. Old, responsible and married. Anita and I bought a hotel in Brighton and filled the bar with old guitars. She cooked and I talked music until two in the morning."

"What did you play?"

"Bass guitar. The one that holds it all together. That makes it sound cool. But doesn't get the glory. Or the groupies."

Brady smiled. "And then you sold the hotel and went back to touring?"

"A developer knocked on our door. The proverbial offer you can't refuse. So yes, in slightly more comfort than the back of a knackered Transit."

"You're parked by the cliff path?"

He nodded. "The same place we park every year. Music festivals in Europe in the summer. Back home in the winter. But if it's September it must be North Yorkshire. There's a lane that runs down to the cliff top. Widens out at the end so two or three vans can park there. So we more or less walked out of the front door and on to the cliff top."

"It sounds idyllic."

"It is. It absolutely is."

"And this Sunday night..."

"We're just walking along the cliff top. I had a bit of a heart scare about three years ago. Well, more than a scare if truth be told. Not so much Born Too Late as damned near died too early. So I do my ten thousand steps a day. I had three thousand more to do. Half an hour give or take."

"And you passed Diane Macdonald?"

"We passed someone. I didn't know it was her. Just as it

started to rain. That's what I said to her. But she didn't reply. I think she was worrying where her dog was."

"She was just... There's no other way to put it. Just a normal person walking her dog?"

"Very much so. Jacket, jeans, dog biscuits in her pocket no doubt."

'I had three thousand more to do. Half an hour give or take.' On the cliff top...

"Your three thousand steps, Mr Adams... If you're doing them on the cliff top presumably you walk in one direction, turn round and come back?"

He laughed. "It's pretty much all you can do, isn't it? Set a timer for fifteen minutes. Sea on your right. Turn round. Sea on your left. Back to the van."

"So had you reached your fifteen minutes when you saw Diane Macdonald?"

Keith Adams nodded. "Did we see her on the way back you mean? No, just the once. Maybe two minutes after we turned round."

Brady nodded. "Did you see anyone else?"

Keith nodded. "That's the reason I'm here. I know you've not said anything official. About it being suspicious. But we overtook someone. And he was... I don't know. God knows I've seen my share of bouncers and roadies but I wouldn't want to meet him on a dark night. Or any night come to that. We said that when we were back in the van."

"Can you describe him to me?"

"In a word? Dark. Dark jacket. Jeans. Some sort of beanie hat. Sort of hunched. This sounds stupid. First impressions – "

"No. Go ahead."

" – But hunched. Dark. Mentally and physically. Collar turned up."

"Did you speak to him?"

"No. Because he gave off this 'don't speak to me' vibe. You know how it is. You get on the train. You need a seat. But some people... 'Don't sit next to me' is coming off them in waves."

So we need to find him...

"Nothing else?" Brady said. "He was the only person you saw?"

Keith Adams nodded. "Half an hour on a cold, wet clifftop in September? Nights drawing in? People have better things to do."

"How long are you staying in Whitby?"

He shook his head. "We're not. My wife's delving into our family history. She's discovered one of her great-grandmothers came from a village in Northumberland. We're off to look at gravestones. So September's not North Yorkshire after all."

"I can ring you? If I need to ask you anything else?"

Keith Adams nodded. "Of course. Anything we can do to help."

Brady stood up. Shook hands with the retired bass guitarist. Wished him well. Told him to enjoy the gravestones.

Walked back to his office. Googled *Born Too Late* so he could impress Siobhan...

11

"Mike? Geoff. I promised to phone you when the lab came back to me."

"What did they say?"

"Exactly what I expected. Feared. The sample I sent them was too far gone. Just bumps."

"Bumps?"

"The sample goes through something called an electropherogram, Mike. It produces a graph. Which in a perfect world is a series of peaks. Diane Macdonald having her hand in the water for thirty-six hours is *not* a perfect world. As far from perfect as you can get. So yes, just bumps."

"So nothing useful? No blood group? DNA? Identikit picture of a killer?"

"Bumps, Mike. I'm sorry."

BRADY WALKED into the main office. "Spare me a minute, Frankie?"

"Diane Macdonald," he said when Frankie had closed

the door. "Geoff found some skin under her fingernails. On her right hand. He's just got the results back from the lab."

"Which – seeing as that's your frustrated face – didn't tell us anything."

Brady nodded. "Nothing at all. Geoff said her hand had been in the water – that rock pool, remember? – for too long. The sample was 'too far gone' in his words."

"But you're putting two and two together..."

"Maybe. Going over the cliff edge is statistically unlikely. Having skin under your fingernails is statistically unlikely. What did Goldfinger say? 'I don't like coincidence, Mr Bond.' Something like that."

"She could have been having sex, boss."

"Before she fell?"

"Probably not on the cliff top. Not in the rain, anyway. But she could have a lover. You're making the assumption she was fighting with someone. At least lashing out. I've obviously led a very sheltered life but I understand there's something called rough sex? Other ways to get skin under your fingernails? Her husband's in Hungary after all..."

"So I need to interview every bloke in Runswick Bay between twenty and fifty?"

"It's September in North Yorkshire, boss. You can probably rule out the pool boy."

Brady tapped his middle finger on the desk. Stared out of the window. "We need to have a look in the house, Frankie."

"On what grounds, boss? The stats say she had a lover not a fight. That she fell rather than she was pushed. There's nothing to say a crime's been committed."

She's right. No grounds. And Graham Macdonald isn't going to give me permission...

"Is that it, boss?"

"Yeah. Sorry, Frankie. I said to Geoff last night – this case is turning into a mess. There are only three reasons why she went over the cliff – "

"Murder, accident, suicide."

"Right. And I'll feel a lot happier when I've ruled two of them out. I'm going out for a walk. I need a bit of space."

Frankie nodded. Smiled sympathetically. "You need to do some thinking?"

"I do."

"By the harbour? The water? The boats? Helps you think more clearly?"

"Exactly that, Frankie."

"Say 'hi' to Dave for me, boss..."

12

Brady walked past the empty fishing sheds. Glanced across the harbour. St Mary's Church up on the hill. His house at the end of Henrietta Street. Low tide, the high water mark clearly visible on the harbour wall. The sea flat, a yellow marker buoy bobbing listlessly, a seagull perched defiantly on top of it.

"Haven't seen you for two days," Dave said. "Thought you'd given up on me."

"You're joking, Dave. You know I get withdrawal symptoms when you close for the winter?"

Dave laughed. "You'll have to go to rehab, Mike. Like that singer."

"Amy Winehouse? Ash is suddenly into her. *Back to Black*. All I can hear from her room. I'm ashamed to say I quite like it."

"I thought you'd be strictly classical now. Impress that new girlfriend of yours. Not so new, mind. Two months? Three?"

"Four now, Dave."

"Serious then. How's it goin'?"

"Yeah, good. I think. She's in London right now. Seeing the record company. Back at the weekend."

Dave handed him his bacon sandwich. Pressed the lid onto the coffee cup. "I can't wait," he said.

"What for?"

"You, mate. I'll turn the telly on one night and you'll be there. BAFTAs or whatever they're called. Sitting there in your posh dinner jacket – "

Brady laughed. "I'm going to sit by the bandstand. I need to do some thinking. And I probably don't fit into my 'posh dinner jacket.' Too many bacon sandwiches, Dave..."

BRADY WALKED over to the bandstand. Exchanged 'good mornings' with an old couple. Sat on the same bench he always sat on.

'Serious then. How's it goin'?'

'Good. I think. Four months now...'

He'd decided to take Archie with him. Knocked on the pale blue door with the roses growing up a trellis at the side of it.

'We'd better not come in. Archie's rolled in something. I've come to pay my debts.'

'Case closed?'

'Case closed. Other than the paperwork, we're done.'

He'd hesitated...

'But I'm not doing paperwork on Saturday. Come round in the afternoon. I owe you a walk. And then I'll cook dinner.'

And at four o'clock Siobhan had rung the doorbell. Dark grey jeans, a pale green jumper, a bottle green body warmer that looked like it could cope with whatever the North wind threw at it.

A bag in her right hand.

'And I brought some clothes. I thought I should change for dinner.'

They'd walked on the beach. Stood under the pier at low tide. Brady had told her about coming back to Whitby. Told her about Patrick. Didn't tell her about Jimmy Gorse.

She'd filled in the gaps in her story. Taken his hand as they turned to walk back to the car. Only let go of it to throw sticks for Archie.

'I'll leave you to cook. Can I have a shower? Get changed?'

'Of course. Your bag's at the top of the stairs.'

Brady hadn't known where to put it.

Half an hour and she was back. A short summer dress. Navy, random pink flowers. Her legs long and tanned. Almost as tall as Brady in her heels.

'I was going to ask you to stir the sauce while I had a wash. But...'

She'd laughed. Told him it would be fine. Laughed at his jokes over dinner. Made him realise how much he'd missed being with someone.

'Would you like coffee?'

She'd shaken her head. Stood up. Walked over to him. Taken his hand. Pulled him to his feet. Looked into his eyes. Sensed how difficult the first time would be for him.

Kissed him. Broke it off. Held his eyes again. Brought her hand up and undid two buttons on his shirt.

Took a step back. Reached behind her. Never broke eye contact.

Let the navy dress with the random pink flowers fall to the floor...

"I'M SORRY TO INTERRUPT. How long will it take us to walk to Sandsend?"

Brady looked up. The old man. White hair, a neatly-trimmed white beard. Tanned, fit. Straight out of an insurance company's pensions ad.

"Half an hour? Maybe a little longer. And there's a lovely walk up on the cliffs. Just through the car park. Beautiful views."

Where I scattered my wife's ashes...

"Thank you. Enjoy your day."

"You too. And turn right as you come out of the car park after your walk. There's a little café."

"Thank you again. And... If you don't mind me saying... I hope you find the answer. I was a psychiatrist. I recognise someone making a difficult decision."

Brady watched them walk down the slipway onto the beach. Stood and walked over to the railings. Looked across the harbour to his house.

Looked at the cliffs behind the house.

Saw Diane Macdonald falling...

'You need to add murder to your list of options. There's skin under her fingernails.'

'Definitely not hers?'

'I've been over the body with a fine-tooth comb. A very hi-tech fine-tooth comb. No, it's not hers.'

'There are other ways to get skin under your fingernails, boss.'

'We overtook someone. I wouldn't want to meet him on a dark night. Or any night come to that. Dark. Mentally and physically.'

Brady shook his head.

'I recognise someone making a difficult decision.'

So make a bloody decision. Before Kershaw makes one for you.

Brady screwed the bacon sandwich bag into a ball. Threw it towards the waste paper bin. Missed hopelessly.

Bent down to pick it up. Shook his head in frustration. Knew what he had to do.

I need to see inside the house...

13

"I need to be in that house, Frankie."

"What's changed, boss? In the time it's taken you to eat a bacon sandwich? Talking to Dave doesn't give you grounds. Macdonald's in Hungary, his daughter's in Italy. And the key will be with the next door neighbour. Mrs Stokes, or whatever her name was."

Brady shook his head. Smiled. "Except it's not is it, Frankie? It's downstairs in a plastic bag. Along with a couple of quid in cash and half a dozen dog biscuits."

"Her phone's with the techies?"

Brady nodded. "In the never-ending queue. But maybe we won't need it – "

"If we can get in the house? We've got the key." Frankie smiled. "And we've got the trump card."

"What's that?"

"We've got Reggie. At least for a couple of days. No-one needs to know he's with Lochie at Hutton-le-Hole."

Brady grinned. "Genius, Frankie. Bloody genius."

"It doesn't tick the ethics box, boss."

"No, it doesn't. But neither did Graham Macdonald

when he ran off across the field and left Lizzie Greenbeck to die."

Brady reached for the phone. Dialled the British Embassy in Budapest. Found himself talking to the same person. "Hello, this is Detective Inspector Michael Brady ... That's right, I rang to speak to Mr Macdonald ... Yes, it's absolutely tragic ... I know how busy he is, I'm guessing he's not available at the moment? No? Well perhaps I could ask something? One of my colleagues is taking care of his dog ... Reggie, a cocker spaniel ... But she needs a few things to make him comfortable ... his bed, maybe a favourite toy or two ... Obviously we can't enter the house to get them without Mr Macdonald's permission ... I wonder if you'd ask him? I'll send my sergeant ... not more than ten minutes. Yes, sadly we have a key in his wife's personal effects ... my Detective Sergeant ... yes, very responsible. And of course. *Absolute* discretion. Thank you so much."

Brady put the phone down. Looked at Frankie. "Let's see shall we?"

Was surprised how quickly the call was returned.

This meeting not so important, Graham? Or are you feeling guilty...

Walked into the main office. "Frankie? Macdonald's house. He's says fine. Or the person on the phone says fine. Reggie's bed is in the kitchen. There's a cupboard above it with his food in it. See if you can find a squeaky toy or something. Make it convincing. He doesn't think she'll have turned the alarm on. If she did it's four – five – eight – nine."

"What am I looking for, boss?"

"Anything that helps us. Don't touch anything – although I'm guessing Macdonald wouldn't know if you did. But take your shoes off, no footprints on the carpet. I'll leave it to you, Frankie. You'll understand Diane Macdonald better than me – "

"Late forties? Only her dog for company? Lonely walk late at night? Thanks, boss."

Two hours and she was back.

"First things first. You remembered Reggie's bed?"

Frankie laughed. "It's in the car. Plus a supply of dog food and the squeaky toy you ordered. Lochie will be delighted."

"He's alright with it?"

"He's fine for now. Said he took Reggie running yesterday morning. But he's away in a fortnight. Three days at some dusty conference for museum curators."

"That's not a problem though. Macdonald's back at the weekend. However much of a shit he was on the phone he'll want his dog back. More importantly," Brady said, "What did you find?"

"OK, I didn't stay too long. I didn't want to risk Mrs Stokes telling him, 'there was a car parked outside for half an hour.' So I thought ten minutes was consistent with getting the dog's bed."

"Lounge, bedroom, bathroom?"

"In that order. Tidy, impersonal. A bottle of gin on the side." Frankie checked a note on her phone. "An Dúlamán. Irish maritime gin. Reassuringly expensive as the ads used to say."

"So a lonely gin in the evening."

"And then to bed. Reassuringly untidy. Not a woman who saw the need to make the bed if she was alone in it."

"What did you say to me? 'There's more than one way to

get skin under your fingernails.' There's more than one way to untidy the bed as well."

Frankie shook her head. "Absolutely no evidence, boss. I checked all the bins. And the post-mortem didn't suggest she'd had sex."

"Bathroom? Your ten minutes must be nearly up by now."

"Nothing you wouldn't expect. No sign of anti-depressants. Nothing you or I wouldn't have in the bathroom cupboard."

"So you drew a blank?"

Brady looked at her. She smiled back at him.

"Except you didn't draw a blank did you, Frankie? Because I know that smile. Half knowing, half butter-wouldn't-melt. What is it you're not telling me?"

Frankie tapped her phone to open it. Scrolled through her pictures. Opened one. Passed the phone to Brady.

"What's this?"

"Lounge, bedroom, bathroom," Frankie said. "Maybe eleven or twelve minutes. The office. Or study. Two desks. One with a picture of their daughter. One with a picture of Graham Macdonald shaking hands with the Prime Minister. So it wasn't hard to guess which was her desk..."

Brady looked at the photo. A spiral bound notebook open on the desk.

Judging by the pen next to it, A6. Small enough to fit in her handbag. A phone number. Firm, decisive handwriting. 0 – 2 – 0 – 7. London.

There was a name written under the phone number. Underlined. Toby Padgett.

"Are you going to tell me who Toby Padgett is? Or do I get the pleasure of looking it up? Phoning him?

Frankie smiled. "I'll tell you, boss. He's a solicitor. Even more reassuringly expensive than the gin. And he specialises."

"What in?"

"According to his website, 'My clients are the wives and partners of high net worth and ultra-high net worth individuals.' He specialises in divorce, boss."

Brady raised his eyebrows. "This was definitely on her desk?"

"Next to her laptop."

"The underline is in a different colour. Which suggests – "

"That she wrote the number down and then underlined it later. Reminding herself."

"Confirming it. Saying to herself, 'I'm definitely going to do this.' You think Macdonald knew?"

Frankie shrugged. "I don't know. He must have had some idea."

"We need to know, Frankie. If he knew what she was planning he had a motive. Money. Jealousy. Two motives."

"He was in Hungary."

'I wouldn't want to meet him on a dark night. Or any night come to that. Dark. Mentally and physically.'

"You're right, Frankie. The stats still say she fell. But he wouldn't be the first husband to delegate the dirty work."

14

"The bloody techies, Frankie. How hard can it be? Recently dialled numbers on her phone. Her daughter, the dentist, pizza delivery – "

"You order a pizza online now, boss. Ash will walk you through it..."

"And there's me thinking standing in the shop for ten minutes added to the flavour... I'll chase them up. Let's see who the unfortunate Mrs Macdonald's been talking to."

"HERE YOU GO, Frankie. Hot off the press from Diane Macdonald's phone."

Brady handed her a sheet of A4. Watched her scan quickly down it.

"Annabel Cowling?"

"Married to Roger. MP since 2010. Safe seat, junior minister and happily married, at least according to his official bio. Maybe not for much longer."

"What are you going to do?"

Brady shrugged. "Call her. What's the worst that can

happen? She won't co-operate. I can probably fill in the gaps myself. I'd just like someone to confirm them."

Brady decided that a mobile phone number she didn't recognise had more chance of success than the police station's 'number withheld.' Reached for his phone.

It didn't. The phone clicked through to the inevitable answerphone message. "Good afternoon, Mrs Cowling. My name's Mike Brady. I'm a Detective Chief Inspector with North Yorkshire police, based in Whitby. You've no doubt seen the news regarding Diane Macdonald. I gather she was a friend of yours and... I can only offer my condolences. I wonder if you'd give me a ring when you get the message? This is my mobile number, so feel free to phone me in the evening if that's more convenient."

SHE DID. Brady had just opened a beer. Discovered that it wasn't warm enough to sit outside. Hadn't closed the balcony doors.

"Michael Brady."

"Annabel Cowling, Inspector."

"Mrs Cowling. Thank you – "

"Annabel, please. The less I hear the words 'Mrs Cowling' the happier I am."

"Thank you for coming back to me – "

"What in God's name is that noise, Inspector? It sounds like you're under attack."

Brady laughed. "It's seagulls. I'm in Whitby, overlooking the harbour. There's a fishing boat coming in. One minute."

Brady put the bottle of San Miguel down. Closed the balcony doors. The seagulls fell silent.

You were right, Chris. The cold, the noise. Triple-glazing was worth it...

"Annabel, you obviously know what happened to Diane. I can only offer my condolences. And while we're not treating her death as suspicious, she was the wife of an MP. Falls from the cliffs are rare. Especially cliffs we walk on every day. I'd like to ask you some background questions. If you'd prefer not to answer them, I understand. At this stage I've absolutely no authority to make you."

"What can I tell you, Inspector?"

"Can I ask how well you knew Diane?"

There was a brief pause. "Reasonably. We met at some Parliamentary reception or other. The terrace at the House of Commons is a splendid place to have a glass of Pimm's on a summer's evening. Then your husband abandons you for someone who might advance his career. So we found ourselves talking. Exchanged phone numbers. So like many friendships these days it was far more phones and Facebook than in person. But yes, we were friends."

"And you gave her Toby Padgett's number?"

"I did. As you have obviously worked out I will not – praise God – be Mrs Cowling for much longer. Thanks to Toby my soon-to-be-ex-husband will be significantly poorer. But what does the bastard need of money when he has a flat stomach and firm tits to console him?"

Brady couldn't stop himself laughing. "And Diane Macdonald was... considering the same path?"

"She was. Our husbands were cut from the same cloth. Like a great many men. The longer you knew them the less you liked them."

"Diane was definitely going ahead with the divorce?"

"Yes. We had a long conversation... I can tell you the exact date if you want. The Friday of Royal Ascot. Obviously a crucial fact-finding trip for Her Majesty's Elected Representatives."

"Did her husband know?"

"If you're asking had she told him, to the best of my knowledge the answer is 'no.' He must have had some inkling. Unless he was totally oblivious to the signs. Which being a man is entirely possible, I suppose."

Brady laughed again. "I'd better not comment had I? Mars and Venus doesn't even come close? Thank you for your help. And... am I allowed to say 'good luck?'"

Her turn to laugh. "Thank you. I shall miss the Pimm's and Royal Ascot. But two-thirds of a parliamentary pension and the house in Tuscany is adequate compensation. Phone me if you need anything else, Mr Brady."

"WHAT DID SHE SAY?"

"Exactly what you'd expect, Frankie. She'll shortly be going back to her maiden name. Thanks to Toby Padgett she's been amply compensated for however many years of marriage it was. And Diane Macdonald was treading exactly the same path."

"So her death was good news?"

"For Graham Macdonald? On the assumption that he's not stricken with grief – which he certainly wasn't on the phone – bloody good news. God knows I'm no expert on the parliamentary pension scheme but based on what Annabel Cowling said... That and a house in Tuscany? A million quid?"

Frankie nodded. "A good enough motive."

"Plus the publicity. Or lack of it."

"So where do we go from here, boss?"

Brady sighed. "In the short term? I'm going to see Kate. I haven't seen my sister for a week. And Maddie's off to university next week. As far as this case is concerned? In search of something concrete. It's unlikely that she fell. She wanted a divorce. Keith Adams said he saw someone. 'Dark, physically and mentally.' Where does that get us? There's skin under her fingernails but it's inconclusive. None of it adds up to anything."

"You going to appeal for witnesses? The cliff-top?"

Brady shook his head. "Maybe. But then I've got Kershaw asking why I'm spending so much time on the case. 'It's clearly an accident, Michael.' I need to make some progress. There's only one bloody positive at the moment."

"What's that?"

"Reggie. At least the dog's happy."

15

"You look worried," Kate said.

Brady laughed. "You're the second person to say that to me this week. Kershaw's away. I'm in charge. It's my job to look worried."

"Graham Macdonald's wife?"

"Who else? And right now she's just a series of loose ends."

"Probably not the best choice of words, Mike."

"No. Especially – "

Especially with what the seagull did to her eye...

"Especially what?"

"No, nothing. I'm not going to say it while you're eating your breakfast."

"But you're worried?"

"Worried isn't the word, Kate. I'm frustrated more than worried."

"Why?"

Brady finished his tea. "Have you got five minutes? You want to hear the story?"

"I was a copper's wife? I'm a copper's sister? If I can't listen to a story who can?"

Brady nodded. "Go back to last year. When Gina Foster was found I *wanted* it to be murder. I'm not even remotely proud of that – "

"But it's the truth?"

"Right."

"Mike, if you can't tell your sister the truth who *can* you tell?"

"Not only did I want it to be murder, Kate. I *needed* it to be murder."

"Because you had to prove yourself."

"Yes. But not just to other people. To myself. To prove that I still had it. That... Sitting by Grace's bedside. That I hadn't lost it."

"I understand that. You want some more tea?"

Brady shook his head. "I'm fine, Kate, thanks. Forty-four next month. Ash has started coughing significantly when the incontinence ads come on."

"Teenage sarcasm, Mike. You'll miss it when she's gone. Next weekend I load the car up and take Maddie."

"Is she in? I need to see her before she goes."

Kate shook her head. "Tearful goodbyes with the boyfriend. She's going to Reading, he's going to Stirling. Four hundred miles of unrequited love. Tell me about Diane Macdonald."

"She was murdered, Kate. I'm certain of it. I was talking about it with Frankie. It's – "

"How's she doing?"

"She's good. Lochie – "

"Lochie? Who's Lochie?"

"Her new boyfriend. The guy she met at the Folk Museum."

"I thought you said his name was Graeme?"

"I did. I *thought* his name was Graeme. But apparently when he was little his grandad – who's called Lochlan – took him fishing. He caught a fish with his first cast. So grandad calls him, 'Lucky Lochie.' The name sticks. When he goes to school there are half a dozen Graemes in his class, so he tells the teacher, 'Grandad calls me Lochie.' The teacher heaves a sigh of relief, all his friends call him Lochie – "

"And now only his mum calls him Graeme."

"The same in all families." Brady shook his head. "Where the hell was I, Kate? Ash is right. I'm starting to ramble."

"Discussing it with Frankie."

"Thank you. There are parallels with Gina Foster. The farmer's wife. You remember. You don't fall where you walk every day. Or frequently in Diane Macdonald's case. You don't commit suicide in front of your dog. But I can't bloody prove it. Which is where we came in five minutes ago. If I look frustrated it's because I am. She's been murdered: I can't prove it. And I'm running out of time."

"So what are you going to do?"

"Stare out of the window? Try and work out what I've missed? Answer pointless e-mails from Kershaw? More importantly, see what Macdonald has to say for himself. The not-very-grieving widower."

"When are you seeing him?"

"Monday afternoon. He flies back on Saturday. But he's decided his dead wife can wait another two days. I cannot understand it Kate. Except..."

'If you don't tell your sister who do you tell?'

"Keep this to yourself – "

"Obviously..."

"She was going to divorce him."

Kate raised her eyebrows. "Was she? You think that puts a different slant on it?"

"Yes. But it doesn't move me any further forward. We still have the three options. Accident. Murder. Even suicide."

Kate shook her head. "Two options, Mike."

"Why?"

"Because I'm a woman. You know things weren't good between Bill and me. You know what I was planning to do. As soon as Lucy went to university. Bloody hell, I had the date in my phone. Two reasons to celebrate my youngest daughter's A-level results. So you rewind two years – before the selfish bugger got cancer – and I was unhappy. I was fed up. I was counting the days. But what I wasn't was suicidal. Because I'd made a plan. I had a *future*. It was five or six years away, but I had a future."

"So never mind the dog?"

"It's not the dog. Not this time. What did you just say? No-one commits suicide in front of their dog? No woman commits suicide the day before she phones the solicitor."

Brady nodded. "That's what we think. But like I say, I've no proof. And no proof equals no murder investigation. Talk to me about something happier. How's it going with Doug?"

Kate smiled. "Good. Better than good. It's... Bloody hell, Mike, I'm within spitting distance of fifty and I'm having to think about contraception. It's ridiculous and wonderful at the same time."

What's Ash say? 'Too much information?' But I'm clearly supposed to reply...

"Didn't Bill..."

"Bill had a vasectomy after Lucy, Mike. But he could have saved himself the bother. As far as Bill was concerned, 'golf's on the telly, love' was all the contraception we needed."

16

'I need a name, Scholesy. Someone like you. But in this part of the world. I've moved.'

'Someone unofficial. Who'll give me the information the police techies can't. Or won't.'

Who won't need Graham Macdonald's password...

Brady drove up the coast road. Sandsend, Hinderwell, Boulby. Through Loftus. Brotton. A forty minute drive.

Brady remembered the first time he'd been. The elegant apartment in what had once been the Zetland Hotel.

Mozart's simple instructions.

Drive to Saltburn. Park your car. Stand across the road from the Zetland Hotel. Monday 11am.

"You're looking well."

Mozart hadn't changed. Still looking like a man who'd become a Maths professor at a ridiculously young age. The same olive green jumper, the leather patches on the elbows marginally more worn.

He laughed. "I'm looking tanned you mean. Outwardly well. I've been to my desert island. My client's desert island. I'm tempted to build some sort of bug into his software system that kicks in twice a year and demands my attention. March and September, maybe." Mozart spread his hands. "But what can I do? Those wretched professional ethics. Even in my profession."

He smiled. "You'd like some tea. Earl Grey still? Give me five minutes."

Mozart disappeared into the kitchen. Brady walked over to the window. Looked down at the pavement. Where he'd stood for ten minutes.

Stand across the road.

'You can learn a lot from watching someone stand still, Michael.'

What did you learn from watching me, Mozart?

"You must be in the new house by now. How is it?" Mozart was back with his elegant art-deco tea set.

"It's lovely. I'm pleased. My daughter loves it. I've finally located my fridge. It's good."

"And you're recovered?"

For a moment Brady was baffled. Then he realised and laughed. "Yes, I was bloody cold for a few days. But no lasting damage."

Mozart smiled. "My clients usually like to keep a lower profile than ten thousand YouTube hits. The colleague you rescued from the harbour?"

Brady nodded. "Col? He's fine. Happily retired, tending his allotment – and his daughter's about to present him with a new grandchild."

Mozart sipped his tea, looked at Brady over the cup. "The simple pleasures. Sadly not granted to men like us – "

Because we need more? You're right...

"So whose grubby little filing cabinet would you like me to rifle through today?"

"He's an MP," Brady said. "Graham Macdonald. As much

as you can. Whatever's at the back of what could be a *very* dirty filing cabinet."

"The Palace of Westminster, Michael. Possibly the least secure computer network in the Western world. I wouldn't be surprised if the Russians and Chinese didn't use it as a chat room."

Brady laughed. "Why's that?"

"Because fifty per cent of our elected representatives use their dog's name as a password."

"What about the other half?"

Mozart shook his head sadly. "Their mistress, mostly."

Brady nodded. "I know it won't be your greatest challenge. I'll try and do better next time. And I know a lot of it is in the public domain. I've known Macdonald since I was a teenager. Met him at conferences. Read Wiki. But – "

"The unfortunate Mrs Macdonald has fallen off a cliff."

"Yes. His wife has fallen off a cliff and she was planning to divorce him."

And it's personal. I want him to be guilty. Implicated. I want him to pay for Lizzie Greenbeck. Why don't I come out and say it?

"Leave it with me, Michael. I'll be back to you in a couple of days. I suspect the longer this case goes unsolved – "

"The more pressure I'm under? Something like that. And I want it to be simple, Mozart. Something that starts and ends in Whitby. That business with Eric Kennedy... You'll understand this. I don't want to go tiptoeing down the corridors of power again."

Brady looked at Mozart. Wondered for the hundredth time about his past. About the real nature of the work he did...

'He's called Eric Kennedy. He's a maths professor at Cambridge.'

'No. I'm sorry, Michael. Eric Kennedy? No. It's not that I can't do it, Michael. I won't do it. Even for someone I now consider a friend as well as a client. Professionally... It's just somewhere I won't go.'

...And why there were some boundaries he couldn't – or wouldn't – cross.

Mozart nodded. "I'll do my best. But starts and ends in Whitby? There are no guarantees for people like us. Especially when politicians are involved..."

17

Michael Brady walked down the stairs. Out of the Zetland. Crossed the road to his car. Looked at this watch.

Half an hour to drive back. Forty minutes maybe. Time to walk Archie and make sure Ash is alright. Not much time to tidy the house before Siobhan comes round...

"HAVE you got everything you need, sweetheart?"

"Have you got everything *you* need, Dad? Fresh flowers? You've checked that Archie doesn't smell of dead fish? Mince for the Spaghetti Bolognese?"

"There you are, Miss Clever Dick, I'm not cooking Spag Bol. Bruschetta."

"That's – "

"Right. Sophisticated – "

"How did you stumble across the recipe?"

"You want the truth?"

"Of course. And nothing but the truth..."

"I fell asleep in front of the football and woke up in front of a cookery programme. Ciabatta. Slice it. Rub it with garlic. Olive oil. Pepper. In the oven for ten minutes. Finish it on the griddle. Top it with tomato and mozzarella. Avocado wrapped in Parma ham. Sprinkle with parmesan and chopped basil. Red wine. Think about entering *MasterChef* – "

"Not *too* much red wine, Dad. Remember your age. You don't want to fall asleep on your hot date. Anyway, that sounds like Fiona's car. She says she's jealous of our view. Jess showed her a picture from my bedroom. She says will you rent it to her when I've gone to uni?"

Brady laughed. "Go on. Off you go. And good luck tomorrow. Who are you playing?"

"Acklam Grange."

"I remember playing them at football. Get stuck in. No mercy. Don't take any prisoners."

"Thanks for the team talk, Dad. I'll see you Saturday night. Love you."

"Love you, sweetheart."

Michael Brady kissed his daughter. Waited until she was out of the door. Reached for his phone. Checked the recipe. Wondered how long it would take him to wrap slices of avocado in Parma ham...

THE DOORBELL RANG JUST as Brady realised the answer was 'three times longer than the chef on TV.'

He poured Siobhan a glass of wine. Walked to the front door.

Four months now...

The same pale yellow jacket and skinny jeans she'd been wearing when he'd met her. Dark hair tumbling to her shoulders, green eyes, high cheekbones. Overnight bag in her right hand. She put her hand on his cheek. Kissed him.

"A week. I've missed you, Michael Brady."

"I've missed you too."

She laughed. "You've been too busy to miss me. I saw the news. The MP's wife. Someone said the dog stayed with her all the time."

"He did. Reggie. He's a hero."

He reached down. Took the bag from her. Kissed her again. "Come on. I've poured you a glass of wine. I'll put this in the bedroom."

Michael Brady walked into his bedroom. Put Siobhan's bag down. Looked at the bed.

Wondered if he'd ever stop feeling guilty...

"You mind if I have the last one?"

Brady shook his head. "Help yourself."

Siobhan took a bite. "I'm impressed."

Brady laughed. "I confessed to Ash so I may as well confess to you. I fell asleep in front of the football. Woke up in front of some midnight chef."

"So it's been a tough week?"

"Not tough... Inconclusive. Frustrating. You've seen the news about Diane Macdonald. There are too many loose ends – "

"That you can't tell me about?"

"Not that I *can't* tell you about. It's – "

"Friday night and you want to talk about something different?"

"Maybe. I'm just unwinding from it all. That's why there's another bottle of wine open."

"You don't need to get me drunk, Michael Brady."

"I know. I – "

Don't want to make the same mistake I made with Grace. Never switch off from work...

Brady stood up. Took two steps across the balcony. Bent down and kissed her. Breathed in her perfume. Realised how much he'd missed her.

"And it's personal," he said.

"How?"

"Graham Macdonald. Her husband. He was brought up in Whitby. We go back a long way. As the saying goes, we've got history."

"What happened?"

"You're sure you want the story? You're not too cold out here?"

She shook her head. Ran her hand through her hair. "No. Tell me. If you want to tell me..."

"It was Christmas Eve. Years ago now. We were eighteen or nineteen. Just back from our first term at uni. So four of us went to Robin Hood's Bay. Why we didn't just get pissed in Whitby I'll never know but..."

"The follies of youth?"

"The stupidity of youth. The plan was simple. One of us was going to stay sober. Well, sober enough to drive back."

"But you were eighteen."

"I was nineteen. But no wiser. So come midnight we're freezing cold and phoning for a taxi."

"On Christmas Eve..."

"Right. And it's looking like the next taxi is on Boxing Day. So Lizzie – "

"Your girlfriend?"

Brady shook his head. "No. We'd been out a couple of times. But nothing serious. And she had this prodigious work ethic. And an incredibly protective father. So she had to get back."

"What happened?"

"Lizzie gets into a car driven by a boy called Graham Macdonald. His dad's the Chief Constable. The car's owned by John Clayton, whose dad has two or three hotels. Whitby's *jeunesse d'or*. But Clayton's too pissed to stand up, never mind drive. So Macdonald is driving."

"This isn't going to end well."

"No. A miracle occurs. A taxi turns up. So we – "

"You and..."

"Patrick – my best friend – and a girl called Angie Carter. Angie Carmichael as she now is. Channel Four on Sunday mornings. So we jump in the taxi and we're about half a mile behind them. And we're the first ones on the scene. After the police."

"There was a crash?"

Brady nodded. Saw the blue flashing lights. Saw the Astra crushed against the tree. John Clayton lying on the ground.

"Yes, there was a crash. Lizzie died at the scene. When we got there John Clayton was on the grass. Graham Macdonald wasn't there. A crash that killed Lizzie, he escaped with a few bruises. The son of the Chief Constable was running away. Scampering across the fields, hand-in-hand with his guardian angel."

"What happened to him?"

"What happened? The guardian angel went into overdrive. Clayton took the rap for driving the car – no-one bothered to check for prints on the steering wheel. He got about 200 hours community service, joined the army and died in Afghanistan. The other guy in the car suffered an even worse fate: he became an estate agent. And Graham

Macdonald, complete with new found belief in law and order and family values, became – still is – an MP."

"And married to the woman who died?"

"Married to the woman who died. Diane Macdonald. And that's probably where I shouldn't tell you any more."

Siobhan was silent. "So what you're saying to me is that two of the four of you that went out that night – that Christmas Eve – are dead. Is it safe to be around you, Mike? Should I wear body armour? Increase my life cover? Or take better care of you?"

Brady laughed. "All three probably. Macdonald's back tomorrow. I'm meeting him on Monday."

Siobhan raised her eyebrows. "May you live in interesting times, Mr Brady..."

Brady stood up. Walked over to her. Reached his hand out. Pulled her to him. "Time to talk about something else. Or don't talk at all. I've missed you..."

18

"How did it go in London? I'm sorry, I didn't ask you last night."

She leaned over to him. Traced the back of her fingernail down his chest. "Because you had other things on your mind, Michael Brady..."

Brady laughed. Held her hand. Stopped it going any lower. "Well I'm asking now. How did it go?"

Siobhan half-turned in the bed. Pushed the pillow up behind her. Leaned back. "Serious conversation?"

Brady nodded. "Serious conversation. And then I'll do us some breakfast." He leaned across and kissed her. "Or maybe not..."

She pushed him away. "Serious conversation. And the answer is... Not well. At least in the short term. Long term? I don't know."

"Tell me..."

"You remember that Saturday morning we had breakfast? The café at Sandsend?"

When Kershaw phoned. Gleefully told me I was all over the internet. How could I forget...

"Remember what I said? Lucy's getting married and moving to the US? Emma's body clock is ticking?"

"Sure..."

"Well the wedding's been brought forward. Something to do with his job. Some promotion. Chicago, I think. And Emma's body clock isn't ticking any more. It's ticked. She's three months pregnant."

"So where does that leave the band?"

"Changing our name probably. Not so much *Levata* as *Tramonto*."

"Sunrise to sunset at a rough guess..."

She nodded. "Got it in one. Realistically, Mike, it leaves Helen and me. Do we want to look for two new members? Spend that amount of time? Auditions? Rehearsals? Another tour? For both of us the answer's probably 'no.' And as the cynical – but sadly correct – boss at the record label pointed out, 'you're not the only pretty girls who can play classical music.'"

She reached across. Took his hand. Brought it to her lips. Kissed his fingertips.

"So short term it's bad news."

"But long term you don't know."

She nodded. "Long term I don't know. I don't want to give up playing. Because – "

"Because there's nothing else like it and once it's gone it's gone?"

"Right. Exactly. But in the short term I'm going to compose. Buy all of Amazon's sheet music paper."

"All those squiggles I'll never understand?"

She laughed. "Never, ever understand. But that's the short term sorted. The long term can take care of itself for now. Which just leaves the here and now..."

Siobhan threw the quilt back. Turned towards him –

Brady's phone rang.

He glanced at the display.

The station.

"Michael Brady."

"Boss, it's Sue. I know it's Saturday, I'm sorry. There's someone to see you. He was sitting outside when I arrived this morning."

"Sitting outside?"

"Sitting on the front step."

"Who?"

"His name's Donoghue. Gerry Donoghue he says. He's not... Well, you'll see for yourself. He says he was on the cliffs. The night Diane Macdonald died."

Brady was already out of bed. Reaching for his clothes. "Ten minutes, Sue. Fifteen at the most. Make him a cup of tea. Keep him there. Lock him up if you have to."

"I'm sorry," he said to Siobhan. "Really sorry. I need to see this guy. From Sue's tone of voice he isn't going to wait around."

He leaned over. Kissed her. Looked at her. Naked, still with the quilt thrown back. "You're beautiful," he said. "Just beautiful. But I have to go. Help yourself to breakfast. The shower. I'll call you when I'm done."

19

Dark hair. Dark, heavy eyebrows. Long sideburns, a week of stubble. A face that had seen its share of suffering. A camouflage jacket, a check scarf, dark green trousers, pockets on the side. A faded orange backpack, a sleeping roll attached to it.

He looked at Brady. Assessed him before he spoke. "I thought I'd come to you before you came looking for me."

'I wouldn't want to meet him on a dark night. Or any night come to that. Dark. Dark jacket. Jeans. Some sort of beanie hat. Dark. Mentally and physically.'

Very clearly the man on the cliff top...

Brady held his hand out.

"Michael Brady. You want to talk?"

A firm grip. He looked into Brady's eyes. Assessed him for a second time.

"Gerry Donoghue. Maybe. I'd rather eat breakfast though."

This is a murder enquiry. Might be a murder enquiry. This is the last person to see Diane Macdonald alive. In theory the only suspect I've got...

"I can get you something from the canteen."

"I was in the Army. I've done canteens if it's all the same to you."

'So the suspect – the only bloody suspect: the obvious bloody suspect – walked into the station on Saturday morning. Gave himself up. And you took him out for fucking breakfast?'

Brady ignored Alan Kershaw's policing manual. Knew instinctively that Donoghue had been in far tougher places than Whitby's interview room. Made a decision. "There's a café down the road. How's a full English sound?"

"MORNING, MR BRADY."

"Morning, Tracey. How's things?"

"Can't complain. What can I get you?"

"Two coffees. And can we have some breakfast? Full English?"

"For your friend? He looks like he needs a bit of feeding up. What about you?"

I'm being unfaithful. But I need some breakfast...

"Bacon sandwich, Tracey. Plum tomatoes if you've got some."

"Coming up. He's alright with black pudding? Some folk are a bit funny with it."

Brady didn't bother asking. "He was in the Army, Tracey. Give him double. And give my love to Ruby when you next see her."

GERRY DONOGHUE PUT his fork into the last piece of black pudding. Pushed his remaining baked beans onto it. Didn't waste much time chewing. Put his knife and fork down.

"Not bad," he said. "Not bad at all. The British Army can

fuck plenty of things up but it can cook breakfast. So I'm a fair judge." He looked up. Caught Tracey's eye across the café. Shouted, "Thanks, love."

Brady finished his coffee. Sat back. Knew he didn't need to say anything.

"What were you doing on the cliff top on Sunday night, Mr Donoghue? That's your opening question. Then again..."

Donoghue paused. Weighed Brady up for a third time. "Maybe not. You're not a man that plays by the normal rules. If you did we'd be sitting in your interview room. What can I tell you?"

Why you walked into the police station. But you're not going to answer that one...

"Sunday night. What you saw..."

Donoghue shrugged. "I was walking. I walk a lot. And yeah, I saw her. Her and two other people." He hesitated. "Three for definite. Maybe four."

Maybe four? Am I making progress?

"Diane Macdonald first."

Donoghue shook his head. "There's nothing to say. A woman walking her dog. Looking like she wanted to get home before it rained. Said 'hello' to me. 'Good evening' maybe. And then she was off. Telling her dog to keep up."

"That's it?"

"That's it. A woman walking her dog."

"What about the other two?"

My bass guitarist and his wife...

"They overtook me. I wasn't going very fast. Thinking." He shrugged. "Think too much sometimes but what can you do? A tall bloke. Angular. His wife. Looking like she didn't much want to be there."

"Nothing else about them?"

A second shake of the head. "That was it. Just the impression that she was doing her duty. Body language. You know."

The last person to see her alive. 'Your obvious bloody suspect, Brady.' Or maybe not the last person to see her alive...

"What about the fourth person. The person you might have seen?"

Donoghue nodded. "You know how it is on the cliff top. The path winds round on itself. Inlets. So I've just passed the woman and her dog. There's one of those. As I walk round it I look behind me. Back the way I've come. See what the weather's doing. See how wet I'm going to get."

"And you see someone?"

"Maybe. You can see a long way there. Back up the hill. And maybe there's someone at the top. *Maybe.* The light's going. Give me a pair of night-viz and I'll tell you for definite. But..."

He shrugged.

"No-one else passed you?"

"No. Definitely not."

"And you're not walking very quickly?"

Another shake of the head. "No. Doesn't make much sense seeing as it was starting to rain but no."

"You want another coffee?"

"Sure, if you've got time. You look like a man who should be somewhere else."

Brady smiled. "Maybe. I'll owe someone an explanation. And a bunch of flowers. But this is more important."

"Never apologise, never explain. That's what they say isn't it?"

"It's not a bad motto. I've known a few coppers that lived by it. What about you? You said you were in the army?"

Tracey came over with the coffee. "Anything else, Mr Brady?"

"We're good, thanks, Tracey. Tot it up, I'll come over and pay you."

"Sergeant," Donoghue said. "Staff sergeant. High enough to have a few blokes under me. Not so high that I had to read the fucking memos."

This time Brady laughed out loud. "How many blokes?"

"Thirty. Plus the fresh-faced knob from Sandhurst who thought he was in command."

"All your life?"

He nodded. "From sixteen. Army family weren't we? Germany. Hong Kong. Army schools. Didn't spend a lot of time with the Careers Master."

"But not now?"

Donoghue shook his head. Tore open a sugar sachet and poured it into his coffee. Held his spoon the wrong way, stirred it with the handle.

"Not now, no..."

A faded orange backpack, a sleeping roll attached to it. Why do I already know the answer to the next question?

"What do you do?"

Donoghue smiled at him. "Walk on the cliffs. Help a couple of mates out occasionally. Tell a copper what he already knows in exchange for my breakfast. I'm a stat, aren't I?"

"A stat? A statistic?"

"Sure. A stat. Five hundred. A thousand. Five thousand. Depends who you believe. Homeless ex-servicemen. Take yourself down to a railway arch one night. Half the blokes there will tell you their service number."

Brady nodded. Didn't reply. Didn't know what to say...

"Thank you for your service," Donoghue said. "That's

what they say now, isn't it? Thank you for your service but now you can fuck off and sleep in that shop doorway."

...Had even less idea what to say. Retreated into police procedure.

"I might need to talk to you again."

"You *will* need to talk to me again. Inevitable. And no, I don't have a mobile."

"So how do I get in touch with you?"

"We'll shake hands. Trust each other. The old religion. I'll phone you in a week."

Brady reached his hand out. Shook hands with the homeless ex-serviceman. Knew he'd phone.

"Supposing I need to see you before then?"

Donoghue smiled. "Magic."

"Magic?"

"Magic Pockets. Fuck knows what his real name is. You'll find him on the seat halfway up Blue Bank. He likes the view. Or doing the church garden the other side of town. He wears a big old coat. With magic pockets."

20

Brady put his key in the door. Guessed Siobhan had gone home to start working her way through Amazon's sheet music. Wondered how Ash's hockey had gone.

Pushed the door.

At exactly the moment someone opened it from inside.

"Bean! Jess, sorry. What are you doing here?"

"I'm just going, Mr Brady."

"I thought you were playing hockey?"

"It was cancelled. The other school couldn't raise a team. Some bug they've got. So we drove to Guisborough. Then they phoned and we turned round."

"Where's Ash?"

"Upstairs in her room. We're going out later."

"Ash?" Brady stood at the bottom of the stairs and shouted hopefully. Amy Winehouse told him she wasn't going to rehab. His daughter didn't reply.

He walked up two flights. Knocked on the bedroom door.

"Go away, Dad. I don't want to speak to you."

"Ash, What's the matter? Can I come in?"

"No. You'll only make it worse. Go away."

What the hell have I done? Or not done? It's not my fault the hockey was cancelled...

"Ash. Just – "

"No, Dad. I'll come downstairs when I'm ready. Probably in a fortnight. Or next year."

Brady shook his head.

Just when I thought I had her worked out...

Walked downstairs. Rang Siobhan. Apologised again for having to go out. "It's low tide this afternoon. Archie says there are still some dog biscuits in your pocket..."

She laughed. Told him she'd be ready.

Brady made himself a coffee. Sat on the balcony. Still couldn't work out what he'd done wrong...

THE DOOR OPENED. Ash was finally downstairs. There was no preamble.

"It's *our* house, Dad. Yours and mine. *We* planned it. *We* went shopping for furniture. And then – "

"Ash what are you talking about?"

"I'm talking about your girlfriend, Dad. I come home and she's coming out of your shower. And before you ask, no, I'm not spying on you. I heard a noise and I was looking for Archie."

"You and Bean? Jessica – "

"Yes, me and Jess. Because hockey was cancelled. And Jess's room at home is being decorated. So – "

"Ash, I'm sorry. It was a one-off. A complete one-off.

Someone had turned up at the station. Someone I had to see."

"So you left her in *our* house?"

"Ash, she's got a house of her own. You know that."

"But she was *here*. When I came in. Do you want me to move out, Dad? So that you've got some privacy? Then you can have as many bloody girlfriends as you like."

"Ash, you're being irrational."

"No, I am *not* being irrational. Supposing you came home and my boyfriend was just wandering out of the shower?"

"You haven't got a – "

"How do *you* know whether I've got a boyfriend or not? When was the last time you took any interest in what I'm doing?"

"Last weekend when I took you shopping. The other day when we talked after school – "

"That's not the point."

"Well what is the point?"

"The point is that Jess and I came home and it wasn't *our* house. Because she was here."

"Ash, 'she' has a name."

"You know what I mean."

"Look, Ash, it was an emergency. A one-off. You know that MP's wife was found on the rocks. Someone I needed to speak to had turned up at the station."

"Well why didn't you arrange a time to talk to him? Like a normal person?"

"Because you can't do that, Ash. Look, sit down, let me explain something to you."

"I don't want – "

"No, Ash, humour me. In fact, just for once do as you're told. I know you think I'm old. Nearly past it. But I still know a few things, so listen to me. Five minutes, no more."

Ash reluctantly sat down. Looked warily at her father.

"You want to be a human rights lawyer."

"You know I do."

"Right. And you know what, Ash? It's going to be a lot like being a copper. You're going to know what's right. You'll be *convinced* it's right. But you'll find some bloody bureaucrat says it's wrong. Or politics will rear its ugly head. You'll have to fight for what you *know* is right. You're going to deal with people that are frightened and afraid. Not thinking straight – "

"Dad, being frightened *is* being afraid."

Brady laughed. "Like I said, not thinking straight. Above all, Ash, you'll have to talk to people. Get their story. And you'll have to talk when they're *ready* to talk. And that isn't always going to be at ten-thirty in the morning. Or when you've made an appointment. And it sure as hell isn't going to be in your nice, comfortable office. It's going to be at midnight. Quite possibly in some bloody hell-hole in a foreign country. And you know what, Ash – "

Brady felt the tears prick his eyes. Couldn't stop them.

"– You know what? I'm your dad. And when I say the words 'hell-hole in a foreign country' I am bloody terrified for you. And at the same time I'm so proud I could burst. And that's how it was with me. The guy I needed to talk to turned up. He's homeless. There's no way of contacting him. Except through someone called 'Magic Pockets.' So I had to go. And yes, Siobhan was here. I had to leave her. And I'm sorry about that. I understand your point. But I can't promise it won't happen again because that's what I do. And that's who I am. And one day, Ash you're going to do the same. You're going to look into someone's eyes and say, 'Yes,

I love you. Yes, I want to have dinner with you. But I've had a phone call. And this is what I do. And this is who I am.' And that's a long speech. And I'm sorry. But it's the truth."

Brady stopped. Wiped his eyes. Made no attempt to hide the tears. Looked at his daughter. "There. You made me cry. Because I love you. Now come here and give me a hug. You want pizza tonight? Fish and chips? Maybe you should get me that drone you were talking about. We could fly it to every fish and chip shop in Whitby."

21

It was Scholesy who said it to him.

'I'll be back to you tomorrow, Brady. Assuming those scouse bastards don't beat us and I have to call the Samaritans.'

'Tomorrow's Sunday.'

'Right. You think your dirty little secrets know it's Sunday? Or maybe crimes committed on a Sunday don't count any more? You're a copper. Phone the Home Secretary. Suggest it as a way of making the figures look better. Sit back and collect your knighthood. Tomorrow morning, kemosabe.'

Brady clicked Mozart's e-mail. Opened the attachment. Entered the password that had just appeared on his phone.

'Your secrets don't know it's Sunday.'

Let's see what Graham Macdonald's secrets have to say on the Sabbath...

GRAHAM MACDONALD WAS ELECTED as the MP for mid-Hampshire in 2005. He made it to the final three of the selection procedure –

possibly as a result of being married to the Chairman's daughter – but even so was 'unimpressive' and 'a distant third.'

That would probably have been the end of his political career had not the chosen candidate been arrested for indecency in a public toilet the day before nominations closed. The runner-up in the selection process was, by that time, committed to standing elsewhere and, with no time to re-open the selection, the 'unimpressive' Mr Macdonald became the candidate for a very safe seat.

And who told the local police where to find the candidate? Or am I getting far too suspicious in my old age?

Macdonald had some family money behind him (the Chairman's daughter. And his own parents were still alive at that point – although their money was ultimately swallowed by care home fees). Nevertheless Macdonald quickly bought a house in Kennington SE11, with a mortgage from the Bradford & Bingley.

He paid £270,000 for the house, with a £30,000 deposit. If that was his cash it was all the cash he had.

Macdonald's first two years in the Commons appear to have been uneventful. His maiden speech was described as 'lacklustre and unoriginal' and he achieved nothing of note. In 2008 he found himself appointed to the Defence Committee, a role for which he had no obvious qualifications, unless you count four years in the Career Cadet Force at boarding school.

Following the 2010 General Election he was briefly appointed a (very) junior minister, but resigned eight months later, saying that it 'took too much time from looking after the vital interests of my constituents.'

Judging by the way Macdonald's bank balance began to increase around this point I suspect it took too much time from looking after the vital interests of Graham Macdonald.

There is little else to report regarding his House of Commons career. He remains resolutely on the backbenches. He supports the Government, his majority rises and falls with the Conservative Party's national fortunes. If he ever says anything publicly it is to call for more spending on defence or harsher penalties for offenders.

Financial

Macdonald entered the Commons with little money: he would now be described as wealthy. Clearly some of this can be accounted for by property appreciation. But...

You know that I do not like to speculate. But there are too many unexplained deposits in Macdonald's bank account. I have listed them on a separate appendix, and also cross-referenced them to foreign visits by the Commons Defence Committee.

Brady looked at the appendix. Counted eight deposits, the smallest £10,000, the largest £100,000.

A hundred grand? A hundred bloody grand? More than I make in a year. Way more than I make in a year.

Shook his head. Looked at the appendix again.

Four deposits from the Middle East. Two from Eastern Europe. One from Central America, one from South America. Totalling... Enough to buy the holiday home in Runswick Bay.

Did his bank not ask any questions? No, because it's in the Cayman Islands...

Macdonald has also mastered the art of the expenses claim. He has twice been among the top 5 MPs for expenses claims – a not insignificant achievement – and briefly enjoyed his 15 minutes of fame when he claimed for a taxi to take him 200 yards as 'my weather app said it was going to rain.'

Brady finished the report. Walked to the fridge and got a beer. Braved the cold and sat on his balcony.

Is he taking bribes? Selling information? Had Diane found out? Was she threatening him?

But Macdonald was in Hungary. Gerry Donoghue thought he saw a runner. Macdonald's as far from a runner as you can get. Then again... I've only got Gerry Donoghue's word that there was a runner.

And it wouldn't be the first time I've found myself liking a murderer.

It's time to take Frankie for a walk...

22

'The path winds round an inlet. So I've just passed the woman and her dog. There's one of those. I look back the way I've come. See what the weather's doing. See how wet I'm going to get.'

'You can see a long way there. Back up the hill. And maybe there's someone at the top. Maybe. But the light's going.'

"This has to be it, Frankie. The only possible place. A mile from Runswick? Maybe not that. But far enough for Diane Macdonald to give her dog a good walk."

"And be in a hurry to get back if it starts to rain."

Brady walked along the cliff-top path. Only wide enough for one person as the path bent round to the left. "Here," he said. "Just before he turns. He's going to glance back up the hill. I'd do it, most people would do it. Rain or no rain."

"So where's Diane Macdonald?"

"The other side of the inlet? More or less opposite him? Let's walk back up the hill, Frankie."

She shook her head. "Walk across the Moors, 'walk up this hill, Frankie.' No wonder we don't have any overweight coppers in Whitby."

"Despite our best efforts with the fish and chips. Come on..."

"Twelve minutes," Brady said. "So what's that? Two-thirds of a mile? But it's a clear line of sight. If there's someone at the bottom of the hill we could see them. Easily. So Gerry Donoghue could have seen someone."

"Except you said it was nearly dark. And it was raining."

"Let's suppose there *is* someone, Frankie. A killer. Somewhere – " Brady started walking back down the hill. "Somewhere around here – definitely before the path – he meets Diane Macdonald. But it all depends *where* he meets her."

"I don't follow you."

"Walk to the top of the hill, Frankie. The cliffs go straight down. Push me off there and I'm dead. Go two hundred yards down the hill – where the path is, where the cliff slopes – and I'm definitely *not* dead. You push me off there and I'm going to fall what? Ten feet. And I'm going to fall onto earth, not rock. So I'm going to be hurt – "

"Especially at your age, boss."

"Thanks, Frankie. But you see the point I'm making. There I'm alive, at the top of the hill I'm dead. And right here – more or less where she went over the edge – it's what? Fifty-fifty?"

"So it's the same questions as Billy and Sandra Garrity?"

"It's *exactly* the same. Why them? Why kill them when they did? Why like that? Here we go again. *Two* questions. Why Diane Macdonald? And just as importantly, why here?"

"Three questions, boss. Why now?"

Brady nodded. "Assuming we ignore the divorce... But concentrate on 'why here?'

Frankie was silent. She looked down at where Diane Macdonald had died, the rocks washed clean by half a dozen high tides. "Pushing someone off a cliff isn't a spur of the moment decision."

"No, it's not. Maybe it is if you're married. But if it's a stranger..."

"Then you're going to check. Rehearse. Scout it out beforehand."

Do your reconnaissance. Like in the Army. Like Gerry Donoghue would have been trained to do...

"What you just said, boss. 'Maybe it is if you're married.' What her friend said about the house in Tuscany. We can't ignore the divorce. Whatever way you look at it her death is bloody good news for Macdonald. You think he knew?"

Brady shook his head. "My gut feeling is no. The number was written on a piece of paper. Torn out of a pad. My guess – "

"*Why*, boss? Why is the number written on a piece of paper? If someone gives me a phone number they just share the contact. The number's on my phone, not on a piece of paper."

Brady nodded. "But you're not getting divorced are you, Frankie? They've been married for twenty-two years. The number probably is in her phone. But I think she wrote it down as well."

"So she saw it?"

"Every time she sat down at her desk. 'This is what I'm going to do on Monday morning.' Cross the Rubicon. Make the first appointment."

"Why Diane Macdonald? Why here? Why now? We've definitely ticked the last box, boss."

"Maybe. Let's see what happens this afternoon. I'm seeing Graham Macdonald. He's paying North Yorkshire the honour of a state visit."

23

No *sign of a suit.*

But no sign of his jeans either...

Macdonald was wearing a mid-grey jacket, a pale blue open-necked shirt, a pair of chinos. A man dressed by a catalogue. The middle-aged man who'd seen the 25-year-old model with the flat stomach and thought, 'Yep, that's me.'

Even the white-soled Skechers all the young football managers are wearing...

"Thank you for coming," Graham Macdonald said. "Obviously not good for me to come in to the station. Some bloody tourist with an iPhone."

As if a 'tourist with an iPhone' is going to recognise a back-bench MP...

He led the way into the lounge. A room dominated by the view. A picture window, the rooftops of Runswick Bay falling away to the beach in front of them.

A pale pink settee facing the fireplace. Another settee along the far wall. A wood burning stove that looked like it had never been used. Expensive paintings of ships at sea. The longest footstool Brady had ever seen, ornately covered, copies of the *Economist* and the *Spectator* thrown on it.

And this is what 'casual politician' reads. Wants you to think he reads. Where's Jack Reacher...

"Mornings," Macdonald said. "That's when the house is at its best. Like everything on the East Coast. Fine at seven, rain by eleven. Or is it the other way round? Anyway, mornings. And bloody early ones in June and July."

"How much time do you spend here?"

He shrugged. "Five weeks? Six weeks? My wife and daughter are here more often than I am. It was an impulse buy. Where I grew up. But my wife likes it. Liked it. Now? With my daughter in Italy for a year? Who knows?"

Macdonald sat at one end of the settee. Gestured for Brady to sit at the other. Ostentatiously rested his right ankle on his left knee.

"She fell," he said. A simple statement of fact.

Brady nodded. "Your wife certainly fell. The question is what – or who – caused her to fall."

Macdonald shook his head. "Diane fell. It's obvious. It happens. Her own fault. I'm not even sure why we're discussing it."

"I agree, Graham. People do fall from cliffs. But it's rare. And you're a public figure. So we need to dot the I's – "

"Cross the bloody T's? There are no T's to cross. And I'd have thought you'd have better things to spend police resources on. God knows you're always complaining you don't have enough. I was talking to Alan Kershaw the other day..."

'I know your boss.' Dropped not very subtly into the conversation...

"...But fortunately he can see the bigger picture now he's in London."

...Clearly I need to retaliate.

"I think your wife did fall, Graham. An unfortunate accident..."

Like Lizzie Kershaw was an 'unfortunate accident.'

Don't say it. Save it for later.

"But we have to rule out the other possibilities."

"Which are?"

"There are only three possible reasons for the fall, Graham. Accident, murder or suicide."

Three simple words. Let's see how he reacts...

"You're being stupid now, Michael. God knows I meet plenty of idiots in the Commons but murder and suicide..." Macdonald shook his head. "Diane was happy. She had everything she needed. Didn't lack for money. What more does a woman want? And she didn't have any enemies. The most contentious thing she did was judge the Victoria Sponge at the village fete."

"And nobody with a grudge against you?"

Macdonald laughed. "A few journalists. The prick that ran the story about the taxi. The feeling's mutual, I assure you. That leftie comedian I made mincemeat of on *Question Time.* No wonder the BBC didn't ask me back. No, is the answer. You've been watching too much TV."

Or I've been standing in Billy and Sandra Garrity's lounge...

Brady glanced across the room. A single shelf over the wood-burning stove. A vase of fading flowers at one end.

...But you're safe. No-one's going to tie you to that fireplace, Graham.

"What about Diane, Graham. No-one with a grudge against her?"

Macdonald laughed dismissively. "Only the old bat who

came second in the Victoria Sponge competition. Diane was a political wife, Michael. Her job was to smile on the front of the election leaflet. Trust me, no-one had a grudge against her."

"And the two of you – "

"What are you asking me now? Were we happy? We were a normal married couple. And as you know – "

Brady held his hand up. "I'm sorry, Graham. My job. Not for one second did I think anything else."

"So we're done are we, Michael? Can I get on with some work? Make sure this plays out properly?"

"Plays out properly? If you mean the investigation – "

"I mean the bloody press, don't I? Grieving widower back at his desk after his wife's tragic accident. There's a big new estate in my constituency. Full of first-time buyers. Fucking Lib-Dems to a man. But this should be worth two or three thousand votes. Enough to stem the yellow tide for another five years. So I'll get back to London. Talk to my press people."

And get back to whoever was wearing those heels...

Brady stood up. Knew that Diane Macdonald had been murdered. Knew he was never going to prove it. Spread his hands. "Of course. When are you going?"

"First thing tomorrow morning."

"I'll get my sergeant to bring Reggie tonight then shall I?"

Macdonald looked at him blankly. "Reggie?"

"Your dog."

"The dog? What do I want with the bloody dog? I can't take a dog back to London. What do you expect me to do? Take it into the House of Commons? Train it to shit on the Opposition benches?"

"You can't just abandon your dog – "

"It's not my dog. It's my wife's. Was my wife's. Where's the bloody thing now?"

"Someone's looking after him. Out in the country."

"Well that's perfect, isn't it? Tell him to send me the adoption papers. Fed-Ex. I'll sign them tonight."

24

"The five stages of grief," Brady said, throwing his pen down on his desk. "Five bloody stages of grief. Denial, anger, bargaining, depression, acceptance."

"Exasperation..." Frankie murmured.

"Not in Graham Macdonald's world. Bluster, belligerence, bargaining... I don't know about bargaining so much as outright bloody spin. *Lack* of depression. And opportunism. You know what Diane Macdonald's pal said to me? 'The longer you know him the more you dislike him.' Talking about her husband but... Bloody hell, I thought he was a prick when he was eighteen. Now? Kershaw on steroids. And then – "

"Can I get you a blood pressure tablet, Detective Chief Inspector?"

"Then he says – not so much acceptance as bloody opportunism – then he says, 'Diane dying will play well with the voters. Two or three thousand votes. Hold back the yellow tide for another five years.""

"Are you displaying your political prejudices here, boss?"

"I haven't got a political bone in my body, Frankie. I do have a hypocrisy bone. I do have a nose-in-the-trough bone. I do have a… Well, I'm not going to use the word."

"What about the investigation. If there is one…"

"Right now there isn't. That's why I'm frustrated – "

"Honestly, boss, you can't tell… You think he knew about the divorce? What she was planning?"

Brady shook his head. "You know what? I think he barely knows his wife. 'Her job is to smile on the front of the election leaflet.' That's what he said. I think the rest of the time they live separate lives."

"Except that if a woman dies – "

"Her husband is the first place you look. But we've made no bloody progress at all, Frankie. *I've* made no bloody progress. Death by misadventure. But there's something there, Frankie. There's absolutely something there. But right now we've no evidence. Nothing. You want to walk down to the harbour and get some fish and chips? One of the last days it'll be warm enough to eat them outside?"

"I'll get my coat."

"And Frankie. You might need to phone Lochie. The Honourable Member for mid-Hampshire does not want his dog back. 'What do I want with the bloody dog?' was his exact quote. So prove it was murder, solve the bloody murder and find a new home for Reggie."

Frankie smiled. "Not in that order of importance though, boss…"

"Come on Archie, the tourists have all gone home. We've got the beach to ourselves again."

Brady told Ash he'd be back in an hour. Clipped Archie's

lead on, checked he had some biscuits and opened the front door. Wondered if he'd ever get tired of the view across the harbour. Knew the answer was 'no.'

"We need a bridge, mate. Never mind Ash and her drone, we need a bridge. Straight across the harbour and onto the beach. Come on." He opened the tailgate of the Tiguan. Archie jumped in, looked at him expectantly. "Honestly, Archie, I'm not sure jumping into the car really deserves a biscuit. But... I need you, Arch. Common sense at the end of a crap day." He ruffled the dog's head. Closed the tailgate. Drove slowly down Henrietta Street. Even more slowly down Church Street. Glanced out of the window.

Another happy couple having their photograph taken under the 'Arguments Yard' sign...

Brady pulled Archie's ball out of his pocket. Held it in his hand for a moment...

Thirty minutes of picking it up covered in Archie's slobber.

...Drop-kicked it across the beach. Watched the Springer scamper after it. Set off walking towards Sandsend. Checked his watch.

Half-six. Sunset in what? Forty minutes? Fifty? Another month and the clocks go back...

Brady walked down to the water's edge. Waited for Archie to drop the ball. Started to bend down. Saw the slobber glistening on the ball. "Christ, Archie, even by your standards that's impressive." Straightened up, spun round, kicked the ball in the direction Archie hadn't been expecting.

'She fell. It's obvious. Her own fault. I'm not even sure why we're discussing it. I'd have thought you'd have better things to spend police resources on.'

'When are you going back to London?'

'First thing tomorrow morning.'

So case closed. Because I can't prove anything. For all my suspicions, for all that Gerry Donoghue 'might have seen someone,' I can't prove a thing.

Brady kicked the ball again. Archie sprinted after it. Brought the ball back and dropped it.

"Here." Brady bent down. Gave him a biscuit. Patted him. Ignored the slobber dripping from Archie's mouth and put his hands either side of the dog's head. Tilted it up slightly. "You're a bloody good dog, Arch. And you'd do that, wouldn't you? Sit by my side until the helicopter turned up?"

Archie looked back at him. Brady laughed. "I know that expression, Arch. Cut the crap and kick the ball."

Did as he was told.

'It leaves Helen and me, Mike. Do we want to look for two new members? Spend that amount of time? The answer's 'no.' So in the short term I'm going to compose. Buy all of Amazon's sheet music paper.'

He'd reached Sandsend. Looked up and saw Siobhan's cottage.

"The band's broken up, Archie. So she's going to be here a lot more. Not just weeks in London and weekends in Sandsend. Is that good news, mate? I don't know."

'It's our house, Dad. Yours and mine. We planned it. Went shopping for furniture. And then I come home and she's coming out of your shower.'

"I don't know what to do, Arch. Walk across and knock on her door? Or tell her it's only weekends? Bloody hell, mate, all you need is a beach, a ball and a biscuit. I'll come back as a spaniel."

Brady turned round. Walked back towards Whitby, felt the wind picking up off the sea. "Come on, mate. We need to walk faster. Get home before it's dark. Spend some time with Ash."

25

She was sitting on the balcony, reading on her iPad.

"Hi, sweetheart. You warm enough? What are you reading? Homework?"

"Nadia Murad, Dad."

"Who? I've never heard of her."

Ash shook her head. Looked up at him.

"That's your you-spend-too-much-time-watching-football face, Ash."

"She's an Iraqi Yazidi, Dad. She was kidnapped by Islamic State and held for three months. She's going to write a book with Amal Clooney. You need to stop watching illegal streams of Middlesbrough games and take an interest in world affairs. Besides, supposing you got arrested?"

"No-one's ever been arrested for watching a football match, Ash."

"There's always a first time, Dad. How was Siobhan anyway?"

Brady shook his head. "I don't know, I didn't see her."

"I thought she was your dog walking buddy now?"

"No. Archie's my dog walking buddy. Or you. And Ash..."

"What, Dad?"

"I'm sorry again. About Saturday. Seeing it from your point of view. Well, I'm sorry."

"Dad..."

"What, sweetheart?"

"About Saturday. I need to ask you a question."

"That sounds like a serious question. Can I make myself a coffee? The wind was picking up on the beach."

Ash nodded. "Decaf at this time of night, Dad. And remember coffee makes you pee. Good job your bedroom's next to the bathroom..."

'Teenage sarcasm, Mike. You'll miss it when she's gone.'

I will, Kate, I will...

IT WAS DARK NOW. Ash had come back inside. "Did you lock the doors?" She nodded. Sat down on the settee.

Now it's her serious face...

"Saturday morning, Dad. When we were talking. When you were lecturing me."

"I wasn't lecturing you."

"I was joking, Dad. But Saturday morning..."

"What about it, love?"

"You said to me... You said one day I'd tell someone I loved them, but that I had to go – couldn't have dinner with them – because I had to work. Is that what you did, Dad? Tell Siobhan you loved her but you had to go?"

Brady stood up. Walked over to the settee. Sat down and pulled her to him. Held her. Thought for a moment. Then pushed her away so he could look at her.

"I understand the question you're asking me, Ash. Not

just 'do I love her?' But 'do I love her like I loved your mum?' And 'can I have those feelings for anyone else?'

Ash looked at him. Blinked away tears. "And what are the answers?"

Brady took a deep breath. "Right now the answers are 'no' to the first one. And so 'no' to the second one. And the third one? Long term? I don't know, sweetheart. I honestly don't know."

"But you like her? It's not just sex?"

Brady laughed. "Yes, of course I like her. She's funny, she's intelligent – "

"Good looking?"

"Yes, sure. And she makes me laugh."

And she's away in London most of the time. Or she was. And that was perfect. Because it stopped the relationship going any further. Except now she's sitting in Sandsend composing. Every day of the week. And I don't know how I feel about that...

Ash nodded. "Thanks for telling me, Dad. I... Well, I'm not sure how I feel if I'm honest."

Brady wrapped his arms round her again. "You and me both, sweetheart. One day at a time. Like we've always done. And nothing – and no-one – will ever come between us."

Ash pulled away. Smiled sweetly at him. "By the way – the other day when I said you didn't know whether I had a boyfriend or not. It's probably time you met Angel."

Brady stared at her. "Angel?"

Ash nodded. "I've been seeing him for three months. He's thirty. He has a motorbike. And a neck tattoo. Earrings. And a stud through his nose."

Brady considered what she'd said. Smiled back just as sweetly. "Of course, darling. That's lovely. It's a bit late tonight. I'll put your room on Airbnb tomorrow..."

. . .

He kissed her. Told her to sleep well. Fetched his fleece. Unlocked the balcony doors. Sat and watched the lights reflect off the harbour.

Tried not to think about Diane Macdonald.

Failed.

'You need to add murder to your list of possibilities, Mike. There's skin under her fingernails.'

But it's degraded. So no evidence. Nothing. Except for one witness. Who doesn't even have a phone. But does have a friend called Magic Pockets...

Brady pulled the zip of his fleece up. Heard Jim Fitzpatrick talking to him. His first boss, his mentor.

'Sometimes you know they're guilty, Mike. Sometimes you know what happened – almost like you were there. But you can't prove it. And you've got to accept it. Move on. Solve the cases you can solve. The ones with enough proof to convince a jury.'

'What about the bastards that get away with it, boss?'

'Write their name down in a notebook if it makes you feel better. Leopards don't change their spots. There'll be another day.'

Brady shook his head.

Not for Graham Macdonald.

'When are you going back to London?'

'First thing tomorrow morning.'

Where he'll spend his days in the security of power and privilege. And his nights with whoever owned the heels that clicked across the Embassy floor...

Brady locked the balcony doors. Went to bed angry and frustrated.

Wished he'd opened a beer instead of taking Ash's advice.

Woke up at two and stumbled to the loo.

Made a mental note not to buy any more decaf.

26

"Dan. How are you doing? Good to have you back. Training course good?"

Dan Keillor shook his head. "Two weeks of police college food, boss? They're probably still re-heating the stew from when you were there."

"Relatively fresh then? I reckon I ate Dixon of Dock Green's leftovers. A few plates of fish n' chips'll sort you out, Dan. And riding that bike of yours over the Moors."

"Pickering and back eight times a day, boss. I must have gained half a stone."

"Have a word with Frankie and she'll fill – "

Brady glanced down at his phone. Sighed. "Sorry, Dan, I need to take this. Our Lord and Master..."

"Michael. How are you?"

Michael? 'Brady' if I'm in trouble. 'Mike' if he wants to be friends. 'Michael?' I've no idea...

"Alan. Good afternoon. And I'm well thank you. Better than the sneak preview of winter Whitby is giving us today."

"Michael, I won't waste your time. A government whip's just collared me as I came out of a meeting. Asked me about Graham Macdonald."

Macdonald? Where's this going?

"I saw him yesterday. Spoke to him about his wife, obviously."

Kershaw clicked his tongue dismissively. "Too bloody high-strung if you ask me. I met her at some do. And now she's tipped herself over a bloody cliff. More importantly, on our patch."

I've no idea where it's going...

"Anyway, Macdonald was supposed to be in a Select Committee meeting today. Didn't turn up. No-one's heard from him apparently. And according to the Chairman of this bloody committee, as I'm from Whitby, and Macdonald was brought up there, I obviously know his every movement."

"As far as I know he was catching the first train back to London this morning. He didn't say any more."

Apart from offering to sign Reggie's adoption papers...

"If you hear anything let me know will you? So I'm fore-armed next time I bump into the pompous arse."

"I'd have thought the obvious answer was that his wife's death has caught up with him. He's probably at his house in London."

Kershaw laughed. "Like I said, I've met his wife. I've met his girlfriend as well. I doubt he's grieving. But it's on our patch, so keep me posted. You never know when you can use an MP's influence. Even one as thick as Macdonald."

Do I say anything to him? My doubts? The divorce...

"Mike?"

"Sorry, sir, I was thinking."

"Well don't waste any more time thinking about Diane Macdonald. We've nothing to gain and plenty to lose if it gets messy. Fight the battles you can win, that's what I say. And don't forget to come down here. Have dinner with me. Parliament won't be paying the bills for ever."

Brady promised to keep Kershaw up to date. Crossed his fingers behind his back and promised to have dinner with him. Ended the call.

'Solve the cases you can solve. The ones with enough proof to convince a jury.'

'Fight the battles you can win.'

The best boss I've ever had and one of the worst. Both saying the same thing. Maybe I should pay attention...

BRADY CLOSED HIS OFFICE DOOR. Walked into the main office. "Dan, have you seen Frankie?"

"She was in early, boss. So she finished early. Something about a date? Some guy called Reggie? I thought she was seeing a Scottish bloke?"

Brady laughed. "You're out of the loop, Dan. Way, way out. Let me get a coffee. I'll bring you up to date."

27

"You're wearing your best shirt again, Dad. Except you've worn it so often lately you probably need a new best shirt."

"I told you, I'm taking Siobhan out for dinner. But it's my birthday next month. Large."

"You'll need to transfer me some money if that's a subtle hint."

"I don't doubt it, sweetheart. And I won't be late. Siobhan's got a call early tomorrow morning. Something about some music for a film."

Brady reached for his car keys. Kissed his daughter. Bent down and patted Archie. Closed the front door behind him and walked over to the car.

Ten minutes, he texted to Siobhan. *Table booked, gin and tonic waiting...*

HIS PHONE RANG as he was driving past the golf club, looking across the fairway and out to sea.

If it's Kershaw I'll ignore it...

It wasn't Kershaw.

"Graham, I wasn't expecting to hear from you."

"I need to see you. Something's happened."

"What's happened? You've thought of something? Tell me on the phone."

"No. I need to see you. Now. Tonight."

Brady braked. Pulled over into a parking space on the right. Saw Sandsend in front of him. Someone walking their dog on the beach. Knew this wasn't good news.

"Tell me on the phone."

"I can't. I need to see you. Now. It's urgent."

"Is this about Diane? And how the hell can you see me tonight, Graham? You're in London."

"It's about who killed Diane. And I'm not in London. I'm in Runswick Bay."

What's made him come back?

Brady heard a noise.

Glass clinking. Phone in his left hand, pouring a drink with his right hand. His hand shaking. The bottle hitting the glass...

"I'm in Sandsend. I'll see you in ten minutes. Fifteen at the most... No, half an hour. I have to see someone first. And don't drink too much, Graham."

Because I need you sober.

So you can explain to me.

After I've done some explaining of my own...

BRADY INDICATED. Turned right down Ellerby Lane towards Runswick. Replayed the conversation for the tenth time in ten minutes.

'I'm really sorry. All I do is apologise to you.'

'Can't it wait until morning?'

'No, it can't wait. And I can't tell you why. Just that he was

drinking – and I can't take the risk of him changing his mind. Or getting cold feet and going back to London.'

'I – '

'You don't have to say it, Siobhan. You look lovely. Beautiful. Beyond beautiful.'

'I wasn't going to say that. I was going to say I'll still be here when you're driving back.'

'I don't know how long I'll be.'

'It doesn't matter. I'll compose. I might have got changed though...'

He parked outside Macdonald's holiday home.

Turned the engine off. Closed his eyes. Took a deep breath.

What did I say to Frankie once? 'This is who we are.' Right. Every bloody time...

He pushed the image of Siobhan out of his head.

Switched off Mike Brady, who made a career out of letting people down. Switched on Detective Chief Inspector Michael Brady, who knew that Diane Macdonald had been murdered.

But who can't prove it.

Not yet...

28

"You want a drink, Mike? Michael? Which is it today?"

'You want a drink?' Asks the man who got away with it. Who drove a car when he was drunk. Who killed Lizzie Greenbeck and ran away across a field.

"No thanks, Graham. I'm driving. And Mike or Michael. I'm easy."

Macdonald shook his head aggressively. "Don't be stupid. You're the bloody police. Who's going to arrest you? Besides, it's unlucky to drink alone."

Brady watched him pour two whiskies, one a double, the other a final eliminator for an Olympic drinking contest.

The face hadn't changed much. Brady could still see the arrogant teenager. But the hair was greyer. Red veins charted a steady course across his nose and cheeks. A big face, but even so his mouth seemed disproportionately large. A smile that exposed as much gum as teeth.

"What's happened, Graham? We only talked on Monday. You were rushing back to London."

So fast you didn't want to see your wife's body. Or worry about your dog...

"Why are you back so quickly? And why the urgent phone call?"

Macdonald took a deep breath. Stood up.

"Are we off the record here, Mike? Like the press? Or don't the police have 'off the record?'"

Not if you're going to tell me you paid someone to push your wife off a cliff...

"I'm in your home, Graham. You invited me here. You know what I do. You know how far my authority goes."

"North Yorkshire?"

"Right. North Yorkshire. And right now I have no evidence to suggest there's been any crime in North Yorkshire that's connected to you."

Suspicions? Yes. Evidence? No.

Macdonald walked across the lounge to the picture window. Spoke with his back to Brady.

"I went back to London. Went to my house. I was getting out of the taxi when my phone rang."

"And that call's the reason you phoned me? Why you're here?"

Another deep breath. Macdonald slowly turned round.

What did I think last time? Casual politician? Now? As far from casual as you can get. Dishevelled politician. Worn, worried politician. Bloody terrified politician.

"Someone made a threat. A very serious, very personal threat. I don't know any other way to put it."

Brady shook his head. "I'm sorry, Graham. I don't understand. I saw you on Monday. Your wife had died. You didn't even want to see her body. You didn't want your dog. You were rushing back to London. I can't say I approved of your choices, but that's what you'd decided. Now you're here..."

Brady spread his hands. "...telling me you're being threatened."

And looking at you – and the amount of whisky you're drinking – I believe you. But you're going to have to say a lot more than, 'I've been threatened...'

"Look, I went to London – " Macdonald broke off. Walked over to the sideboard. Poured himself another Olympic whisky.

"How long were you there?"

"I came back this morning. Nine o'clock from King's Cross."

So you were threatened and you ran away. Like you did after Lizzie Greenbeck...

Brady shook his head. "I'm a police officer, Graham. You asked to see me. Your wife's dead. I have trouble believing she slipped and fell. But there's no evidence. The verdict would be 'death by misadventure.' Except now you tell me you've been threatened."

And I'm a copper. I swore an oath to uphold the law. And that applies to someone I think is a complete shit as much as it applies to someone who goes to church three times on Sunday.

"You're back in Runswick. We've known each other a while so I can be blunt. You look bloody awful. So clearly something's happened. But I need more than the words, 'I've been threatened.' Who by?"

Macdonald turned round. Stared out of the window again.

Even from behind I can tell he's not seeing anything...

Lifted his whisky glass to his lips. Drained it. Finally spoke.

"I don't know. It sounds stupid but it's the truth. I don't bloody well know."

Brady stood up. Put his untouched whisky down on the

sideboard. Tried to keep the frustration out of his voice. "You *must* know."

"No, I don't. I simply don't."

He finally turned and faced Brady.

"You understand the biggest divide in politics, don't you? The biggest divide in the Commons? Across the pond in Congress? Probably the same in the Chinese fucking politburo for all I know."

"I'm clearly wrong if I say left and right. So no, I don't understand – "

"Money," Macdonald said. "Pure and simple. Conservative and Labour? Leave and Remain?" He shook his head. "Money. Nothing more, nothing less. Wealthy and skint. Straight out of the City. Family money. Or me. Boracic and fucking lint."

'Macdonald entered the Commons with little money: he would now be described as wealthy.'

Brady raised his eyebrows. Did his best not to look sceptical.

"That's how it is in the Commons. Remember what someone said about Heseltine? 'He bought his own furniture.' Same as Biden. 'I was the poorest man in Congress.' Well, I was the poorest man in Parliament. Third in the selection process. Working for my father-in-law. Selling industrial shelving for fuck's sake. Mansfield on a pissing wet Tuesday afternoon. By Wednesday night I'm the candidate. A month later I'm an MP. And a skint one. I'm the MP for mid-Hampshire. The bloke sitting next to me on the backbenches *owns* mid-fucking-Hampshire."

"You didn't go to school in Whitby. You were privately educated."

"I was. On the cheap. It wasn't Eton or Winchester. And where was I afterwards? Not Balliol bloody College.

Southampton Uni. Not taking port with the Master. Having a pint down by the docks. Hoping some bloody docker didn't stick one on me."

"Your father was the Chief Constable."

"You want to know the truth about my father? I'll tell you. A family secret no-one knows. And if they did know they're dead now. North Yorkshire's Chief Constable was an alcoholic. And you can make a lot of stupid decisions when you're pissed. In uniform and out. Easy pickings for the wide boys in sharp suits."

Macdonald was back at the sideboard. Poured another whisky. Made a 'help yourself' gesture at Brady.

"School fees? My mother paid them. And then she gets dementia. And the nursing home chews its way through what my father hasn't drunk. Or invested in Nokia – on the day the iPhone was launched."

Is he expecting me to feel sympathy for him?

"So I did what any sensible MP does."

"Make money?"

"There are six hundred of us in that den of iniquity. Two hundred mad bastards who think they'll be Prime Minister. Two hundred deluded simpletons who are true believers. And two hundred of us who know it won't last and we need to make the most of it."

"And that's what you do?"

"That's what I do. Because my mother and father left me no fucking choice."

"That still doesn't explain why you're being threatened. Why you're back here."

Another trip to the sideboard. Another whisky.

The apple doesn't fall far from the tree...

"I'm on the Defence Select Committee. You know the most useful thing I own? The *only* thing I own that's of any real value? Apart from the houses?" He pointed at a picture on the wall. "That's a Norman Wilkinson. Four grand? Five grand? It's not worth one percent of my address book. My contacts. So that's what I sell. Access. Introductions. Gossip. Who's carelessly been filmed with a Commons researcher. And my considered opinion on which way the wind's blowing."

Brady nodded. Kept his feelings to himself. Hoped they didn't show.

"But none of that – your opinion, introductions – none of that gets you threatened. None of that – with the greatest possible respect, Graham – accounts for the amount of Macallan you're drinking."

Macdonald slumped down on the sofa. Put his elbows on his knees. Spoke to the carpet. "You want it in one word?" he said quietly. "One fucking word? Greed. That's what accounts for it. Pure fucking greed." He shook his head slowly.

An addict admitting it...

"And once you start you can't stop."

"How much greed?"

"Two hundred and fifty grand."

"Two hundred and fifty grand? A quarter of a million? Pounds?"

"Well not lira. And not the Chinese fucking yuan either. Not that we won't all be using it in thirty years' time."

"That has to be for a lot more than information."

"Yes," Macdonald said to the carpet.

"What for?"

"No comment. Can't comment."

Like any bloody suspect in the interview room. 'No comment. My solicitor says I can't comment.' Not that I can't find out with a phone call to Saltburn, Graham...

"Who offered you the money?"

"An intermediary."

Brady nodded. "So not the first time he'd approached you. Or paid you."

Macdonald stared at him. "How do you know?"

"Because you accepted the offer. Because that amount of money comes under 'too good to be true.' Unless you know the person making the offer. And they know you. And what you're prepared to do."

Brady looked at the painting on the wall. *'That's a Norman Wilkinson. Four grand? Five grand?'*

What have I got? Two sculptures I paid a murderer three hundred quid for.

"Alright, you won't tell me *why* they made the threat, Graham. Can you at least tell me what they said?"

"They said – "

"This is as you're getting out of the taxi? Standing outside your house?"

Macdonald nodded. Finished his whisky. "They said – *he* said, it was a man's voice – "

"Accent?"

Macdonald shrugged. "None. English, I think."

Bloody hell, every English voice has an accent. Brady didn't press it.

"So what did he say? And I'm guessing this isn't the intermediary?"

"No. He said... He said that what happened to my wife would happen to my daughter. Or to me."

"That's it. Just those words?"

"No. He said... As I'm standing in the street outside the house. Shaking like a bloody leaf. He took the piss. He said, 'Don't forget to pay the taxi.'"

"So he was watching you."

Or someone was watching you for him...

"I need police protection," Macdonald said. "Armed protection. Round the clock. Twenty-four seven. Someone on duty outside."

Brady shook his head. "Graham, two days ago – two fucking days ago – you told me your wife fell. Stop wasting time, you said. 'I thought you'd have better things to spend police resources on.' Your exact words. Now you're telling me you want round-the-clock protection."

"This is different. Obviously this is different."

Brady looked at his watch. Decided that he'd listened to Macdonald's self-pity for long enough. Worked out how many years he needed to work to earn a quarter of a million pounds. "Graham, I realise this is difficult. Let me try and summarise. Interrupt me if I make a mistake."

If you're capable of interrupting after three Olympic whiskies...

"Someone – you won't tell me who because you're too frightened to tell me, or because you don't know – has offered you a bribe. For which – "

"A consultancy fee – "

"Oh for fuck's sake, Graham, you're back in Yorkshire now. And you've drunk half a bottle of whisky. So let's use simple words we can both understand. In return for this bribe you were due to do something. Which you didn't do. Which pissed someone off. So they sent you a warning. Or used your wife to send a warning. And yesterday this was made very clear to you. Resulting in your thinking 'what the fuck do I do?' And your first instinct – "

Like it was twenty-five years ago.

" – Was to run away. Put some distance between you and the man who told you to pay the taxi. About five hours' distance. Which isn't very much. And as you're standing here drinking whisky and staring out of the window you realise that. So who can help? Maybe that useless prick Mike Brady can help. He is the police after all..."

Macdonald walked towards the sideboard. Reached for the whisky bottle. Brady stretched his hand out. Stopped him. "When I'm gone. No more for now. So am I right or am I wrong?"

Macdonald shook his head. "Right. More or less."

"Good. So we know where we're starting from."

"What are you going to do about it?"

"Tonight? Nothing. Get a patrol car to drive past a few times. But wittingly or unwittingly you've bought yourself some time. Whatever you were supposed to do, it clearly isn't something you're supposed to do in Runswick Bay. But you can't put off going back to London forever. So like I say, I'll get a patrol car to drive past. And I'll think. Long and hard."

Brady stood up. Very reluctantly shook hands. Turned to go.

Paused.

Decided Macdonald had drunk so much it was worth the risk.

"Graham. One thing... If this *does* have something to do with your wife... Does she have a study? A desk? Would you mind if I had a look?"

Macdonald shook his head. "Help yourself. Study. Second door on the left."

"Thank you. Two minutes. A quick look. No more."

'Two desks. One with a picture of their daughter. One with a picture of Graham Macdonald shaking hands with the Prime Minister.'

Brady pulled a pair of gloves out of his jacket pocket. Found an evidence bag in the other pocket. Carefully put the notebook with the solicitor's number into it. Sealed it. Tucked it in his inside pocket. Stripped off the gloves.

Because you'll sober up at some point, Graham. And I can live without you knowing what she was planning. The waters are muddy enough already...

BRADY BRAKED as he started down Lythe Bank. Squinted as a car came up the hill with its headlights on full beam.

Hadn't realised how tired he was. Turned right at the bottom. Drove along the sea front. Turned right again. Saw the house with the pale blue door, the roses growing up the trellis at the side of it.

'I wasn't going to say that. I was going to say I'll still be here when you're driving back.'

'I won't be late, Ash.'

Make your choice. A difficult conversation with your girlfriend? Or a difficult conversation with your daughter?

It wasn't even a debate. Brady slowed down, turned left over the bridge in Sandsend.

More bloody apologising.

But I'll be home in ten minutes. At least Archie loves me...

29

Brady looked at his phone.

6:59.

"She'll be up by now won't she, Archie? Everyone's up by now. Apart from teenage girls, obviously."

She answered on the eighth ring. Didn't sound like someone who'd been up since sunrise.

"Frankie, are you OK?"

"Ah... Sort of, boss. What's up?"

"I know it's early. I need to talk to you."

"I'll be in for nine."

"Before everyone else gets in, Frankie. Ash is getting a lift to school so I'll see you at Dave's? Fifteen minutes?"

"Boss... I'm at Lochie's. At Hutton-le-Hole. What time is it?"

Has she moved in with him?

"It's seven."

"OK, I can be in for eight. Maybe just after. I'm not dressed. And I need a shower."

. . .

"I ASKED Dave to wrap it in silver foil," Brady said, handing her the bacon sandwich. "But..."

Frankie nodded. "Yeah, sorry. It's three-quarters of an hour on a good day. But what can I say? North Yorkshire. The world's slowest tractor." She unwrapped the bacon sandwich. Shook her head. "Don't worry, God's punished me. The bread's gone soggy with the tomato."

"Everything alright out there?"

"Lochie? He's good. Reggie's even better. Lochie's next door neighbour is a retired teacher. Walks five miles across the Moors every day. He's started taking Reggie with him. Lochie's at that conference next week. I think Reggie's going to move next door. But..."

Brady laughed. "I didn't phone you at seven in the morning to check on Reggie? No, I didn't. I saw Macdonald last night. That – "

"I thought you were going out to dinner last night? Oh... Right."

Right, Frankie. You understand.

"As I say, I saw Macdonald. Or I watched him drink whisky."

"The same Macdonald that was going back to London?"

"He went back to London. And bounced straight back to Runswick Bay. As fast as LNER and a bloody expensive taxi from York could carry him."

"Why?"

Brady shook his head. Looked out of the window. Sighed. "Because the plot thickens, Frankie. Thickens a lot. And confession is good for the soul. Even Graham Macdonald's."

"You've short-changed me, boss. This sounds like a two bacon sandwich story..."

Brady laughed again. "Sorry. It probably is."

. . .

"He's being threatened, Frankie. *Says* he's being threatened."

"And this has something to do with his wife's death?"

Brady nodded. "Macdonald has a house in Hampshire. Another one in London. Half a million quid's worth of Runswick Bay that he lives in for four or five weeks a year. Money in the bank. *Plenty* of money in the bank."

"How – "

Brady shook his head. "Don't ask. And he's regularly at the front of the queue for expenses. Despite all that he poured me a glass of very expensive whisky and invited me to feel sorry for him. Explained the emotional trauma of becoming an MP with no money behind him. 'I was the poorest man in the House of Commons, Michael.' The even greater trauma of his mother's nursing home fees."

"He's been taking backhanders?"

"I'm appalled, Detective Sergeant. What sort of expression is that? You'll be saying 'bribes' next. Consultancy fees. Paid straight into his account in the Cayman Islands."

"What does he consult on?"

"He doesn't Frankie. He delivers results. Contacts. Information. Access to ministers. And so far so good. Until now. Until someone offered him more money than he'd ever been offered before."

"And it went wrong?"

"He *says* it went wrong. Just the same as he *says* he's being threatened."

"But we've no evidence?"

"None at all. The only evidence we have is that he's back in Runswick."

"Meaning?"

"Meaning that he doesn't particularly like Runswick Bay. Not compared to London. He didn't love his wife. He's left his mistress in London."

'I've met his girlfriend.' The heels clicking across the parquet floor of the Embassy. 'I doubt he's grieving.'

"But in fairness to the man he looked terrified. And he drank half a bottle while I was there."

"Why us, boss? He's an MP, he's being threatened. Why not go to the security forces? The Met?"

"Don't think I haven't asked myself that question, Frankie. About a hundred times – and that's since I brushed my teeth. Because we're investigating his wife's death? Because if we weren't before we are now."

"But he's an MP. He's in London. Why doesn't he go to the Met?"

"Because he's got to confess, Frankie. 'Why have you received a threat, Mr Macdonald?' 'Because I've been taking bribes. And this time I didn't deliver.' And he can't do that."

"So he comes up here? Trusts us to save him?"

"You know the story, Frankie. The frog carries the scorpion across the river, the scorpion stings it. 'I'm sorry. That is my nature.' What's Graham Macdonald's nature? It's to panic. To run away. Whether it's from the crash that killed Lizzie Greenbeck when he was eighteen – or what may or may not have happened in London. There's something else as well. A reason he might trust us. Or tolerate us."

"What's that?"

"Something Bill said to me. When he was telling me why Kara had killed Patrick. He knew far more than I did. Was taking the piss out of me. He said, 'You thought we were just simple fucking plod in Whitby. All we do is roll up at two in the morning and catch some poor sod pissed on the beach.'

I can hear him saying it. See him banging his whisky glass down on the table."

"And Macdonald thinks the same?"

"Maybe. Maybe he thinks we're bright enough to keep him safe. And not bright enough to take it any further. That we'll decide what happened in London can stay in London."

"Doesn't say much for his opinion of you, boss."

Brady shrugged. "Trust me, Frankie. The feeling is mutual. More than bloody mutual."

"Come on, Frankie, walk down to the harbour with me. I seem to need the sea air to think these days."

"Do I get another bacon sandwich?"

Brady laughed. "No, Ms Thomson, you get the wind off the sea. The alluring scent of diesel. The screech of the seagulls. The heart stopping excitement of the dredger going under the swing bridge. If you're lucky..."

"Maybe the railings will get a blue plaque, boss."

Brady laughed. "You think? 'On this spot DCI Brady and DS Thomson ate fish and chips? Attempted to solve another murder?'"

"We've only got two options, boss."

"Right. He's lying to us or he's telling the truth. So let's be charitable. Start by believing him. He failed to deliver. Very clearly on something important. And with a serious amount of money involved. Someone uses his wife to send a warning. And it goes wrong. His wife dies."

"You're saying they didn't mean to kill her?"

"I'm saying go back to that morning we were on the cliff. That's what I can't get out of my head. Places where there's *no* chance of dying if you go over the edge. Five hundred yards further up the path you're guaranteed to die. Diane was fifty-fifty. So it *had* to be a warning."

"Because if I'm going to murder you by pushing you off a cliff I'm going to do my homework?"

"I hope so, Frankie. Don't tell me all those years of police training have been wasted."

"You asked him about the bribe? Consultancy fee, sorry."

"I did. At which point he started staring at the carpet. 'I don't know. It was always through an intermediary.' Jesus, Frankie, you'd think someone putting his career at risk would want more than a bloody intermediary."

"Except he doesn't see it that way, does he? He wants the money. And it's not putting his career at risk. It's business as normal."

"Until it goes wrong."

Frankie looked across the harbour. Asked Brady the question he'd already asked himself.

"If it's a warning, boss, it's a bloody serious one. Where's your wife on the scale of warnings?"

Don't say it, Frankie. Because I've already worked it out. Already imagined it happening to me...

Frankie did say it. "She's above your dog and below your daughter."

Brady nodded. Didn't reply.

"You think whoever did it knew she wanted a divorce?"

"I don't think it matters, Frankie. I'm convinced Macdonald doesn't know. But he's a frightened man."

"Why? Because he's had a warning? Or because it's option two. He's lying. He found out she wanted a divorce, worked out how much it'd cost him and did something about it?"

"And relied on Whitby's 'simple fucking plod' to get

away with it? Suppose that's it, Frankie? Suppose he did kill her? Suppose yesterday was an elaborate charade and I'm too stupid to see it?"

"He was in Hungary, boss. We know that for certain."

"He *was* in Hungary and... You know what I think, Frankie? I think he's telling the truth."

"Why?"

"Because the man's a bloody shambles..."

Frankie shook her head. "But like you said, boss, he wouldn't be the first husband to delegate the dirty work. How much organisation does it need?"

"More than Macdonald has got." He looked at Frankie. "We're married, Frankie. You've had enough of me. Do I think you're efficient enough to organise a hitman while you're away somewhere? Damn right I do. Macdonald? I think it's unlikely. Very unlikely."

"But what do we always say, boss? Occam's Razor. The simplest solution is the most likely. And our simple solution has one lead..."

"The man who saw a runner. *Says* he saw a runner."

"So they're both lying to us?"

"It's the simplest explanation, Frankie. Macdonald found out. Worked out the cost of a divorce. Somehow found Gerry Donoghue – "

"Another of his intermediaries?"

"Probably. I asked Donoghue how he coped. He said 'I do a bit of work for a couple of pals.' Ex-army? Homeless? Bitter?"

"It's not exactly a leap of faith..."

"Except, except... Macdonald's vain, Frankie. He's arrogant. Admitting he's terrified can't come easily to him. And Donoghue. There's no other way to put it. I liked him. Felt I could trust him."

"So unless Macdonald's a bloody good actor – "

"And I'm a crap judge of character. But the cost of a divorce. You know what they say. Money is the root of all evil."

"The *love* of money, boss. Timothy, chapter six, verse ten. For the *love* of money is the root of all evil. They have pierced themselves through with many sorrows. Something like that."

"You never cease to amaze me, Frankie."

"I paid attention in RE, boss. Didn't spend the lesson staring out of the window thinking about football."

Brady laughed. "You're supposed to lick your finger now. That's what Ash does when she scores a point off me. Licks her finger and chalks an imaginary 'one' in the air. You want a coffee? Celebrate the breakthrough we haven't made? Sod it, Frankie. You want to walk down to Dave's? If Sherlock Holmes can have a two-pipe problem I don't see why we can't have a two-bacon sandwich problem."

"Thought you'd never ask, boss..."

Brady started to walk towards the swing bridge. Stopped. Turned back to Frankie.

"What's the difference between a professional and an amateur?"

"Getting paid?"

"That. But a pro gets the job done and moves on. An amateur meddles. Can't resist. And gets caught."

"So you're saying Macdonald's the amateur? He's meddling. And Donoghue's the pro. He's moved on?"

"Right. Which means we have to find him. And that means I need to find a tramp. One called Magic Pockets. After I've eaten the world's largest slice of humble pie..."

30

"There's no point you apologising every time, Mike."

"No, you're right. We sat here four months ago. What did I say? Something about an alcoholic."

"You told me to have breakfast with him. Or start a relationship with a drug dealer. Or a compulsive gambler. You said, 'they're all better bets than a copper. Especially this copper.'"

She reached across the table and took his hand. "What did I say to you?"

How can women do this? Remember a conversation you had four months ago? Four years ago for Grace...

"I don't know. Not to worry?"

"I said, 'Let me be the judge of that.' And you told me I was mad. Well four months on I'm not mad. And I'm still here."

"I don't want to keep letting you down, Siobhan. What I do – "

"I know what you do."

Brady shook his head. "No, you don't. It's not just Wednesday night. It's..."

How the hell do I explain?

"It's long term, Siobhan. The people I deal with... They don't say, 'Oh, Brady's taking Siobhan out for dinner, I'll murder my wife tomorrow. Oh hang on, tomorrow's Parents' Evening at school. Friday night then. Oh fuck it, Middlesbrough are playing.' They just crack on and murder her. Reach for the bread knife and Parents' Evening and Middlesbrough have to pay the price."

"Or the person you're having dinner with."

Brady sighed. "Yes, or the person I'm having dinner with." He reached his hand up. Stroked her cheek with the back of his finger. Held her eyes. "No matter how much I want to have dinner with her. Or how many times I've let her down in the past."

"So next Wednesday?"

Brady nodded. "Next Wednesday, I promise. I'll re-book the table. What are you doing this weekend?"

"I'm going to see Lucy. Before she goes to the States. Drink gin, go for a walk in the park. Reminisce about the band. And I need to speak to Helen. I want to talk to her about the film."

"They came back to you?"

"They did. It's a short. Thirty minutes. About a girl going back to Dublin. So I tick the local knowledge box."

Brady laughed. "Even though it's a hundred and fifty miles from Killarney?"

Siobhan put her finger to her lips. "Shhh... I don't think Geography's their strong point. One of the guys is American. He was seduced by my accent."

"So when are you going?"

"Tomorrow morning. I'm back on Monday."

She paused. "There's something else I want to say, Mike."

"That sounds serious."

"Maybe... When I first met you – "

"When our supermarket trolleys romantically crashed? Or when I drove into the back of your car?"

"The supermarket. Four months ago. You were working on that case. The couple."

Brady nodded. "Billy and Sandra. The trial starts the week after next."

"You were tired. You said to me, 'when this is over I'm taking a week off.'"

I said it to myself as well...

"Where did you go?"

"I didn't. You know that."

"No, you didn't. And you've not had a proper holiday since – "

"Since before Grace died. You don't need to say it."

"Right. So when this is over we're going away for a weekend. And I'm going to take you home. May or June. When the sun shines warm upon your face."

Brady looked at her. "Home? Ireland?"

She nodded. "Fly to Dublin. Hire a car. Drive to Killarney. Show you where I grew up. Out to the Atlantic coast. The Wild Atlantic Way. *Real* waves, Michael Brady, not the pretend ones you have in Whitby. Steak and chips and the fiddle in an Irish pub. Back to our four-poster bed in a converted castle..."

"It sounds perfect, Siobhan. Better than perfect. Except – "

"You've got Ash and Archie? Didn't you have Ash's friend for a week when her mum went away?"

"Ten days in August. I've never seen the fridge empty so fast."

"There you are then. And a hundred-and-one people would volunteer to look after Archie."

Frankie for one. Lochie may as well open a kennels...

"You've thought it all through."

She laughed. "Mike, it's a holiday. It doesn't take much thinking through. And it's what you need."

And it's another step. Another step away from Grace...

"Let me deal with Diane Macdonald, Siobhan. You go to Wales and drink gin."

"And we'll sort out a date when I'm back."

Brady nodded. Couldn't shake the feeling he'd been out-manoeuvred.

31

Brady turned his computer off. Pushed the keyboard away. Decided he'd read enough memos and policy briefings for a Friday afternoon. Looked up as Frankie tapped on his office door.

"I'm off, boss. The high road is calling."

"Scotland for the weekend?"

Frankie nodded. "Long weekend. The A19. A1. Crawl past Newcastle. And then the high road."

"As opposed to the low road."

"Over the hills to Jedburgh. Lochie's mum is sixty-five. There's a party."

"So you're going to meet the family?"

She nodded. "Brother and a sister. A niece. A nephew. Sundry friends, no doubt."

"You ready for it?"

"Four months, Mike. I guess that's about par for the course. And Reggie's going next door on his holidays. You? The Golden Lion? A pint of the black stuff and Siobhan playing the fiddle?"

Brady shook his head. "Billy No Mates. Ash is away with

Jessica, as I consistently forget to call Bean. And one of Siobhan's friends is off to the States. So it's a long goodbye over several gins."

"Just you and Archie, then?"

"Me, Archie and the beach or the Moors. And Middlesbrough away to Everton, thanks to a fifteen year old genius in Ash's class."

"I thought you watched on dodgy streams with Chinese commentary?"

"I did. But Spencer's upgraded me. South African TV now. Just don't tell the police..."

"Don't get depressed if they lose."

"*When* we lose. Even at this stage of the season I'd bite your hand off for seventeenth."

"And don't sit on your balcony at three in the morning – "

"Brooding on Diane Macdonald? I think we're done with that one, Frankie."

"You're sure? Despite what the not-very-Honourable Gentleman said?"

"Almost *because* of what he said, Frankie. Is he being threatened? I think the answer's probably yes. But one, what Macdonald has or hasn't done isn't our problem. And two, we've no evidence. So I'm going to take the weekend off and follow Alan Kershaw's advice."

"Kershaw's advice? You need me to take you to A&E, boss?"

"Fight the battles you can win. That's what he said. More or less the same as Jim Fitzpatrick once said to me. 'Accept it. Move on. Solve the cases you can solve.' Maybe I'm wrong about Diane Macdonald. Maybe she did just fall. Enjoy your weekend, Frankie. Good luck with Lochie's family."

Maybe I'm getting old. Finally come to my senses. 'Fight the battles you can win.' That's what I'll do. And go online. Google the Wild Atlantic Way. See how wet Ireland is. And look at pictures of four-poster beds...

32

'I*'m going to fight the battles I can win, Frankie. Move on. Start by taking the weekend off.'*

Brady clipped Archie's lead on. Started up the slipway. "Beach in the morning, Moors in the afternoon, sausage from Dave's. Life doesn't get any better than this, Arch. Breakfast, mate. Come on."

Brady waited as Dave served two optimistic-looking fishermen. Said good morning to them. Wondered if fishermen ever looked anything but optimistic first thing in the morning. Wished them luck. Avoided Dave's meaningful glance.

"Mornin' to you, Mr Brady. And the boss."

"Morning, Dave... I'd best not say anything."

"You'd best not. Cheat me out of the last fishing trip by nicking the bloke that was taking us."

"Dave, Greg Chadwick was arrested on two counts of murder."

"First offence. You could have bailed him while he took us fishing."

Brady laughed. "We'll go before the season ends. Promise."

"Only a couple of weeks. Weather's starting to change. You can feel it. Smell it in the air. Anyway, what'll it be? Not that I need to ask."

Dave put three rashers of bacon on the grill. Gave the tomatoes a stir, reached for an oven bottom cake. Brady's phone rang. "Give me a minute, Dave. It'll be Ash. She's away for the weekend. I forgot to transfer some money into her account."

Brady didn't bother looking at the display. "Morning, sweetheart. I'm just at Dave's. I'll – "

"Boss? It's Sue."

"Sue? Bloody hell. Sorry. I didn't look. Just assumed it was my daughter. What – "

"He's here, boss. The same as last Saturday. Sitting on the step again."

"Donoghue?"

"The guy you took for breakfast, boss."

'It's the simplest explanation, Frankie. Macdonald found out. Worked out the cost of a divorce. Somehow found Gerry Donoghue – '

'So the suspect – the only bloody suspect: the obvious bloody suspect – walked in to the station on Saturday morning. Gave himself up. And you took him out for fucking breakfast?'

'There's no other way to put it, Frankie. I liked him. Felt I could trust him.'

BRADY MADE A DECISION.

"I've just come off the beach with Archie, Sue. I'm having breakfast at Dave's. Give him directions. Tell him I'll see him in five minutes."

Turned to Dave. "Take mine off the grill for five minutes will you, Dave? I've got company."

Dave raised his eyebrows. "Work company by the sound of your voice. It's Saturday."

Brady nodded. "Weekend off. I said as much to Frankie yesterday. What time is it?"

"Just gone eight."

"There you are. I've been up since six. Two hours off. What more does a man need?"

"Never mind what a *man* needs. Here." Dave leaned over the counter. Tossed Archie a sausage. "Mebbes you can wait five minutes. The boss can't."

THE SAME CAMOUFLAGE JACKET, check scarf, dark green trousers. Faded orange backpack over his shoulder, his stubble a week longer.

"You could have left your backpack with Sue," Brady said.

Donoghue shook his head. "No, you're alright. And thanks."

"Breakfast, it's no problem. It's – "

Donoghue shook his head. "Not breakfast. For trusting me. Textbook says I'm a suspect doesn't it? Probably your only suspect. Not many coppers would let me wander through Whitby."

"Then I'm not most coppers am I? Besides..." Brady gestured at Archie. "...We've been on the beach."

Donoghue glanced down. "Nice dog," he said. Bent down to pat Archie.

Archie stiffened. Stared up at Donoghue. Backed away behind Brady.

"What's the matter, mate? Don't be silly."

"It's not important," Donoghue said. "Not the first time it's happened."

Brady nodded. “I’m sorry. He’s usually friendly. Too friendly. Let me get you some breakfast. We’ll sit by the bandstand. Admire the view.”

And you’ve saved me a job. First thing Monday: find Magic Pockets. No need now...

“THANKS, DAVE.” Brady took the two bacon sandwiches and the coffees.

“Mike.”

“What, Dave?”

“Leave the boss with me. You need to talk. Archie not liking the bloke won’t help. Leave him here. He’ll be fine.”

Brady walked over to the bandstand. Handed Gerry Donoghue his breakfast.

“Bacon sandwich and coffee. The best Whitby has to offer.”

“On a perfect morning.”

Is this right? Sitting here? Where I sat with Patrick? Four days later he was dead.

Donoghue looked out to sea. “Like being a rock star,” he said with no preamble. “Being in the army. On patrol. It’s like being a rock star.”

Brady started to laugh. Stopped himself. Sensed he shouldn’t. “Sleeping in the barracks? The canteen? The chance of getting shot?”

Donoghue did laugh. “No, mate. The adrenalin. Like being on stage. You know – you just fucking know – that you’re never going to feel that alive again.”

“When there’s a chance of being killed?”

He nodded. “*Because* there’s a chance of being killed. Because you’re never more alive than when there’s a chance of dying. Because if someone woke up that morning and his

God – whatever passes for his God – said to him, 'You want to kill 2 – 5 – 0 – 3 – 2 – 4 – 0 – 6 Staff Sergeant Donoghue today?' he wouldn't fucking hesitate. He'd stretch, scratch his bollocks and say, 'fucking right, mate, I'll have some of that.'"

He paused. Drank some of his coffee. "Like your job."

"The chance of getting shot? Maybe not..."

Except for Jimmy Gorse. 'Aye. I shot your dog. I meant to kill him. But I see now this is better. Gives us chance for a wee chat.' Jimmy Gorse, who could have shot me as easily as he shot Archie.

"...But working on a case? Pulling all the strings together? Adrenalin for sure," Brady said. "Usually at three in the morning."

"You want to talk. Something's happened? Fair enough. Let me finish breakfast. Then we'll talk."

Brady stayed silent. Donoghue finished his sandwich. Drained his coffee. Fished in a pocket. Found a tin. A cigarette paper. Barely filled it with tobacco. Smiled at Brady. "Life's luxuries, eh? Got to make it last."

"You want me to... I don't even know if I'm doing the right thing in asking. You want me to find you somewhere? Even for a night? Hot bath? Soft bed? Full English in the morning?"

"B&B?" Donoghue shook his head. "No, you're fine. One night? Strange bed? I wouldn't be able to sleep. Then I wake up in the morning knowing it's over? No, mate. Thanks for the offer. I'm sorted for tonight." He paused. "But..."

"But what? Oh, right." Brady laughed. Reached into his pocket. Found a twenty pound note. "All the cash I've got. I'm sorry."

Donoghue didn't look at him. Stared out to sea again. "Why'd you do that? To make yourself feel better?"

Brady shook his head. "You want the honest answer? I

don't know. Three in the morning. I'll work it out then. Because you're more or less my age. Because I'm going home to my daughter."

Except she's away...

Donoghue turned to look at him. "Wife? Someone else's wife?"

Brady shook his head. "My wife died. She was killed in a hit and run. Meant for me. They hit her."

Donoghue sucked his breath in. Nodded. "That's shit. You want revenge?"

Brady took a long time replying. "I did. Then I didn't. Now..."

"...Now I don't know. I've met someone else."

"And you can't move on?"

"It's complicated."

Why am I telling him this? A stranger? My only suspect...

Donoghue nodded. "You know the old saying? 'If you want revenge, dig two graves.'

"I do. But maybe it's time to move on. I can't do that if I don't..."

"Draw a line under it?"

"Yeah. A nice way of putting it. Draw a line under it."

Or under someone...

Gerry Donoghue nodded. "You're doing the right thing. You've got to know why. Understand. Even if you don't like the answer. That's the problem with the army. You stop thinking for yourself. That's why we can't cope when we come out. That and..."

"What?"

"The ghost. The fucker with the AK-47. Except he's real. Real life. On patrol, some frozen shithole in Afghanistan. That's real life. Then I'm on leave. Back home. The wife wants to go round Tesco. I can't do it. Thursday morning I'm in Bagram. Saturday afternoon I'm in Tesco's. She says, 'What sort of pasta do you want, Gerry?' I'm thinking the fucker with the AK-47 is in the next aisle. Breakfast cereal or whatever the fuck it is. She says, 'tagliatelle or fusilli, Gerry?' I don't give a shit. Whatever the Army puts in front of me. PTSD. Whatever you call it the end result's the same. Couldn't do it. Couldn't hide it either."

DONOGHUE STOOD UP. Held his hand out. "Simple things, eh? That was right up there. Fucking good bacon sandwich. Thanks."

Brady passed him his scrunched up paper bag. Watched him walk to the bin, limping slightly.

"Gets worse in the cold and damp," Donoghue said without looking round. "November's a shit month."

He walked back. Sat down. Rolled another cigarette. Carried on staring out to sea.

"You ever killed someone?"

Brady shook his head. "Too much paperwork." Tried to make a joke of it.

Jimmy Gorse? Did I kill Jimmy Gorse? No, because he threw himself in the sea. Would I have killed Jimmy Gorse? Him or me? I hope so...

"You think you could?"

Brady took his time replying. Slowly nodded. "I think so. Yes, if my daughter was threatened."

"Everyone thinks they could, don't they? 'If my daughter was threatened.' 'If it was him or me.' Every fucker in the fish and chip queue who thinks he's Daniel Craig."

Donoghue shook his head. "They couldn't. Nine out of ten. Ninety-nine out of a hundred. I'm not saying *you* couldn't. Maybe you're one in a hundred. But it ain't easy."

"You could?"

"Could. Did. And that's probably why I spent last night in a church doorway. Somewhere different tonight. But it has its compensations. Perfect view of the North Sea. Watch the sun rise every morning. Well... when it's not pissing down."

Does he want me to ask the obvious question?

"How many?"

"Three." He paused. Put the cigarette to his lips. Inhaled. "Four maybe. I couldn't see for certain. It was pissing down."

Brady didn't reply.

'Couldn't see for certain. It was pissing down.' Like Sunday night on the cliff top...

"You're disappointed? You were expecting a number like that *American Sniper* guy? Three or four's enough. You want to know how?"

Brady shook his head. "Not straight after breakfast. Where next?" he said, trying to change the subject.

Donoghue shrugged. "North. Seaham. Seahouses, I like Northumberland."

"Walk?"

"Walk. Get a lift. There's worse things than walking up the east coast. But you want to talk. Go over what I saw on the cliff top. You said something's changed."

Do I tell him? Yes. Let's see how he reacts to Graham Macdonald. But a normal conversation. Don't ask too many questions...

"Her husband's back. Graham Macdonald. He's an MP – "

"So the shit's hit the fan?"

"So the shit *could* hit the fan." Brady paused. Weighed his next words carefully. Wanted to give Donoghue a chance to comment.

"I can't make up my mind about him."

"He's a politician. That's all you need to know."

Brady laughed. "That sounds like you don't have a high opinion of them."

Donoghue looked out to sea. Turned back to Brady. "I wouldn't piss on one if he was on fire. That do you?"

Brady nodded.

"Macdonald," Donoghue said. "Why not?"

"Because I can't make up my mind whether his wife fell. Or whether she was pushed."

"Which is why you want to talk to me."

"Yes. Go over Sunday night. See if there's anything I've missed. You might have missed."

Donoghue shook his head. "That bloke and his wife. The wife that looked like she didn't want to be there."

"The guy you *might* have seen," Brady said. "Let's talk about him."

"Any chance we could talk about another coffee?"

Brady laughed. "Yeah, sorry. Too focused on the job. Anything else to eat?"

"You've twisted my arm. Same again. Thanks."

Brady walked back to Dave's. Apologised to Archie while Dave grilled the bacon. Promised he'd only be ten more minutes. "The Moors this afternoon, OK? Ten minutes, no more." Walked back to the bandstand.

DONOGHUE WAS GONE.

The faded orange backpack was gone.

Replaced by a family eating ice creams.

"There was a guy sitting here. A camouflage jacket. An orange backpack."

"No-one sitting here when we came, mate. Jason, you're dripping ice cream down your front."

Brady ran back to the public toilets. Found the attendant. Realised he was still holding a bacon sandwich in one hand and a coffee in the other. "Has a guy come in here? Camouflage jacket? Orange backpack?"

"Just come on haven't I, love? Not seen no-one though."

What the hell do I do? Stand outside the toilets for ten minutes? He could be half a mile away.

Brady sprinted down the slipway. Looked along the beach. On the pier. Under the pier.

Nothing.

Ran back up the slipway. Up the Khyber Pass. Stood outside the Fisherman's Wife. Down the steps at the side of it. Another long look along the beach.

Nothing.

'There's no other way to put it, Frankie. I liked him. Felt I could trust him. Unless I'm a crap judge of character.'

Which I clearly am...

"Fuck," Brady said. "Fuck, fuck, fuck."

Finally threw the bacon sandwich in a bin. Tipped the coffee down the drain.

Walked back towards Dave's. Asked again at the toilets. Got the same answer. Collected Archie. Didn't tell Dave what had happened.

Walked back to the bandstand.

'On patrol, some frozen shithole in Afghanistan.'

So outwitting a thick copper in Whitby wasn't going to be a problem.

Waited 20 minutes.

Nothing.

Started to walk home. Past the Magpie. Past the fishing sheds.

'So the suspect – the only bloody suspect: the obvious bloody suspect – walked in to the station on Saturday morning. Gave himself up. And you took him out for fucking breakfast?'

'No, sir. I took him out for breakfast twice. Then I let him run away...'

Michael Brady swore again. Threw in an extra 'fuck' for luck.

33

A *basic, basic, basic, bloody mistake.*

When was the last time I was so stupid?

Sarah Cooke. When I was twenty-six...

"Come on, Archie. It's an ill wind. And it's only taken us a whole summer to get here."

Four months since Bobby Brownley told me about it.

Let's see if he's right. Let's see if it calms me down...

Brady clipped Archie's lead on. Walked down to the Scarborough road. Waited for a stream of cars to pass. Crossed the road, up the stone steps on the other side. Reached the top and saw the radio mast that marked the end of the Lyke Wake Walk.

The radio mast Paul Jarvis and Andy Boulding would have reached. If they hadn't found Becky Kennedy's bones...

He unclipped Archie's lead, watched him race away after a scent. Set off walking through the heather, the path narrow, gradually uphill, scattered with loose stones, a solitary tree on his right.

Brady walked for five minutes, came to a direction post, a wider track on the right running back towards the road.

"It's on our right, Archie, so it needs to be on our left on the way back. I can hear Ash now. 'You and Archie took a wrong turning on a straight path, Dad? All I did was leave you alone for the weekend.' We can live without that, old son..."

Brady felt a few spots of rain. Looked up at the clouds. "Maybe getting soaked will calm me down, Archie." Knew as he spoke that it was only a shower.

Five minutes, no more.

"Another marker, Arch. So it's right, left coming back."

The rain stopped. Brady looked up. The radio mast was closer.

Half a mile? Hard to tell.

"How far have we walked, Arch? I should have used the app on my phone."

He hadn't noticed the end of the loose stones. Now he was on a bridleway, sloping steadily uphill to the radio mast.

'And there's this pond. Comes out of nowhere. The water's flat. Flat as a mill pond.'

"Where is it then, Archie? This mythical pond he told me about? That appears out of nowhere?"

A dozen more steps and it was there. Half-hidden by the tall grass growing up around it. Twenty yards long, five yards wide, the water flat, the clouds reflected as the sun reluctantly came out.

'It's quiet. More than quiet. Still. Silent. You can't hear the traffic. No-one else around. Just you. The Moors. Nothing else.

Bobby Brownley had been right.

Silence.

Not even a breeze.

Brady stopped, looked up at the radio mast. Turned to his left, saw Stony Marl Moor fall away to reveal the sea. Turned again, looked back the way he'd come, saw the

Moors stretching away on the other side of the road, the path eventually leading to the Lilla Cross.

Where they found the bones...

Made the final turn. South towards Scarborough, a line of trees, the start of a small wood in the distance.

Looked back at the flat, unbroken surface of the water. Wouldn't have been remotely surprised if a hand had appeared. The Lady of the Lake offering him Excalibur...

Stood still. Listened to the silence.

Let it wash over him.

"Just us, Archie. Miles and miles of the Moors. We could make a picnic. Bring Siobhan."

Knew as soon as he'd said the words that he wouldn't. That this place was special. That he'd keep it for himself.

"Just us then, mate. You and me. And silence."

Realised his anger had gone.

Dissolved.

That the Moors had healed him.

"We'll walk up to the radio mast, Arch. Remind me to start the app when we get there. See how far it is back to the car. And then we'll go home. Have some tea. And think. And we'll keep thinking until we've worked out what the hell's going on."

34

Brady pulled the pad of A4 towards him. Reached for his pen, drew a line down the middle of the page. Wrote, 'what I know' on one side: 'what I only know because I've been told' on the other.

Made notes for five minutes. Wasn't surprised to find he had as many notes in the second column as the first.

DM dead. Lay there 36 hours. Cause of death was drowning

Dog stayed with her all the time – found by two local kids

Skin under her fingernails.

Married to an MP

Had solicitor's number on her desk

Macd was in Hungary when it happened

Now back in RB. Prick/coward

Gerry's homeless – Archie didn't like him

I've no proof of anything

Brady had a battle with his willpower. Lost. Flicked the TV on. Tried to find some football. Forced himself to turn it off. Fought down the tiredness. Focused on the second column.

Adams saw DM on top of the cliff. Saw Gerry

Gerry saw Adams. Wife looked like she didn't want to be there.

Might have seen a runner. Serious runner? Serious runners don't go on clifftops in fading light

Adams/wife to Northumberland.

DM wanted a divorce

Macd is being threatened. Drinking heavily

Brady looked at the lists.

Two weeks of worrying and that's all I've got...

Ripped the sheet off the pad. Started screwing it into a ball.

Stopped. Smoothed it out again.

Read through the lists a second time.

She definitely wanted a divorce. What Annabel said. The number on her pad. That's reason enough to kill her. Except I've no evidence. Nothing. All this bloody time and Frankie's right. I don't have a crime to investigate.

Shook his head. Decided he'd wasted enough time.

Admitted defeat.

Reached for the remote. Sat down on the floor with his back against the sofa. Patted the carpet next to him. "Come on, Arch. Come and watch football with me." Turned the TV on.

"Solve the cases you *can* solve, Arch. And this is one we can't solve. So death by misadventure it is. And if Graham Macdonald is being threatened it's his problem, not ours."

Wondered how Siobhan's weekend was going. Heard Ash's voice.

'Why do you pay Sky so much, Dad? All you do is watch football. And you fall asleep in front of that.'

Managed ten minutes.

Woke up at two in the morning with a stiff back. Told Archie it wasn't time for breakfast. Fell into bed.

Not for long...

35

"Four-oh-four," Brady told Siobhan later. "Four minutes past four in the morning. Pitch black, sunrise two hours away."

"Who phoned you?"

"A fireman. Once he'd sniffed the cold, clear morning air. And realised it was arson. And whose house it was."

FIVE MINUTES TO GET DRESSED: 15 minutes to drive there. Brady parked behind the fire engine. Walked 20 yards up the road and found Dan Keillor.

"The last bloody thing we need," Brady said. "How long have you been here?"

"Five minutes? I've kept out of their way. Let them get on with it."

"No sign of Anya and her scene of crimes van?"

"Not yet. She moved didn't she? Robin Hood's Bay?"

"She did. I'm getting forgetful in my old age." Brady pulled his coat round him. "Half an hour to Runswick. So where's our boy?"

Dan Keillor nodded to the left. "Next door. Sitting in his neighbour's kitchen."

"Mrs Stokes? The woman who reported Diane missing?" Brady shrugged. "Then again it's fifty-fifty. Neighbours on both sides."

"Lucky to find someone in. No lights on at the other side. Looks like that's a holiday home as well."

Brady glanced at the house. Nodded. "Find out who it belongs to, Dan. Give them a ring. Tell them they'll be needing a new fence."

BRADY KNEW the Fire Investigations Officer from the touchline. He had a daughter in Ash's year. They'd shivered through hockey matches together. Had the stilted conversations parents always have on the touchline.

Punctuated by me trying to encourage Ash without embarrassing her. Or sounding like an over-the-top touchline dad...

"Bad business, Mike. Especially at four o'clock on Sunday morning."

"Bad business at any time, Pete. But I take your point. Be nice to have some daylight."

"Don't need it, Mike. At least as far as your side is concerned. There's broken glass down there. One piece with a Smirnoff label. Remnants of the cloth he used as a wick. And a healthy smell of petrol. So strong even our lads couldn't miss it."

"What are you saying? Home-made Molotov cocktail?"

"I am. And not the slightest attempt to disguise it."

"Scene of crimes is on her way. But she's moved to Robin Hood's Bay. So ten more minutes."

"But you and I know he'll have worn gloves..."

Brady sniffed the morning air. Smelled the petrol more

strongly. "It's a hell of a risk, Pete. Throw a Molotov cocktail and just saunter off into the darkness. I know Runswick Bay isn't Benidorm, but there has to be a chance of someone being around at four in the morning."

"Right. Where's an incontinent dog-walker when you need one? Got up for a pee and couldn't get back to sleep."

Except Runswick has more than its share of side streets and back alleys. And empty houses. Especially now the schools have gone back. Anyone who knows the place could disappear. Duck into someone's garden. Sit on the back step and listen to the sirens...

"How much control would he have, Pete?"

"You talking about damage? Asking me what he was trying to do? 'Enough' is probably the answer. No wind to speak of. Light from the streetlights."

"Yeah. You think he stands here? The end of the drive? Throws the bottle?"

"My guess – and that's all it can be, Mike – is that he was *aiming* at the porch. Brick walls. It'll be a UPVC door. But a wooden porch. And the fence to next door. They've gone up like it's Bonfire Night."

"So that's what he wanted? Controlled chaos?"

Brady saw Pete nod in the half-light. "Something like that. Enough damage to send a message – a bloody powerful message. But danger to life and limb? Possible but unlikely."

"What would you do, Pete? If you wanted to do real damage?"

"What are you trying to do, Mike? Make me go to confession? It's obvious. I'd put it through a window. Throw that into a house and all bets are off. But these windows look new. You stand here and throw a brick – it's probably going to bounce off."

So criminal damage. Not attempted murder. And aimed at

Graham Macdonald? Or just someone who owns a second home? Or third home in Macdonald's case...

Brady shook hands. "Thanks, Pete. I'll go and see Macdonald. God only knows what state he'll be in. I'll see you on the touchline."

"Saturday morning. Long-range weather forecast says it's going to be a bad winter, Mike. So wear your big coat."

Brady laughed. "North Yorkshire, Pete. When do we wear anything else?"

36

"You alright here, Dan? Sort Anya out when she comes? I need to go next door. See what Macdonald has to say."

Nothing good. 'I told you I needed protection.' Four in the morning. He'll have rung Kershaw already. Let's hope he didn't want to sleep through the night...

The house was ablaze with lights. Brady looked up and down the road.

Remembered when he'd been growing up.

A fire at Mrs Garrett's. The whole street turned out to watch. Fire engines, police cars. Everyone had their lights on. Here? Half a dozen houses at best. 'Don't worry, sir. Your holiday home wasn't damaged...'

Maggie Stokes answered the door, a thick white dressing gown pulled tightly round her, fading blonde hair hurriedly pinned up. "Morning," she said. "Not sure I can say 'good' when the house next door is in flames. But come in, Inspector." She shook her head, a rueful, almost bitter, expression. "The perils of living next door to the Macdonalds."

She turned, led the way back along the hall. "Can I get you anything? Tea? Coffee?"

Brady glanced into the kitchen. Saw a cup lying smashed on the tile floor. A laptop open on the kitchen table, what looked like an onion on the screen. "No, I'm fine, Mrs Stokes. And I can only apologise for this. Like you say, the perils of living next door to a politician."

Maggie Stokes nodded. "I'll go back to my work then. I'm not sure..."

Brady smiled. "You're not sure flashing lights and sirens are conducive to a good night's sleep?"

She laughed. "Something like that. But scholarship – I'm sorry, that's a pretentious word – but work is for some reason. I'm no stranger to three in the morning."

Brady nodded. "You and me both. It's better to do something – "

"Than lie in your bed worrying?" She nodded. "It's better to do anything than lie in your bed worrying. The Honourable Member is in the lounge. First door on your left."

"Thank you. I'll need to come back and see you. Procedure. Ask you if you saw or heard anything."

She nodded. "I'm away for a week. From tomorrow morning. My mother is in her eighties."

So you need to see her. The questions will keep...

"That's fine. It's only routine."

Unlike Graham Macdonald...

HE WAS DRESSED. Brady tried not to let his surprise show. Clearly failed.

"What did you expect? Striped pyjamas and a dressing gown? A House of Commons nightcap?"

Two out of three. And a glass of whisky in your hand.

"I couldn't sleep. So I was dressed. Sitting by the window with a cup of tea. Thinking. Waiting for the dawn."

Which means you'd been in the kitchen. Next to the porch. Just before the bomb...

"What have they found?"

He sounded resigned. Brady had expected belligerence. Aggression. An attempt to mask the fear.

Couldn't see any point in not telling the truth. "So far? A broken bottle. Remnants of a piece of cloth. And a distinct smell of petrol."

"I told you didn't I? I bloody well *told* you about the threat. The phone call I had. There should have been someone on guard all night."

Brady didn't bother to explain the budgetary constraints of North Yorkshire Police a second time. Decided Macdonald could spend his time more usefully.

"Take me through it, Graham. You're in the kitchen, making a cup of tea."

"No milk. There's never any fucking milk. And when there is it's off. Diane drank Earl Grey. Put lemon in it. Didn't like breakfast cereal either. So half the time we had no milk."

Brady nodded. "Black tea. I can sympathise with that. What happens next?"

"I take my tea into the lounge. Stand by the picture window. Wonder what time sunrise is. Wonder how many lights I'll see come on."

Says the man whose lights are only on for five weeks out of fifty-two...

"Then what?"

"Then what? Then bloody what? Then someone opens the gates of Hell. I heard a noise – glass shattering, I thought some local louts had thrown a stone through a window – I went into the kitchen and there are flames. Bloody *flames*. Halfway up the kitchen door."

"What did you do?"

"Ran into the garden."

"Not through the front door?"

Macdonald shook his head. "There's a door in the conservatory. I suppose I should be grateful. The fire people came out – with me being an MP – and advised me to put it in. Diane didn't want it. Said it spoiled the look of the bloody thing. I told her not to be stupid. I'd put it on expenses. And spoil the look? Not as much as bloody Reggie sprawled all over my sofa."

He's fine by the way...

"So you're out in the garden..."

"And I phoned 999. 'And don't pay any attention to the speed limit.'"

"And they're here in fifteen minutes?"

"Twelve. I timed it. Twelve minutes. While I watch my fucking house burn down."

A slight exaggeration. But we'll let it pass...

37

Brady sat in his car. Turned the engine on, turned the heater up.

Wondered how long it would take Kershaw to ring.

Decided it was a small price to pay.

Because now there's a case to investigate. And it involves an MP. So it doesn't matter how much it costs does it, Alan? Time, money, manpower. All of a sudden they're not important.

And while I'm investigating one crime...

BRADY PUT the car in gear. Indicated, turned left on to Ellerby Lane, up towards the Moors road. Glanced at the clock.

Six forty-five. Sunrise. Daylight. I should be on the beach with Archie. Meeting Frankie to talk about it. Where is she? Scotland.

I need to go into the office. Start making notes. Wait for Anya to come in with her report. But Ash is away. Siobhan's away. So Graham Macdonald and official police procedure will have to take second place. To something far more important. Archie's breakfast...

He left the car at home. Could still smell petrol. Hoped some clean, crisp Whitby air would wash it away. Was halfway down Church Street when his phone rang. Glanced down. Saw the inevitable *Kershaw* on the display.

"Alan, good morning."

"A good morning is what it's emphatically not, Brady. Seven-thirty on Sunday morning and I've had that useless prick Macdonald on the phone. Is it true?"

"Yes, sir. His house was firebombed. I got the call at four in the morning. Four-oh-four to be precise."

"He says it's burned down – "

Inflating his expenses claim already...

"No, sir. His porch has been badly damaged. The door will need replacing. His neighbours will need a new fence."

"Is he hurt? He told me he was in shock."

Probably because he was only drinking tea...

"Physically he seems fine, sir. Obviously it was a shock – "

"Well find out who did it, Brady. The whole of bloody Westminster will know about it by Monday morning. I can do without the snide bloody comments."

"So I can devote whatever resources I need?"

"Don't be naïve, Brady. Of course you bloody can. This is a politician who's been attacked. On our patch. It's my – our, I mean – reputation on the line. Nick someone. And quickly."

"Four in the morning, sir. There probably weren't any witnesses."

"Just fucking find some, Brady. And keep me informed. Before I'm drowning in fucking sarcasm."

The line went dead. Brady put the phone back in his pocket.

'So I can devote whatever resources I need?'

'Of course you bloody can.'

I've got what I want. Time. Time to find whoever killed Diane Macdonald.

So thank you. Whoever firebombed Macdonald, thank you.

Not that I don't know...

38

Brady sat at his desk. Ran his hands through his hair. Despite the best efforts of Church Street and the sea air could still smell the smoke, the petrol. Looked at his watch.

Just gone eight. At least Dave will be open...

Pulled a pad towards him. Started to make notes.

Was still making notes when Anya walked in. Black jeans, a black leather jacket, hair – so black it almost looked blue in the office light – tied back in a bun, secured with the inevitable pencil.

"Not the best start to your Sunday, Anya. I'm sorry. You want to run me through it?"

Anya reached for her notebook. "Probably me who needs to apologise, boss. I'm not going to tell you anything you don't know. Or can't guess."

Brady nodded. Didn't speak.

"Broken glass. From the label a standard size bottle of vodka. The remains of a cloth wick among the debris. If you asked me to guess I'd say a chain store T-shirt. A very definite smell of petrol and that – what's the word? Sheen? That distinctive pattern you get when petrol mixes with water. Blue, purple, streaks of yellow."

"You've got photos?"

"Photos and samples. The FIO has done the same. Put samples in a paint can to preserve the fumes. But it's petrol, boss. If you want me to have another guess it's the petrol everyone has in their garage."

Brady nodded. "Top up the lawnmower once a year. Fingerprints? DNA?"

Anya shook her head. "Fire? Water? And the fact he almost certainly wore gloves. I'd say that's the definition of optimism, boss."

"What are your thoughts, Anya? Assuming the only thing we can prove is that someone took a leaf out of Comrade Molotov's book?"

"You're saying we can't even prove Macdonald was the target?"

"Right now? No."

Brady spun his A4 pad round so she could see the jumble of arrows, names and question marks. "Right now we can't prove anything. Assuming there are no fingerprints and DNA. So what do you think? Graham Macdonald specifically? Or a random attack on a holiday home?"

"I think there are a lot of houses in Runswick Bay, boss."

"So the chance of choosing the only one owned by an MP is slim? I agree with you. But it's the same five words we always use, Anya. We need to prove it."

Brady watched her walk out of the office. Pulled the pad towards him again. Heard Jim Fitzpatrick again.

'Sometimes you know they're guilty, Mike. Sometimes you know what happened – almost like you were there. But you can't prove it. And you've got to accept it. Move on. Solve the cases you can solve. The ones with enough proof to convince a jury.'

Right. Maybe I don't have enough to convince a jury, Jim. But I'm working on it. And like Kershaw says, I can do whatever it takes.

Starting with someone who'll know all about Molotov cocktails.

Who 'wouldn't piss on a politician if he was on fire...'

39

"You were working late last night, Dad."

Brady parked in the lay-by outside school. "Not really, love. Just making notes. Thinking. Wishing it was still warm enough to sit on the balcony."

"You're looking tired, Dad. You need a break. Why don't you take Siobhan away for the weekend?"

Brady nodded. "Maybe. When this case is over – "

"You said that last time. You need to take care of yourself. Your birthday next month. Another year older. Maybe we need another dog. Twice as much exercise."

Brady laughed. "Twice as much rolling in dead fish. Whose turn is it to wash Archie?"

"Yours."

"It's always mine. Go on, have a good day. I'll see you at tea-time. Love you."

He pointed the car back towards the police station. Drove down Prospect Hill.

Changed his mind.

'Magic Pockets. Fuck knows what his real name is. You'll find him on the seat halfway up Blue Bank. He likes the view. Or

doing the church garden the other side of town. He wears a big old coat. With magic pockets.'

Went right round the roundabout, back up the hill. Turned right on to the Moors road and then left towards Sleights. Drove through the village, started up Blue Bank. Slowed down as he passed the seat. Two walkers enjoying the view and a flask of tea.

Neither of them remotely wearing 'a big old coat.'

He turned round in the car park at the top. Briefly caught sight of the Moors, the hills falling away, the patchwork of fields.

'Stop and smell the roses.' Stop and look at the view if you're in Whitby. When you've the time...

Drove back into town. Through Sandsend, past Siobhan's front door –

Back today. Composing. Working her way through 'all of Amazon's sheet music.'

'They came back to you about the film?'

But they don't make many films in Whitby...

– Up Lythe Bank and into the village. He parked the car and walked a hundred yards back to the church. Pulled his collar up against the drizzle. Could see even without going in that the churchyard was deserted.

What was Siobhan's blessing? 'May the rain fall softly on your fields.' It's falling softly on the church garden. And whoever Magic Pockets is, he clearly has better things to do than get wet...

BRADY PARKED THE CAR. Walked back to the office.

"Boss... Boss?"

"Sorry, Sue, I was miles away. What's happened?"

"There's been another break-in up on the estate. Paul Devlin from the paper's been on the phone. Wants to know if you've a comment for the local people, 'worried sick about this crime wave' according to Paul."

"I thought he was due to retire about now?"

"He's staying on to the end of the year. I saw his wife the other day. I was at school with her."

Whitby. You're related to one half of the town: you were at school with the other half...

"I'll give him a ring. And dead bat his questions on Macdonald's fire..."

BRADY PROMISED Paul Devlin he'd come to his retirement do. Finished the call. Went into the main office.

"Dan, can I ask you to do me a favour in the morning?"

"What's that boss?"

"I want a pound on a longshot. An outsider. Are you still going out on your bike? Specifically up the Moors road, across and back down the coast road?"

Dan Keillor nodded. "Most mornings."

"Tomorrow?"

"If it's not raining."

"Will you do me a favour and stop at a church? St Oswald's at the top of Lythe Bank? I'm looking for a tramp. I've been up there today but there's no sign of him."

"What's he look like, boss?"

"I have no idea. But there can't be that many tramps doing the church gardens. And my guess is he starts early in the morning."

"Longshot sounds about right, boss. You don't want me to go now?"

Brady laughed. "You mean the sun's come out and your bike's calling you? I need you to go out to the estate. We need to nail these break-ins. And talk to Anya. See what she's found. So tomorrow morning's fine. And if he's there, ring me straightaway will you? Thanks, Dan."

"Definitely not this afternoon?"

Brady shook his head. "No, I'm out this afternoon. On the mobile if anyone wants me."

40

"You remember the first time you came here? What I said?"

Brady looked at him. Suspected Mozart would be disappointed if he didn't give the right answer. "Not the computer screens," he said. "That was a reply to a question I asked. You advised me to raid my piggy bank. Buy some Bitcoin."

Mozart laughed. "I'm still advising you to buy some Bitcoin. But..."

"You told me to stand outside for ten minutes. 'You can tell a lot from watching a man stand still. I don't trust impatient people.' Words to that effect."

Mozart nodded. "I did. And the first time you came you did exactly that. Your wife had died, your best friend had been murdered and you'd crossed the Rubicon. You'd brought his laptop to me. But you stood still. You were at peace with yourself."

"Because I knew I'd made the right decision."

Brady hesitated.

It was the right decision. For me. For Ash...

"Now you're saying I'm not at peace with myself?"

Mozart poured the Earl Grey tea. Looked up briefly. "You don't even need me to tell you."

No, I don't. Today I would have been pacing. Two minutes down the hill, two minutes back up. Looking at my watch. Checking my e-mails every thirty seconds. Obsessing about Diane Macdonald...

"Men of our age, Michael. We – "

Brady raised his eyebrows. Mozart saw the implied question. Smiled. "I would have been in the year below you at school," he said. "And that's enough information. All you need now is the name of my first pet and you'll have access to my entire life."

"I'm sorry. You were saying..."

"Men of our age. We get restless. We feel the hot breath of younger colleagues on our necks. Competitors in my case. Then we look at the ones above us. Flushed, overweight, their belts loosened another notch, counting the days to retirement."

Or to St Mary's Church in Bill's case...

"We feel trapped. We start to feel threatened. And I suspect having a teenage daughter doesn't help."

Brady laughed. "If by that you mean she's not only arguing with me, she's arguing logically and winning the bloody argument most of the time, then you're right."

"So we make rash decisions. Buy motorbikes. Have younger girlfriends – "

"Investigate cases we should leave well alone. Is that what you're saying?"

"I'm saying we're prepared to cross boundaries, Michael. *Some* of us. Most of us look at those older colleagues and think, 'well, he doesn't look *too* bad.'"

"And mentally loosen our belts?"

Mozart nodded. "Mentally and physically. But you're taking the opposite approach. Another birthday coming up. Another year older. Felt the hot breath on your neck and started running faster. You're determined to prove yourself. Determined you won't be beaten."

And determined not to have an unsolved murder in Whitby...

"Even someone like me," Mozart said. "I was at the top of my tree. Some people I admired – "

"Eric Kennedy?"

Mozart nodded. "Some I regarded as equals. They say mathematicians peak in their mid-twenties. Maybe it's ten years later. My business is exactly the same. But now... Now there are countries where computer hacker – "

"I thought you didn't like that term?"

"I don't. But it's a convenient shorthand. Countries where it is a recognised career path. Where the careers master says, 'Hacker? In that case, Dimitri, you should talk to my cousin. And order yourself a BMW.'"

"And the Chinese?"

Mozart sighed. "Exactly. How many are in the British Army? A hundred thousand? The good gentlemen – and ladies – at the Foreign Office will tell you the Chinese Army has a hundred thousand *hackers*. The North Koreans probably aren't far behind."

He reached forward. Poured Brady some more tea. "There you are, proof positive that I'm getting old. Harking back to the good old days."

"Deal with the world as it is. Not as you want it to be?"

Mozart nodded. "Who said that? One of those quotations everyone lays claim to. But here we are, Michael. Two gentlemen in early middle age taking tea and gently fraying at the edges. But I worry about you."

"You worry about me? I thought – "

"You thought I was dispassionate? Maybe I was once. But... Why do I do this, Michael? Take tea with you? Chat?"

More or less what I said to Gerry Donoghue. Maybe we all need someone who understands...

Brady shook his head. "I don't know."

Mozart looked at him. "My father died last week. The funeral's tomorrow – "

"I'm sorry. I – "

Mozart held his hand up. "No. Don't be. It was degenerative. Trapped in his own body. I only wish I'd had the courage to..." Mozart shrugged. Spread his hands. "What can I say? Take action. Spare him the pain. The indignities."

He reached forward. Poured himself some more tea. "But I find his illness has made me more reflective. More protective of the few people I value. Care for. I worry you'll find Whitby too small. Too suffocating."

"And I'll do something stupid?"

Mozart nodded. Didn't speak.

"No," Brady said. "No. You don't need to worry. I've got Ash. The new house. People I'm responsible for. You don't need to worry about me."

Mozart smiled. "Good. And enough of our middle-aged introspection. What would you like me to do for you?"

Brady hesitated.

'Prepared to cross boundaries. Determined to prove yourself. Determined you won't be beaten.'

Yes, I am...

"Macdonald was firebombed. He's convinced it's connected to a threat he received. He – "

"A specific threat?"

"Yes. He was told – *says* he was told – that what happened to his wife could happen to his daughter. Or to him." Brady shook his head. "No doubt the second option is at the top of his priority list."

"You think they're connected?"

"Maybe. Logic – maths – says the chances of his wife dying and his house being firebombed and it *not* being connected are too high. So they have to be connected."

Mozart shook his head. "Maths is greatly overrated. What are the chances of a family having three children all born on the same day? One in a hundred and thirty thousand. But there are millions of families with three children in the UK. How many people do you need at a party to have a fifty-fifty chance of two of them being born on the same day? Someone will say, 'a hundred and eighty.' The answer is twenty-three."

"So you're saying – "

"I'm saying don't jump to conclusions, Michael. So tell me what you want me to do. Let us see where our grubby research leads us. And I'm guessing it's two people this time? One old, one new."

Brady laughed. Accepted that it wasn't just his daughter who could read his mind. Told Mozart what he wanted. Gave him the service number...

2 – 5 – 0 – 3 – 2 – 4 – 0 – 6. Easy to remember, Gerry...

41

'I *want a pound on a longshot.'*

And sometimes you collect your winnings...

Brady parked the car in the village. Walked a hundred yards down the road.

Right at the top of Lythe Bank. If walking up a hundred and ninety-nine steps to the Abbey is a test of your piety, what's walking up Lythe Bank to confess your sins?

Brady pushed the lychgate open. Walked up the gravel path towards the church. Paused. Read the inscription on one of the gravestones.

In memory of Revd. William Haworth. First incumbent and vicar of this parish for 40 years. After having lived a blameless and exemplary life he died universally beloved and lamented on the 28th February 1883. 'Mark the perfect man, and behold the upright life. For the end of that man is peace.'

'Blameless and exemplary.' I'll do my best...

He was kneeling at a grave.

Definitely not mourning... Gardening. Kneeling like a gardener...

"Magic?"

"One minute, cock. Let me finish this."

What's the accent? Geordie? No. Softer. Carlisle maybe?

Brady waited. Watched him doing something with his right hand. Unhurried.

He slowly straightened up. Turned to face Brady. Tall, well over six foot. Dark, matted hair. A beard that had been haphazardly trimmed in the last two weeks. A cautious, watchful face. A blue jumper over a check shirt. A faded red cord holding his jeans up. A jacket. An overcoat on top of that. Brady lost count of the layers.

The overcoat was long. Might once have been navy blue. Might once have had a hood trimmed with fur. Flared out as it reached the ground.

A one-man pyramid...

Brady glanced at Magic's right hand. He was holding a pair of scissors.

"Good morning," Brady said.

Magic dropped the scissors into one of the coat's pockets. Hitched his jeans up. Re-tied the red cord.

"Morning to you," he finally said. "You were reading the Reverend. Everyone does. Did him yesterday." He nodded at the grave he'd been working on. "Alice Cundle. She was overdue a trim. But you're not the vicar. And you're no grieving relative of hers. So you'll be Brady."

"I am..."

So he was expecting me. How? Donoghue.

"...And I've come prepared."

Brady unslung his backpack. Unzipped it. "Here." He handed Magic two paper bags.

"What's this, mate? A bribe?"

"Breakfast. I took a guess that you'd like tomato with them. He's wrapped them in silver foil so they'll still be hot. And there's tea in the flask."

Magic Pockets raised his eyebrows. "Sugar?"

"Half a dozen sachets in my pocket. And a stirrer."

"What were you then? Chief boy scout?"

"Of course."

Magic laughed, "Aye. Me n' all. Come on. Sun's shining, we may as well have the table by the window."

BRADY FOLLOWED the tramp's flowing coat through the graveyard to where it ended. "Here," Magic said, gesturing at a bench overlooking the sea. "Second best view in the world. An' I know what you want to ask me. Just let me work my way through these lads first. An' two sugars'd be perfect."

Brady unscrewed the flask. Poured the tea. Added the sugar and handed it to Magic.

He took it. Nodded. Waited until he'd finished the first bacon sandwich. "Thought I'd miss it," he said. "Don't at all."

Brady followed his gaze out to sea. Saw a long, low cargo ship heading north. "Thought I'd miss the sea. But I don't. This – " He gestured behind at the graveyard. "Does me good. Keeps me... Fuck knows what the word is. Sane, probably."

He started on the second sandwich. Brady kept quiet. Looked at the cargo ship. Wondered what had made him come ashore.

Magic finished the sandwich. Smoothed out both the paper bags. Folded them. Put them in another of the pockets.

Brady smiled, "Magic pockets," he said.

"One of the local kids. It stuck."

"You stay in Whitby all the time?"

"Pretty much. Whitby. Up an' down. But east coast or

west coast. Day comes when you have to make your mind up. Sunrise or sunset. Wind off the sea or pissing down."

"You knew who I was. So you can probably guess why I'm here."

"Gerry."

"Yes. I need to find him."

Because I need to question him. And not over a bacon sandwich this time...

"I got the feeling he... That his range was a bit wider than yours."

"Younger isn't he? Not by much but a few years make a difference. This isn't a life that lends itself to old age."

Brady nodded. Felt Magic's 'wind off the sea.' The slight chill of approaching autumn. "I can imagine."

"No, mate. You can't. Slept rough, have you? One night? For charity? You an' a few of your pals? Decent dinner then you all kip down at the football ground knowing there's a hot bath an' a full English in eight hours' time? St John's Ambulance standing by? No, mate, you can't even begin to imagine."

"I'm sorry, I – "

"No, you don't need to apologise. An' I'm not being critical. Walk a mile in my shoes? Spend a winter in my fuckin' coat more like."

Brady didn't speak. Didn't know what to say.

"Anyway, you want Gerry. What's he done? Not that it's any of my business."

"Nothing at all – "

Apart from firebombing Macdonald's house. Disappearing halfway through a conversation...

" – I just need to speak to him."

"That lass that went over the cliff? No phone, no internet an' we still know more than most folk."

"Maybe. But I do need to speak to him."

"Here." Magic reached into one of the pockets. Passed Brady a bacon sandwich bag. "Write your number down. Can't promise, though. He's his own boss. An' people like me an' Gerry. We don't do 'official.'"

Brady did as he was asked.

"You know his story?" Magic said.

"Gerry's? Some of it."

But not the important parts...

"Like I say, not my business to share it. But you'd do well to listen the day he tells you."

Magic stood up. Unerringly went to the correct pocket. Brought the scissors out.

"How do you do it?" Brady said. "Right pocket every time?"

The tramp shrugged. "Filing system. Paperwork, hardware and personal. And this one." He patted a pocket Brady hadn't seen him use. "Gobstoppers for the kids. An' now – " He pushed himself to his feet. Opened and closed the scissors three or four times. "You need to let me get on. Old Mother Marston. Eighteen fifty-three. She's well overdue..."

42

Brady rolled out of bed. Walked naked to the bathroom. Ignored Siobhan's wolf whistle.

"Eighty point seven," he said as he came back.

"Eighty point seven what? The temperature outside? Not even in old money..."

"Kilogrammes," Brady said. "Eighty point seven kilogrammes. You're bad for me."

"Why? I like eighty point seven. It looks good from this angle."

She threw the covers back. Reached for him.

Brady stepped back. "Stop it. I'm serious. And I'm forty-four next month."

"The thirteenth. It's in my diary. In blood."

"Right. And on the thirteenth I'm six years away from being fifty – "

'Flushed, overweight, their belts loosened another notch, counting the days to retirement.'

No way, Mozart. Absolutely no way...

" – And I need to be under eighty kilos. Otherwise I'm

never going to be under eighty kilos again. Maybe I should start going to the gym."

"No," she said quietly. "Don't do that."

"Why not? I'm only joking. When do I get time to go to a gym?"

"Well don't. Walk Archie more. Run up the steps to the Abbey. Get back into bed with me. But *don't* go to the gym."

Brady laughed. "Why not? What harm can going to the gym do? Apart from being embarrassed if I'm on the exercise bike next to Dan Keillor?"

She shook her head. "I'm Irish. I'm superstitious. That's why."

"I still don't understand."

She sighed. "Because when a man – especially one in his thirties or forties – suddenly announces he's going to the gym... Most of the time it's got nothing to do with getting fit and everything to do with a new woman in his life."

Brady shook his head. "You're being ridiculous, Siobhan. Bloody hell, our relationship consists of me letting you down. How do you think – "

"I don't. Not for one minute. But once bitten..."

"Oh. Right. I'm sorry. Alan – "

"The EMI guy. The O'Briens do not speak the name of their enemies." She pushed the quilt even further down. "Now get back into bed. Eighty point seven or not you're going to lead this good Catholic girl into temptation – "

"I'm going to take you to Dave's for a – "

"Right. So you might as well work it off before you put it on..."

BRADY STIRRED THE BOLOGNESE SAUCE. Tasted it. Remembered Kate telling him to sprinkle some sugar into it.

'Just a pinch, Mike. it takes away the acidity of the tomatoes.'

Reached for the sugar bowl. Sensed her come into the kitchen. Turned to look at her.

She smiled, hair still wet from the shower.

"That smells good. I'm hungry."

"I've put some sugar in it. Just a pinch. My sister told me it improves the sauce."

She looked at him. Held his eyes. "Eating it with you improves the sauce."

He laughed. "You're just saying that."

Siobhan shook her head. Walked towards him. Reached up and kissed him. "I've something I need to tell you."

"What's that? You're away at the weekend? Another film? More composing?"

"No. Something more important."

Something about her expression. She's pregnant. Oh fuck. She's on the pill. How the hell has that happened? What in God's name will Ash say?

"I wanted to tell you this when I was sober."

"What are you talking about, Siobhan? I haven't even opened the wine."

She smiled. "I don't mean 'sober' like that. I mean in the cold light of day. Not when we're in bed together. When you know I really mean it."

"Mean what?"

She reached her hand up. Pulled his head down. Kissed him. Kissed him again. Harder. Broke off. Kept her hand on his cheek. Looked into his eyes.

"I love you, Michael Brady."

"I – "

Don't know what to say. Don't have a clue what to say...

"I – " Brady said again.

I like her. Really like her. But Ash. Grace...

Siobhan smiled at him. "You remember what I said? That night? After the gig at the pub?"

"You told me you were going to London."

"I told you I liked complicated men. I do. Especially you."

"I – "

She held her hand up. Stopped him speaking. "You don't have to say anything. I understand. But I wanted to let you know. In case..." She took a step forward. Put her hand on the front of his jeans. Ran her nails up and down. "In case you hadn't guessed." She stepped back. Held his eyes again. "There's something else I need to tell you, my love."

Christ. What now? She is pregnant. Ash...

Brady tried to hide his nerves. Failed. "What's that?"

"The Bolognese sauce is burning."

43

A Sunday afternoon. A long walk on the beach. Holding hands with Siobhan, throwing sticks for Archie, dinner waiting when they got back, a bottle of wine already opened...

Perfect.

Except that Brady felt his phone vibrate. Just as they turned round at Sandsend. Tried to fight the urge to check the message.

Failed.

Threw Archie's stick extra hard. Told Siobhan it was her turn to wrestle it out of his mouth. Watched her run across the beach.

Surreptitiously checked his phone.

Mozart.

The report. Exactly as promised. Shit.

Can I wait an hour to read it? I'll have to...

"You want a coffee? Let me make you one. Find a film for us to watch. I'll make you a coffee and get dinner started. Or do you want a glass of wine?"

Brady turned the Bolognese sauce on low. Poured Siobhan a glass of wine. "What did you find?"

"The Hateful Eight? Have you seen it? It won Best Original Soundtrack. Ennio Morricone. So I'm going to listen to the music, make mental notes and sort-of watch the film. Come and sit with me."

Brady shook his head. "I won't be long. I just need to sort dinner out."

"You did the sauce this morning. You want me to pause the film?"

"No, no. I'll pick it up. Five minutes, no more."

Brady walked back into the kitchen. Forgot about dinner in the ten strides it took him to get there. Reached for his phone. Started reading Mozart's report.

YOU ASKED me to look at two people for you. I have started with the least interesting: the continuing saga of the elected representative for mid-Hampshire.

I have little to add to my previous comments – thank goodness, as it would mean I'd missed something – other than to say that another significant deposit has appeared in Graham Macdonald's bank account.

The amount is a relatively modest £25,000. The source is the same East European account responsible for the two previous deposits.

Macdonald's just back from Hungary.

'How much greed?'

'Two hundred and fifty grand.'

So what's this? The first instalment?

Brady poured himself a glass of wine. Scrolled down. Started reading again.

As you know from my previous report Graham Macdonald married the daughter of John Channon, at the time prosperous local businessman and Chairman of the Conservative Association.

Diane Susanna Channon enjoyed a conventional middle-class upbringing, largely paid for by her father's company, which supplied equipment and components to the motor industry.

You may though, be aware of the phrase 'clogs to clogs in three generations.' It is supposedly of Lancashire origin but applies equally well to manufacturing companies in Hampshire, especially when they are suddenly exposed to competition from the Far East and a downturn in the UK motor industry.

John Channon's company – started by his grandfather in the 50s and aggressively expanded by his father – went into liquidation last year. There were substantial personal guarantees attached to the bank borrowing. He has resigned as Chairman of the Conservative Association and there would have been little, if anything, for her to inherit.

Brady stirred the sauce. Sipped his wine. Started reading the second section of the report.

The one I've been waiting for...

"Mike? I thought you were coming to watch the film?"

"I am. Five minutes, Siobhan."

"You said 'five minutes' five minutes ago. I feel guilty watching it on my own."

"Seriously. I'm just checking the football scores." Took a step forward and kissed her. "Five minutes, I promise."

GERRY ROYSTON DONOGHUE was born in Germany on 2nd April 1978, the son of a sergeant in the Royal Electrical and Mechanical Engineers.

The childhood was exactly what Gerry had described in

the café. Different schools in different countries. Inevitably joining the army at 16. Married at 22. One son, born two years later.

He didn't say anything about that...

25032406 Donoghue G. was transferred to the Parachute Regiment and ultimately promoted to Staff Sergeant. In March 2010 he was in Afghanistan.

What age is he? Thirty-one...

Details of his service record at that time are almost non-existent. However with some judicious research – Her Majesty's firewall is not quite as fireproof as it once was – he appears to have been tasked with a rescue operation in the north of Helmand Province.

I am speculating now but that is the exact time Lieutenant Leo McMahon disappeared. As you may know, there is a general belief that McMahon was undercover and was captured and tortured by the Taliban. His body has never been found.

Brady put his phone down. Sipped his wine. Stared at the kitchen wall.

He's in Helmand. Working with someone who's undercover...

"Mike!" This time she didn't walk to the kitchen door. "Are you coming to watch the film or not?"

"Yes. I told you. But there's something I need to read."

"I thought you were checking the football?"

"I was. I am..."

Brady picked his phone up. Tapped *Leo McMahon* into Wiki. Read the story.

Captain Leo Francis McMahon (20.2.77 to 13.3.2010) was a British Army officer in the Parachute Regiment. He was abducted in Bagram, the most northerly district in Helmand Province, while serving in Afghanistan. It was McMahon's third tour of duty as a Military Intelligence Officer. His body has never been found.

Thirty-three. Bloody hell. 'His body has never been found.' How do his parents cope with that? How do they even know what date he died?

Was Donoghue complicit in some way? Responsible for McMahon's death?

'What do you do?'

'Walk on the cliffs. Help a couple of mates out occasionally. Tell a copper what he already knows in exchange for my breakfast.'

Supposing a politician was responsible for McMahon's death? 'I wouldn't piss on one if he was on fire. That do you?'

Diane Macdonald. The firebomb. Donoghue has all the skills. And the cynicism.

Brady closed Wiki. Scrolled back to the top of Mozart's report. Started reading –

"Mike." Siobhan was standing in the doorway. He hadn't heard her. "You're working."

"Sorry, love. Something came through. I had to read it – "

"Work?"

"Yes, work."

"It's Sunday afternoon."

"I told you before, Siobhan. The people I deal with – "

She shook her head. "It doesn't matter. I'm not feeling very well. Maybe I'm coming down with something. I'm going home. I'll have an early night."

"What about dinner?"

"It doesn't matter. Freeze it. Give it to Archie. And you wouldn't have enjoyed the film."

Brady stepped towards her. "No, don't kiss me. If I've got something there's no point you catching it. I'll text you when I'm home."

Brady stood at the door. Watched her drive slowly down

Henrietta Street. Walked back inside. Looked at an expectant dog. “No, Archie. Just no. It’s going in the freezer.”

Felt his phone vibrate for the second time that afternoon.

Siobhan home already?

It was Ash.

We’re at Jess’s. Can you collect us? Jess is staying over ‘cos her mum has to go early in the morning. Is there anything to eat? We’re starving.

“So it’s not going in the freezer after all, Archie. It’s going in Ash and Jessica. I’ll share a tin of beans with you...”

44

"Clearly a good weekend. You've caught the sun."

"A lovely weekend," Frankie said. "His parents made me feel welcome. They took me out for Sunday lunch, they forgave me for being English. And his eight year old nephew destroyed my castle and killed all my men."

Brady laughed. "I thought you were walking up hills, not playing video games?"

"Hills? I must have been off sick when we did the Cheviots in Geography. Hills and more bloody hills. But at least the sun was shining."

"Let me bring you up to date. Come into the office. Assuming you're not too stiff to move."

"Graham Macdonald was firebombed," Brady said as Frankie closed the door.

She nodded. "I know. The early hours of Sunday morning. "

"The very early, still-dark hours of Sunday morning. I

was out there with Dan and Anya. The remains of a Smirnoff bottle and someone's old T-shirt."

"Home-made Molotov cocktail? That's about as far from Runswick Bay as you can get. Did you talk to Macdonald?"

"In his neighbours' lounge. Said he was up and dressed when it happened. Couldn't sleep. Heard what he described as 'the gates of Hell opening.' He thought at first someone had thrown a stone through his window. Then he saw the flames and ran into the garden."

"How much damage was there?"

"Damage to the house? He'll need a new porch. A new door. The neighbours on the other side will need a new fence. Damage to Macdonald? None. But it was a message, Frankie. A warning. I talked to Pete. He – "

"Pete Warren? The FIO?"

Brady nodded. "Definitely a firebomb. But it needed to be in the house to do real damage."

"So what have we got? Someone standing at the top of Macdonald's drive at four o'clock on a Sunday morning? Choosing the house at random? Or do they know it's Macdonald's?"

Brady shook his head. "It *can't* be random, Frankie. You don't stand in your garage, make a Molotov cocktail and then wonder what you're going to do with it. Macdonald's been threatened. Says he's been threatened – and I'm starting to believe him. His wife goes over the edge of a cliff. Now he's been firebombed. They *have* to be connected."

"Suppose they're not?"

"Diane dies? Macdonald's threatened? His porch burns down at four in the morning? Three separate incidents? That's stretching things, Frankie."

"Except that right now there's only one incident. The firebomb. We've no evidence that Macdonald's been threatened. Only his word for it. And like you said, even if he has it's the Met's problem, not ours. And much as you want Diane to be murder – "

"I don't *want* it to be murder, Frankie. It *is* murder."

"But you've no proof. And you're contradicting yourself."

'You're determined to prove yourself. Determined you won't be beaten. Don't jump to conclusions, Michael.'

Is that what I'm doing? No, because Diane Macdonald was murdered. All I need is the proof...

"How am I contradicting myself?"

"What you said before. The professional does the job and moves on. The amateur meddles and gets caught. Supposing – just supposing – Diane *was* murdered. For whatever reason. Why complicate it by firebombing Macdonald?"

"Because they're both warnings, Frankie. That's obvious."

Frankie shook her head. "No, boss, it's not." She hesitated. Looked away. Looked back at Brady. "With respect, boss, it's only obvious if you want it to be obvious. If you've made your mind up."

"Whether I've made my mind up or not, Frankie, we need to get to the bottom of this. Or however much Kershaw likes London and his expense account he's going to be back."

"You think that's likely?"

"I think it's inevitable. Kershaw's not going to sit back while an MP's firebombed on his patch."

My patch. I like it being 'my patch...'

"Wales," Frankie said.

Brady raised his eyebrows. "That's a touch cryptic, Detective Sergeant. "The country? Or are they doing a remake of *Free Willy* off Whitby?"

"The country, boss. Back in the seventies and eighties the Welsh Nationalists bombed homes owned by the English. The Sons of Glendower. Why not here? Runswick, Robin Hood's Bay, Staithes. It's not just people being homeless while Macdonald's in his house for four or five weeks a year. It's local kids on minimum wage trying to buy a house. And not just the kids, their parents as well. How would you fancy Ash living in your top bedroom when she's thirty?"

"So firebombing holiday homes is the answer? The Sons of Captain Cook?"

"No, obviously it's not the answer. But on one level... It's understandable."

"I didn't have you down as a militant, Frankie."

"I'm not, boss. But being out at Hutton-le-Hole with Lochie has brought it home to me. That village is going the same way. *And* the village where his parents live. Another thing..."

"What's that?"

"Your Molotov cocktail. It's easy. Go on YouTube and there'll be half a dozen videos telling you how to do it. And that's before you go anywhere near the Dark Web."

"But if it's someone local – "

"Then we're back where we were. With two, maybe three, unrelated crimes. But it makes as much sense as them being connected. Like you said, you've only Graham Macdonald's word that he's being threatened."

"Bloody hell, Frankie. That's more loose ends than a bowl of noodles. They *have* to be connected."

Brady hesitated. Looked at her. "Frankie, I'm sorry. I'm not trying to fall out with you. Just... Graham bloody Macdonald. We've got history. You know that. I can still see the car wrapped round the tree. I see it every time I drive to

Scarborough. So I need to sort this out. Before bloody Kershaw decides to come home."

"Which none of us want."

"Right. Talk to me about something else, Frankie. It's none of my business but I'm glad you had a good weekend. That it's going well."

She nodded. "It is. Except Lochie might have a decision to make."

"Why's that?"

"There are rumours of a couple of jobs coming up."

"That's good. Whereabouts?"

"North and south. The Institute of Modern Art in Middlesbrough. And one in Scarborough. There's a place called Woodend. Used to be a natural history museum, now it's part creative centre, part gallery and part venue."

"I thought he was happy where he is? Heavily into the folklore? Knew everything there was to know about North Yorkshire's witches?"

Frankie nodded. "He is. But he's ambitious. And heavily into surfing as well. And there's a chance to develop the job in Scarborough. There's an art gallery and another museum. He's going down there this week."

Brady nodded. "Wish him luck. And sorry again, Frankie. Like I said – "

"No problem, boss. And it's my turn to apologise. I didn't ask. Good weekend?"

"Apart from four o'clock on Sunday morning – "

And falling out with Siobhan. And eating baked beans for Sunday dinner...

" – Yeah, it was fine. Dave was open. Archie found a dead fish to roll in."

Frankie laughed. "Story of your life, boss. I'll leave you to it."

"I'm going online. See if YouTube will teach me how to make a Molotov Cocktail."

"Careful. Big Brother will be watching you."

"Some nerd down at GCHQ more likely. But I need to know what I'm talking about."

When I ask Gerry Donoghue why he firebombed Macdonald...

45

Brady reached for his keyboard. Stopped as his phone started playing classical music.

Siobhan. Another apology I need to make...

Read her message. Read it a second time.

I wasn't ill. I just thought you needed some space. Maybe we both do. So I'm going to see Helen in the morning. Sort out what we're doing. Write some music. Walk on the hills. Drink gin. I'll be away for a week. I'll miss you. But you need space.

Signed with an emerald green heart. But only one....

Brady sighed.

What the hell can I do? Killers don't care what day of the week it is. Mozart probably doesn't know what day of the week it is. 'What difference would that make to me, Michael...'

He started to write a reply. Saw *Kershaw* flash on the display before the phone even had chance to ring.

"Michael. Good morning."

'Michael' this morning. Maybe he's not had time to get in a bad mood yet...

"Good morning, sir. Macdonald?"

"In a word, yes. Before I go into that fetid swamp that

passes as the Mother of Parliaments. Some fucking committee today. So bring me up to date. Witnesses?"

None...

"As I explained, sir. It was four o'clock on Sunday morning – "

"For Christ's sake, Brady. An MP's been firebombed. Have you done a house to house?"

"We have. With absolutely no results."

Mainly because it wasn't a house-to-house, it was a holiday home-to-holiday home...

"We need a conviction for this, Brady. We need some results. Macdonald's no more use than a chocolate bloody fireguard, but he's got powerful friends."

Who can no doubt help your career, Alan...

"I'll go and speak to Dan Keillor and Jake Cartwright again, sir. Double-check everything."

"Do that. And put Thomson on it if you have to. God knows she's a pain-in-the-arse at times but she's got some brains."

The line went dead.

You're right, Alan. She has. Maybe I should listen to her...

"FRANKIE, I know we've just finished talking. Spare me another five minutes, will you? I've had Kershaw on the phone."

"So you need to make progress?"

Brady laughed. "Understatement of the year. I need to make progress or Macdonald's 'powerful friends' might send Kershaw back to the sticks."

"Which none of us want. That's your I've-got-a-theory face. What is it?"

"Humour me. Gerry Donoghue. Ex-army. Homeless.

You've not met him. But I like him. Felt he was someone I could trust. Came in after Diane went over the cliff. Told me he *might* have seen someone."

"The only witness we had."

"Right. But I can't detain him. And he's homeless, so he's hard – bloody nearly impossible – to contact. But he turns up again a week later. He asks for another cup of coffee, I go to Dave's. When I come back he's gone. Why?"

"Why did he turn up again? Or why did he go?"

"Both. I can't work out a reason. Half of me thinks he's taking the piss. Taunting me – "

"He wouldn't be the first killer to pretend to help with the investigation."

"Right. You think he *wants* to get caught?"

"Why?"

"Because of something he said. Being on patrol in Afghanistan. The adrenalin. 'Like being a rock star' he said. Then he said, 'You know – you just fucking know – that you're never going to feel that alive again.' 'Despite there being a chance of getting killed?' And he said, '*Because* there's a chance of getting killed.'

"So your theory is he killed Diane Macdonald? But that wasn't enough for him? That he gets the adrenalin buzz from taunting you?"

"Something else. He told me how many vets were homeless. 'Take yourself down to a railway arch one night. Half the blokes there will tell you their service number.' I checked the stats. He's right. He was in Helmand. Undercover. Suppose he's got PTSD? Something tipped him over the edge? Suppose Donoghue wants to swap the army for prison? 'You stop thinking for yourself,' he said. 'That's why we can't cope when we come out.'"

"So he wants to swap one set of rules for another? If he's

homeless – can go wherever he wants – I'd have thought prison... It'd be like a bird in a cage. Besides, boss, if he wanted to be caught why did he disappear?"

Brady shook his head. "I don't know, Frankie. But it's a theory."

"Half a theory. Maybe not even that."

"But right now the only theory I have. I need to find him, Frankie. Before Kershaw books himself a one-way ticket back to Whitby."

FRANKIE TURNED TO GO. Changed her mind. Turned round. Put her hand on Brady's arm. "Boss, before you go looking for him... Can I say something?"

"Of course you can."

"Donoghue. You know a lot about him."

Brady nodded. "I did my research."

"Some of that research... Undercover. Helmand. I'm surprised it wasn't behind a firewall. A bloody big firewall."

Brady raised his eyebrows. Didn't reply.

"You need to be careful, boss. I know it speeds things up. I know you get frustrated by the techies. By Whitby always being last in the queue. But one of these days your 'research' is going to land you in trouble."

"It's fine, Frankie."

"It's fine until it goes wrong, boss. Or something happens to whoever's doing the research for you."

"Trust me, Frankie. And I'm going to be out for the rest of the afternoon – "

"Looking for Donoghue?"

Brady nodded. "Looking for someone who might know where he is. But no 'research,' I promise."

"What do you want me to do?"

"It's your turn to be frustrated. Chase the nerds, will you? Diane Macdonald's bank account."

Mozart would have done it in an afternoon. But Frankie's right. One of these days...

46

Church of St Oswald
Parish of Lythe
Sunday service 9:30am
Please see notice board in porch

BRADY WALKED past the green and white sign. Decided the only notice he needed to see was one telling him where Magic was. Walked round the churchyard to check he wasn't working behind one of the gravestones. Knew he was wasting his time.

Looked at the gravestones, half of them tilted drunkenly towards the sea.

A hundred years of the prevailing wind and they've finally conceded defeat...

Stood for a minute looking out to sea. Shook his head in irritation. Turned to walk back to the car.

"Perfect day."

Brady looked up. Saw a man in his early fifties, his elderly mother supported on his arm.

"Yes," Brady said. "The last of the summer. Enjoy it while we can."

"We will. Won't we, mum?"

He turned. Held his mother more tightly as she stumbled. Gave Brady a look which very clearly said, 'Not many more times I can bring her.'

"You take care," Brady said to the old lady. "Enjoy the sunshine."

Her son steered her slowly back down the path. Brady saw them pause briefly by one of the gravestones.

Husband? Father? One last visit before it's too cold for her?

He looked round the churchyard again.

Like I can make him appear out of thin air. Maybe I should pin a notice in the porch. 'Wanted, man with large overcoat. Knows someone who makes Molotov Cocktails...'

Shook his head in frustration. Walked back to his car.

47

"Boss?"

"What is it, Frankie?"

"You wanted the details on Diane Macdonald's bank account. They're here."

Brady looked up. "Finally. How long is it since we asked for them? The bank statements will be in tanners and threepenny bits."

"Sorry, boss. I'm – "

"Don't say it, Frankie. You're not as old as me. It's my dad's fault. He didn't believe in decimal currency. Converted everything – including my pocket money – back to pounds, shillings and pence."

"So..."

"A tanner. Sixpence in old money. So two-and-a-half pee. Five of them in half a crown. But you're dying of boredom. Let's see what Diane's bank statements have to say."

"One thing, boss. And not so much 'say it' as 'shout it out loud.'

Frankie handed him the bank statements. One entry circled in red.

"Seventy-five grand?" Brady said. "Seventy-five grand?"

Looked at the statement a second time. "Global Books? Seventy-five grand?"

"It's an advance," Frankie said. "It's all it can be."

"So Diane Macdonald has written a book? Wrote a book before she died?"

"Like I say, it's all it can be. It's not royalties because it's an even amount. You know, royalties would be like seven thousand, six hundred and twelve. So it has to be an advance – "

"We're in the wrong job, Frankie. I thought authors got about five grand?"

"They do. Ten minutes' research says it's way more than normal. Way more. Unless you're a celeb or you've written the next *Fifty Shades* advances are nowhere near that."

"So is that what she's done? *Fifty Shades* – "

"*Fifty Shades* set in Westminster, boss? She is a politician's wife after all."

Brady nodded. "So there'll be someone's dirty washing hanging on the line. You don't get paid seventy-five grand for keeping secrets."

"So if someone's found out about the book. What's in it – "

"Bloody hell, there's a lot of supposition in this. But she'll have made enemies. Maybe powerful enemies. We need to read the book, Frankie."

"It'll be on her hard drive."

Brady shook his head. "Which means we'll be waiting for the bloody techies *again*. We need to recruit our own nerd, Frankie."

"You said, boss."

"I know. Sorry. But four, five years from now half the bloody crime we're fighting will be online. We can't fight it with coppers whose IT skills are limited to going home and playing *Grand Theft Auto*. Let's get the hard drive. And tell them it's urgent. More urgent than anything else they've got. And make a phone call, Frankie."

"Who to?"

"The publishers. Global Books? We can't kick Macdonald's door down and take her computer. Maybe there's a short cut. Tell them we need the manuscript. And while you do that I'm going to gossip."

"Football?"

"No. Sex."

Frankie smiled. "What else, boss? Then you've only got food to go and you've covered everything men are interested in..."

She was out of the door before Brady could reply.

48

Brady reached for his phone. Dialled Annabel Cowling's number. Didn't get the answerphone this time. Didn't waste much time on small talk.

"They didn't..." He wasn't sure how to phrase it. "Diane and her husband – they didn't have a physical relationship any more?"

Annabel Cowling laughed out loud. "Are you asking me if Diane still had sex with her husband?"

"Yes, I suppose I am."

"They hadn't had sex for nine years. She told me having sex with Graham was like having a very large wardrobe fall on top of you. With a very small key sticking out."

"So why were they still married? Because he's an MP?"

"Goodness me, Mr Brady. I had you filed under 'sharper knives in the drawer.' Don't disappoint me."

"So he's a source of gossip?"

"Was. He gave her gossip and introductions. She gave him a dutiful wife – at least the appearance of one – and therefore votes. But all that changed when she got the whopping advance for the book."

Let's see how much you really know, Annabel...

"The fifty thousand?"

"Is that all she got?"

So maybe not as much as you think...

"Good God. I'd have expected twice that. At least."

"For the book you didn't tell me about."

"Surely, Inspector Brady, 'helping the police with their enquiries' means answering their questions? Not holding their hand."

Point taken. One-all...

"Fifty grand. Or the hundred she should have got. It clearly wasn't a first novel."

"An insightful political memoir, Inspector. The personal background to one of the most important periods in our history." She laughed. "Or who the cabinet ministers were shagging when they fucked-up so spectacularly. A Westminster kiss n'tell. And she didn't stop at the bedroom door. Or the office door. Or the lift in the Conference hotel..."

"You've read it then?"

"No. Just a teaser. Ten pages. That's all. Obviously I know the gossip, the people involved. But no, I've not read the book. Anyway, I assume you've got her hard drive. You can read it yourself."

Not yet...

" – But the publishers have read it. And once they started salivating everything changed. Telling your husband you want a divorce doesn't instantly improve your cash flow. It was two years before I saw anything. But Diane's advance changed everything. Set her free..."

And gave Graham Macdonald a problem...

"And she could write, I'll give her that. Short, sharp and funny. Not that you have to try hard to be funny about some of their peccadilloes. Especially her husband's. And... If I'm honest, she was vindictive as well. Diane had a mean streak in her. She was settling a few old scores. Slights. Real *and* imagined. Not that I should gossip."

Of course not, Annabel...

"I don't know the people involved like you do, Annabel. And if the publishers were getting excited she'll have named names. Who's got a reputation he daren't lose?"

"Not he. She. Certainly based on what I read. You'll need to turn your hypocrisy filter off. But the good news is you don't have to drive far. No five hour schlep down the M1. Sixty or seventy miles should do it. Home for lunch. One word of warning though..."

"What's that?"

"Moths. Flames. Don't get too close to her."

49

Brady glanced out of his window. Saw the two telecoms vans. "What did they say, Frankie?"

"Half an hour before we get the phone line back. The guy in charge says there's some flood damage from last night's rain."

"Use your mobile. I don't want to wait half an hour. You do that and I'll pray."

"Pray there isn't a crime epidemic while the phones are off?"

"Right. But it's Thursday morning. No-one commits a crime on Thursday morning."

"The Great Train Robbery was on a Thursday morning, boss."

Brady shook his head. "You know too much, Frankie. Like I say, use your mobile. A copy of the book. That's all we need."

Frankie was back in ten minutes. "They say 'no,' boss. Not without a court order."

"What?"

"They say 'no.' They said – "

"Who did you speak to?"

"Amanda Millard? One of the directors."

"And she said 'no?'

"She said in view of Diane's recent death – and the extreme sensitivity of the subject matter – they'd decided not to go ahead with publication. They'd stopped editing the manuscript and would be deleting the files they had."

"Unless we had a court order?"

"Unless we had a court order."

"That's..." Brady shook his head in frustration. "That's bollocks, Frankie. One, Diane's pal told me the publishers were 'salivating.' The exact word she used. And two, there must be a thousand books published posthumously – "

"Girl with the Dragon Tattoo."

"Was it? There you are. Ring the woman back. Tell her I'll get a court order. This afternoon if I can. And tell her if she destroys the files she'll be committing an offence."

"The file – files, maybe – they'll still be on Diane's laptop, boss. All she's done is attach the Word doc to an e-mail. Press send..."

'Not that you have to try hard to be funny about some of their peccadilloes. Especially her husband's...'

Brady shook his head.

"I've changed my mind, Frankie. Leave the hard drive where it is. Macdonald's still our most likely suspect. I don't want to alert him to anything. God knows he's not very bright but he's capable of pressing delete."

Frankie looked doubtful. "Assuming he has his wife's password."

"OK, he's capable of hitting a laptop with a hammer. Or dropping it into the harbour."

Like I thought about doing with Patrick's laptop. And if I'd done that I wouldn't be sitting here now...

"You still think we should go to Runswick and get it?"

Frankie nodded. "I do."

"We'll still be behind York in the queue for the techies."

"But we'll be in the queue, boss. And it's procedure."

"Not now, Frankie. Procedure can wait. We'll have to agree to disagree on this one."

Brady pulled his keyboard towards him.

'The good news is you don't have to drive far. Sixty or seventy miles should do it. One word of warning though. Don't get too close to her.'

Sixty or seventy miles. Even with the sea on one side that's still a bloody big area. So what do I have to do? Trawl through every MP in the North of England?

He didn't.

Frankie tapped once on Brady's office door. Walked straight in.

Punched the air.

"One minute, boss?"

"Always, Frankie, even if we have just fallen out. And I've crashed into a dead end." Brady looked at her. "Or maybe not. I know that expression, Frankie. It's your 'I've made a breakthrough' expression."

"I've had a phone call. Someone at the publisher."

"They'd got your number? How?"

"The phone lines are off remember? I rang them on my mobile. We're in white van man's debt. I've got a mole."

"At the publishers?"

She nodded. "He wouldn't give me his name – "

"Easy enough to trace the call. He must have known that."

"He said he was motivated by the public's need to know. That and starting a new job on Monday."

"So what did he say? And you can go back to your normal expression now..."

"He spoke for five minutes. Chapter and verse. Quoted some passages from the book. Specifically about Lilian Beale."

"Lilian Beale? She's – "

"The Government's rising star. Shooting star. The youngest cabinet minister for a thousand years. Something like that. A glowing reputation built on traditional values. Hard work. Thrift, Family, Honesty. She's written a book. *The Seven Pillars of Integrity.* Very popular with right-wing talk shows in the States. And happily married, obviously."

Brady raised his eyebrows. "You wouldn't be wearing that expression if she was happily married, Detective Sergeant."

Frankie smiled back. "Her researcher, according to my mole. Several researchers. And two or three less-than-Honourable Members."

"An affair? Several affairs?"

"Apparently the pleasantly old-fashioned term they use in the Whips' Office is 'fornication.'"

'She didn't stop at the bedroom door. Or the office door. Or the lift in the Conference hotel...'

"So she has a motive."

"A very obvious motive."

"Good. Bloody excellent. Find out everything you can."

Frankie closed the door. Brady nodded to himself.

What did I say to Mozart? 'I don't want to go tiptoeing down the corridors of power again.' I don't. But if it leads to Diane's killer... And I won't be tiptoeing.

50

"Chapter and verse, Frankie?"

"Chapter and verse, boss. Lilian Beale has a French mother, an English father. Went to a moderately expensive boarding school, played hockey for England girls. Then Brasenose College, Oxford. The same college as David Cameron."

"At the same time?"

"No. Much later. She's still in her early thirties. A year in the States as some sort of super-scholar. Joined a hedge fund. Stints in Hong Kong, Moscow and London. Rapidly became a director. Married a gold mine along the way."

"A gold mine? Are you serious?"

Frankie nodded. "I am. Among other trinkets. She's married to Antoine Pavard, the youngest son of Raphaël Pavard who – depending on how Microsoft and Amazon shares are doing – is the richest man in the world. Jewellery, watches, vast swathes of real estate, a stake in an F1 team. Everything you and I can't afford – "

"And a gold mine?"

"Yes. The family part-owns a gold mine in South Africa."

"Children?"

"Raphaël has seven. Three marriages, seven children. But Antoine and Lilian?" Frankie shook her head. "*Non. Pas des enfants*. In fact..."

"Go on..."

"She wouldn't be the first politician to have a marriage of convenience. The guy at the publishers suggested as much."

"So what are we saying? Her husband is gay?"

"And Lilian's twenty-something researcher very definitely wasn't..."

"And the old man doesn't approve of his son's lifestyle? How old is he?"

"Eighty. And *very* old-school."

"So he can't – or won't – accept Antoine. Somehow meets Beale. She sees an opportunity. Offers him a solution. A veneer of respectability."

"In return for the keys to the gold mine..."

"She marries him. Raphaël is happy. Rumours about his son are very clearly just rumours. She's free to pursue her political ambitions. Antoine is free to pursue whatever he wants to pursue. And both of them free to benefit from the gold mine. Bloody hell, there's a way to solve your cash flow problem – "

"I didn't know you had a cash flow problem, boss."

"I don't. Not until Ash gives me her next list of clothes and sports kit that she simply *cannot* live without."

"There's something else."

"What's that?"

"Raphaël. He gets direct access to a British cabinet minister."

"So if she's in Diane's book. If the stories about her are true..."

"The shit hits the fan. Her career's over – "

"And Raphaël is publicly embarrassed. Humiliated. And Lilian's golden tap is turned off."

Frankie nodded. "And it doesn't really matter if the story is true or not. Once it's out there the damage is done."

"So she had a motive."

"She did. The whole family did. A gold-plated motive. No doubt she was somewhere else when Diane went over the cliff – "

"But if Macdonald can hire someone, so can she."

Brady looked out of the window. Remembered his last conversation with Annabel Cowling.

'You'll need to turn your hypocrisy filter off. Your neck of the woods as well. Not that I should gossip.'

"Annabel Cowling knew. She said something to me. 'Your neck of the woods.' Where is she the MP for?"

"East Craven. A large slice of the Dales."

Brady laughed. "So about a hundred miles? 'Appen one part o' Yorkshire is much t'same as another to t'Southerners. Thanks, Frankie. Thank you very much. I'll make an appointment. See what Ms Beale has to say for herself."

MICHAEL BRADY REACHED for his keyboard. Tapped 'Lilian Beale affair researcher' into Google. Visited some of the more salacious sites on the internet. Spent 20 minutes reading. Not just about Lilian Beale.

But no gossip on Macdonald. A shame.

Found the number for her constituency office.

Let's see how committed to family values you really are, Lilian...

51

Brady made a decision. Knew he was going to have another argument.

"I can't ignore this, Frankie."

"You're going to see her?"

Brady nodded. "I am. It'll only take one day."

"Three days. Tomorrow's Friday. Saturday, Sunday – nothing's going to happen until Monday."

"You think I'm wrong?"

"Can I be honest with you?"

"Frankie, when have we been anything other than honest with each other? You do think I'm wrong."

"I think our time would be better spent on the laptop. I think the answer's closer to home."

"...Which is why I don't want to alert Macdonald. But I have to rule this one in or out. And I can do it in a day."

"What about finding Donoghue?"

'Moth. Flame. Don't get too close.' Is that what I'm doing? Before I've even met Lilian Beale?

"How the hell do we find someone like Donoghue,

Frankie? He's homeless. He's almost certainly been undercover – "

"Boss, look at it logically. Let me concede for one minute that Diane Macdonald *was* murdered."

"Am I finally making progress?"

Frankie shook her head. "No. It's hypothetical, boss. You know, like Elvis being found on the moon."

"Like Kershaw putting someone else first?"

"Not *that* hypothetical, boss. But hear me out. Assume for one minute she was murdered. Assume it's linked to the firebomb. And there's a link between the cases."

"There is. There *has* to be."

"Not in my opinion. But if you want a link, I'll give you a link."

Brady looked at her. "Is this a breakthrough, Frankie? Or are you winding me up?"

She gave him a butter-wouldn't-melt look that Ash would have envied. "You're a senior officer, sir. I would never wind you up. But you want a link – and there is one..."

"What?"

"Incompetence."

"Incompetence?"

"Yes. Sheer bloody incompetence. Ineptitude. Captain Cock-up. Whatever term you want to use. Diane's pushed off the cliff at the very spot where she has a fifty-fifty chance of dying. Macdonald's house is firebombed – and there's probably more damage to the neighbours' fence. They had one job – "

"But if they're warnings..."

Frankie shook her head. "They're *not* bloody warnings, boss. We've already had that conversation. Down by the harbour. Warning number one, Diane goes over the cliff.

Number two, someone burns his porch. Warnings are supposed to escalate, boss. Ignore the first one, the second one is more serious. The warnings are going the wrong way. De-escalating. What are they going to do next? Let his tyres down?"

"But you could be convinced by the cock-up theory?"

Conspiracy or cock-up? Maybe she's right. However much we want it to be the first one, it's nearly always the second...

"Yes. And cock-ups happen in Whitby. Not a hundred miles away. And not with someone who – whatever she may or may not have done in a conference lift – clearly isn't incompetent."

Brady nodded. "Your comments are noted, Frankie. But I'm still going."

Frankie shook her head. "You're a bloody good copper, boss. The best. I could be a copper for a hundred years and not find anyone I'd rather work with. But you're wrong."

"Wrong or not I'm still the boss. And I've made a decision."

"You have. So enjoy your day out." She hesitated. Added the word to underline her disagreement. "Sir..."

52

Deborah Eastwood. The relationship had only lasted six weeks. But in that time she'd dragged a 17-year-old Brady along to a Young Conservatives meeting.

Chairs shoehorned into an office overflowing with constituents' files and polling leaflets. Winston Churchill glaring down at him from one wall. Margaret Thatcher admonishing him from the opposite wall.

Lilian Beale's office caught him by surprise. A desk made from reclaimed wood, an Apple Mac, a single file with a Mont Blanc pen resting on it. Former Prime Ministers replaced by Hockney's industrial Yorkshire.

She stood up, stepped forward to greet him. Dark hair loose around her shoulders, a navy blouse, white blazer with the sleeves pulled up to her elbows.

Focused. Driven...

She held out her hand. Red nail varnish. No rings, no jewellery. Flicked cool, calculating blue eyes up to meet his.

"What can I do for you, Mr Brady? I have – " She glanced pointedly at an oversized Tag Heuer wristwatch. " –

Seven minutes. Eight hundred and forty words according to my speechwriter." She gestured for Brady to sit down.

"I won't waste them then. I'm investigating the death of Diane Macdonald. Who as you know had written a book – "

"Which suggested I'd had an affair with my researcher. I'm aware of the gossip. Every politician makes enemies. Especially one with convictions. And people sling mud. Never more than when they have a book to sell."

Brady pursed his lips. "Your researcher's now in New York. Working for the UN. A long way from the British press."

She smiled. "I admire your diligence. Clearly he wasn't the only one who did his homework. What can I say? He was offered a good job. Late-twenties. Who wouldn't want to work in New York?"

"So there's no truth in the story?"

She shook her head. "No truth at all. I'm a happily married woman, Mr Brady. I met my husband at Oxford. The Brasenose Ball. We married four years later. Again, as I'm sure you already know."

The son of one of the richest men in the world. Who makes no secret of his traditional values...

"A second researcher is in LA. And the woman who wrote the book is dead."

Lilian Beale shrugged. "Diane Macdonald? As I understand it she fell off a cliff. Accidents happen, Mr Brady. You didn't need to drive ninety-four miles to discover that."

The exact distance? She's checked how far it is? What does that tell me? Attention to detail...

"Why North Yorkshire, Ms Beale? It's a long way from home."

She tilted her head to one side. Slightly backwards. Gave

Brady the impression she was looking down at him. "On the contrary, Mr Brady. It *is* home."

"Officially..."

"Safe seats aren't always where we want them to be. What would you have me do? Wait for the Honourable Member for Rural Surrey to die? I don't have time."

"You're an ambitious woman."

"Is that an offence? A woman knowing what she wants? Hard work? Ambition? They're not fashionable values these days. But the wheel turns, Mr Brady. My time will come. Here – "

She turned, reached behind her. Brady saw the inside of her wrist.

A tattoo. A night sky. A snake emerging from a cloud. Winding its way round a crescent moon.

"Let me give you a signed copy of my book. Then your – "

She followed his gaze. Held her arm up so he could see it more clearly. "You thought people like me didn't have tattoos? This is a Wojciech Grabara. New York. Good ink costs, Mr Brady. It says as much about you as the car you drive or the art on your wall. And as you can see, a snake. The symbol of power, strength, re-birth."

"Treachery?"

She laughed. "Only in the Garden of Eden. Let me sign the book for you. Then your morning won't have been entirely wasted."

She opened the book. Wrote rapidly on the title page. Handed it to Brady.

"Thank you. I'll make sure I read it."

She stood up. Walked round the desk. Held her hand out a second time. "I'm sorry I couldn't help you, Mr Brady.

But I've enjoyed our meeting. You have a certain... reckless naiveté. I find that attractive."

Lilian Beale smiled at him. Walked across to the door. Turned the key in the lock. Walked back to Brady. Held up the middle finger of her right hand. Traced the bright red nail across his cheek.

Laughed.

"A shame we didn't have more time, Michael..."

Brady stood on the pavement. Shook his head. Knew she'd been playing with him. Looked at her picture on the cover of the book. The cool, calculating blue eyes stared back at him.

Opened it. Read the dedication.

To Michael. There are three sides to every story. Yours. Theirs. And the truth. With love, Lilian

Realised he felt slightly dirty...

53

C*offee. Then ninety-four miles back home. And an apology to Frankie. Except she'll have finished for the weekend...*

Brady's phone rang. He glanced down at the display.

Six – nine – nine. I should recognise that number.

I do...

"Good morning," Brady said. "How are you, Simon? Am I being invited to watch Emma's ducks again?"

Simon Butler laughed. "Clearly I need a less memorable number. I'm well? You?"

Brady looked up to check the traffic. Walked across the cobbles in the market square. Remembered their meeting.

Emmanuel College, Cambridge. My age. Fair hair, a neatly trimmed beard. Six foot. Eyes that were wary. Had seen their share of combat zones. A man used to giving orders.

'So what are you? Home office? Special branch? MI5?'

'All of them. None of them. Do you want a reference?'

Butler had reached for his phone. Scrolled through his contacts. Offered it to Brady.

'Call her. I'm one of six numbers she'll answer immediately.'

She was Home Secretary. Now she's Prime Minister. How much trouble am I in...

"I'm good, thank you, Simon. I've just been to see Lilian Beale. But then you already knew that."

"I did. How is she?"

"She's... I don't know. It was the first time I'd met her. A force of nature? She struck me as a woman using North Yorkshire as a stepping stone if you want me to be blunt."

Another laugh. "I'd never want you to be anything other than blunt, Mike. And I still owe you a pint. Except – "

"Except now it's two pints, because I'm going to forget I ever talked to the fragrant Ms Beale. Or heard any gossip about her."

"You know me too well, Mike."

Brady sat down on a bench.

'Your neck of the woods as well. Not that I should gossip.'

Took his time replying.

"Where does this leave Annabel Cowling? Or do I forget her as well?"

"People will always gossip, Mike. But gossip is one thing. A book that's front and centre in Waterstones is quite another."

"A book whose author is dead."

Brady heard the noise of traffic in the background. "Where are you, Simon? Back in Cambridge?"

"I'm on the Embankment. Cradling a flat white. Enjoying the last of the summer sun."

"And warning me off again."

'I thought I was supposed to be warned off by a six foot thug with a broken nose? Not someone I could enjoy a pint with.'

'I suspect we could. But appreciate that I'm the velvet glove, Mike. And yes, there is an iron fist.'

"Not warning you off. Asking for your co-operation. And wondering what the odds are..."

"I'm not sure I understand."

"The first time I ever came to London. With my parents – I was twelve, maybe thirteen. We stayed in a hotel in Bayswater. Got a cab from King's Cross. Two days later we got a cab back to King's Cross. The same cab. I remembered the number. A few years later I realised how unlikely that was. Now I'm asking myself the same question. What are the chances of me talking to the same copper twice in a year?"

"Especially one from a quiet backwater in North Yorkshire?"

"Exactly..."

"Maybe your cab driver lived near Bayswater."

"Maybe he did. And maybe my copper from Whitby is – "

"A tough bastard. That's what you called me."

Except I'm not a tough bastard. No-one with a teenage daughter is a tough bastard...

"But you remember what else I said? 'Even tough bastards need help occasionally.' Our paths seem destined to cross, Mike."

Eric Kennedy. Lilian Beale. Maybe you should send me a list of the people you're protecting, Simon...

"I still have a murder to solve."

Brady heard a tourist bus go past in the background. Briefly caught some of the commentary.

"Eric Kennedy was guilty," Butler said. "If only of youthful stupidity. Lilian Beale is innocent. Whatever happened to Diane Macdonald, it was nothing to do with her."

"But she's still dead. And her death was bloody convenient."

Brady almost saw Butler shrug. "Sometimes you get lucky. But you know the book would never have seen the light of day. As for Lilian Beale, you have my word. She's a woman who gets what she wants. But that doesn't make her guilty."

"She can't have been the only politician mentioned in the book."

"She's not. But trust me. Backbench MPs? All they care about is fiddling their expenses and getting re-elected. Another five years on the gravy train. They don't have the brains or the balls for murder. Especially the member for Mid-Hampshire."

Something about the tone of voice...

"So you know all about Graham Macdonald?"

"We do. We certainly do. And we'll reel him in when the time's right. But not just yet." Butler paused. "Do you know your Hobbes, Mike. *Leviathan?*"

"They don't teach philosophy in Whitby schools, Simon. But I know what you're going to say. Nasty, brutish and short."

"Right. The life of man. Solitary, poor, nasty, brutish and short. Like I say, when the time is right. And when Macdonald's end comes I suspect it *will* be nasty. And brutish. But I doubt it will be short..."

"So I need to sit by the river?"

Butler laughed. "What are we doing now? Trading quotes? You do. And the body of your enemy will float past, I promise you."

Brady nodded to himself. The dog's been tossed a bone...

"Good to talk to you again, Simon. You should come to Whitby for the weekend."

"Seeing as you've mentioned Whitby... One last question, Mike."

"What's that?"

"How is the town treating you? Well, I hope. Or are the boundaries starting to close around you?"

'I worry you'll find Whitby too small. Too suffocating.'

The second person to say that to me...

"No, I have a daughter – "

"I know you do. And a view my wife would kill for. But if... If you ever want a bigger challenge than Whitby, ring me. There are more important crimes than Diane Macdonald. Human nature doesn't change, no matter how far up the ladder you climb. And you're relentless. My lord and master likes relentless. We'll talk again, Mike..."

54

Ninety-four miles. Three hours. Brady parked the car. Switched the engine off. Hadn't realised how tired he was.

What did Frankie say the other day? 'The world's slowest tractor? And all its mates...

Looked at his phone. Two messages while he'd been driving. Anya and Ash.

Work first.

I'm sorry, boss. There's nothing on the firebomb. Every test has come back negative. I'll go through it in detail on Monday. Really sorry. Have a good weekend. Anya.

And Ash. Fish and chips? I'm too tired to go out again. We'll send the drone...

The message was short and simple. And filled Brady with foreboding.

Drive carefully, Dad. I need to talk when you get home.

Brady opened the car door. Ignored the view. Walked across Henrietta Street. Wondered if he'd even have time for a beer...

55

"Dad, I need to talk to you."

Brady sipped his bottle of Peroni, looked at his daughter.

More and more like her mother. Maybe slightly... Softer?

And can I see my mum in her?

"I've got your list. What do you want to do? Order it online? Or do you fancy a day shopping with your dad? We could go over to York if you want? Have some lunch? Maybe see a film?"

Ash shook her head. Hesitated. "Not that. I want to talk to you about something important."

"You want to go for a walk? Take Archie?"

Like we did before...

'You want an ice cream when we get to Sandsend?'

'Maybe. But there's a question I need to ask you. Something you need to tell me.'

The sinking feeling in the pit of his stomach. The question he'd been dreading. The question she was bound to ask one day...

'Why did Mum die?'

He'd told her. The case he was working on. Corruption. Drugs. Prostitution. Organised crime. The day all the pieces fell into place.

And then the next day.

The day their world fell apart.

AND NOW. Brady had known there'd be a follow-up.

The same feeling in his stomach. He knew what was coming...

"No, Dad. I mean... We can talk here, can't we? Every important conversation we have... It doesn't have to be on the beach. Besides..." Ash gestured at the window. "It's raining."

Brady nodded. Did his best to delay the inevitable. "You want a drink or anything?"

"No, Dad. I..."

"Is it easier if I guess, Ash?"

She nodded.

"You want to talk about Mum?"

Ash shook her head. "No. Yes. It's like I said that time on the beach. I do and I don't."

"You asked me why she died."

Ash nodded. Reached for a tissue. Brady stood up, walked over to her. "No, Dad. Don't. I know you want to hug me. But I can't talk to you like that."

"What do you want to know?" Brady said quietly.

"You explained, Dad. That case you were working on. You told me why. Sort of told me why. And I miss her so much. I miss her *more*, Dad. I don't miss her less, I miss her more. And it's easier for you 'cos you've got Siobhan now – "

"No, I haven't. We've – "

"Don't stop me, Dad, 'cos it's hard to say this and I need

to say it before I start crying. And I do, I miss her more, not less. And you're my dad and you do the best you can. I know you do. And Frankie. I talk to Frankie. But she's just a friend. And – "

"And no-one can replace your mum. I know."

"That's right. No-one can. So I need to know. I need to know."

"What, sweetheart?"

As if I don't already know the answer...

"I need to know who killed her, Dad. Who took her from me. From both of us. Because... Out there. Somewhere out there. Is the person who killed her. And if I don't know... Well, I don't know if I can cope with that. And I don't know how *you'll* cope with that. Forever. I'm not making much sense."

Brady shook his head. "You're making perfect sense, Ash. And I understand, I really do."

"Except you're not fourteen. And you can replace a wife – "

And you can't replace your mum. You don't need to say it...

"Ash... Can I hug you yet?"

Ash shook her head. "No. Not yet. Not 'til we've talked."

Brady nodded. "When your mum died. You know, we were in that sort of limbo for six months. Then – "

"Then you turned the machine off."

"Don't say it like that. But yes, I took that decision. With the doctors. Because you and I had to move on with our lives. Start to heal. And – "

"But I *can't* heal, Dad. I can't. That's what I'm realising. Every day I realise it more. While I don't know everything – "

"I know. I know. Just let me finish what I was saying. One day, Ash, you'll have a child. And you'll love that child, like...

I don't even know how to put it into words." Brady hesitated. Tried to find a comparison. Said, "Do you love Archie?"

"Yes, of course I love Archie."

"Right. Well take how much you love Archie. Multiply it by ten thousand. And another ten thousand. And you're nowhere near how much you love your child. And when you have a baby of your own you'll realise. And you'll think, 'Bloody hell, did my dad love me this much?' And I do, Ash. I absolutely do. And you're making me cry."

Brady reached for the box of tissues. Passed one to Ash. Took two.

"Other people, Ash... They learn to live with grief. I thought we could do that."

"But you're not 'other people' are you, Dad? You're Detective Chief Inspector Michael Brady. So you *don't* have to live with it. You can *do* something."

And here we come to it. The harsh fucking realities of my job.

Brady shook his head. "I can't, Ash. Because I'm in Whitby. North Yorkshire. I can't wander over to Greater Manchester and demand they re-open the case. It doesn't work like that."

"So how *does* it work?"

Brady shook his head. "In the short term, I don't know. You want me to be honest with you, Ash? In the short term it doesn't work."

"So you just accepted it?"

"*No*, Ash, not with one fibre of my being did I accept it. But I had a decision to make. Except I didn't have a decision to make, because I had you. And nothing – nothing on this earth – was as important as you. As protecting you and taking care of you."

Protecting you. Because if they can come for you they can come for your daughter...

"So we came to Whitby?"

Brady nodded. "Yes, we came to Whitby. Because we needed a new start. Because Kate was here."

"We didn't run away?"

"No, not in a thousand years did we run away."

"But you're not doing anything. To find the person."

"No..."

Because it's dangerous. Because it's a sleeping dog and I'm letting it lie, Ash. Because you're all I've got. And I'm frightened...

"Why?"

"I told you. Procedure. The way the police is structured. I've no authority in Manchester."

'Procedure.' Bloody procedure. I ignore it with Frankie. Hide behind it with Ash.

But what can I do?

"You remember what else we said, Dad?"

"I remember it all, sweetheart."

I do. The whole conversation. Almost word for word.

"Remember what else we said – no more fighting. Because you're too old."

Her second question. Jimmy Gorse.

'Supposing he'd killed you?'

I tried to play it down. 'He didn't kill me. Supposing I got cancer? Like your Uncle Bill.'

'Anyone can get cancer, Dad. Not everyone fights a madman on the end of the pier.'

"I told you. I've got younger, fitter coppers to fight my battles."

"Good, 'cos you're all I've got, Dad."

Brady nodded. Smiled. "We said that last time as well. You're all I've got, Ash."

"What about Siobhan?"

"We've fallen out. She's in Wales."

"Why?"

"Because that's where her friend lives."

"Dad..."

"Because she wanted me to watch a film and I was reading a report."

And I'd already explained to her. 'The people I deal with...'

"This case? The one that means you don't answer when I ask you a question?"

Brady laughed. "Was that the question about the new sports kit you need? Parents have selective deafness, Ash."

"Don't try and change the subject, Dad. I know you'll solve it. But can you do it without fighting?"

Brady hesitated a second time. Weighed his answer carefully. "You want to be a human rights lawyer, Ash. Because – what did you say before? There's injustice, unfairness. And you want to put that right. That's what you believe. That's who you are. And I'm beyond proud of you. I'm – "

"But – "

"No. Let me finish saying this. I'm a copper. A simple copper who can't stand the political crap. I just think people who commit crimes should be caught. But the people who commit crimes – the people I deal with – they don't care if it's Sunday. They don't care if I'm going out to dinner – "

"This is why you fell out with Siobhan, isn't it?"

"Yes. Because I'm not sure she understands. That she'll *ever* understand. But... But the hard part, Ash, is that they don't care if my daughter's worried either. Whoever did this... He's not going to say, 'Oh well, Brady's daughter is worried, so I'll give myself up."

"So you're saying you *will* fight."

"No. Absolutely not. I'll do anything I can to avoid it. You're right. I am getting old. Thirty-nine next birthday."

"Forty-four, Dad..."

Brady laughed. "Don't rub it in, sweetheart. Come here. I'm going to hug you whether you like it or not. And we will go to York to do your shopping. Have a day out, just the two of us."

"So long as you let me choose the film, Dad..."

BRADY NODDED AT THE WINDOW. "It's stopped raining, Ash. You want to take Archie out now?"

Ash nodded. "Yeah, I'd like that, Dad. But..."

Not another question...

"Before we do, there's something else."

"What's that?"

"I want you to meet someone."

"Who?"

"The other day... When I said I was going into town with Bean. Jessica. You've got me doing it now, Dad. The other day... I did go into town to meet someone. Just not Jess."

"And I'm guessing not Frankie either?"

Ash blushed. Nodded. "His name's Spencer, Dad. Spence. And I... I like him. I don't want secrets between us."

Brady nodded.

Her first boyfriend. Or the first one she's told me about. Another bridge crossed...

"Spencer. He's the one..."

"The one that told you about the illegal football streams. So you could watch Middlesbrough. He's really clever. Computers and stuff."

"And he's your boyfriend?"

Ash shook her head. "No. Not officially. But... We've met a couple of times."

"So more than once?"

Ash laughed. "Criminals don't stand a chance with you

do they, Dad? Yes, a couple of times. And... Well, I like him. We talk about politics. He doesn't think Emmanuel Macron is a potential centre forward he needs to scout on YouTube."

"And you want him to come round?"

And you'll be up in your bedroom. And I'll be downstairs. Wondering what the hell's happening...

Ash nodded. "You'd like him."

"He doesn't have an earring? Or tattoos? He doesn't own a motorbike?"

"He's fifteen, Dad."

"He doesn't support Manchester United?"

"He's not into football."

"So what will I talk to him about?"

"You don't have to talk to him, Dad. Just say 'hello.' Don't say anything embarrassing."

"When?"

Ash shrugged. "I don't know. Soon, I guess. But nothing formal, Dad. Not Sunday lunch or anything – "

"Why? Doesn't he like Spaghetti Bolognese?"

"Be serious, Dad. And you're not to interrogate him. Just be cool."

"I *am* cool."

"No, Dad. You're not. Well maybe a bit. Jess thinks you're quite cool, so maybe."

Brady laughed. "OK. I'll take that. So long as my football stream keeps working he can come round."

56

Brady kicked the flat stone with the outside of his right foot. Watched it spinning along the beach, curving back to the left as it slowed down.

"Why's that happen, Archie? Kick a ball like that and it curves to the right. Kick a stone and it curves to the left. You tell me, mate."

Archie wasn't interested. He was under the cliffs, investigating what was left of a lobster pot, washed up by the high tide.

Brady felt the first spots of rain. Pulled his zip up a few inches, wondered why the rain always started when you were furthest from the car.

"Come on, Archie, it's starting to rain. We need to get back."

Except Brady carried on walking. Didn't turn round.

Bloody genius. 'You want to think differently? You need to be somewhere different. So let's try a different beach, Archie.'

Right. One where we can be a mile from the car when it starts to rain. Sod it. I'm going to get wet. Archie's going to get wet. So we may as well stay here and work it out...

The rain was harder. Brady hunched into his coat. Archie was still at the foot of the cliff. "Doing your best to keep dry, Arch?"

Am I talking to my dog more? Is that a sign I'm getting old? Or that I've fallen out with everyone else...

Brady looked up at the cliffs. Saw Diane Macdonald's body falling. Lying on the rocks. Turned round. The waves 20 yards away. But the tide going out.

'Incompetence. Ineptitude. Whatever term you want to use. Diane's pushed off the cliff at the very spot where she has a fifty-fifty chance of dying. Macdonald's house is firebombed – and there's more damage to the neighbours' fence. They're not bloody warnings, boss. They're cock-ups. And cock-ups happen in Whitby.'

'Lilian Beale is innocent. Whatever happened to Diane Macdonald, it was nothing to do with her. She's a woman who gets what she wants. That doesn't make her guilty.'

I should have listened to you, Frankie...

The rain turned itself up another notch. Brady swore. Pulled his hood up. Walked across the rocks to the foot of the cliff. Shouted to Archie. Found part of the cliff where the rocks at least made an attempt at an overhang. Crouched down, did his best to keep Archie dry as water dripped on to his back. Watched the rain splashing into the rock pools. "Someone you love, Archie. Lying out on the rocks while the rain pours down on them and the bloody seagulls peck out their eyes. You'd stay with me, wouldn't you pal?"

'Someone you love.' Or who says they love you...

'I wanted to tell you in the cold light of day. Not when we're in bed together. When you know I really mean it. I love you, Michael Brady.'

I should phone her. As soon as I get back...

Brady reached forward and ruffled the top of Archie's

head. "I can't say it to her, Archie. Not yet. Maybe never. Maybe when Ash goes it'll be just you and me. Two lonely old blokes shuffling along the beach together. Come on, mate, it's stopping. We may as well walk to the end. Gives us more time to dry out. Maybe the car won't smell quite as much. And we need to do something about the car. Even Frankie says it smells. And she grew up on a farm..."

He found a stick. Put it across a rock and stamped on it. "Find one get one free, Arch."

Brady threw the stick towards the waves. Watched Archie race after it. Did it a dozen times. Knew Archie would never get bored.

He was back. Dropping the stick at Brady's feet. Spraying him with seawater as he shook himself dry.

"Christ, Archie, you've covered the stick in gob." Brady fumbled in his pockets for a tissue. Didn't find one. Wiped his hand on his jeans.

"Two minutes, Archie. No more. Walk up the beach with me. That cliff in the distance. I need to think. And I can't think if I'm throwing sticks."

Archie looked up at him. A look that clearly said, 'If you're not going to throw the stick at least give me a biscuit.' Brady did as he was told.

They'd finally reached the end of the beach. More rocks, the cliff towering over them. Brady watched Archie scampering about searching among the rock pools.

If Cam Stokes can do it...

Reached for his phone, opened the camera.

"Archie! Lift your head up. Look at me. Let me get a photo with the waves behind you."

Archie heard him. Fleetingly glanced in Brady's direction. Brady pressed the button on his phone. "Thanks, Arch. Although I don't know if I've got your head or your arse."

I'll look at home...

"Come on, pal. Breakfast. I'll drop you off at home. Give you a rub down with your towel. Extra rations for getting wet. And Frankie secretly likes the smell of wet dog..."

Brady started walking back along the beach.

What have I sorted out? Nothing. Nothing at all. I'm not as wet as I was. But I'm no closer to finding Donoghue.

Or Magic.

'I can't help you. And if I could I don't know if I would. He hasn't done anything wrong. So he's entitled to his privacy.'

And what do I say to Ash?

'I don't want you fighting, Dad. You're all I've got.'

Except now there's Spencer. And yes, you're only fourteen. And Spencer won't last. But one day I won't be all you've got...

Brady turned and looked at the sea. Spray coming off the waves. A lonely seagull swooping across the surface of the water.

'I need to know who killed her, Dad. Who took her from me. From both of us. Somewhere out there is the person who killed her. I don't know if I can cope with that. And I don't know how you'll cope with that. Forever.'

No, sweetheart. Neither do I...

But never mind me.

I need to give you an answer.

Or one day I'll lose you...

57

"Bloody hell, didn't expect to see you this morning, young man."

Brady laughed. "Given the state of the rain, Dave, I doubt you expected to see anyone."

"You're right there n' all. Reckon the seagulls'll be eating most of these bread buns. Not that I bought many."

"Well cut one in half for me before you throw them out will you? And you can stick an extra rasher on if you think you'll have some spare."

"Three's enough for any man. Don't want you suing me when you have a heart attack."

Brady laughed. Watched Dave put three rashers of bacon on the griddle, cut an oven bottom cake in half, stir the plum tomatoes.

"Just you is it?" Dave said over his shoulder.

Brady nodded. "Just me. I took Archie out to Kettleness. Change of scenery. But I figured he was entitled to a rub down and a few biscuits. So yep, just me. Girlfriend away. Daughter in bed."

"Billy No Mates?"

If I can't tell Dave who can I tell?

"You want the truth, Dave? I'm Billy No bloody Mates at all."

"How's that then?"

"How's that? Because I've fallen out with everyone. Siobhan – "

"Lovers' tiff. You'll be fine."

"Maybe. And I'm not speaking to Frankie. Or we've agreed to disagree."

Dave turned and looked at him. "Bloody hell, how did you manage that?"

Brady shook his head. "You tell me. We're too alike for our own good. Both of us convinced we're right."

"An' who is right?"

"This time? I thought I was. Now? I'm not so sure."

Dave started to hand Brady his bacon sandwich. Changed his mind. Put it on a plate. "It's pissin' down," he said. "Come inside. There's something I want to say to you."

"What?"

"No, do as you're told for once. Come in here. It's not something I want to say over the counter."

Brady walked round to the side of the kiosk. Glanced across the harbour. Couldn't see his house the rain was so heavy. Opened the door, did his best not to drip too much water on Dave's floor.

"Here." Dave passed him the plate. "Sit down. I want to say something."

"I'm wet."

"It's a wooden chair, Mike. Next stop, the tip. Sit yourself down."

"What's up then, Dave? That's your serious face."

Dave nodded. "Aye, it might be. I'm off to Spain next month. Not back until spring, you know that. I'll be sitting in

Maria's café, drinking *mi cerveza* and watching the world go by. An' I don't want to be worrying about Michael Brady."

Is Dave putting it into words for me?

"We'd known each other, what? A month? After Patrick – poor bugger, I still think about him – had introduced us. Remember what I said?"

Brady nodded. Looked at him. Realised how much he missed him through the winter. Knew that Dave's wife, Maria's café and *mi cerveza* would win one day. That someone else would be selling bacon sandwiches.

"You asked me if I was happy."

"I did. And you weren't. Because you weren't in control."

"I remember your exact words. 'Are you happy? No you're not. So I've another question for you. What are you going to do about it?' That's what you said."

Dave nodded. "I did. An' I reckon I could ask them two questions again. Cos you're not happy, Mike."

"I – "

Dave held up an enormous hand. "Hear me out. You and I – we sat in this kiosk that night. Waiting for Jimmy bloody Gorse."

Dave charging. The knife flashing down. Dave lying on the cold, wet steps. Frankie arriving...

"An' it nearly killed me. I wouldn't change a thing. 'Cos I reckon we saved a life that day. Mebbes more than one."

And maybe one of them was mine...

"An' I reckon it gives me a right to be honest with you."

"That and being my friend."

"Aye, that n' all. But someone's got to tell you what you don't want to hear."

What I've already worked out for myself...

"What happened to Patrick... You were desperate to be involved. Bill in charge, buggering up the investigation. A blind man could see how much it frustrated you. With what happened to your wife... You needed it, Mike. An' it's the same now."

"Except Bill's dead. And I am in control now."

Dave shook his head. "Except you're not are you? Sure, Kershaw's away. You're making the decisions. But it's not just work, Mike. Not just this case you're working on. It's personal."

"And personal's affecting work?"

"Siobhan. She's a bonny lass. An' I've seen the way she looks at you. But something's holding you back, Mike. An' we both know what it is."

"And that's why I'm falling out with everyone?"

Brady finished his bacon sandwich, passed Dave the plate. "Thank you. And for what it's worth, I agree with you. But you're forgetting something, Dave. Or someone."

"Ash."

"Right. I've got a daughter. And I will never, *ever* do anything that puts her at risk. She's all I've got. *I'm* all she's got. I'd rather – " Brady gestured across the road at the amusement arcade. "I'd pack it all in and give out change on Enzo's bingo before I'd do anything that puts my daughter in danger. Yes, you're right. What happened to Grace – knowing there's someone out there who did it – eats away at me. Every bloody day. But if I have to live with it to protect Ash it's a small price to pay. A very small price. So the eagles can go on pecking at my liver."

BRADY PULLED the collar of his coat up. Walked back along Pier Road. Past the Magpie. Past Gypsy Sara's cabin.

You're right, Dave. I'm not in control. Whoever killed Grace is in control.

But I've got Ash. But I'm in Whitby, not Manchester. So I can't do anything about Grace. And if it costs me Siobhan, it costs me Siobhan.

'I love you.' She can say it as many times as she likes. But until I know who killed my wife I can't say it back. Not to her. Not to anyone.

Brady crossed the swing bridge. Turned left into Church Street. Wondered if he could get any wetter. Wondered if it was pouring down in Wales. Stopped outside the jet shop where he'd bought Grace the teardrop earrings.

The first time I brought her to Whitby.

'You have to promise to wear your hair up. You know I'm powerless when you pin your hair up...'

Didn't hear her reply.

Heard his wife say something else.

'*Take action, Michael. It's simple. Either you control your life or someone else does.*'

So what can I control? Diane bloody Macdonald. Either she was murdered or she wasn't.

Time to sort it out one way or the other.

And that starts with finding Magic.

'The second best view in the world.'

Where's the first? Where you live.

So let's find it...

58

Brady reached for the notepad. Found a pen in the kitchen drawer.

Ash. It's 6am. I'm taking Archie out early. There's someone I need to find. Early morning's the best time. I phoned Fiona last night. She'll collect you and give you a lift to school. I'll sort out dinner for tonight.

Love you, Dad x

AN HOUR later he was apologising to his dog...

"You don't have to say it, Archie. I can see it on your face. The stupidest walk ever. But at least we've seen the sunrise. We're alone on the cliff top. The sun glistening off the water. A hint of autumn. Beyond beautiful... You don't care, do you? Five more minutes, I promise. Then we'll go home. Double rations for sticking with it."

Brady turned left off the cliff top path. Glanced down at the app on his phone.

'Second best view in the world.'

So the best view is the one you see every morning, Magic.

I don't think you live far from the cliff top.

But coming up to three miles. Knock off a mile for dead-ends and detours. We're two miles from Lythe. Forty minutes. He can't live any further from the church.

Brady walked up another path towards another distant farm. Still didn't know what he was looking for. Knew he'd recognise it when he saw it.

The path was overgrown, still wet from yesterday's rain. A tangle of hedgerow and blackcurrant bushes on one side. Weeds, long grass, some red/orange flowers that Brady thought he'd seen growing in a pond.

Water? On the cliff top? But what the hell do I know about –

There. What's that? A gap...

Barely even a gap. Brady forced his way through, felt the blackcurrant bushes snag on his jacket. Came out into a field of wheat stubble, a tumbledown farm shed at the far end.

Knew he'd found what he was looking for.

Smiled to himself. "Come on, Archie. Breakfast. And remind me to tell Frankie to wear a thick coat. After I've apologised to her."

59

"So how did it go, boss?"

Brady shook his head. "First things first, Frankie. I'm sorry. You were right, I was wrong. There's no other way to put it. So I'm sorry, I should have listened."

Brady smiled at her. "Kershaw told me you had a lot of brains. Clearly I need to pay more attention."

"Kershaw said that? I'll ask for a pay rise. And you don't need to apologise, boss. But I'm glad we're friends again. What about Lilian Beale?"

"She gave me a signed copy of her book. I'm thinking of giving it to Ash – "

"Good luck with that. Make sure you're wearing full body armour."

"Right. Other than that? Interesting is an understatement. I'm driving back through the Dales. Slowly. What you said about tractors... But it's a beautiful day. Early autumn, the leaves starting to turn. I should be enjoying the journey. But all I can think is 'who does Lilian Beale remind me of?' I finally got it at the top of Blue Bank."

"Who?"

"Marko Vrukić. A good looking thirty-something sitting in her office in an English market town. And a sixty-year-old Serbian warlord – "

"Now comfortably retired in the English countryside."

"As you say. But the force of personality was the same. *Exactly* the same. Almost electric. And... Sorry, Frankie, I'm turning lyrical in my old age. You know the Hole of Horcum? The story of Wade the Giant? Striding across the Moors? That was the feeling I had. Lilian Beale striding over North Yorkshire. Using it as a stepping stone. And I had a phone call."

"Kershaw? Macdonald?"

"Neither. Far more interesting. Simon Butler. The man I met in Cambridge. Who very politely told me we couldn't go after Eric Kennedy. Or his father. This time he told me to lay off Ms Beale. And said she had nothing to do with Diane's death. Gave me his word."

"Despite the stories?"

"Despite the stories. And I'm inclined to believe him. Especially given what you said..."

"What I said?"

"The cases being linked by incompetence. Whatever Lilian Beale is, she isn't incompetent. And he told me Diane's book would never have seen the light of day."

"What about the seventy-five grand?"

Brady shrugged. "You know who she's married to. In Lilian Beale's world that's petty cash. So I was reminded of my place in the world. Then Simon Butler looked up from the feast and tossed the dog a bone."

"What was that?"

"*Who* was that. Macdonald. He implied that they – whoever the hell he works for – knew all about him. 'We'll reel him in when the time is right' were his exact words. Suggested that it wouldn't end well for him."

Then he offered me a job. And not-very-subtly told me he knew where I lived. But I'll keep that to myself...

"Why do you think they're going to such lengths to protect her?"

"What did you say to me? Rising star? Shooting star? And you're not telling me Raphaël's cash isn't a factor. But if you want the real reason – "

"Obviously."

"Butler said something. 'My boss likes relentless.' I suspect he likes backing winners as well. Maybe that's why she reminded me of Vrukić. One thing you can say about Lilian Beale. She's a winner."

A winner who drew her nail across my cheek. 'Moth. Flame. Don't get too close...'

60

The phone on Brady's desk rang. He glanced at the display. Mouthed 'Geoff' at Frankie.

"Mike, spare me a minute?"

"Now?"

"If you're not busy."

"I've got Frankie with me. OK if I bring her as well?"

"Of course."

"DIANE MACDONALD," Geoff said five minutes later. "I'm sorry, Mike. I think I may be getting old. Or I've been married too long. Or I'm reading the wrong books. Or 'flu hit me harder than I thought. Or all four."

Brady laughed. "I'm not sure I'm following you, Geoff. But it's clearly leading somewhere."

"Maybe," Geoff said. He reached into a folder, pulled two pictures out, laid them on top of each other.

"Look at the marks on her hands. I'd assumed they were made by her clutching at bushes as she fell. Scraping over whatever was on the cliff."

"You were fairly definite on that."

Geoff nodded. "I am, I still am. But I was lying awake last night – even an ageing bladder has its compensations – and realised there was something I'd missed. Or I'd seen and not seen. Too busy focusing on the cause of death, the broken bones. Not her hands, her wrists. Look..."

Geoff reached for his pen, used it to point. "Here, on her right wrist. The faintest of faint marks."

Brady bent over and looked. Wondered how long 'reading glasses' had been on his to-do list. Stood back so Frankie could see.

"Like something's been tied?" she said.

"A wrist band?" Brady said. "Everyone wears them these days. Ash wears half a dozen at the weekend."

Geoff pointed to a faint discolouration of the skin.

"I don't think so. It's a line. Tied, not worn. And definitely not your daughter's wristbands, Mike."

"You don't tie someone's hands before you push them over a cliff."

"No, you don't," Frankie said. "Not this side of *Game of Thrones*, anyway. You're going to show us her other wrist aren't you, Geoff? And put the pictures side by side?"

The pathologist nodded. "I am. You know what I'm going to say?"

Frankie smiled. Winked at him. "I do. But Detective Chief Inspector Brady has led a much more sheltered life."

Geoff Oldroyd laughed. Placed the two photos next to each other.

"Just as faint. But there. Once you know what you're looking for."

"And sloping," Frankie said. "Inside of her wrist to outside."

"You're saying she was tied to something?" Brady said.

Frankie shook her head. "No. What I'm saying – and what our learned colleague is delicately hinting at – is that she was tied to a bed."

"Willingly, Geoff?"

Geoff Oldroyd nodded. "I think Frankie's right, Mike. I'd say, looking at the marks, the angles – and there's not a hope in hell this would stand up in court, but it fits – I'd say that she was on her back and tied to the bed. And that she didn't struggle."

"Leather handcuffs," Frankie said. "Something like that..."

Brady was silent. Looked at the photographs. "We've no way of telling when? The day she died? Or one or two days earlier?"

Geoff shook his head. "Given that she was in the water? That her right hand was in the water long enough to degrade the skin sample? No. If I was betting with your money I'd say two or three days but honestly, Mike, there's no way of being precise."

"But whilst Graham Macdonald was away?"

'They hadn't had sex for nine years.' Why am I even asking?

Geoff nodded. "Yes. I'd bet on that with *my* money."

"If she was tied up... We're saying the skin sample would still have been the attacker's?"

"It doesn't matter whose it was, Mike. Lover. Attacker... The sample was too far gone."

"What about semen, Geoff? A nice healthy DNA sample?"

"Nothing, I checked. You always check. Clothes, vagina, nothing."

"Mouth?" Frankie said. "Stomach?"

"No, not a chance. One, they're both designed to break food down. Two, she swallowed half the North Sea."

"So no evidence," Brady said.

"No evidence at all, Mike. But suspicion? Plenty. Especially given that her husband was away when it happened. When it *might* have happened."

"You said there was no evidence in the bedroom, Frankie."

"Not when I was there. If it was Thursday or Friday she'd have tidied up, boss. And I didn't have time to go through her drawers. Or check the bookcase for *Fifty Shades*."

Brady nodded. "So we're no further forward. Except we are. Because if she had a lover it's someone local."

"Assuming her phone confirms it."

"Let's hope it does. And let's hope she texted him half a dozen times before he tied her up."

Frankie shook her head. "We've checked her phone, boss. Nothing like that. But she wouldn't be the first woman to have two phones – "

Frankie's phone rang. She laughed. "Right on cue. And my only phone as well. Sorry, boss, I need to take this. The break-ins on the estate."

"Thanks, Geoff," Brady said. "And don't blame yourself. This case... Even proving there's a bloody case."

"Thanks, Mike. But I'm embarrassed. I should have seen it. I was too focused on what killed her."

"It's my fault, Geoff. I was obsessed by the fall. Distracted by that bloody seagull. No wonder that's all you looked at."

Was obsessed? I'm still obsessed...

"Let me take you for a pint of Doom tonight. Ash is back late. My way of saying 'sorry.'"

"What about Archie?"

"His once-a-week treat. A girl a few doors down has started a dog-walking business. Half a dozen miles on the

Moors and as many biscuits as he can eat. Archie ticks off the days..."

Geoff laughed. "In which case I'll see you at six."

BRADY WALKED SLOWLY BACK up the stairs to his office.

'It doesn't matter whose it was, Mike. Lover or attacker...'

Suppose it's not lover or attacker?

Suppose they're one and the same...

61

Twenty past six. Geoff still hadn't appeared. Brady was fighting a battle with the notebook in his pocket.

Filling another bloody page with notes and question marks. And arrows leading nowhere...

"Sorry, Mike. A report I needed to finish. I should have phoned you. But I couldn't face going in early tomorrow."

"No problem, Geoff. Here." Brady nodded at the pint of Doom Bar on the table. "The fates have rewarded you."

"Thank you. Sharp's Doom Bar, Michael. Proof that God exists." Geoff lifted the glass to his lips. Sighed in satisfaction. Drank some more. Smiled. "*Definitely* exists..."

"You got your report finished?"

"I did. Like I said, I'm getting too old for early mornings. Or late nights come to that. But what can we do? Not so much a pound of flesh these days as a pound of bloody paperwork."

"Mind if we join you, boss?"

Brady looked up. Saw Frankie. Black jeans, black jacket, hair not pinned up for once. A man standing at her side.

Stood up. "Frankie, of course we don't. Sit down. You want a drink?"

She held up a glass of wine. "We're good. And this is Lochie."

Brady shook hands. A firm, no-nonsense handshake. Curly brown hair he could have wasted all day trying to control. A neatly trimmed beard. Clear blue eyes.

"Mike Brady. And Geoff Oldroyd, our sifter through the bones."

Brady offered Lochie his chair. Made a 'can I take your spare' gesture at the people on the next table.

"Lochie was at Whitby Museum," Frankie said.

"A wee bit of work on Master Scoresby and the whaling –"

"So I said I'd collect him and show him the seamier side of Whitby."

Brady laughed. "I thought that was Grape Lane in the old days?"

"Grope Lane, boss. Tactfully re-named at some point..."

"Good to meet you," Brady said to Lochie. "Cheers. And thank you. I'm sure Frankie's said it on our behalf. But thanks for taking care of Reggie."

Lochie shook his head. "It's nae bother. Or it wasn't after Frankie arrived with his bed and a car boot full of toys. And it's not me you need to thank. It's Bob next door. Two years telling his wife they needed a dog. Reggie arrives and she's sold in a day. But I'm allowed to borrow him when I need some exercise."

"Even so, I appreciate it. And say 'thank you' to Bob and Mrs Bob."

Lochie laughed. "I'll do that for you."

Geoff's phone rang. He glanced down at the display.

"And this is Mrs Geoff. I'll take it outside. Convince her I'm not in the pub."

Brady watched him weave between the tables, push the door open. Found himself facing Frankie and Lochie.

Slightly old to be playing gooseberry. What the hell do I say?

"Frankie said you might be moving to Scarborough?"

Lochie pursed his lips. "Maybe. I've been invited to apply for the job but... ach, I don't know. It's a big decision. Frankie's probably mentioned I'm a surfer. Scarborough's not Newquay but Cayton Bay's nae bad. But... It'd be more admin and not so much academic if you know what I mean."

Brady nodded.

I know exactly what you mean. Give me more policing: a lot less paperwork...

Found he liked Lochie's honesty, his openness.

"So the wee boy's helping me decide."

"Reggie?"

Lochie laughed. Nodded. "I walk him to Lastingham and by the time I'm there I've made my mind up. Then I have a pint in the Blacksmith's, walk him back and I've changed my mind."

"But you like living there? Hutton-le-Hole?"

"I do, but I miss the sea. Frankie's probably told you, my parents are in Kirk Yetholm now. I grew up in a place called Burnmouth. Just a wee fishing village. Seagulls singing me to sleep."

"And waking you up at five in the morning if it's anything like Whitby."

The door opened. Brady looked up expecting to see Geoff. Saw a middle-aged Goth couple instead. "Two months early," he said. "First weekend in November this year isn't it, Frankie?"

She nodded. "Goth weekend and Bonfire Night. What more does a town need? I've promised Lochie the full tourist package."

Like Patrick promised me. Sitting by the bandstand. Eating our bacon sandwiches. 'I'm a Goth. Don't laugh. Kara spent a year in black leather and ripped stockings as a teenager. Share your wife's interests. So twice a year I have to dress up like a Victorian gentleman and listen to Siouxsie and the Banshees.'

And get murdered by Jimmy fucking Gorse...

"So you miss the sea?"

"I do. It's a rare thing. You've lived by the sea. It's hard to move away..."

Brady nodded. "It pulled me back."

"Frankie told me what happened. Your wife. I'm sorry."

Frankie stood up before Brady could reply. "You want another drink, boss?"

Brady shook his head. "No thanks, Frankie. I need to be back before Ash gets home."

Lochie reached across. Put his hand on her arm. "My round. Let me."

He walked to the bar, leaving Brady and Frankie alone.

I need to say something...

Frankie beat him to it. "He's good for me. Stops me dwelling on things. I get home and he's got some story to tell me about a standing stone on the Moors. A witch in the middle ages."

Brady nodded. "I can see that. I can absolutely see that. He seems like a good guy."

"He listens. Doesn't interrupt. I like that."

Brady stood up. "Frankie, I don't mean to be rude. I'm worried about Geoff. His wife rang ten minutes ago. I'm just going outside. It's not like him to leave a pint half-finished."

He pushed the door open. Looked up and down Church

Street. Saw the rain glistening on the cobbles. Didn't see any sign of Geoff Oldroyd.

'And this is Mrs Geoff.' Something serious? I bloody hope not...

"ALL OK?" Frankie said.

Brady shrugged. "I don't know. He wasn't there. That's not like him. Not just his pint. To go without saying anything."

"Some domestic crisis, boss. Nothing to worry about. Or Anne telling him dinner's ready."

Brady nodded. "Hopefully..."

Because it's only six months since we lost Henry. I can't lose another one...

"Frankie was telling me," Lochie said. "Your body on the beach..."

"Yeah, I'm sorry. It's the price we pay, Lochie. Someone always finds a body when you're having breakfast. It's always inconvenient. A year ago I got a call at my brother-in-law's funeral."

Lochie shook his head. "No, not that. Frankie warned me on the first date. What the seagull did. You know it's symbolic?"

Frankie looked guilty. "Sorry, boss, I probably shouldn't have mentioned it."

"No, you're fine, Frankie. I asked the teenagers to keep it to themselves. Which obviously means the whole of Whitby knows."

Besides, we all need someone to talk to...

"Symbolic in what way?"

Frankie laughed. "Careful, boss. Genie. Bottle. Just don't ever ask him about surfing. Apparently there's this village in Portugal – "

"Ericeira. Fifty foot waves."

The same expression as Geoff tasting his pint...

"See what I mean?"

"No, I'm interested. You were saying."

"You're sure you want to hear? She's right. Once I get started..."

"Be brave, Lochie. Ignore her. What's symbolic?"

"Taking her eye out. Blinding."

"You talking about the Middle Ages? I thought it was just punishment? Torture?"

Lochie shook his head. "No. And stop me if this turns into a lecture. But blinding as a punishment has been around for ever. Revenge, torture. It crops up any number of times in Greek mythology as a punishment from the gods. Blinding your enemy as a tactic – if he's blind he can't lead an army against you. Then there's Basil the Second. He captured thousands of Bulgarian soldiers after a battle. Put them into groups of a hundred and blinded ninety-nine of them. The last guy only had one eye gouged out. It was his job to lead the others back to their commander."

"In the kingdom of the blind?"

"The one-eyed man is king. Exactly right. And so it goes on. Even Shakespeare. Gloucester in *King Lear*. Not just your enemies though. It's been a punishment for adultery – the Athenians thought adultery was a far worse crime than rape."

"Why? I can't see that."

"Very droll, boss."

"Sorry, Frankie. No pun intended."

"Because rape was just violence," Lochie said. "Adultery undermined the family. The key thing Athenian society was based on."

Brady finished his beer. "Are you this expert on everything?"

Lochie laughed. "Folklore? Mythology? Surfing? Yeah, I probably know too much for my own good. Maths? Frankie'll tell you, I can't add up a shopping list. It's fascinating. You read your history books and it's all there. But it's kings and queens. It's everyday life that does it for me. Ordinary people. Your witch post out on the Moors. Or drive up into the Dales. There's plenty of villages that would have been cut off through the winter."

"No option but to police themselves?"

"Right. In any way they could. And if witches, spirits and curses – and unusual punishments – helped to do it – "

"You can understand it?"

"Aye, you can. And..." He glanced at Frankie. "I probably shouldn't say this but in terms of cruel and unusual punishments... It was the women as much as the men."

"Why's that?"

Lochie laughed. "Who knows? I'm nae a psychologist. Childbirth? If you've been through childbirth in the twelfth century – nae epidural, nae gas and air – well... You probably think having your eye put out stings a wee bit."

Brady looked at his watch. Stood up. "Time to go. Or I'm in trouble with Ash." Shook hands with Lochie. "It was really good to meet you." Told Frankie he'd see her in the morning. Pushed the door open. Stepped out into Church Street.

Wondered for the tenth time what had happened to Geoff...

62

"Frankie? Take a look at this will you? And it was good to meet Lochie. I liked him."

She nodded. "Like I say. He's good for me. Although he insists on porridge for breakfast."

Brady laughed. "I'll tell Dave to branch out."

"Sorry, boss. You wanted me to look at something."

Why am I doing this? Showing her a photo of my dog. Like some sad bastard who doesn't have a life. Or friends...

Brady opened his phone. Scrolled through his photos. "Tell me what you think. It's Archie on the beach at Kettleness. I took it at the weekend."

Frankie took the phone. Looked at the photograph.

"I don't have a really good photo of him," Brady added. "I thought... You know, maybe I should. While he's young and fit."

"Like you in your twenties, boss? What am I expected to say? 'Don't give up the day job?' There are people – "

"Proper photographers. I know. I was looking at some of Cam Stokes' photos. One of a cormorant. You see the cliff? It's the same cliff as the picture he took. The same angle."

Frankie shrugged. Gave the phone back to Brady. "Here's Whitby Abbey. It's the same Abbey in thousands of pictures. Here's the end of the pier. Whitby's a good place to take photos, boss. It's a beach. Everyone takes photos on the beach."

"Right," Brady said. "And he's a wildlife photographer. And I'm a copper. And I'm talking crap. Ignore me, Frankie."

She was staring out of the window. Not listening.

"Frankie? I said – "

She turned to face him. "We need to go to Macdonald's house. Right now. There's a photo of her on the desk. I swear to God it's that same cliff in the background."

"I've looked at her desk. I didn't see – "

Because I wasn't looking for it. Because I was focused on the notepad. The phone numbers...

"Are you saying you believe me now? She was murdered?"

Frankie shook her head. "No. It doesn't prove anything. Even if it is the same cliff. You took a photo there, Cam Stokes took a photo there. What do we do if there's a murder at the Abbey? Arrest everyone who's ever taken a photo there? But – "

"We're coppers aren't we? That's what we do. Investigate. Eliminate. Until all that's left is the truth." Brady stood up. Reached for his jacket. "Come on. Macdonald's going back to London tomorrow. We can discuss the odds on the way there."

"Assuming it is the same cliff.

"Assuming we can tell from a photo."

Frankie smiled. "Don't be so negative, boss. Let's see what develops..."

Brady stared at her. "Are you thinking of doing stand-up, Detective Sergeant? 'Don't give up the day job?' Isn't that what you just said? I'll tell the Edinburgh Festival you're busy. Come on, Frankie. Before Macdonald gets pissed for the day."

BRADY PUT the key in the ignition. Turned the engine on. Paused. Reached forward and turned it off again. "Hang on, Frankie. Before we go charging out there, let's think this through."

"You've changed your mind walking downstairs?"

"No, I haven't changed my mind. And I'm conscious of what I said – "

"About him getting pissed? It's only ten, boss. We've a two-hour window."

Brady laughed. "You're getting cynical in your old age, Frankie. I was going to say three. Look, we've got a photo. I took a photo of Archie. Cam Stokes took one of a cormorant. I'm convinced it's the same cliff. The same beach. You say there's one of Diane on her desk. Even if it's the same cliff – "

"You *have* changed your mind – "

Brady shook his head. "No, I haven't. But Macdonald's an MP. He knows Kershaw. I can live without his sarcasm. 'You thought the best idea was to go through his photo album, Brady?' I don't need it."

"Right. We need to do two things. We need to speak to a photographer. An expert. And we need to ask Macdonald a simple question."

"Did you take the photo of your wife?"

"Exactly." Frankie reached for her phone.

"Paul's on holiday isn't he?"

Frankie nodded. "Karen's pregnant again. I'm not sure it's going all that well. He's taken a few days off. Fortunately – "

She opened recent calls. Tapped the top one.

Lochie.

Put it on speaker. Held it up so Brady could hear clearly.

"Hey you. What's up? I'm just going into a meeting. But if you want to say something dirty to me I can be two minutes late."

"I'm in the car with Detective Chief Inspector Brady. You're on speaker, Romeo."

"Oh. Shit. Sorry. Am I under arrest?"

"Not yet. That photographer who came to the museum last week. Did the publicity shots for you. Text me her number will you?"

"You want it now?"

"Hampering police investigations, McRae. Five years in Barlinnie."

"I'll take that as a 'yes.' Give me a minute, officer. And remember to bring your handcuffs home."

"Add another five years for sexual harassment. See you tonight."

"I'm sorry," Frankie said, pressing the red button. "He's, er... romantic."

Brady laughed. "You don't need to apologise, Frankie."

Frankie's phone beeped with the message. "You want to ring her?"

Brady shook his head. "You know what you want to ask her. But keep her on the speaker."

She answered on the fourth ring. "Linnhe Harrison. Good morning. Or possibly afternoon. I've not drunk enough coffee."

"Ms Harrison. It's still morning. Comfortably. My name's Frankie Thomson. I'm a Detective Sergeant with North Yorkshire police."

Linnhe Harrison didn't reply. "You're not in trouble,"

Frankie said. "And we're not ringing with bad news. I got your number from Lochie McRae at the museum. We need an opinion. Maybe it's relevant, maybe not. But we need it quickly. Hence the call."

A nervous laugh. "Right. No problem. Ask away. It's just that when someone phones and says it's the police – "

"Right. Like the Inland Revenue. Or the school if you've got kids. Sorry to startle you. It's a simple question."

"I didn't mean to over-react. What do you need to know?"

Frankie hesitated. "I don't know if I'm asking this in the right way. But do photographers have favourite places? The view, the light, that sort of thing?"

Linnhe laughed. "You mean are we creatures of habit? Of course we are. Me? Falling Foss. And abandoned industrial buildings. Don't ask me why. But yes, of course."

"So if a photographer has a favourite place for... I don't know – say, wildlife. He might take other pictures there?"

"I'm not sure I follow you. I mean if he's photographing wildlife he's not going to take a photo of his kids there is he?"

No he's not. But he might take his girlfriend...

"But I suppose... If the light's good. Maybe if the sun's coming up at the right angle. Something like that. But do we have favourite places? Of course we do. Favourite places, favourite subjects, favourite cameras. We're only human. And we're superstitious. 'I got a good one here last week.' You know how it is."

"I do," Frankie said. "Thank you. Thank you very much. And sorry again if I worried you."

She ended the call. Turned to Brady. "So he *might* have taken the photo. That beach *might* be one of his favourite places. What are we suggesting, boss? Diane Macdonald was having an affair with the next door neighbour? One photograph isn't much proof."

"She had skin under her fingernails. She'd been tied up."

"Kama Sutra one-oh-one, boss. If you're tied up you can't get skin under your fingernails."

"You know what I'm saying. She can't have been tied up all the time."

"It still doesn't prove it was her next door neighbour."

"No," Brady said.

He stared through the windscreen. Didn't see the car park. Saw Cam Stokes' house.

I could see straight through the house. Dining table. Glass doors. Conservatory. Settee, coffee table. Something else. A running machine...

"No," he said again. "But maybe the running machine does."

"The what?"

"The running machine. The one in Cam Stokes' house. Siobhan said it to me the other day. I told her I needed to lose weight. Or not gain any. Made a joke about going to the gym. She said no. Said that when a man in his thirties or forties starts going to the gym it's nothing to do with keeping fit and everything to do with another woman."

Frankie shook her head. "A running machine and a photo? It still doesn't add up to much."

"Maybe not. But it's a motive. The start of a motive." Brady hesitated. "And what Lochie said last night."

"His lecture?"

"Blinding as a punishment. For adultery – "

"What did you just say to me, boss. 'You're getting cynical in your old age.' Are you turning superstitious? Starting to believe in omens?"

Brady laughed. "I thought omens were from the Gods? Not from seagulls. But it's enough to visit Graham Macdonald. Look at the photo."

"And get her computer. Read the book. See what else is on the hard drive."

"Right. However many times Simon Butler gives me his word. And we'll strip the bed as well. See what Geoff can find on the sheets. Nip back inside, Frankie. Give Jake Cartwright a shout. Tell him to follow us. With plenty of evidence bags. While I work out what lies I'm going to tell Macdonald."

63

"Graham, good morning. And let me introduce Detective Sergeant Thomson. And I've a constable waiting outside in the car."

Macdonald looked Frankie up and down. Black leather jacket, maroon T-shirt, black jeans. Hair pinned up.

Gave her a second look.

"You're the one that came for the dog's bed? I should have been at home."

And a third.

Finally turned to Brady. "Three of you, Mike. Have you come to arrest me?"

Only if being a prick is a criminal offence, Graham...

"No, Graham. Not in the slightest. But..."

'While I work out what lies to tell Macdonald.' His ego. That's all you need...

"I've been talking to someone, Graham. I can't give you his name. You'll need to trust me on that – "

"Security? MI5?"

Brady smiled. "More or less. The first time I met him I asked him if he was Home Office, Special Branch or MI5. He said all of them. And he gave me a reference. A number to ring. Not Number Ten. Well, not then..."

"But now? They take my security that seriously? I told you, Mike. I told you."

Clinging on to his ego like a drowning man clinging on to a rope.

Brady nodded. "They know about you, Graham – "

'So you know all about Graham Macdonald?'

'We do. And we'll reel him in when the time is right. But not just yet.'

Yep, they definitely know all about you, Graham...

" – So like I say, I need you to trust me."

Macdonald looked sceptical. "I'm a bloody politician, Mike. When someone at Westminster says 'trust me' all it means is the bastard is going to stab you in the front, not the back."

Brady laughed. "And I'm as far from a politician as you can get. So like I say, trust me. And – "

Brady gestured at Frankie. "Graham, I trust Sergeant Thomson implicitly. But this is *very* confidential. Would you mind if she waited somewhere? Your wife's office, say?"

Macdonald shook his head. "Wait where she likes. Second door on the right."

Frankie glanced at Brady behind Macdonald's back. Raised her eyebrows. Made a mocking 'I'm only a woman' gesture.

"You want one, Mike?" Macdonald said as soon as Frankie was out of the room. "Bit early, but bloody stress. You know what doctors say about it being bad for you." He reached for a bottle of Macallan. "Just the one at lunchtime. Helps me think more clearly. What did you want to say? And pretty little thing. Nice arse. Are you fucking her?"

Maybe I will arrest you for being a prick, Graham...

Brady smiled. "I'm her boss, Graham. And she has a partner. And so do I."

"Fuck's sake. Never stopped anyone at Westminster. Why do you think the Commons sits so late at night?"

Brady ignored the comment. "Graham, like I said. Your security. This is a delicate subject – "

"Delicate? Bloody life and death if you ask me."

"Right. The warning you got in London."

The one that made you run back here...

"The warning mentioned your wife, Diane. 'What happened to her could happen to you.' Words to that effect."

"That's right."

"I want to – I'm sorry, Graham, there's no simple way to say this – I need to make sure Diane wasn't involved in any way."

"Plotting against me?" Macdonald snorted in derision. "The woman didn't have the brains."

She had a lot more brains than you thought...

"So what I need to do is take a few things away. Do some analysis."

"What sort of things?"

"Certainly her laptop. Anything else we find is relevant. I'd like to focus our search on her office. And – she had a separate bedroom?"

"Of course she did." Macdonald shrugged. "Take what you want. And I don't want it back. Take the whole bloody lot. Save me the bother of carting it to the charity shop."

For most people it's painful. Really painful. Explaining to Ash that I was taking Grace's clothes to Oxfam. That someone else would be wearing them. Not you, Graham...

"We'll take an inventory of everything. Give you a copy, obviously."

Macdonald shook his head. "You don't need to bother.

Just do what you have to do. And I'll let you crack on. I've got a constituency problem I need to deal with. They want to expand that housing estate. More bloody Lib Dems. The yellow fucking peril..."

BRADY OPENED the door of Diane's office. Saw Frankie with the picture in her hand.

She looked at Brady. Shook her head. "You don't even need your phone, boss. It's the same cliff. No question."

Brady shook his head. "How the hell did I miss it?"

"You didn't miss it, boss. You weren't looking for it. And it wasn't important. Not then."

Brady reached into his pocket. Found some disposable gloves. Pulled them on. Flexed his hands to make sure they fitted properly. Picked up the photo frame.

Diane Macdonald. Half-turned towards the camera, framed by the cliff on one side, spray from the waves on the other.

Something else. Her expression. The way Siobhan looked at me when she told me she loved me. Before the argument...

Brady put the picture down. Stripped the gloves off. Reached for his phone. Opened the picture of Archie.

Nodded. "The same cliff. Same shape... What do you call it? Not big enough for an overhang. Bulge? Outcrop?"

"A nose," Frankie said.

"A nose? That's a technical term is it? A-level Geology?"

Frankie laughed. "No. But that's what it looks like doesn't it? The way the cliff sticks out."

"It does. But we need to rule out the obvious."

Brady put a new pair of gloves on. Picked up the picture. Walked out of the room.

. . .

'I've got a constituency problem I need to deal with.' And whisky's clearly the best way to deal with it...

"Graham. A question if I may. This picture of your wife. Did you take it?"

Macdonald stared at him.

Like I'm suggesting he gives his expenses to the homeless...

"Did I take it? How on earth would I have taken it? Number one it would require me to walk on the beach with my wife. Which I haven't done since God was in short pants. Number two she's smiling. The last time she smiled at me was when I trapped a nerve in my back and couldn't put my socks on. Bloody woman stood there laughing while I shovelled Ibuprofen into my mouth."

Brady suppressed a smile. "Have you any idea who did take it?"

Macdonald shrugged. "One of her friends, I assume. They were always coming to stay. Walked on the beach, talked until God knows what time in the morning, drank all my gin and fucked off home."

You must know that can't be true. This is far too good to be taken on an iPhone. Or maybe he's like everyone. Believes what he wants to believe...

"If anyone comes to mind let me know, won't you?"

"Why? Is it important?"

Brady shook his head. "Almost certainly not. But that's police work, Graham. Ninety-nine times out of a hundred we're wrong. But you know what Churchill said. Keep buggering on. Like your constituency work. I'll leave you to it..."

"So did he take it?"

"Did he take it? I'm not sure he's even seen it before. 'Living separate lives' doesn't come close."

"So Cam Stokes took it?"

Brady nodded. "I think so. Macdonald said maybe one of Diane's friends took it. But three people? The same cliff? The same angle? Unlikely, to put it mildly."

"Cam Stokes then?"

"Yes. And there's another reason. It's a bloody good photo. My photo of Archie... That's all it is, a photo. That picture of Diane... It tells a story."

"What's that?"

"You don't need me to tell you, Frankie. The expression on her face. Siobhan said something to me the other night. The way she looked at me when she said it... It was the same way Diane Macdonald was looking at the photographer. At Cam Stokes."

Frankie didn't reply. Picked up the picture. Looked at Diane Macdonald. Turned to Brady. "She looks like she wants to fuck the guy holding the camera. Right there on the beach."

"She does. And that was Cam Stokes. Her next door neighbour. Tell Jake to bring the evidence bags in. The office and her bedroom. I'll square it with Macdonald. And Frankie – "

"Boss?"

"You were right. I'm sorry again. This is where I should have been. Not buggering about with Lilian Beale."

64

"Graham, we're done. Finally. And I'm sorry it took so long."

Macdonald nodded. Didn't seem to register what Brady had said. "I'm back in London tomorrow. A bloody three-line-whip to save that waste of space in Number Ten. What do I do? Supposing I get another threat?"

Brady shook his head. "Be careful. Do what I told you to do. Speak to the Met. There must be someone who gives MPs advice? And remember what I told you. About your security."

"I want to believe you, Mike. Maybe you've watched too much TV. The PM can have as much security as she wants. A lowly backbencher gets exactly what you offered me. A bored copper driving past twice a night." He shrugged. Sighed. "But there's no bloody alternative. I have to go back."

For the three-line whip? Or to guarantee your next payday? Greed trumps fear...

"Trust me. We're working on it."

Macdonald shook his head dismissively. "You already said 'trust me' once. When someone says it a second time you know you're fucked. Never mind my bloody wife. You can't bring her back. Just find out who firebombed me. And make bloody sure they can't do it again."

Brady didn't speak. Held his hand out.

Shook hands with the man who'd killed Lizzie Greenbeck and run away across a field. Who hadn't wanted to see his wife's body. Who at best was taking bribes and at worst selling out his country. Who stood in his lounge looking frightened. Shrunken. Left hand shaking as he clutched his whisky glass. Sweat glistening on his forehead.

'We'll reel him in when the time is right. But not just yet...'

Brady was disappointed to find he felt a pang of sympathy.

Suppressed it as quickly as he could.

Brady leaned in through the car window. "You sure you've got it all, Jake?"

"Everything, boss. Shame there's not a car boot sale on the way back. I'd make my fortune."

Brady laughed. "Just book it all in. I'll be back soon. I need to talk to Frankie for five minutes."

He watched Jake drive off. Turned his collar up against the first spots of rain. Climbed back into his car.

Stared through the windscreen. Watched the rain start to fall, the black clouds over the distant hills.

"I said something to Macdonald. Police work is being wrong ninety-nine times out of a hundred. Not this time.

Cam Stokes was having an affair with Diane Macdonald. And murdered her to protect his wife."

"Protect her? What are you talking about, boss?"

Brady watched some more rain hit the windscreen. "I think she's ill, Frankie. I think she's got some sort of degenerative condition. MS maybe. She stumbles. Drops things. I was in the churchyard the other day. Watched an old woman stumble. Someone said something to me about his father. 'Trapped in his own body.' It all fits. I think Cam Stokes was having an affair with Diane, realised he was going to have to care for his wife, told Diane it was over – "

"They had an argument on the cliff top and he pushed her over? That doesn't fit with the witnesses, boss. It doesn't fit with the cliff. Where we think she went over the edge. It was fifty-fifty. If I was going to push someone off a cliff I'd choose a place where it was a lot more than fifty-fifty."

Brady shook his head. "If you were cold. Dispassionate. But Cam Stokes wasn't thinking clearly. A crime of passion. Or the consequences of passion. Apart from the fifty-fifty cliff it ticks all the boxes, Frankie."

"Except the witnesses. They saw Diane Macdonald. Not Diane and a plus one."

"Maybe he followed her. When I was talking to Annabel... She said Diane could be vindictive. She had a mean streak. Suppose she pushed him too far?"

"So what are you going to do?"

Brady looked at her. "Right now? Wait for the techies to get the book off the hard drive. Lie awake thinking. And do the one thing I have to do. Go and see Maggie Stokes."

"The DNA? Doesn't that give you a problem, boss?"

Brady nodded. "With Maggie Stokes? It does, Frankie. I like her. I admire her courage."

"But you're going to turn her life upside down? 'Good

morning, Mrs Stokes. Could we take your husband's toothbrush? Just on the off chance he murdered your next door neighbour?' If what you say is right – if she's ill – what the hell is going to happen to her then?"

Brady shook his head. "I don't know. It's not meant to be easy is it? I wish I was one of those coppers that didn't have any empathy, but – "

"We are what we are?"

Brady nodded. "Come on, let's get back. Start the ball rolling. See where it takes us."

Brady reached forward. Turned the engine on. Shook his head. "Graham Macdonald," he said. "I told him a complete cock and bull story in there. Diane maybe being involved in the threats against him. But I tell you, Frankie, there's nothing that man won't believe if it flatters his ego."

"Like all men," Frankie said softly.

"Sorry, Frankie, I didn't catch that over the rain."

Frankie smiled at him. Shook her head. "Nothing, boss. It wasn't important. After all, I'm only a woman..."

65

'Good morning, Mrs Stokes. Could we take your husband's toothbrush? Just on the off chance he murdered your next door neighbour?'

And there's no simple way to say it...

Brady opened the car door. Looked across and saw the white van. *Peter Cooper. Fencing Repairs.*

The neighbours on the other side haven't wasted any time...

Looked up at the dark clouds, wasn't surprised to see the solar pump still wasn't working. Reluctantly knocked on the door.

Jeans, a University of Michigan sweatshirt, hair still wet from the shower.

What did I think the first time I saw her? A face that had accepted some pain. Some harsh truths.

And here I am. Ready to deliver another one...

"I'm sorry, I slept in. I was late back last night."

"Your mother? How is she?"

Maggie Stokes shrugged. "How is anyone in their eighties? She's been lucky. Good health all her life. Now? She's lost her enthusiasm for gardening. I'm worried. But..."

"But I'm not here to ask about your mum's garden? I'm not Maggie. Can we – " Brady gestured at the kitchen. "Can we sit down?"

"Can I make you a coffee? Or show you where everything is and let you make your own coffee?"

"No. Thank you. What I'm here for... I'm not sure you'll want to make me coffee."

She raised her eyebrows. "That sounds rather ominous, Mr Brady. I thought you wanted to ask me – "

"About the firebomb? I did. I probably still should do. But events have moved on while you've been away. I... I don't quite know how to say this – "

Because I know you're ill. And I don't know what this will do to you. But Diane Macdonald was murdered...

Maggie Stokes looked at him across the table. Lifted her pale grey eyes to meet his.

"Why do I think this is about my next door neighbour? My late next door neighbour?"

Brady sighed. "Because it is, Maggie. Because – there's no simple way to say this so I'm just going to come right out and say it – because I don't think Diane Macdonald fell. I think she was pushed. Very possibly by your husband. I'm truly sorry to tell you this, but I believe Cam and Diane Macdonald were having an affair. And I need a sample of his DNA to confirm it. A hairbrush. A toothbrush. Something – "

Maggie Stokes reached her hand across the table. Put it on Brady's arm. Shook her head. "He didn't kill her. But were they lovers? Of course they were lovers. It was my idea."

. . .

BRADY HAD CHANGED HIS MIND. Cradled his coffee. Listened to the story.

"We were adults, Mr Brady. No children. Pursuing our careers. And we were adults who decided we didn't want to lie to each other. You've met Cam. By any standards he's good-looking. A cameraman. Photographer. Away for three, four months at a time. What's he supposed to do? What am *I* supposed to do? So we had an agreement. An understanding. Absolutely faithful when we were together. Discreet, careful when we were apart. And it worked. And when we were together it was good. A lot more than good."

"So Diane Macdonald..."

She nodded. "Was my idea. She came round for coffee sometimes. When she was here on her own – "

"Which was fairly often?"

Maggie nodded. "I could tell she was attracted to Cam. And that the feeling was mutual. So I suggested it to her. Here, in the kitchen, she was sitting where you're sitting."

"I – "

"You find it hard to believe? I wasn't the first woman to do it and I won't be the last. Maybe it was unconventional but..." She shrugged. "I've reached a stage where convention no longer matters. But you've already worked that out."

"Because of your illness..."

She nodded. "How did you find out?"

Brady paused before answering. "I didn't find out. You're not the only one who's awake at three in the morning, Maggie. You said to me that Diane Macdonald's house 'felt empty.' Didn't feel right. It was the same principle."

"And twenty years of being a cop?"

"Right. What you said about arthritis... You don't stumble against the wall if you've only got arthritis."

She nodded. Picked her coffee up with two hands.

"I thought at first it was MS. But someone said something to me. It stayed with me. Talking about his father. 'Trapped in his own body.' I saw an old lady stumble in a churchyard. Visited Doctor Google. Everything fell into place. "And that." Brady nodded at the coffee cup. "It reminded me of my dad."

Towards the end. But I don't need to say that...

"So three in the morning is when you're on Google? Working out that Diane Macdonald's next door neighbour has Motor Neurone Disease."

Brady smiled. Tried to make a joke. "When I've finished checking the football, yes."

"I watch old films. Tiptoe into the spare room when Cam's home and re-trace my life through films. *Thelma and Louise* was the last one. I've a lot of sympathy for them."

"How do you cope with Cam being away?"

She shrugged. "Badly. But this is his last trip. And he's been home more."

Maybe two or three nights before Diane died? I don't need to ask...

"So Cam's going to give it up – " Brady gestured towards the hall. "To look after you?"

She nodded. "In sickness and in health. I'm not sure either of us thought we'd have to take it so literally."

"Will he..."

"Will he resent giving up his trips to Antarctica? Possibly not. He said the cold was starting to get into his bones. Will he miss catching the train to Edinburgh and two days stalking red deer in the Highlands? Absolutely, irrevocably, without question. But he knows it's only in the short term."

She looked at him. Blinked.

Not a shred of self-pity. Would I be this brave? Not a chance...

"As you now know, I don't have a long-term. Or even a

medium-term." She made no attempt to hide the tear that rolled down her cheek. "Once I had the diagnosis everything changed. Cam and me. Something switched itself off –"

Like me. Sitting by Grace's bed. Until I met Siobhan...

"– Certainly for me. And for Cam too, I think. The knowledge that you're going to be wiping someone's arse isn't one of life's aphrodisiacs is it? But at the same time..."

Another tear. Brady felt in his pocket. Couldn't find a tissue. Stood up. Walked across the kitchen. Tore off a piece of kitchen roll. Handed it to her. "Thank you. Where was I? Aphrodisiacs. But our relationship changed. It became even deeper. Like everything we'd shared – always being honest with each other – like it had been preparing us for this. Sex? Sex wasn't important. Not even remotely. Diane Macdonald was a need Cam had like... I don't know, beer and pizza on a Friday night."

"I'm sorry, Maggie," Brady said gently. "I still need his toothbrush."

She nodded. Pushed her chair back. Put her hands on the table. Started to push herself up.

Brady reached across. Stopped her. "Just tell me where the bathroom is. I'll get it."

"The top of the stairs. Straight across. It's red. I'll tell him I threw it away."

Because you still want to protect him. I'm sorry, Maggie...

BRADY PUT the toothbrush into an evidence bag. Walked back downstairs. Into the kitchen. Maggie Stokes looked up at him.

"Why are you a policeman, Mr Brady? Why do you do it?"

The question caught him by surprise. "Because it's who I am. I thought I could change it. I couldn't."

She nodded. "That's Cam. That's what he is. A photographer. That's how he sees the world. We were in Amsterdam. We'd been together for a month. We were walking back from a bar. Most men would be thinking about sex. I was *definitely* thinking about sex. Cam stopped and stared at a door. He's excited. Looking at a bloody door. I couldn't see it until he explained. Steps going up to a glass door. More steps through the door. A geometric progression from the outside to the inside. I shivered in my mini-skirt while he took photos. That's how he sees the world. Through a lens."

She needs to tell me this...

"But he's like all creative people. He's insecure. Needs reassurance. I don't know who'll do that. After I'm gone..."

He's guilty, Maggie. All I need is the DNA match and I'll be back. And they don't do reassurance in prison...

She shook her head. Looked at Brady. Lifted her coffee cup with two hands. Sipped it.

He watched a small drop escape, land on her sweatshirt. She nodded. Acknowledged the small indignity. "It's shit, Mr Brady. Like Cam missing the Highlands. Absolutely, irrevocably, without question, shit."

"So the trip to see your mother..."

"Yes. Was to say goodbye. Apologise for being such an arse as a teenager. While I still could."

All I want to do is stand up and hug her...

"And to see my consultant. He's good. He doesn't sugarcoat it. MND. Google told you it gets progressively worse? It does. Except in my case I'm not sliding downhill. I'm walking down steps. Down the steps and onto a landing. Remission. Call it what you like. Where I am now. And then one morning there'll be some more steps. Another landing.

One day I'll be at the bottom. Unable to speak, unable to swallow, unable to move. Like your friend's father. A prisoner in my own body. And finally unable to breathe."

Brady nodded. Didn't trust himself to speak.

"Or maybe I'll get on a plane. 'Welcome to Switzerland, Mrs Stokes. Or can we call you Maggie?' Like I said, absolutely, irrevocably, without question, shit."

Brady willed himself not to ask the question. The one he'd been thinking about since he worked out she had MND.

The one that would keep him awake. Staring at the ceiling. Wondering...

Geoff Oldroyd's First Law of Hypochondria. 'Whatever you Google, you've got it the next day.'

Failed.

"It's none of my business. None at all. But... Why you? What do they think caused it?"

Maggie laughed. "What do they think? Or what do I know? I was skiing. Val d'Isere in France. I'd done a winter there when I was twenty. Thought I knew every inch of the slopes. Clearly it's not just men who think they're invincible. Or immortal. I hit a tree. Knocked unconscious. Airlifted to hospital. In for a week."

"And you think that's what triggered it?"

"The doctors say no. They say they can't pinpoint the cause. It could be hereditary they say. But my parents were fine. My grandparents. Pops – my mother's father – climbed a mountain for his seventieth birthday. So the doctors say no, I say yes. I didn't have headaches before, I did afterwards. I think I fractured my skull. I think *les bons docteurs* missed it." She shrugged again, spread her hands. "But we'll never know. So I slide gradually downhill. Walk down my steps."

'I think I fractured my skull.'

Gary Cooke. My first case. Running down the alley. Goading me. Right hand smashing into my head. Jerking back as I fell. Cracking my skull against the brick wall. The briefing room spinning. Waking up in hospital.

Brady stood up. "I've taken up enough of your time, Maggie. I can only apologise again. I'll get this back to the lab."

"And if you have your match you'll be back to see Cam. He's many things, Mr Brady. Driven. Talented. Insecure, like I said. He's many things. But he's not a killer."

66

Brady handed Frankie the evidence bag. "Cam Stokes' toothbrush."

"Leave it with me, boss. I'll get it off to the lab. How quickly do you need the results? Ten minutes?"

Brady laughed. "Faster than that. Tell them it's urgent, Frankie. And then nip up to St Mary's. See if you can enlist some Divine help."

"Leave it with me. And good news. The break-ins on the estate. Dan Keillor's got someone downstairs."

"Good. Tell him well done from me. And I'll catch up with him later today. I'm just going down to see Geoff."

"Maggie Stokes? How was it?"

"Interesting. To put it mildly. I go in there with no idea what I'm going to say. 'Your husband's having an affair with your next door neighbour.' She looks at me across the kitchen table and says. 'I know. It was my idea.'"

"Because she's ill?"

Brady nodded. "It's a long story. Wouldn't work for me but seems to work for them. But yes, MND. Motor Neurone

Disease. That's why I need to see Geoff. Ask him a couple of questions. Then I'll bring you up to date."

BRADY PUSHED the door of the morgue open. Saw Geoff Oldroyd bending over a corpse.

"Morning, Geoff. Another satisfied customer?"

The pathologist straightened up. Rubbed the small of his back. Turned round and started peeling off the surgical gloves. "Mrs Rivington, Mike. And it might be a new record for Whitby. She's more or less embalmed herself with gin. What can I do for you?"

"First things first, I haven't seen you since the pub. Is everything OK?"

Goeff nodded. "Sorry, Mike, I meant to tell you. I've been pre-occupied with Mrs R's liver. It's Anne. *Was* Anne. She's fine now. But..."

"What's the problem? Anything I can do?"

Geoff shook his head. "Remember I told you? When you asked me about Diane Macdonald? She gets these bloody migraines. Seem to be getting worse as she gets older. And before she gets them she has these flashes. Disturbance to her vision. Sometimes it's shimmering lights. Sometimes it's a bloody hole. That's what it was the other night."

"A complete hole? Where she can't see?"

"Yep. 'Black hole,' she calls it. Technically, it's a retinal migraine. And it's harmless. Short-lived and your sight goes back to normal. And the trained, logical part of me knows all that."

Brady nodded. "But in the middle of the night – "

"Right. When we're both convinced it's something way, way worse. She gets frightened. So when it starts the least I can do is abandon a pint of Doom and be with her. How was it with Frankie and Young Lochinvar?"

Brady laughed. "He's alright, Geoff. Knows his stuff. Gave me a whistle-stop tour through Greek mythology and the middle ages. I liked him. And like Frankie said, he's probably good for her."

"Stops her dwelling on – what did she say? The darker side of Whitby?"

"Seamier, I think. That must be you and me. And she said he listens."

Geoff looked surprised. "Listens? All men listen don't they?"

Brady laughed. "Absolutely. It's what we're best at isn't it?" Hesitated. "Geoff – you mind if I ask you a serious question?"

"A pint of Doom Bar, Mike. Pointless asking a question when you already know the answer."

Brady shook his head. "Geoff, I'll buy you a pint any night of the week. But this isn't one for the Black Horse."

"Work then?"

"Personal. A personal question."

Geoff nodded. Walked over to Brady. Draped an arm across his shoulder. "It's alright, Mike. I understand. You're dating a woman who's ten years younger than you. She's got that wistful, not-quite-satisfied look. You need the advice of a real man. There's no need to be embarrassed."

Brady laughed. "Geoff, I suspect you fall asleep in front of the TV faster than I do. Screw your professional head on for a minute. I want to ask you a medical question."

"Sorry, Mike. You know what they say. Women talk, men hide behind banter. But why me? Why not your GP? Police doctor? Except the fact that you want to ask me is answer enough."

"Yes. Informed but unofficial – "

"Unrecorded?"

"Very much unrecorded. A completely unofficial answer. But I'd value your opinion, Geoff. And I've no-one else to ask."

"Go on then..."

Brady nodded. Hesitated. "What I'm going to ask you. It's been on my mind. Like a lot of things in life, you don't realise how much until you ask someone."

"I'm listening. And I'll not make any jokes."

"Not until you know what it is? Cheers, Geoff. Can we talk over there? I know it's normal for you but talking over a dead body. It seems – "

"Disrespectful? To Mrs Rivington's liver?"

"THIS CASE," Brady said. "Diane Macdonald. I saw Maggie Stokes yesterday, the next door neighbour. She's got Motor Neurone Disease – "

Geoff sucked his breath in. Shook his head.

Like the garage mechanic looking at my first car...

"Not good. How far along is she?"

"Far enough, she says. And I suspect a good deal further than 'far enough.'"

"She knows the prognosis?"

Brady nodded. "Yes. She was philosophical. She's in remission. For now. Maybe that's the wrong word. She said it wasn't a consistent decline. More a series of steps going down. Then, she reaches a landing – "

"Has a rest and then goes down some more steps. Brave lady. I don't envy her. Knowing what's coming. There's a bloody lot to be said for getting yourself up on the Moors and having a short, sharp heart attack, Mike."

"There's a bloody lot to be said for not dying at all, Geoff, but Maggie Stokes knows she's going to die and she's meeting it head on. But – "

"But she said something that's made you worry. And that's why I'm not holding a pint of Doom."

"She did, Geoff. I asked her how it started. What caused it."

Geoff shook his head. "No-one knows for sure. There's a genetic link. Contact sports. Rugby. That's pretty well documented now. Even the military, although I doubt that Mrs Stokes was either a prop forward or a paratrooper. I could go all technical on you and talk about neurones and nerve impulses. But for most people it's the effect, not the cause."

Brady took a deep breath. "She told me all that, Geoff. Not in so many words. But then she said that she'd fractured her skull. Skiing. She hit a tree. Said she would have died if she hadn't been wearing a helmet. She started having headaches. And found out later that she'd fractured her skull and the medics in France had missed it."

"She thinks that's what caused it?"

"She's convinced."

"She's possibly right, Mike. But she's *probably* wrong. Like I said, no-one knows. Least of all me." Geoff paused. Looked at Brady. "But it's clearly struck a chord with you. Or we wouldn't be sitting here."

"The same thing happened to me, Geoff," Brady said quietly.

"Which is why we're having this conversation..."

Brady nodded. "I was twenty-six. My first case as a detective. I chased someone down an alley in Manchester. Gary Cooke – "

"He's the guy you were telling me about once? That footballer's girlfriend shot him?"

"Charlie Irvine's girlfriend. She shot him in the leg. I put a tourniquet on it. Saved his life I suppose. She'd hit an artery. He got twenty years."

"And he's the one that's due out soon?"

Brady nodded. "He'd have been out sooner. He broke a warder's jaw in there."

"So go on. You're chasing him down an alley..."

"He's a big bastard. Twice the size of me when I was that age. We have a fight. He slams my head into a brick wall. I black out, he gets away."

"And you fractured your skull? Is that it, Mike? The parallel with the skiing accident?"

"That's the problem, Geoff. I don't know. I've spent seventeen years wondering. Too frightened to find out. Like I said, I blacked out. The same again back at the station. My old boss is doing a briefing. The world starts spinning. I wake up in hospital. I was supposed to rest for... Honestly, I can't remember now. A fortnight."

"But you didn't."

"No. I discharged myself. Worked out who'd done it."

Geoff laughed. "Well you're consistent, Mike, I'll give you that. Jimmy Gorse on the end of the pier. Jumping in the harbour to save Col Appleby. You don't do things by halves." He paused. Looked at Brady. "So maybe you fractured your skull – and now you're worried it's coming home to roost."

"Since I spoke to Maggie Stokes, yes. You know – Google..."

"*Don't.* Just don't. You know my well-known Law of Hypochondria. Whatever you Google – "

"You've got it the next day. Except you can't stop yourself. And I dropped my keys the other morning. Coming out of the house. One minute they're in my hand, the next minute they're on the floor."

"Christ, Mike. I drop things all the time. You know why? Because I'm not thinking. My hands are emptying the dishwasher, my mind's down here. Or worrying about one of the kids. The more I see of my daughter's boyfriend the less I like him. But they're in love. So what do we do?" Geoff shook his head sadly. "Old age. Where the hell was I?"

"Not thinking..."

"Right. Next thing one of the new plates is on the floor. John Lewis deliver it on Wednesday, I drop it on Thursday. Thirty-five years together and I didn't know she could be that sarcastic. I know what you want me to say, Mike. And I know why you wanted to talk to me."

"Because we're friends – "

"And because you didn't want anything official. That's fine. I'd have done the same. But I'm not an expert, Mike and even if I was I couldn't give you a definite answer. I'd say it's unlikely. You *and* Maggie Stokes. Bloody hell, *most* things are unlikely."

"But something gets us all in the end?"

"It does. The wife in my case if I drop another plate."

Brady laughed. Held his hand out. They shook hands. "Thanks, Geoff. I just... I needed to hear someone talk some common sense."

"Except it won't stop you worrying."

"What does? Ash was talking about this boy the other day. Her first boyfriend. Now all I can think about is her taking him up to her bedroom – "

Geoff laughed. "To help with my revision?' There's not a teenager alive who's not used that line. She'll be fine, Mike. How many times have I met her? Twice? I doubt there's a more sensible teenager on the planet. Now stop worrying. And get this case cleared up. The Black Horse won't wait for ever."

Half an hour later Michael Brady turned left into Henrietta Street. Walked the two hundred yards to his front door. Put his key in the lock without dropping it and braced himself for an excited Springer Spaniel.

'Except it won't stop you worrying.'

It won't, Geoff. And yes, something gets us all in the end. But just let me get my daughter settled. Settled and happy. Then I'll take my chances...

67

Brady looked up from the report he was reading. "Is that you, Frankie? I've gone cross-eyed trying to make sense of this crap. What's up?"

"All seven planets, boss. Or nine. Or however many there are this week. They're in line."

"Cam Stokes?"

"Cam Stokes' toothbrush. Diane Macdonald's sheets. The report says the DNA's degraded – "

"But not degraded like being in sea water overnight?"

Frankie shook her head. "No. It's a match. Diane Macdonald had sex with Cameron Stokes."

"And we've got Graham Macdonald to thank."

"Macdonald? Why?"

"For being too lazy to change the sheets. That's brilliant, Frankie. Thank you."

"It doesn't prove he killed her, boss."

"No, it doesn't. But it does leave him with long list of bloody awkward questions to answer. I've been doing some checking..."

"Tomorrow, boss?"

Brady nodded. "Tomorrow. I'll sort it out. Cometh the hour, cometh the suspect. And you'd better do what Lochie suggested on the phone."

"Boss?"

"Bring your handcuffs, Frankie."

68

Brady looked at his watch for the thousandth time.

Like waiting for a football match to kick-off. Part of the job I hate. Maybe I should have joined the KGB. Kick someone's door down at four in the morning.

But right now it's questioning. Nothing more. So it'll come soon enough. Patience. Do some paperwork...

Brady sighed. Reached for the report he hadn't finished yesterday. Had read two paragraphs when his phone rang.

"Boss? Have you got two minutes? There's someone downstairs."

Brady felt his pulse quicken.

Donoghue. Brilliant. Bloody brilliant. I don't have to go looking for him...

"Is it Donoghue, Sue? Make sure you keep him there. I'll be straight down."

"No, boss. It's not Donoghue."

So who the hell is it? And why did she sound amused?

Brady half-walked, half-ran down the stairs. Pushed the fire door open. Into what passed for reception.

The pale yellow jacket, skinny jeans –

The same clothes she was wearing when we met...

– dark hair falling to her shoulders, green eyes sparkling. Clearly sharing the joke with Sue.

"You're back from Wales."

She laughed. "And you haven't lost any of your detective skills, Michael Brady."

"I – "

We can't have a bloody conversation standing in reception...

"Can you give me five minutes? Finish what I was doing? I'll take you for coffee."

Siobhan nodded at a bench by the door. "I'll sit down, shall I? Pretend I'm a suspect..."

SHE TOOK his hand as they walked into town. Forced him to stop. Kissed him. Told him she'd missed him. Kissed him again.

"I missed you as well. I texted you on Saturday night. You didn't reply."

"Because there was no signal on the mountain."

"What did you just say? I thought – "

"I did. There was no signal on the mountain."

"So you didn't compose music and drink gin?"

"We did. Take me for coffee. I'll tell you the story."

"TELL ME..."

"We did. We composed music. Drank too much gin. Made decisions. And went up a mountain."

"To forget about your unreliable copper in Whitby? I thought the plan was to talk about your future?"

"It was..." She paused. "And that's why we got the tent out of the attic. Helen lives at the foot of *Cadair Idris*. Idris's Chair to a man without a drop of Gaelic blood. And there's a lake. And a legend."

"Don't tell me. The legend says if you go on the mountain in the dark you fall in the lake."

Siobhan shook her head. "You are the least romantic man on the planet, Michael. The legend says that if you sleep on its slopes alone you wake up a madman. Or a poet."

"You weren't alone."

"Technically. But two girls in a tent on the side of a mountain? It's close enough."

"So what are you? Mad? Or a poet?"

"I'm a composer. And that's why it was symbolic."

"You're not a musician any more?"

Siobhan shook her head. "I'll always be a musician. Especially at the Golden Lion. But we've taken the decision not to replace Lucy and Emma in the band. Not even think about replacing them. To recognise that all good things come to an end. Accept that the cynic from the record company was right. That we're not the only pretty girls who can play classical music."

Brady reached across the table. Took her hand. "I think that's... I don't quite know how to put it into words. But I think it's the right decision."

"Something else."

When Ash said 'something else' it was a boyfriend. Now what...

"The film company. The one I told you about. They rang me."

"The one in Dublin?"

"The short film. The Irish girl going home. They *definitely* want us to write the music. And – "

"Siobhan, that's brilliant. Absolutely brilliant. I'm proud of you. Really proud."

Siobhan nodded. "We're pleased. Beyond pleased. There's no money. Not much anyway. Start-up film company, start-up composers."

"Everyone has to start somewhere."

"They do. But it's a start that means we have to go to Dublin. They want us to meet the cast. The director. Go through the script. See the locations."

"When?"

"October? Maybe for two to three weeks. Some of it is out on the Dingle Peninsula. Where they filmed *Ryan's Daughter*. And where the rain sweeps in off the Atlantic..."

Brady laughed. "You know I'll have to Google that?"

She squeezed his hand. Looked into his eyes. "I thought – when this case is over – maybe you could come over for a few days."

Brady nodded. "I'd like that. I've never been to Dublin – "

"You've never been to Ireland."

"Very true. But October? Assuming nothing else rears its ugly head. I'd like that. Although I don't like Guinness..."

"There are plenty of other things to drink. And..." She hesitated. "I'm sorry. About going away like that."

Brady shook his head. "No, it was my fault. I... When I'm working on a case. It takes over. Completely takes over – "

And I can't stop it...

" – It's me that should say 'sorry.'"

"You don't need to. I'm back. And... I've missed you." She reached across the table. Traced her finger across his lips. "You're the boss, Ash is at school..."

Brady took her hand. Kissed the tip of her finger. Shook his head. “I can’t. I’ve an appointment.”

Doing what you suggested, Siobhan. Making an appointment at a civilised time...

“This case?”

Brady nodded. “I’m getting there. It won’t be long.”

Two o’clock this afternoon, Cam. ‘Bring your handcuffs, Frankie...’

69

"You ready for this, Frankie?"

She nodded. "Always. And..."

"What?"

"Maybe it's me that should apologise. You were convinced she'd been murdered. I wasn't."

Brady laughed. "Frankie, we wouldn't be here without you. Besides, how long has it taken me to get here? What's that saying? A thousand monkeys with a thousand typewriters and sooner or later they'd write *Hamlet*? They'd be in the pub having a beer by now."

Brady put his hand on the door handle.

"You want to run through it one more time, boss?"

Brady shook his head. "There's nothing to run through, Frankie. They've got – had – an open marriage. No children. Both pursuing careers. That's what she said to me. 'Faithful when we were together, discreet when we were apart. Always totally honest with each other.'"

"It sounds like a nice theory," Frankie said. "Nice theories fall down in the real world."

"And it has, hasn't it? He was seeing Diane. She knew

about it. Encouraged it. "Because he had a need. 'Like a pizza or a beer,' she said."

"A pizza doesn't have feelings, boss. It can't talk back to you. Make you laugh. It doesn't have a birthday. Mannerisms that should irritate the hell out of you. But that you somehow find endearing."

"It doesn't matter, does it? Something went wrong with the relationship. What that was... Cam Stokes can fill in the blanks. Come on, Frankie. I don't want to do this. I like her. I don't want to tear her world apart."

"So you'd rather be Kershaw..."

"Dispassionate? Sometimes. Waltz in there, ask the questions, an hour later Cam Stokes is down the station asking for a solicitor? Sometimes..."

"Except Kershaw would have dismissed it as accidental death. Given Macdonald the verdict he wanted. And a killer walks free..."

Brady sighed. "Come on, Frankie. Let's do this."

He climbed out of the car. Paused to look at the solar pump in the garden. "The fourth time I've been here. It's never been working."

"You should have put solar panels on your roof, boss."

"You want the truth, Frankie? I'd run out of money. 'Here's an estimate, Mr Brady. Double it. Add any number greater than a thousand. Double it again. Come on, I'm wasting time. Delaying the inevitable."

Cam Stokes answered the front door.

Looking tired.

No, Cam. I wouldn't have slept much either.

. . .

"You know why we're here. I won't insult your intelligence by beating about the bush. Where were you the night Diane died, Mr Stokes?"

"I was on Lindisfarne. Holy Island. Filming for the BBC. And shooting photographs for a wildlife magazine."

"You weren't a hundred-and-twenty miles down the A1? With Diane Macdonald?"

"No, I've just told you where I was."

Brady nodded. "You have. Except that it was pouring down."

Stokes didn't reply.

"It was pouring down all that day. We've checked with the Met Office. Spoken to the production company."

Brady was conscious of Maggie looking at him.

She knows me too well by now. She knows where this is going. We all do...

"...And it was a Sunday. So rain or no rain there was no filming. And I suspect any wildlife was firmly tucked up in its den. Or cave." Brady smiled. "You'll excuse me, Mr Stokes. Where wildlife goes to get out of the rain isn't a specialist subject of mine."

Cam Stokes shook his head. "You're a policeman. I'm a photographer. Your job is facts. Although fuck knows we're rapidly heading into the realms of fantasy. My job's not. It's about light. Angles. Location. More than anything it's about patience. You see that?"

He pointed at one of the pictures on the wall. A red deer. A stag. Standing on the side of a Scottish hill. Staring defiantly back at the camera. The ground behind him sloping down to a loch. Early morning mist rising off the water, framing the stag, half its antlers shrouded in the mist.

"How long do you think that took? The right light? The right angle? The bloody thing looking at me with that expression. Proud. Haughty. 'What are you doing on my land?' Twelve hours – "

"No-one's denying you're a good photographer, Mr Stokes."

"With respect, Mr Brady, that's like me saying... I don't know, Tiger Woods is a good golfer. I don't play the game. I've no bloody idea what 'good' means. But time. Patience. Twelve hours of stalking. Bloody starving. The sheer bloody-minded will to get the photo. That's 'good'"

The sheer bloody-minded will to prove you're guilty. And it takes as long as it takes...

Brady nodded. "I appreciate all that. And you're right. I don't have a clue what I'm talking about."

Brady glanced at Maggie.

An expression halfway between fascination and foreboding...

"But on Sunday you weren't stalking a stag. You hadn't nipped across to Farne Island to watch the puffins. Because when Detective Sergeant Thomson spoke to the production company and found they weren't filming that day, she also spoke to Fern. Who as you know books all the accommodation. Who told her you were staying at Mrs King's B&B. Do I need to go on?"

"Yes," Maggie said quietly. "You do."

Brady nodded. "I'm sorry. As you know, Mr Stokes, Mrs King confirmed that you *weren't* there on the Sunday night. Your room was paid for: your bed wasn't slept in. She didn't see you again until Monday morning. By which time Diane Macdonald was lying on the rocks. Dead or dying."

And with a seagull pecking her eye out. But we'll save that for the trial...

Brady was surprised. He'd expected to see Cam Stokes slump. Start to admit the truth.

He didn't.

"I was out late. Scouting locations. It was light until half-eight. Me and the director. Then we went to the pub. One too many. Bloody hell, we'd been working for twelve hours. I slept on his sofa."

Maggie looked at him. "You didn't tell me."

"I didn't want to worry you. You know Tony. You know how much he can drink."

"And Tony could confirm that, could he?" Brady said.

Cam Stokes shrugged. "If he remembers. He's got a big drinking problem. Everyone in TV knows it. But when he's sober he's bloody brilliant."

"And then Monday morning came and you went back to Mrs King's? Back in time for breakfast?"

Stokes smiled. "I did. Full Northumberland. Extra sausage. No tomato. As Mrs King will confirm."

"So..." Brady said. "While you were sleeping on the director's sofa. Which he may or may not remember. And then eating your hungover breakfast..."

I'm sorry for this, Maggie. Truly sorry...

"...Who was driving your car, Mr Stokes?"

Cam Stokes didn't reply. Didn't look at Brady.

And daren't look at his wife...

"That's the trouble with a personalised numberplate," Brady said. "I'd have checked anyway, but CAM 77S... Even a dim copper like me can remember that. And you know what? If I'd had to spend 12 hours stalking you to find out where you were that night I'd have done it. Twelve hours. A hundred and twelve hours. But sometimes we get lucky. Like the Sunday night Diane Macdonald died. The same Sunday night your car was clocked at eighty-five on the A1. Just outside Durham. Eighty miles south of Lindisfarne. Well on the way to Runswick Bay. But not to see your wife, Mr Stokes..."

Cam Stokes lifted his head.

The same angle as the stag...

Stared back at Brady across the kitchen table. Didn't reply.

"I warned you about the speed cameras, didn't I? But then you were asleep on Tony's sofa. So who gets the three points, Mr Stokes?"

"Don't do this," Stokes said. "Don't."

Brady shook his head. "I don't have a choice. Diane Macdonald was murdered. You were having an affair with her. And it's my job to establish the truth. Which so far has you speeding down the A1. Eight thirty-five. Just as the sun was setting over Lindisfarne. An hour from Runswick Bay. Probably less given the speed you were going."

Cam Stokes shook his head slowly from side-to-side. Looked at his wife.

Pleading. Suddenly he's pleading with her. A little boy's expression. I didn't mean to do it...

"I think you need to give me an answer," Brady said quietly.

"Alright. I *was* driving down the A1. I *was* speeding."

"I don't think any of us are disputing that. Where were you going?"

Maggie stared at her husband. "Not here, that's for sure. Shall I go outside, Cam? Check the satnav? It'll still be in there, won't it? Now I don't drive the car any more?"

"Hannah," Cam Stokes said quietly.

"Hannah?" Maggie said. "Who the hell is Hannah?"

Maggie has taken over. Her and Cam. Frankie and I are spectators...

"You met her once. The opening of that gallery in Middlesbrough. The artist..."

"And you were driving down to see her? In Middlesbrough? Twenty-five fucking miles away? I'm dropping coffee all over the bloody floor and you're in Middlesbrough with – "

"Stockton."

"Middlesbrough, Stockton, it doesn't bloody matter, does it? After what we agreed? After what you said? 'It's different now you're ill, Maggie?' You're twenty-five miles up the road fucking some... some... She's young enough to be your daughter, Cam."

Maggie Stokes put her head in her hands. Shook it slowly. Let out a low moan. Looked up at her husband. "You... you... Fuck it, Cam. You're not even worthy of the word."

"So you weren't in Runswick, you were in Stockton?" Brady said. "And you drove back the next morning?"

Cam Stokes nodded. Didn't speak.

"I assume Hannah has a surname? And a phone number?"

"Lockwood. And yes she has a phone number." He opened his phone. Passed it to Brady.

Brady wrote the number down. Handed the slip of paper to Frankie. "Could you ring her, Frankie? Maybe from the car?"

Spare Maggie some pain...

Frankie nodded. Stood up, took the car keys Brady offered her.

Brady looked at Maggie. Saw the effort it took her not to break down. "I'm sorry," he said. "Truly sorry."

She shook her head. "It's not your fault. The person who uncovers the truth isn't responsible for the lie."

She turned to Cam. Asked him a simple question. Clearly didn't expect a reply. "Couldn't you have waited until I was dead?"

Looked back at Brady. “I told you, didn’t I? Constant reassurance. The fragile male fucking ego.”

Turned back to her husband. “Twenty-five miles. Twenty-five miles from your dying wife, Cam. While I’m struggling to stand up. While Diane Macdonald – ”

The door opened. Frankie was back. She took two steps into the room. Stood behind Maggie. Looked at Brady. Nodded. Mouthed ‘all night.’

Brady sighed. Stood up. “We’ve taken up enough of your time. I...”

What can I do? Apologise again? No...

“Mr Stokes, I’ll leave you to your explaining. Maggie, the person who uncovers the truth. He may not be responsible for the lie, but sometimes he leaves casualties. I’m sorry.”

Yes, then...

“And good luck with your speeding awareness course, Mr Stokes.”

BRADY SAT IN THE CAR. Punched the steering wheel. Punched it again. Shook his right hand to ease the pain.

“I’m not even going to swear, Frankie. That’s as bad as it gets. Worse. Way worse. Fuck. Just fuck.”

“You weren’t going to swear, boss.”

“What else can I do, Frankie? What the hell have I achieved? I’ve just fucked up the last months, years – however long she’s got – of Maggie Stokes’ life. Ruled out the man I was certain – absolutely bloody certain – was guilty. I’ve fallen out with you, I’ve fallen out with Siobhan. I’ve been on a wild goose chase halfway across bloody Yorkshire. When Kershaw hears the story he’ll be in bloody A&E with hysterics. The – "

Frankie reached her hand out. Put it on Brady’s. “Stop it,

Mike. Stop feeling sorry for yourself. You still think she was murdered?"

Brady shook his head. "No, I don't *think*. I know she was murdered."

"Right. So find the killer. You've got two days to work it out."

"Two days?"

"I'm away. That bloody course HR want me to do. Are now *insisting* I do. So go back to square one. Like you always do. Work through it. And *don't* punch the steering wheel again. It's your birthday next month. Old people have brittle bones..."

70

Michael Brady sat on his balcony.

Saw the expression on Maggie Stokes' face.

Saw Frankie mouth 'all night' at him.

'I've fucked up the last months of Maggie Stokes' life. Ruled out the man I was certain was guilty. I've fallen out with you, fallen out with Siobhan. Been on a wild goose chase halfway across bloody Yorkshire. When Kershaw hears he'll be in A&E with hysterics.'

Maybe I should resign.

'Dear Alan. It is with regret that I must resign my position in North Yorkshire Police. Although we have had some limited success since my return it is now clear to me...'

I could get a job on a fishing boat. Persuade Dave to go to Spain. Buy the bacon sandwich business...

What have I got right? Maggie Stokes has MND.

I should have been a doctor not a detective...

Brady finished his beer. Picked up his pen. Reached for the pad. Started in the top left. Finished in the bottom right. Drew a line diagonally through his notes.

'Stop it, Mike. Stop feeling sorry for yourself. You still think she was murdered?'

'No, I know she was murdered.'

'Right. So go back to square one. Like you always do. Find the killer.'

Looked across the harbour to the West Pier.

You found Jimmy Gorse. You found Alice Simpson after twenty years. Got justice for Billy and Sandra.

Frankie's right. She's always right.

Brady picked his pad up again. Reached for his pen –

HEARD A NOISE. Voices. The front door opening.

Ash and Bean.

No, not Ash and Bean.

A boy's voice.

Spencer.

Shit.

Trackie bottoms, hoodie. I haven't shaved for two days and I'm drinking beer. 'Spencer, I'd like you to meet my dad. Someone told him the 'elderly wino' look was fashionable.'

Brady stood up. "Is that you, Ash?"

"No, Dad, it's a random stranger who found our front door key in the street."

"OK, fair enough..."

Ash walked into the lounge. Ripped jeans, her favourite black jumper.

And Spencer, half a pace behind her.

A red and black check shirt over a navy T-shirt. Dark blue glasses, dark hair, brushed back but still managing to fall forward. A ready smile.

A young Clark Kent. But with confidence...

"Dad, this is Spencer."

"Seriously, Ash, I thought it was a random stranger you'd – "

Ash shook her head. "I'm sorry, Spence. My Dad has a middle-aged medical condition. He thinks he's funny."

Spencer laughed. Had the confidence to shake hands. Brady instinctively liked him.

"It's good to meet you. Ash has told me... Well, not very much."

"I hope the stream is still working OK?"

"For the Middlesbrough games? It's working a lot better than the Middlesbrough defence. But thank you. And the commentary is fine. Now you've upgraded me from Chinese."

Spencer laughed again. Ash looked towards the kitchen.

"Is that pizza still in the fridge, Dad? We haven't eaten."

"Sure. Or there's some Spag Bol sauce. I was feeling domestic. I made some, thought I'd freeze it."

"Is that why you've a plaster on your finger?"

"Yep, the knife decided to cut me, not the onion."

"So extra garlic and extra blood. My dad's speciality, Spence. Spaghetti a la Dracula. We'll probably stick with the pizza."

"Help yourself. I'm just here if you want me. Trying to work something out."

Ash nodded at the pad. "Is that why you've drawn a line straight through it?"

BRADY STOOD UP, walked into the kitchen for another beer. Had the distinct feeling he'd interrupted something.

"Is it deep, Dad?"

"Is what deep?"

"Where the onion attacked you."

"No. It's – "

Sunday morning. The firebomb. Maggie Stokes' kitchen. A cup lying smashed on the floor. Her laptop open on the table. An onion on the screen.

Her expression. Almost bitter. 'The perils of living next door to the Macdonalds.'

"SPENCER, CAN I – "

"Spence, Mr Brady. My friends call me Spence."

"Mike then. I'm not sure I'm ready for 'Mr Brady' just yet."

Where have I heard that before? 'I'm not quite ready for Mrs Stokes yet.'

"Spence, can I ask you a question?"

"I told you not to interrogate him, Dad."

"I'm not. It's a simple question. Ash said you knew a lot about computers, Spence. I saw someone the other day. Glimpsed her laptop. There was a big onion on the screen. It looked like an onion. A logo..."

"TOR."

"Tor? Like a hill? Glastonbury Tor?"

Spence shook his head. "T-O-R, Mr Brady. The Onion Routing project."

"That's..."

"The Dark Web if you want to call it that. Anonymous web browsing. If you believe the figures 95% of the web is on the Dark Web."

'But if Macdonald can hire someone, so can she.'

Except it wasn't Lilian Beale, Frankie...

'She was vindictive as well. Diane had a mean streak in her.'

'I trapped a nerve in my back and couldn't put my socks on.

Bloody woman stood there laughing while I shovelled Ibuprofen into my mouth.'

Fuck. Fuck, fuck, fuck.

Brady nodded. "Thanks, Spence. That's great. And let me know what pizza you like best. I'll put it on the shopping list."

MICHAEL BRADY WALKED BACK to the balcony. Looked out across Whitby Harbour. Heard the seagulls. The sounds of late summer. Looked at the West Pier.

Tried not to think about Jimmy Gorse.

About what was coming.

Knew that Maggie Stokes had hired Donoghue.

Knew why she'd done it.

Knew what he had to do.

The lies he'd have to tell.

Felt physically sick.

71

Michael Brady rolled out of bed. Pulled a pair of tracksuit bottoms on. A hoodie over his T-shirt. Sports socks.

Walked into the kitchen. Opened the fridge. Drank orange juice straight from the carton.

"Breakfast when we get back, Archie. I need the beach. You need the beach. Two minutes down the slipway. It's low tide. There'll be plenty of beach."

A HUNDRED YARDS OF BEACH. Enough, not plenty. Brady found a flat stone. Skimmed it across the early morning sea.

Six. A good omen?

'Blinding as a punishment for adultery...'

'Are you turning superstitious, boss? Believing in omens?'

No, I'm not, Frankie.

Watched a seagull fly lazily past. Decide there was nothing worth scavenging.

We're married, Frankie. You've had enough of me. Do I think you're efficient enough to organise a hitman while you're away? Damn right I do. Macdonald? Unlikely.'

'But what do we always say, boss? Occam's Razor. The simplest solution is the most likely. And our simple solution has one lead...'

"It does, Archie. The man who saw a runner. Who *says* he saw a runner. What do you make of that? A bloody poor high tide, I know what you make of that. Not a single stick washed up. I'll have a word with Neptune."

Do I think you're efficient enough to organise a hitman, Maggie? Yes, I do. And I could be knocking on your door in half an hour. But if I do that I'll never see Donoghue again. A killer will go free. And I'm not having that.

So there's only one way.

A trap.

And a trap needs bait.

Which means I'll have to lie to Frankie. Not tell her until it's done. Or she'll talk me out of it.

I'll have to lie to Siobhan.

And Ash...

"I'm not proud of that, Archie. But there's a killer. And it's my job to catch him. And I'm too old for this shit. So I need an insurance policy. Which means you'll get a long walk tonight. After I've been to Runswick. And set my trap."

They were at the far end of the beach now. A narrow strip of sand that would disappear in ten minutes. Brady squatted down. Ruffled the top of Archie's head.

"You know what pisses me off, Arch? Apart from the lies? The danger. All the bloody mistakes I've made. Macdonald pisses me off. Graham bloody Macdonald. 'MP's wife killed by hitman.' The papers will have a field day. Can you imagine how many votes that'll be worth? So much for the yellow peril. He'll be an MP for life. The bastard will probably get a knighthood for long service."

Brady stood up. Looked out to sea. Saw the sun starting to rise. Turning from red to orange. "Sunrise, Arch. Levata. *La levata del sole*. Is that a good omen for me? Or for Siobhan? Come on, mate, breakfast's calling."

Brady started up the slipway, a reluctant Archie trailing behind him. "Keep up, Arch. I told you, a long walk tonight. Somewhere new as well."

Heard his phone ring. Pulled it out of his back pocket.

Ash? Siobhan? Frankie? It's barely seven.

It was Kershaw.

"Good morning, sir."

"I'm not so sure about that, Brady. I heard you went to Runswick Bay yesterday. You and Thomson. Came back with your tail between your legs."

Who the hell has he been talking to?

"DS Thomson and I certainly went to Runswick, sir."

"What for?"

"To interview a suspect, sir. About the death of Diane Macdonald. It turned – "

"Brady, how many fucking times? The woman walked off a cliff. What about the firebomb?"

"We're still no further forward, sir. The good news is we've arrested someone for the break-ins on the estate."

"A council estate? You think my reputation depends on a fucking council estate? Find out who bombed Macdonald. Seven days, Brady. Or I'm on the first train back. And I'm putting it in writing. This cock-up's on you."

"I wouldn't have it any other way, sir."

The line went dead.

Brady shook his head. "What do you think, Arch? Ten

grand for a hitman? Pay him to take care of Kershaw? Cheap at twice the price..."

72

The Audi Q2 wasn't outside the house.

Brady parked. Breathed a sigh of relief. Looked up and down the street, couldn't see CAM 77S.

So maybe sunrise was for me, not Siobhan...

The well-tended hedge, the pond. The view straight through the house. The conservatory, the running machine.

Everything exactly as it was the first time I came.

No...

The solar pump was finally working. Water splashing gently into the pond. The ripples fanning out.

She was wearing the thick, white dressing gown. A T-shirt under it. "I've been expecting you," she said.

Brady nodded. "I'm glad he's away. It makes things easier."

"Will you let me get dressed? Before you arrest me?"

Brady shook his head. "I'm not here to arrest you, Maggie. I'm here to talk. Go and get dressed. I'll make the coffee."

. . .

SHE WAS BACK in five minutes. Jeans, her University of Michigan T-shirt, blonde hair pinned-up.

"How long is he away for?" Brady said.

"Three days. Maybe four. A job he'd turned down before. He went back to them."

"Northumberland?"

"Wales. But he'll find a way to detour via Stockton." She shook her head. "Not that I care anymore."

She held her coffee in both hands. Looked at Brady. "You want to know why?"

He nodded. "Yes. I want to understand."

"It's simple. She mocked me."

'She was vindictive as well. Diane had a mean streak in her.'

'The last time she smiled at me was when I trapped a nerve in my back. Bloody woman stood there laughing while I shovelled Ibuprofen into my mouth.'

"She mocked me, Mr Brady. Sat at my kitchen table and mocked me. Told me my marriage was worthless. That it had been a sham. That Cam was hers. That he'd never loved me. She laughed at our trust. But it was good. And it worked. For twenty bloody years it worked. And maybe it wasn't everyone's idea of a marriage. But it was ours. And it worked. Or... I have to believe it worked."

Brady swallowed. Didn't know what to say. "There must have come a time when – "

"When I told her not to come round any more? Of course. But you can't avoid your next door neighbour. And you've possibly heard of Facebook..."

"So when you told me you went round to check if she was in... You were really going round to see if she was dead."

Maggie looked back at him. Shook her head.

No hint of remorse...

"I was going round to check if my instructions had been carried out."

"But you still reported her missing."

"Of course. Because what else would a good neighbour do? Besides, I live next door. You were bound to knock on my door sooner or later."

"So you thought you'd come to me first."

She nodded. "And you walked into my kitchen. And I knew it was only a matter of time."

"Why?"

"Because – fuck it, you're going to arrest me, and I don't think my sentence will be one day longer if I use your first name – because, Michael, who comes knocking on my door apart from the one copper in North Yorkshire who's far too bright to be a bloody copper?"

"That's – "

"That's not true. That's what you were going to say. You know damn well it's true. I mentioned Aethelflaed. And you said – "

"The Lady of the Mercians? I saw her described as Britain's greatest military commander."

" – You did. And I knew it was only a matter of time."

"But you let the game play out."

"Of course. While there's life there's hope. No-one wants to spend their final days in prison."

"You said – when you went round to the house – you said, to 'check if your instructions had been carried out.'"

Maggie Stokes nodded. "She wasn't there. She hadn't been there all night. That was enough."

"So the instruction you gave – to whoever you hired..."

Donoghue.

"Was to teach her a lesson. But to give her a chance. To let the fates decide."

'Places where there's no chance of dying if you go over the edge. Five hundred yards further up the path you're guaranteed to die. Diane was fifty-fifty. So it had to be a warning.'

I was completely wrong. It was never a warning...

"But you knew she'd be injured. Probably seriously."

She nodded. "I'm not proud of that. But what else could I do? Cam was under her spell. I was dying. I *am* dying. I misjudged her. Totally. There you are. You make a mistake with your first boyfriend. Several boyfriends. By the time you're forty you're supposed to have learned. But I didn't. She sat there mocking me, Michael. Every time I went down another of my metaphorical flights of steps Diane Macdonald was there, waiting at the bottom. Taunting me. Laughing at me. Cam was too good a man to waste on her. She'd have ruined his life. At least..."

She doesn't need to finish the sentence. That's what you thought before he went to Stockton...

"Did she know... about your illness?"

"Honestly? I don't know. She must have worked out something wasn't right."

Or Cam let something slip. Pillow talk. But I won't say that out loud. Because you've been lying awake wondering...

"So you went on the Dark Web?"

She nodded. "I went on the Dark Web. And you're looking at me and you're thinking, she doesn't look like someone who uses the Dark Web. It's not as difficult as you think. I started using it to buy cannabis."

"For the MND?"

"It helps. Relieves some of the symptoms."

"But then you went a step further..."

"As you say, I went a step further." She looked at him. Nodded. "And that's why you're not arresting me..."

Brady knew what he should do. Knew what Frankie

would tell him to do. Knew what the rule book would *demand* he do.

But that means I'll never see Donoghue again. A killer will go free. And I'm not having that. So there's only one way.

Ignored them all.

"THE MAN YOU HIRED. Tell me about him."

"I wish I could. I only know his alias. People like him don't use their name and address."

"How did you pay him?"

"Bitcoin. The same way I paid for the cannabis."

Brady laughed.

Is that why Mozart is always telling me to buy Bitcoin? So I can buy dope and hire a killer?

"What was his alias? Code name?"

"Ares."

"Aries? Like the star sign? March to April?"

Bingo. Gerry Royston Donoghue was born in Germany on 2nd April 1978. Right in the middle of Aries...

"No. A – R – E – S. The Greek God of War. Of battle, technically. He – "

"I thought Athena was the Goddess of War?"

"She was. The civilised part of it. Ares was the brutality. The slaughter."

"The jobs no-one else wanted to do?"

She nodded. "Exactly. And appropriate."

Brady looked out of the window. "Whatever he's called, whoever he is, I have to find him."

"Won't your – "

"Won't our technical people trace him? You've watched too much TV, Maggie. Possibly. Sometime around Christmas. What do I do in the meantime? Let him wander round the country killing people? And no, I'd never know the victims. Some coppers would be fine with that. My boss for one."

"But you're not your boss..."

"No, I'm not. The more people tell me about Diane Macdonald the less I like her. But someone pushed her over a cliff – "

"And I paid. So now I have to help. The accused cooperated fully, Your Honour?"

Brady shook his head. "I'm not promising anything, Maggie." Hesitated. "There's a flaw in my argument. Obviously."

Maggie Stokes laughed. "Hired killers need hiring? I can afford it if that's what you're wondering. Besides, it looks like Cam will spend my money in Stockton. And I'm in your debt. You've stopped me going to my grave as a fool."

"We need to organise it," Brady said. "Set the trap."

Maggie raised her eyebrows. "I'm not an expert in police procedure, Michael, but clearly what you're suggesting is so far removed from official procedure that – "

"That I'm taking a risk?"

"I'd say 'risk' was barely an adequate word. 'Madness' is probably more appropriate."

Brady nodded. "You're right. It's illogical. It's risky. It's dangerous. It probably won't stand up in court. It'll potentially end my career. And it's the only option."

"So you're setting a trap. A trap needs bait."

Brady nodded. "You're looking at the bait."

"You've got a daughter – "

"What do I say to her, Maggie? 'There was a killer. I didn't do anything. No, I don't know how many more people he killed. It was safer to do nothing?" Brady shook his head. "Go online. Contact him."

"What do you want me to say?"

"Nothing. I know who it is."

"So why – "

"Why don't I arrest him? Because he's homeless. Been undercover. Impossible to find. But I've met him. Twice. He's goading me. Taking the piss. Enjoying it. And we've talked. So if I tell you what to say – "

"He'll know it's you?"

"It's not a chance I want to take. So a copper. Getting too close to the truth. You're in danger. His details are on your laptop. Something like that."

She laughed. "You said you weren't going to tell me what to say. You've just told me what to say."

Brady laughed with her. "Right. I'm a man, aren't I? Mr Fixit."

She looked at him. Held his eyes. Reached her hand across the table. Briefly touched his fingers. "In another world, Michael Brady. When things were better. When life was different... I could have spent a night in a hotel with you. Several nights..."

In another world. If I hadn't been married. If I wasn't going to arrest you for murder...

"Send the message," Brady said quietly.

"Suppose he doesn't take the bait?"

Brady shook his head. "It's a risk we have to take."

"It could be tomorrow. The next day. Diane... I contacted him on Friday. It was done by Sunday."

"Good. Because I've looked at the weather forecast. It's raining tomorrow. The cliff top will be deserted."

"Diane... I told him where she went for a walk. She was a creature of habit. Told him what she'd be wearing. And I described the dog."

Brady shook his head. "No. There's no way I'm taking my

dog. He's had one brush with death during his life. He's not going to have another. Number two, what the hell do I say to my daughter? 'I wanted to look convincing so I took our dog?' There's not enough life cover in the world. So Archie stays at home. We need Plan B."

"You'll risk your own life. You won't risk your dog?"

"Exactly. I've got a red jacket. Puffa jacket, whatever they're called. My wife bought it for me. Said she was fed up with navy blue. I didn't have the courage to tell her I didn't like it. I've worn it twice. It makes me look like a Michelin man. But it's red. And it's distinctive. So tell him that. A middle-aged man in a red coat. Walking briskly. Tell him I walk to keep fit. Just before sunset. That should be enough."

She nodded. "Consider it done." Hesitated. "And then you'll be back for me? Handcuffs? The patrol car?"

"I will. When this is over. Like Shakespeare said. When the hurly-burly's done. When the battle's lost and won."

Maggie smiled. "There you go again. Like I said, Michael, I knew it was over the first time I met you. But I've enjoyed watching you."

Brady shook his head. "All you've done is watch me make mistakes."

"On the contrary. You're too clever for your own good. And you're addicted to risk. I shall sit in my prison cell and worry about you. If I make it to a prison cell..."

73

"You a football man are you, mate?"

The big man with the cropped blond hair sighed. Taxi drivers the world over. Total silence or verbal diarrhoea.

"Just you look a bit like one. A footballer, not a fan."

"Neither. Sometimes if there's a game on TV. But no. Not really."

"Wise man. Save yourself some pain. Charlton me. Grew up round the corner. Never had a choice did I? Spent my teenage years in the Premier League. Thought it'd always be like that. Since then? Pain, disappointment and broken promises. Same as getting married, eh? You married are you, mate?"

"No, I'm not."

"Wise man. Save yourself some more pain. Find a woman you don't like and buy her a house. That's what they say, don't they? Ah well, look on the bright side. City are fucked. You see it in the paper? Pretty boy Gustafson. Out for the season. Got himself beaten up. Shagging his teammate's girlfriend. Came home and caught him. That ain't going to do a lot for team spirit..."

"Just here is fine."

"You sure? Bloody steep hill, even if you only live halfway up it. Twenty quid with getting stuck in the traffic. Won't charge you no more to go to the top."

"No, I'm fine. I need the exercise."

The taxi driver glanced in the rear view mirror. "Don't look like it to me. But you're the boss. Twenty quid for cash then, guv. And you have a good day. Remember what I told you. Stay away from wives. And Charlton Athletic."

IT TOOK him ten minutes to walk up the hill. Constantly climbing, not even remotely out of breath when he put his key in the lock.

He walked into the kitchen. Put the leather bag down on the worktop. Flipped through the post.

Looked at the note from the pet-sitter.

Heather? Was that her name?

Willow is limping on her left front leg. I think maybe she's been in a fight? Maybe you should take her to the vet?

He listened. Nothing. The cat must be out. He shrugged. Four o'clock. She'd want feeding soon enough.

He picked the bag up. Walked into the utility room. Unzipped it and started throwing three days' dirty washing on the floor. Socks, pants, jeans, the black top.

How many jobs was that? Twelve. Maybe he should skip the next one and go straight to fourteen. But he wasn't superstitious. Leave that to the Chinese. What he guessed was the Chinese. A gambling syndicate probably. His first job for them.

He heard a noise. The cat flap. A plaintive miaow. 'Feed

me. Not 'I'm in pain.' He bent down. Picked up the black and white cat. Wondered for the thousandth time why the hell he'd agreed. The look on his mother's face. 'Alright, I'll take care of the cat.'

Her left front leg. I think maybe she's been in a fight?

He held the cat. Squeezed her leg. Felt her struggle to get free. "Been fighting have you, Willow? Give it a few days. We go to the vet's there's paperwork. We don't like paperwork do we, sweetheart?"

He bent down. Tossed the washing into the machine. Easy care 40. The only setting he ever used.

'They say he's out for the season. Got himself beaten up. Shagging his teammate's girlfriend. Came home and caught him.'

Two out of three, pal. Beaten up. Check. Shagging his teammate's girlfriend. Check. But no-one came home and caught him...

Bo Gustafson. Ripped jeans, black jumper, pale blue jacket, fucking ridiculous fake dreadlocks.

Out of the lift into the underground car park.

Strolling towards his Range Rover. Smiling.

Two hundred grand a week, Bo. You earn that much you can afford protection. Proper protection. Then again, if you're shagging your teammate's girlfriend there's only one thing protection's going to do.

Decide they're not getting paid enough. Phone the *Sun* or the *Mirror*...

'We want him injured. Enough to be out for the season.' What sort of crap instruction was that? What did they think he was? A fucking physio? Then again it was the Chinese. And they paid well. And the expression on Bo's face when the barbs hit him. Lying there helpless as he stamped on his leg. The crack had echoed round the car park...

He shook his head. It was bollocks. 'Kill them.' That was

the only instruction he needed. Black and white. Pay the money, tell me who you want killing. Leave it to me.

Not like that crap at Whitby. 'Over the cliff but let fate decide whether she lives or dies.' Fucking nonsense. And the bloody woman wouldn't stop talking. Should have tasered her as well...

He walked into the lounge. Flicked the TV on. Some earthquake. Five thousand dead. You should build your fucking houses properly. Good cover for a job though...

Maybe another couple this year. Then two more years. New Year's Day 2020. That was the plan. She'd be long gone by then. So he could buy the place in Portugal. The boat. Maybe half a dozen jobs a year for the Chinese. "There must be a few more footballers, eh Willow? A few more Bo Gustafsons around the world?"

A holiday first though.

The big man with the cropped blond hair opened his laptop.

Tapped Expedia into Google.

Told the cat to wait for her dinner.

Swore. Realised he'd forgotten to phone the care home.

Reached for his phone...

74

B*arely even a gap...*

Brady glanced out to sea. A solitary tanker making its way to Middlesbrough. The cliffs stretching in front of him, climbing steadily to Boulby.

Turned and forced his way through the hedge for the second time. Did his best to avoid the blackcurrant bushes. Told a hesitant Archie not to worry.

Came out into the field of wheat stubble, saw the tumbledown farm shed.

Wondered if it was etiquette to knock when one wall was just a tarpaulin.

"HELLO?" Brady called. "Anyone in?"

The tarpaulin was pulled back. Brady looked up at Magic Pockets. An expression that was half-annoyed, half-impressed.

"Sherlock fucking Holmes. How did you find me?"

"By getting up early. And walking a long way."

"Well, you've found me, so you'd best come in. Who's this you've brought?"

"Archie."

"A Springer? He won't be short of scents in here."

Brady looked around him. Three wooden walls, a workbench at one end. The original rafters. A makeshift bed in the corner.

"You want some tea?"

"If you don't mind. It's been a long walk."

There was a fire smouldering in the far corner. A battered black kettle. Magic poured water into it from what looked like a gallon milk jug. Turned his attention to a shelf overflowing with herbs.

"Mint? That do you?"

"Perfect."

Magic handed Brady a mug that was even more battered than the kettle. "Go on then," he said. "You did more than get up early."

Brady nodded. Knew he had to explain.

"Gerry said you liked the seat half way up Blue Bank. I found you in the churchyard first thing in the morning. What's half way between the two? The middle of Whitby. You don't live there. So it made sense that you lived close to one of them. You were at the church first thing. And no-one in their right mind is going to walk up Lythe Bank every morning."

Magic laughed. "So you set off from the church and walked north?"

"Right. I walked north. And used the clue you gave me."

"Clue? I didn't give you no bloody clue."

"Yeah, you did. When we sat down on that bench. Second-best view in the world, you said. I figured the best view was probably from wherever you lived. Or when you came out of where you lived. After all, you've got the whole coast to choose from. And I knew what I was looking for."

"What was that then?"

"A shelter of some sort. An abandoned shed on an allotment. Abandoned trailer. Farm outbuilding."

"And you'd know it when you saw it?"

"Something like that."

"So you've found me. I'm busted am I? Next thing I know there'll be some arse from the Council telling me I don't have planning permission. That he's going to assess me for Council Tax. Band fucking Z. Desirable country property close to the sea."

Brady laughed. "You're not even remotely busted. No-one knows but you and me. And Archie. And that's the way it's staying."

Brady looked up at the rafters, more herbs hanging from them.

"I can tell you're impressed."

"I am. I..."

"You couldn't live here yourself but for a tramp it's not bad?"

"I wouldn't put it like that."

"I was down the road in Ravenscar. Swansea originally. That's where I washed up ashore. Milford Haven. Spent a summer walking the Coast Path. Chester to Chepstow. Eight hundred and seventy miles. Bloody lovely. But then we had a bad – "

"We?"

Magic shook his head. "Me an' the rest of society's misfits. There's never been a Mrs Magic if that's what you're thinking. No little Magics. I don't do relationships. Never had the knack."

"Sorry. You were saying..."

"Bad winter. Cold. One of the lads zipped his sleeping bag up. Big mistake."

"I don't understand. How can zipping your sleeping bag up be a mistake? Especially if it's cold."

"Cos you're trapped aren't you? Sleeping bag's unzipped you can get out. Chase some drunk who's pissing on you. But if it's zipped up you're fucked."

"What happened?"

"Skinheads."

Magic saw Brady's surprised look. "Yeah, me n' all. Thought they'd died out. But Swansea always was behind the times. Poured petrol on him. Jimmy Shoulder. Survived Belfast. Didn't survive Saturday night in Swansea."

"And you ended up here?"

He nodded. "Ended up here. Ravenscar way for a while. The town that never was, eh? Lived in a stable no-one seemed to want. Then I found my way up here. Anyway..."

"I'm not here for your life story?"

"You're not. What can I do for you?"

Brady sipped his tea. Was surprised at how good it was. "I need you to deliver a message for me."

Magic raised his eyebrows. "There's e-mail."

"He doesn't have a phone. Doesn't do 'official.'"

"I know lots of lads like that."

"Not lads that have only told me half their story. 'You'd do well to listen when he tells you.'"

Magic narrowed his eyes. "Go on then, cock."

"I've a meeting tomorrow night. North of Runswick. Just before sunset. It doesn't have to end badly. For either of us. We can sort it out."

"Bit bloody cryptic."

"Not for the person getting the message."

"*If* he gets the message." Magic shrugged. "No phone, no e-mail..."

Brady nodded. "It's a risk I've got to take. But I trust you."

Magic stood up. "Trust me with those bacon sandwiches next time you come – "

So there'll be a next time. Good...

" – I need to be off. Farmer needs a bit of help before it gets dark."

"He knows?"

"Of course he knows. Help him out when its harvest. A few other times. Like tonight. An' that grave I was doin' the other morning. Alice Cundle. His grandma. Least I can do is take care of her."

"And in return – "

"In return I've got three walls and a tarp. A bed. A kettle. A radio. What more do I need?"

"You don't get visitors? Just by chance?"

Magic laughed. "Only bloody coppers that are determined to find me. Mind you, I did get a courting couple last year. Fancied a quickie, I suppose." Magic stretched. Farted. Scratched his groin. "I said no problem at all. So long as it was a threesome. The lass took one look at me. Changed her mind for some reason..."

75

Brady walked back along the cliff top path. Promised Archie they'd soon be at the car.

'I've a meeting tomorrow night. Just before sunset. It doesn't have to end badly.'

"All day to wait, pal. Never mind, I can spend it telling lies. And polishing my resignation letter..."

"FRANKIE? Five minutes? Down by the harbour?"

She nodded. Mouthed 'scraps' at him.

Brady laughed. Reached for his coat.

"THREE RED AND white fishing boats in line," he said. "What are the chances of that?"

"You *are* getting superstitious in your old age. You'll be telling me you've been to Gypsy Sara next."

"Maybe. She can tell me what my next job will be..."

Frankie finished her chips. Walked across and put the

plastic carton in the bin. Wiped her fingers on a tissue. Looked at Brady.

"That sounds like 'I've done something. And now I'm telling Frankie when it's too late for her to talk me out of it.'"

Brady nodded. "Nail. Head. You know me too well."

"I'm listening..."

"The wife, not the husband. Maggie Stokes hired someone. Not to kill Diane Macdonald. But certainly to do her harm. Plenty of harm."

"Because of the affair? What about – "

"What about Cam being a shit? That was the first she knew about it. She's ill, she thinks he's playing by the rules. Their rules, admittedly – "

"But he's not."

"He's not, neither is Diane Macdonald. Maggie thought Diane was trying to steal Cam – "

"He wouldn't be there to look after her?"

"She said Diane mocked her. Taunted her. 'Every time I went down another of my flights of steps Diane Macdonald was there, waiting at the bottom. Taunting me. Laughing at me. Cam was too good a man to waste on her.' That's what she said. She'd have ruined Cam's life."

"So she hired someone? Despite Cam being a shit?"

"She didn't know that, did she? Not until we told her. I told her. So while he's still St Cam she goes online and finds Donoghue."

Frankie nodded. Looked across the harbour. "Four if you count that one on the far side."

"Four – "

"Red and white fishing boats. Because you're going to tell me what you've got planned, Mike. And I think we need a good omen..."

"I've set a trap, Frankie. I *think* I've set a trap."

Frankie shook her head. "Jesus, Mike. I'm going to say, 'a trap needs bait.' And you're going to say, 'I'm the bait.' Or words to that effect."

Brady nodded. "Maggie Stokes has set me up. Contacted the killer. Told him what I'll be wearing. Where I'll be."

"All of which is, of course, in the official police manual."

"Which says 'go and arrest Maggie.' I'll do that. But I want the killer. Not an interminable wait for a tech trail that may or may not happen. That could get screwed up in one of a hundred ways. Which probably won't be admissible in court. While Donoghue wanders round the country pushing people off cliffs. Under buses. Whatever his next job is..."

"One question, boss. That I couldn't answer as I lay in my Premier Inn bed. If it's Donoghue. If he's doing the jobs, why is he homeless? Because he's earning money. Plenty of money if the stories you read in the papers are right."

Brady shook his head. "I don't know. Maybe he isn't homeless. God knows I've got everything else wrong. Homeless or not, I have to stop him."

"And it's just you. So you're asking me for back-up."

"No, I'm not, Frankie. How can I? This is as unofficial as unofficial gets."

"Seeing as it's unofficial, Mike. Let me say something. This is stupid. It's whatever comes after stupid. How the bloody hell do you know what you're up against? How – "

"I don't."

"Right. So how are you going to plan? Prepare?"

I'm going to wear a red jacket...

"I'm not. But what's the alternative, Frankie? Donoghue walks away? To kill more people?"

Frankie shook her head. "He's not the only hitman for hire, Mike."

"But where's that leave us? Let's not arrest anyone because there'll be another villain along in a minute?"

"Michael bloody Brady. What did I say to you before? I could be a copper until I was a thousand years old and – "

"It was a hundred – "

"Alright, a hundred. And not have a better boss than you. But you're mad. Completely mad. You're putting your life on the line. Not to mention your career. Supposing Kershaw ever finds out? Completely, totally, bloody mad."

"I – "

Frankie held her hand up. "No. Stop it. Don't say anything else. Just tell me two things. Where? And what time?"

76

"I'm playing at the pub tonight."

"The Golden Lion?"

"Where else?"

Brady looked at her. Sensed her hurt even before he'd spoken. "I'm sorry, I can't come. I have to arrest someone."

"At night?"

He nodded. "At night. Don't ask me to explain. It's complicated. This case I've been working on – "

"The woman that went over the cliff?"

"And everything that goes with her. The nice, convenient two o'clock appointment fell on its arse. Caused more problems than it solved. So it's not quite the witching hour. But heading that way. Trust me, I would far, *far* rather be watching you. Play a long encore and I'll get there if I can."

She reached up, held his face. Looked into his eyes. "If you can? Should I be frightened, Michael?"

Brady forced himself to laugh. "No, of course you shouldn't be frightened. What on earth have you got to worry about? I've arrested hundreds of people. I'll be there for the encore. I promise."

He kissed her. Kissed her again.

Knew there wasn't a hope in hell of being there for the encore.

"WHAT ARE YOU DOING, DAD?"

"What am I doing, Ash? I'm getting a coat out of the wardrobe."

"That red one? You never wear that red one."

'I'm going for a walk on the cliff.' Can I say that? No, because she'll ask me why I'm not taking Archie. And there's absolutely no reason why I wouldn't take Archie.

"I'm working, sweetheart."

"In a bright red coat that you never wear?"

"In a red coat that your mum bought me that I think I ought to start wearing."

'I've got a red jacket. Puffa jacket. So tell him that. A middle-aged man in a red coat.'

"What time are you back in your bright red coat, Dad?"

"Blimey, Ash, who's the parent here?"

"I'm not sure, Dad. You're acting suspiciously. If I was a detective I'd say someone suddenly wearing a coat they hadn't worn for three years was grounds for suspicion."

"Well you've nothing to be suspicious about, Ash. It's just the dictates of work. This case I've been busy with. Give me a kiss, and I'll see you later tonight."

"That's suspicious as well. You don't usually ask. You just kiss me. Should I worry about you, Dad?"

"No, Ash. You're far too young to worry. Wait until you have children of your own. I'll see you later tonight, sweetheart."

. . .

'Should I worry about you, Dad?'

'Should I be frightened, Michael?'

Brady reached for his car keys. Opened the front door.

I've lied to Ash. Lied to Siobhan. Frankie's told me I'm mad.

Thank God Archie can't ask me questions...

77

Michael Brady stood on the cliff top. Gazed out to sea. The sky and the sea merging. The fading light making it hard to tell where one stopped and the other started.

Turned his face up. Felt the rain.

'May the sun shine warm upon your face: may the rains fall soft upon your fields.'

The rain is falling on my face, Siobhan. And I'm sorry I lied to you.

'And until we meet again, may God hold you in the palm of his hand.'

Brady shivered.

I hope He does...

Looked along the cliff top path in both directions. Nodded.

You wanted deserted. You've got deserted. But so has Donoghue. So just the two of us...

Reached for his phone. "I'm five minutes behind you," Frankie said. "Exactly like you wanted." She hesitated. "You want me to wish you luck?"

Brady laughed. "You've made your bed might be more appropriate. Give me two minutes. Then start walking. There's one more call I need to make."

"Ash or Siobhan?"

"Neither," Brady said. "Two minutes. Then start walking."

He pressed the red button. Ended the call. Made the second call. She answered on the third ring.

"I wanted to say thank you," Brady said. "You didn't have to do this. And wish you luck – "

If I don't see you again...

"Yes," Maggie Stokes said. "I did. We both know I did. And I'm in your debt. I owe you this. I may be sadder: I'm certainly wiser. I've enjoyed knowing you, Michael. Clearly I was never meant to reach Switzerland."

"I don't – "

But the line was dead.

Brady looked at his watch. Time to go. He looked out to sea again. Somehow expecting to see the sun setting in the sea.

Appropriate. But the wrong side of the country...

Said, "Let's do this." Started walking north along the cliff top.

Had walked a hundred yards when he replayed the conversation.

'I've enjoyed knowing you, Michael. Clearly I was never meant to reach Switzerland.'

Replayed another conversation.

'I tiptoe into the spare room when Cam's home and re-trace my life through films. Thelma and Louise was the last one. I've a lot of sympathy for them.'

Dear God, she's going to commit suicide. Like one of her defeated English Queens. Boudica? I don't bloody know...

Brady grabbed his phone. "Frankie, where are you?"

"I'm about a hundred yards further than last time I spoke to you. Why?"

"Because I want you to turn round. Because Maggie Stokes is going to kill herself."

"What?"

"Maggie Stokes. I spoke to her just now. She said she was never meant to reach Switzerland. Dignitas. That clinic. She'd enjoyed knowing me. Was talking about Thelma and Louise."

"Thelma – "

"Thelma and Louise. They drive into the Grand Canyon. Frankie, she is going to kill herself. You need to go back to the house."

"And leave you alone with the killer?"

"Yes."

You made your bed...

"*No*, Mike, that's not what we agreed. That's... That is just plain bloody stupid."

"Frankie. Listen to me. Maggie Stokes is going to kill herself. Never mind me. Never mind what we agreed. Go back to her house. Stop her. Keep her alive. And that's an order, Frankie."

Brady didn't wait for the reply. Clicked the red button. Carried on walking.

Briskly. You're supposed to be walking briskly.

A middle-aged man in a red coat. Walking to keep fit...

Brady was surprised. Found he felt calm.

Calm before the storm? Is that how it is before a battle? Gerry Donoghue, before he went on patrol in Afghanistan? A moment of calm as he climbs out of the armoured car? But there's half a dozen of them. So no. It's banter. Black humour. Exactly like the police.

Brady forced himself to focus. Turned round, looked behind him.

'The path winds round an inlet. So I've just passed the woman and her dog. I look back the way I've come. You can see a long way there. Back up the hill. And maybe there's someone at the top. Maybe. But the light's going.'

No-one behind me. No-one striding towards me.

And still some light.

But deserted. How you want it.

How Donoghue wants it.

If he turns up...

Brady carried on walking. Pulled the zip up on the red jacket as the drizzle turned to rain.

'Should I be frightened, Michael?'

'Siobhan. She's a bonny lass. An' I've seen the way she looks at you. But something's holding you back, Mike. An' we both know what it is.'

'Should I worry about you, Dad?'

'I need to know who killed her. Who took her from me. From both of us. Because... Somewhere out there is the person who killed her. And I don't know if I can cope with that. And I don't know how you'll cope with that. Forever.'

Dave. Ash. Maybe you're both right. Maybe I'm only just realising it...

BRADY SLIPPED. Looked down. The path was starting to get muddy. Moved to the side. Walked on the grass to avoid a puddle that was forming. Glanced at his watch.

Fifteen minutes until sunset. Then what? Another fifteen, twenty minutes of light.

I should have checked yesterday. Worked out exactly how much light I'd have. Too late now...

Rehearsed the conversation he was going to have with Donoghue...

'Right now, Gerry, I can't prove murder. I can't even prove attempted murder. I can prove conspiracy to commit a crime. Maggie Stokes will testify. But no-one saw you push Diane Macdonald. I can't prove she didn't slip. Maggie's given you an 'out' hasn't she? I doubt she meant to do it. But you've been lucky. 'Let the fates decide.' So it's not murder. Not even attempted murder. Conspiracy to commit GBH? Yeah, there is that. But I'll say you co-operated. The Prosecution Service will take the easy option. Then there's your service record. PTSD. Psychologists' reports. And we'll forget firebombing Macdonald. He had it coming. So five years? And you'll only serve a third of that. What do you say, Gerry? Frankie will be here in five minutes. Less now. So let's do this the easy way. No-one gets hurt...'

Rehearsed it a second time.

Was even less convinced.

Carried on walking. Slightly faster.

Realised he was starting to sweat.

A warm night. Despite the rain. Not nerves. Definitely not nerves...

Unzipped the red jacket as the rain eased.

'How is the town treating you? Well, I hope. Or are the boundaries starting to close around you?'

Mozart. Simon Butler. Both saying the same thing.

Lilian Beale. 'You have a certain... reckless naiveté.'

Are they right? Maybe they're all fucking right.

But it doesn't matter.

This is what matters. Right here. Right now. Me. Donoghue. Ending this. All that matters.

How far have I walked? A mile.

Nearly sunset. 'When the wings of the night start to spread.' What was that? A fairy tale I read Ash?

'He was hunched. Dark. Mentally and physically. Collar turned up.'

Come on, Gerry. Let's get this over and done with. See fucking sense will you? Come quietly. I'm far too old for this physical crap. Especially in the rain...

78

Another bend round another inlet. Brady glanced behind him.

Suddenly felt reassured.

There. Frankie. Definitely. Closer than last time?

Not Frankie. I sent her back. She's with Maggie Stokes. So who –

A local then. A bloody walker.

Go back home, you fool.

Brady looked up. Saw someone on the path.

Thirty, forty yards in front of him.

A BIG MAN.

Five, six inches taller than me...

Not Donoghue.

As far from Gerry Donoghue as you can get...

Brady slowed. Blond hair cropped close to his skull. A black jacket hanging open.

An old fashioned donkey jacket. My dad had one...

Black jeans. No-nonsense industrial boots. He stopped five yards from Brady.

"You're supposed to be walking faster, mate. Red jacket. Walking briskly. But you're the only mad bugger on the cliff top. So it's you."

Brady's rehearsed speech went out of the window.

"You killed Diane Macdonald."

The big man shook his head. "No, mate. I did my job. Over the edge. 'Let the fates decide.' Shit instructions. But I did my job."

The rain picked up again. Brady felt it sting his face. Wiped it out of his eyes. "And what's your job tonight?"

The big man smiled back at Brady. "You are, cock."

"I'm a police officer. I've got back-up." Brady took a pace forward. "Don't make this difficult. I can't prove murder. I can't even prove – "

79

Brady saw him move his coat back. Had a fleeting image of Clint Eastwood in a Spaghetti Western. Then he was holding something in his hand. A yellow gun. A blue tip.

A taser. A police taser. Hadn't even thought...

What would I do?

Make sure people couldn't fight back.

Fuck...

The big man with the cropped blond hair smiled. "Insurance policy." He took a step forward.

"You – "

Brady looked down. Saw two red dots on his chest. Never finished the sentence.

Felt the barbs thud into him.

Felt time stand still.

Two rocks hitting me...

Knew the theory. Knew the drill.

The wires. Windmill your arms. Get the barbs out.

Couldn't. Couldn't do anything.

Lost control.

Tried to step back. Couldn't.

Every muscle in his body in spasm. Excruciating –

Wasps, bees, ants. Crawling all over me. Under my skin.

Brady crashed down onto the cliff top. Still shaking. Every nerve in his body on fire. Shaking. Vibrating. 50,000 volts going through him.

On his back. Staring up at the night sky.

Gasping for breath.

Saw the killer standing over him. Smiling.

"Five seconds," he said. "Longest five seconds of your life. Now you're telling yourself to move. 'I've got to move.' But you can't. Tough shit."

The killer put his foot under Brady's back. Rocked him backwards and forwards.

Two feet from the edge...

Rocked him again. Left Brady facing the cliff-edge. Staring out to sea. Knowing what he'd see if he looked down. Knowing what was coming next.

Still shaking. Still gasping for breath,

"I was expecting you to have a dog with you, mate. Cliff top at night. I'd have put good money on a dog. Fucking Rottweiler though if you're going to meet me. She had a spaniel. Nice little thing. Barked a lot though. 'Specially when she went over the edge. Sort of requiem. Is that what you call it? The music you play when the coffin slides out of view? Fuck knows. I'm probably wrong. Didn't pay much attention at school."

Why the hell is he talking? Listen. Try and speak. If he's talking he's not –

"Fighting mostly. Fighting and getting beaten. Father fucking Kelly. 'I am just God's instrument, boy. God is punishing you, not me.' Got off lightly, I suppose, seeing what happened in some schools. And you know what? Now, I can see his point of view. 'Cos that's all I am. A fucking instrument. Instrument of your death in this case. But I'm not the cause. No, mate, that's your own stupidity. Ah, well, requiem or no requiem, here we go."

Brady struggled to lift his head. Forced his neck muscles to work. Saw him walk to the edge of the cliff. Look down.

"Taser, mate. Made my job a lot easier. Muscle spasms and temporary paralysis. Fucking love it. Sadly in your case the paralysis isn't going to be temporary. Permanent. Very fucking permanent. Not that you'll know anything about it."

Light going. He can't see much. Roll into him. I can't. I can't. He's too far away...

"Sorry, mate, just checking. There's ten feet or so of grass. Sloping obviously. Pretty steeply. So you're just going to roll over that and... well, that's it basically. Straight down after that. Next stop Valhalla. Nirvana. Wherever coppers go. Writing out speeding tickets for eternity."

BRADY IGNORED THE SPASMS. Willed his muscles to work. Somehow rolled over. Pushed himself onto his hands and knees. Forced himself to look up at the killer.

"I've got a daughter – "

"Oh, fuck off, mate. Everyone's got a daughter. Daughter, son, half a dozen fucking children. Me? I've got a mother with dementia. But what you've really got, mate, is fucking shit for brains."

He lifted his right foot. Kicked Brady hard in the ribs. Drove the wind out of him. Brady went down.

Struggling to breathe. Desperate for air.

Forced himself back on to his hands and knees.

The killer shook his head. "You're a tough bastard, I'll give you that. Fucking footballer the other day. Whimpering and bawling. Fucking pansy. Still, all good things come to an end. Here we – "

A shadow.

I saw a shadow.

A shadow.

Behind him.

Distract him.

"Look at me!" Brady screamed. "If you're going to kill me fucking look at me. Be a fucking man."

The killer laughed. "You want me to look at you? You fucking prick, I'll look at you."

He stepped forward. Stood with his legs apart. Bent down. Reached his hand out. Grabbed Brady's hair. Pulled his head up. Stared into his eyes. "There, dead man. That fucking do – "

The army boot was a blur. Within an inch of Brady's face. Between the killer's legs. Straight into his balls.

He screamed. Let go of Brady's hair. Then two hands were round his ankles, pulling his feet away. He crashed down on the path. Just missed Brady.

The hands were pulling him back. Brady looked up. Saw a figure in an army camouflage jacket.

Dark green trousers.

Gerry. Gerry bloody Donoghue. You hero. You fucking hero. I was wrong. Completely wrong...

But the killer was big. Bigger than Donoghue. He kicked. Kicked hard. Broke free. Kicked Donoghue in the chest as he rolled over. Jumped to his feet. Reached into his jacket again.

Holding something. A baseball bat.

Small. Two feet long. Big enough to do serious damage...

Donoghue had scrambled to his feet. Stood facing the killer.

Started laughing.

Dropped his hands.

Laughed at the killer.

"Martin fucking Beck. What have you done to your hair, you poof?"

"Donoghue? Staff Sergeant? What the fuck are you doing here?"

"Stopping you killing a bloody good man. Put that fucking thing down."

Beck shook his head. "No. It's what I do. And I'm fucking good at it."

Donoghue laughed. "Beck, you were never any fucking good at anything."

Beck took a pace forward. "We'll see. We'll fucking – "

Brady had never seen a man move so fast. Donoghue took one stride forward. Leapt up off his left leg. Time stood still. Beck open-mouthed. Donoghue's body horizontal in the air. Then his right foot exploded into Beck's face. Sent him crashing down. The baseball bat spinning away.

Donoghue was on him before he had chance to recover. Slammed his knee into the small of Beck's back. Reached into his pocket. Produced a zip tie. Had Beck handcuffed in twenty seconds.

Looked up. Winked at Brady. "Boy fucking scout. Be prepared. Just one more job..."

He stood up. Looked around him. Took three paces to his right. Picked up the baseball bat from where it had landed. Walked back. Rolled Beck over. Looked down at him. "Like I told you, son. Never any fucking good at anything."

Raised his right arm. Smashed the baseball bat into Beck's stomach. Nodded in satisfaction.

Looked at Brady, still on his hands and knees. Still gasping.

"You want to keep the evidence?"

Didn't wait for a reply. "I didn't think so."

Threw the baseball bat over the cliff edge. Smiled at Brady. "What fucking evidence?"

Stood up. Pulled Brady away from the cliff edge. "Let's not take any risks shall we?" Looked at him.

He cares...

"Try and relax. One muscle at a time. It'll pass."

Heard Beck moaning. Let go of Brady. Walked over to him. "He's got a daughter. He's a fucking good man. So shut the fuck up."

Walked back to Brady. Bent down. Put his arm round Brady's shoulders. Lifted him up.

"What do you want to do with him, boss? There's an easy answer. Gets your girl off the hook. Cut the cable ties. Give him a push. Saves a shitload of paperwork as well."

Brady managed to shake his head. "No, Gerry. I'm a copper. Not judge and jury. I'm tempted. But no. I've a daughter. I have to do it right."

Donoghue nodded. "No problem. We've got company anyway."

Brady forced himself to turn. Still on his hands and knees. Ordered his neck muscles to work. Looked up at her.

"Frankie, meet Gerry Donoghue. Gerry, Detective Sergeant Frankie. And could one of you call the bloody cavalry?"

Michael Brady, forty-four in a months' time, 'far too old for this physical crap,' felt his arms give way. Lay down on the cliff top. Wondered if he'd ever stop hurting.

Felt Gerry Donoghue tugging his shoulder. Rolling him over.

"Sorry, boss. One more job. You've still got the taser barbs in you. You should've kept your coat zipped up, old son." He looked up at Frankie. "You up for this? I'll hold him down, you pull the buggers out. They're barbed. It's going to hurt like hell. So there's no point messing about."

Frankie bent over Brady. Tore his shirt open. Went to work.

80

Brady leaned back against an old fence post. Looked up at Donoghue. "I've got a question. Two questions."

"You in any fit state to ask questions?"

"Yeah. Feel like I've run a marathon. Been in the gym for an hour. Like I've been hit by lightning. All at the same time. But..." He nodded. "I'm good. Well, not bad."

"Go on then."

"Beck. You knew him. How?"

"I told you, didn't I? Thirty blokes under me. For three months he was one of the thirty blokes. Then he was posted to Germany. Heard he got a dishonourable discharge. Not surprised."

"He'd have pushed me over."

Donoghue nodded. "He would."

"Except he talked to me. Wanted to justify what he was doing."

"You got lucky, boss. Don't dwell on it."

"What you did. That was impressive. More than impressive."

Donoghue laughed. Shook his head. "No it wasn't. I could have showed off. Japanese headlock. Remind me to demonstrate."

"What's that?"

"I jump. Land on his shoulders. Legs either side of his head. But it's the sort of bullshit you do on Bank Holiday Monday. Unarmed combat exhibition for the punters. Edge of a cliff? Bloody nearly dark? Kick him in the bollocks. Pull him backwards. The old ways are the best."

"So I saw..."

"No trouble pushing a middle-aged woman off a cliff. But he'd only done basic training."

"And you haven't?"

"Me? No, I spent a few days playing with the big children, didn't I?"

Brady nodded. "I'm glad. Thank you. He had a code name. Alias. Something he used online."

"That sounds about right for Beck. What was it? Superman?"

"Ares."

"Aries? Like the star sign?"

"That's what I thought. And your birthday..."

"You were convinced it was me?"

"That. A hundred reasons. I'm sorry. But Ares. A – R – E – S. The Greek God of war. Of clearing up the crap after the battle.

"Right, we've done that. So we can move on. You had two questions."

"You followed me. How?"

Donoghue gestured to his left. "In the field. A bit bloody muddy. A couple of fences to get over. But yeah, in the field. A hundred yards away. Two hundred. But I was there."

"I didn't see you."

"You weren't looking for me. Head down, focused. Lost in your own thoughts. Hope you don't mind me saying this. You wouldn't have lasted five minutes in Bagram."

Brady laughed. "Just as well I had a guardian angel then."

Gerry shook his head. Nodded at Frankie. "You haven't, boss. You've got two."

Brady forced his neck muscles to work. Looked up at Frankie. Croaked, "I gave you an order."

"You did. I disobeyed it. I turned round. Walked a hundred yards towards her house. Then I realised I had a choice." Frankie looked down at him. "You or Maggie Stokes? I chose you."

Brady nodded. "Thank you. Get my phone out of my pocket will you? Inside pocket. Phone her. Tell her it's done."

"And if she doesn't answer? It doesn't mean anything, Mike. People go to bed."

She did answer.

"Mrs Stokes? This is Detective Sergeant Thomson. I'm a colleague of Mike Brady's. He's asked me to ring you. He's er... Slightly indisposed right now. No, no, he'll be fine. But he asked me to tell you it was done. Yes, those were his exact words. Phone her. Tell her it's done."

"Frankie – "

She paused. Turned to Brady. "What, boss?"

"Tell her I'll see her in the morning."

"Mrs Stokes? Sorry. He's says he'll see you in the morning. Yes, that's what he said."

Frankie ended the call, passed the phone back to Brady. "She's worried about you. And she said yes, tomorrow morning."

"That's good." Brady tried to sit up. Felt the muscle spasms in his chest. "Fuck, I can't do it."

"It doesn't last," Frankie said. "The first five minutes are the worst. Or was it the first five days... But you need to go to hospital, boss. Get checked over."

Brady shook his head. "Ten minutes in the shower, Frankie. Paracetamol. I'll be fine. Did you phone the cavalry?"

She nodded. "Cartwright. Keillor. They're on the way."

"Thanks. Frankie... Just give me two minutes will you? With Gerry?"

She stepped away. Went to check on Beck.

"Magic said something. Said I should listen to your story."

Donoghue nodded. "Yeah, reckon I owe you that. Now?"

"Good a time as any. Bagram. Afghanistan. I was working with – Too late."

He stood up. Nodded at lights in the distance. "The cavalry. My cue to leave."

Brady gritted his teeth. Rolled over onto his hands and knees. Held on to the fence post for support. Forced himself to stand up. Looked at Gerry.

'He doesn't do official...'

"Go on then. Get yourself off."

"He can't," Frankie said. "He's a witness."

Brady shook his head. "No he isn't, Frankie. He's just out for a walk. It was me and Beck. Only ever me and Beck."

"Boss, he tasered you."

"No, he didn't Frankie. I got lucky. Had my coat zipped up. It's a puffa jacket. Windy on the cliff top. The barbs caught in the coat."

Frankie looked sceptical. "In which case, boss, the coat will have rips in it."

"That's fine. I never liked it."

Brady turned painfully to Gerry. "Thank you. Again. I'm not sure I'll ever stop saying thank you."

Gerry shook his head. "You're welcome. Enjoyed it. Like the old days."

"Have you got somewhere for tonight?"

Gerry nodded. "I'm sorted. Little place up the road."

Brady laughed. "Give Magic my best. And tell him thank you. For the message. And Gerry... I know you'll be off. I need to say goodbye properly. Day after tomorrow?"

"Cup of mint tea? I'll be waiting."

81

"You want me to come in with you, boss?"

Brady shook his head. "No, Frankie. It'll be fine. Five minutes, no more. Tell, Jake. And you'll go back with her in the patrol car?"

"No problem. You sure you're alright?"

Brady laughed. "You want the honest answer? No. My ribs hurt like hell. But I can move. And Archie wouldn't take 'no' for an answer."

Brady climbed carefully out of the car. Made his ritual check on the solar pump.

Not working. And I don't see the garden being high on Cam Stokes' priority list...

Was surprised to find the front door slightly open. Pushed it. Stepped into the hall.

"Maggie?"

No answer.

"Maggie?"

Brady walked into the kitchen.

The empty kitchen.

"Maggie? Are you in?"

She can't have gone. Can't have...

'So after you took your original suspect out for breakfast and lost him... Then you told the woman who organised the murder when you were going to arrest her. Gave her the chance to abscond...'

'I trusted her.'

'It's not a problem, Brady. I'm sure the HR department at B&Q will understand...'

"Maggie! Where the hell are you?"

Gone.

Or worse.

'I've enjoyed knowing you, Michael. Clearly I was never meant to reach Switzerland.'

No! No, no, no...

Brady took the stairs two at a time. Stood on the landing. "Maggie! Answer me. Where are you?"

"I'm in the bathroom," she said quietly.

Brady pushed the door open. Found her staring at one of Cam's pictures.

She turned to him. Smiled. "I can't even have a pee without a bloody moose staring at me. Remember me saying that? I realised I'd miss the old bugger. I'm saying goodbye."

Brady nodded. "Thank you..."

For not killing yourself? I can't say that...

"For being here. I was worried – "

"That I was going to run away? Or commit suicide? That if I could buy cannabis and a killer I could buy a convenient cocktail? I thought about it. But... You stopped me."

"*I* stopped you? I didn't do anything."

"You did. You were prepared to risk your life. Because you owed it to your daughter to do the right thing. Suicide is... well, it's not the right thing. Not for me. And – "

"You didn't think Aethelflaed would approve?"

She laughed. "There you go again. Like I said, Michael, too clever for your own good."

Brady hesitated.

I should take her down to the car. Let Frankie and Jake take over. But...

"I've a question."

Gerry. Maggie. All I bloody do is ask questions...

She nodded. "Why did I help you? Apart from being in your debt."

"Yes. I was lying awake wondering."

Along with wondering if that bastard has broken my rib...

"Because you needed it. Because you *had* to find the killer. Because there's something inside you. What are you going to do, Mike? Spend the next ten or fifteen years arresting people in Whitby? I don't think so."

"I've got a daughter."

"Of course you have. And she'll always be your daughter. But she'll make her own life. And it won't be in North Yorkshire. Where does that leave you, Mike? Fifty? On your own in Whitby? So that's why I helped you. I haven't got long left. You have. And you can make a difference."

82

Brady watched Maggie get into the patrol car. Frankie get in after her.

Heard his phone ring. Glanced at the display. Smiled to himself.

Kershaw.

"It's sorted, sir."

"What's sorted? This Macdonald business?"

"Everything. The firebomb, his wife. Everything. Sorted. Resolved. Put to bed."

I can hear the sigh of relief from 200 miles away...

"So I can hold my head up again in this nest of fucking vipers, can I?"

"You can, sir. We've arrested a former soldier. He pushed Diane Macdonald over the cliff. A hired hitman. And we've arrested the woman that paid him."

Although whether she'll ever stand trial is doubtful...

"She paid him to kill Macdonald's wife? And the firebomb?"

"No, not the firebomb. That was on his own initiative. He

hated politicians. Said he wouldn't piss on one if he was on fire – "

"He has my sympathy."

" – Something going back to Afghanistan. There's not enough evidence for a conviction. But there'll be no more firebombs in Runswick."

"I don't care about a prosecution. Just so long as you've put a stop to it."

"I have. With a lot of help from DS Thomson."

"Good. Bloody good, Mike. Well done. Our reputation is intact."

You mean your reputation...

"There's some more good news as well."

"What's that, sir?"

"This task force I'm on. The Home Secretary has extended it for another 12 months. So you'll have to go on coping without me, I'm afraid."

"That's brilliant news, sir. For you, I mean."

"Maybe you'll get chance to come down, Mike. That dinner invitation's always open. Come and sample the corridors of power."

Brady put his right hand behind his back. Did what he'd done as a schoolboy.

"There's nothing I'd like more, sir."

Finished the call. Uncrossed his fingers.

83

"You've got a hole in your chest, Michael Brady. In fact – "

Siobhan traced her finger three inches lower. Across to the right. Stopped above Brady's fourth rib. Felt him wince.

" – You've got two holes in your chest. And a bruise the size of County Cork. Last time I was in your bed you didn't have two holes. What are you doing? Two timing me with a vampire who's lost her reading glasses?"

Fuck it. I've lied to her enough.

"I was tasered."

"Tasered? With a gun? The thing that's on the news? That kills people?"

"On the cliff top."

"And kicked?"

Brady nodded. "And kicked. Hard."

"So the straightforward arrest wasn't even remotely straightforward. And you were in danger."

Brady shook his head. "No, not really. I had back-up. Frankie."

The back-up I told to turn round and go back. Who would have arrived too late. If it hadn't been for Gerry...

Siobhan pushed herself away from him. "I asked you if I should be frightened."

Brady ignored the pain. Reached for her. Siobhan shook her head. "You're forty-four next month – "

"I know."

"And then forty-five – if I'm allowed to look that far ahead. I'd like you to see forty-four *and* forty-five. I'm sure Ash feels the same way."

"I know. We've talked."

She's forgiven me. 'The red coat didn't suit you anyway, Dad.' That sounded like forgiveness...

"Not to mention Archie."

"What is this, Siobhan? Blackmail?"

"No. It's someone telling you what you need to hear. You're too old for it, Mike. You know I like complicated men. Men with a death wish, I'm not so sure..."

"It's not a death wish. It's anything *but* a death wish – "

Because I looked over the edge. And didn't like what I saw...

" – But I told you before. The people I deal with aren't normal people. They don't play by normal rules – "

"And they don't care if they taser you on a cliff top."

Brady pulled her to him. Winced again. "There's something I want to say. I'm going away. A couple of days. Just after my birthday."

"A training course. How not to get tasered on a cliff top."

Brady laughed. "No, not a training course. I'm taking you to the Forest of Bowland. It's beautiful. We're going to walk up Pendle Hill. Chat to the local witches. Stay in a converted manor house with a four-poster bed. You can write the Witch Concerto."

"There's no-one lying-in-wait at the top of the hill?"

Brady shook his head. “I promise. There might be my old boss waiting at the bottom. He doesn’t live very far away. I’d like you to meet him. He can tell you what I was like at twenty-six.”

She leaned forward and kissed him. Traced the back of her nail between the two holes from the taser. “And what were you like at twenty-six?”

“Reckless? Impulsive? Obsessed by the case I was working on? Convinced I knew best?”

“Completely different then...”

84

orning, Frankie. All good?"

"All *very* good, boss. I'm on leave from tomorrow. Apparently my walking boots are calling."

"Scotland?"

"Where else? But I'm assured that 'it's nae midge season nae more' so it should be alright."

"I'm jealous. I'll think of you when – "

The phone rang on Brady's desk. "Boss?"

"What can I do for you, Sue?"

"I just wondered if you'd seen the news this morning?"

"No, nothing. Walk Archie, drop Ash at school, straight in here. Start the paperwork. Not even had breakfast."

Brady glanced up. Mouthed 'Go to Dave's' at Frankie.

"So you've not heard anything?"

"Nothing. What's happened?"

"I won't spoil the surprise, boss. The BBC website is probably a good place to start."

Brady looked at Frankie. "Something's happened. Sue says I need to check the news."

"Before or after Dave's?"

"Judging by her tone of voice, before."

Brady sat down at his desk. Pulled his keyboard towards him. Clicked his shortcut to open the BBC site. Hoped Frankie didn't notice that it opened on the football page.

Clicked news.

Saw the white lettering on the red background: *Breaking.*

Read the headline.

British MP arrested after cash found in taxi

Read the three paragraphs that followed it.

Started to smile...

Conservative MP Graham Macdonald has been arrested after a briefcase – allegedly 'stuffed with cash' – was handed in to police by a London cab driver.

Graham Macdonald has been the MP for Mid-Hampshire since 2005 and is a member of the Commons Defence Committee. Taxi driver Chuck Collins said, "I knew he was important 'cos he kept telling the girl he was with. He said she was his niece. I thought it was odd because she had a foreign accent. Russian maybe. I dropped them outside an apartment building. Then my next fare said someone had left a briefcase in the back. She said I should hand it in to the police so that's what I did. I was proper gobsmacked when I heard it was full of readies."

This breaking news story is being updated and more details will be published shortly. Please refresh the page for the fullest version.

"Well, well," Brady said. "Have you read that, Frankie?"

"Over your shoulder. As you say. Well, well..."

"What in God's name was he doing?"

"We know what he was doing, boss. Not thinking about his briefcase..."

'When Macdonald's end comes it will be nasty. And brutish. But I doubt it will be short...'

Nasty? You might be right, Simon. And brutish? Trial by tabloid ticks that box. Especially when his 'niece' sells her story...

Brady shook his head. "I think the body of my enemy has just floated past me."

"Or driven past in a taxi."

Brady laughed. "Right. And I can tell you one thing for certain."

"What's that?"

"Lochie's neighbour can relax. Graham Macdonald won't be coming back for Reggie any time soon. They don't allow dogs in Dartmoor."

Brady stood up. "I think we should celebrate, Frankie. The Ritz? Champagne and canapes? Or Dave's?"

"Dave's, boss. Every time."

"Dave's it is. And then I'll finish the paperwork. Before we go for a walk on the cliffs..."

85

"What is this, boss? Magical mystery tour?"

"It's the Cleveland Way, Frankie. In all its glory. Early autumn. The sun shining, a seagull floating up to you on a thermal. What more do you want?"

"An idea of where we're going?"

Brady shook his head. "You don't need one. We're here. Once we've squeezed through this gap in the hedge. Mind the blackcurrant bushes."

The farmer had ploughed the stubble. They walked in single file along a narrow track at the side of the field.

"I was worried," Brady said. "My manners. The first time I came I didn't know whether to knock. Magic's got a tarpaulin for a front door."

"Anyone in?" he called. "Visitors."

MAGIC LIFTED THE TARP BACK. Saw Frankie. "You've done it, haven't you? She's from the Council. Come to assess me."

Brady laughed. "Frankie, this is Magic. Magic, Frankie.

And you don't need to worry. I blindfolded her on the way here."

"How are you doing today, boss?"

"And the other miscreant you've already met. Like I said the other night, Gerry. Not good, but not bad. I'll mend."

Magic nodded at a couple of upturned farm crates. "Sit yourselves down. Seeing as we were having company I nipped out to Ikea."

"Tea," Gerry said. "What's it going to be, Frankie? Magic wasn't cut out for a career in hospitality. Mint or nothing. But fair's fair. It's good for your digestion. Chamomile? Helps you relax. Raspberry leaves? Supposed to be good for the change so they tell me."

Frankie laughed. "Not for a few years. Mint's fine."

Gerry reached for a mug. Made a show of finding the least battered one. Put mint leaves into it. Poured hot water onto them and handed the mug to Frankie. Turned to Brady.

"You going to have some, boss? Nettle tea? Magic's got some growing outside. Stops your prostate getting enlarged if you're having problems ... Sorry, Frankie, didn't mean to make you snort mint tea down your nose."

"Whatever's best for healing," Brady said. "Peppermint, is that the one?"

"Your ribs? Still hurting? Cow dung poultice probably. Magic, is there any shit in the fields? I'll make you some peppermint while Magic has a look."

They sat down. Magic swirled his tea round the chipped mug. "Gerry an' his bloody herbs. Healing this, healing that. If he stays any longer I'll live to a thousand. Truth be told there are mornings I'd kill for a cup of Yorkshire Tea."

Brady laughed. "I'll see what I can do. You at the church in the morning?"

"I am, assuming Him Upstairs agrees with the BBC forecast."

"Right. One of my lads will drop you a box in. Fruit cake to go with it alright?"

"Fruit cake'd be champion. Might persuade him to stay."

"No." Gerry shook his head. "I'm getting restless. Need to be off. But before I go – " He looked at Brady. "I owe you a story."

"If that's alright."

Gerry nodded. Stood up. "Bring your tea. We'll stand on the cliff top. Enjoy the best view in the world."

"Frankie? Can I leave you with Magic for five minutes? Persuade him not to make a poultice? Gerry and I – "

"No problem, boss."

86

"You remember what I said? Thirty blokes under me?"

"Plus the knob from Sandhurst who thought he was in charge?"

"Right. And they were knobs. With one exception."

McMahon. But don't say anything. Listen to the story.

"Leo McMahon."

"He was your CO?"

Gerry Donoghue shook his head. "McMahon wasn't anyone's CO. Sort of floated between regiments. Mine for a while. Public school, Oxford, Sandhurst. Everything that should have pissed me off. But it didn't. What the fuck possessed him to join the Army I have no idea. He could have been anything. Done anything. Politics, business, media. Anything. He spoke Pashto for fuck's sake. Brought up somewhere out there. And there he was. The wild fucking west. And we talked. Christ how we talked. Late at night. Tactics. Politics. Military History. Or he talked and I listened. And then one day he disappeared. Not a word. 'Where's McMahon?' No-one knew."

Brady finished his tea. "Undercover?"

"As undercover as it gets. We found out later he was working as a garage mechanic. Don't ask me how. In between Homer and Plato and the fall of Rome he's picked up bloody mechanics."

"How did he – "

"How did he pass for an Afghan? His mother was Italian. So he was dark. Went to sleep clean-shaven and woke up with a beard. Then one day the boss comes for me. Time to get him out. He wants me to drive to a village ten miles east of Bagram. 'It's dangerous, Gerry,' he says. Dangerous? Understatement of the fucking year. But it's McMahon, so off I go in a battered jeep with a shit-scared corporal for company."

"Something went wrong?"

He nodded. "The battered fucking jeep went wrong. I'm fifteen, twenty minutes away. The drive shaft goes. Obviously I improvise. Wave someone down. Tell him to get the fuck out of the car. But I'm twenty minutes late."

"It's not your fault the jeep broke down."

Gerry shook his head. "Of course it's my fault. Rule number one. Test the kit before you go into battle. I should have taken it for a drive. Fifty, sixty miles."

"You didn't?"

"No, I didn't. 'Cos I've got my weekly call to the fucking wife, haven't I? Trying to persuade her not to leave me. 'At least wait while I get home.' 'It's too late, Gerry.' Well I was too fucking late for Leo McMahon, that's for sure. I get there. Pull over. Tell the corporal to stop crapping himself."

He turned. Looked along he cliff path. "From here to that bush. Close enough to see him being bundled into the back of a truck. Hood over his head."

"You were sure it was him?"

Gerry nodded. "Would you recognise your daughter? Of course you would. Someone you love, you recognise their body shape. The way they move. Even with three fucking Taliban holding him."

"Love?"

"Not like that. I cared. He was... fuck knows. I told you before, I don't do feelings. Try not to. But McMahon? Yeah. One part hero, one part teacher, one part the brother I never had."

He paused, finished his tea.

"That do you?"

Brady nodded. "What happened?"

"I drove back to the barracks."

"No-one tried to stop you?"

"No. I was the messenger boy wasn't I? They wanted us to know they had him. One of the bastards – I can see him now – they throw McMahon in the back of the truck and he turns and waves to me. How did he know I'd be there? You tell me."

"What happened back at the barracks?" Brady said.

Not that I don't know the answer...

"I reported to the boss, didn't I? He listened. Made notes. Looked weary. Told me it wasn't his decision. Told me to take the weekend off."

Gerry shook his head. Stared out to sea.

"We had one of theirs," he said. "They could have done an exchange. But the word was the politicians said no. So we kept their guy and the Taliban kept McMahon. You can use your imagination on what they did to him. And now he's on some fucking Godforsaken hill. Baking in the summer, freezing his bollocks off in the winter. Metaphorically."

Brady didn't speak. Didn't know what to say.

"Politicians," Gerry said. "All the fucking same. You know how long they kept him alive?"

"No. I can't guess."

"Three months. Three fucking months. They let us know. Sent us his kneecap back. The one they'd drilled through."

"I'm sorry," Brady said uselessly.

"There you go. That's the story. You read your Dickens? Jacob Marley? 'The chain I forged in life.' That's mine. Leo McMahon. Come on, we'd better get back. Let's talk about something more cheerful. How long will Beck get?"

Brady laughed. "I'm not sure that's the definition of cheerful. It depends on the tech trail. When they've been through his laptop. Diane Macdonald wasn't the only one. And there was a footballer the other week. Tasered and beaten up. Fairly sure he'll recognise our boy if he can limp into the witness box."

Gerry nodded. "Sounds good to me."

GERRY LIFTED THE TARP. Frankie looked up. "Magic's been telling me his story."

Brady nodded. "Saturday night in Swansea? I did some checking. Why didn't you tell me, Magic? Your mate – two weeks after the local politicians refused planning permission for a homeless shelter."

The tramp looked up at him. "No idea what you're talking about."

Brady laughed. "Yeah, you have. I thought at first it was Gerry. Then I realised – "

He'd have done the job properly. But let's not say that...

"But then I realised it wasn't."

"So I'm busted twice am I? Council tax on this place and now I'll be doing Community Service."

Brady looked at Frankie. "What do you think, Detective Sergeant?"

"I'd say there was no evidence, boss."

"Right. Then there's identification. We don't even know the suspect's name."

"Magic Pockets..."

"No chance, Frankie. Magic Pockets? The judge would laugh us out of court. Besides, I've already told Kershaw it was Beck."

"So case closed."

"Case *very* closed, Frankie. Like the Reverend Haworth, eh, Magic? What did it say on his gravestone? 'Blameless and exemplary?' Sounds about right to me. And we need to be on our way."

Gerry walked across to his backpack. "Me too, I'll walk down to the end with you."

"Not going back to Whitby?"

"No. Going north. Going to see my lad. Teenager now. Needs to know he's got a real man for a dad. Not the pasty-faced arse she's living with." He walked across to Magic. Put his arm round him. "Take care, mate. I'll see you again. Let me know when the double-glazing's been put in."

THEY WALKED down the track by the side of the field. Pushed through the hedge. Stood on the cliff top. Frankie looked at Donoghue. Took a step forward. Kissed him on the cheek. "Thanks," she said. "For saving him. I'd have missed the bacon sandwiches."

Gerry laughed. "I figured it was something like that. You take care."

"You too." Frankie started walking down the path. Left them alone.

Michael Brady looked at the man who'd saved his life. "I don't know what to say. 'Thank you' isn't adequate. It'll never be adequate."

Gerry shook his head. "Yeah, it will. And you've one last question."

"I have... If you'll answer it."

"Saturday morning. Why did I piss off?"

"Yes."

"McMahon. Leo bloody McMahon. I thought he was a one-off. I'd never come across him again. And there he was. Sitting by a bandstand in Whitby. Eating a bacon sandwich. Telling me his story."

"Do I want to hear this?"

Gerry shook his head. "You probably don't. But you've got what McMahon had. You're like the fly. And maybe what you want is right in the middle of the spider's web. You know the risks. McMahon knew the risks."

"But he went anyway?"

"But he went anyway. And you'll do the same. So that's why I went. I didn't want to be around to watch it happen. Not a second time."

"Except you came back."

Gerry nodded. "Right. I came back. Must be getting soft in my old age. Maybe I thought I could save McMahon this time."

Brady held his hand out. "You did. Thank you again. Any time you need a bacon sandwich... You know where I am."

"I do. You take care, boss."

He bent down. Picked his pack up. Slung it on his back.

Turned. Started walking north.

Brady watched him.

Until the path bent to the left. Until Gerry Donoghue disappeared.

STOOD WATCHING the path for another minute.

Finally turned. Walked back to Frankie.

"All good, boss?"

Brady nodded. Didn't trust himself to speak.

Finally got his emotions under control.

"We need to get back, Frankie."

"Why the hurry, boss? What did you say? The Cleveland Way in all its glory? Stop and smell the roses. Or the seaweed..."

"I'm cooking. I'd forgotten. Ash is bringing Spence round for dinner."

Frankie looked at him. Smiled. "She's told me about him. She likes him."

Brady laughed. "*I* like him, Frankie. First serious boyfriend. I thought dads were supposed to disapprove."

"Father of the Bride, boss. You'd better start working on your speech."

Michael Brady shook his head. "Not for a good few years, Frankie. There's plenty of water to flow under the bridge first. Down the Esk. And into Whitby Harbour..."

REVIEWS & FUTURE WRITING PLANS

Thank you for reading *The Edge of Truth*. I really hope you enjoyed it.

If you did, could I ask you to leave a review on Amazon?

Reviews are important to me for three reasons. First of all, good reviews help to sell the book. Secondly, there are some review and book promotion sites that will only look at a book if it has a certain number of reviews and/or a certain ratio of 5* reviews. And lastly, reviews are feedback. Some writers ignore their reviews: I don't.

So I'd appreciate you taking five minutes to leave a review and thank you in advance to anyone who does so.

SALT IN THE WOUNDS (MICHAEL BRADY: BOOK 1)

His best friend has been murdered, his daughter's in danger.

There's only one answer. Going back to his old life.

The one that cost him his wife...

Salt in the Wounds is the first book in the Michael Brady series. It's available on Amazon as an e-book, paperback and audiobook.

"Fabulous! Had me gripped from the start. Reminds me of Mark Billingham's detective, Tom Thorne."

"Loved the book from the first page. Straight into the story, very well-written. Roll on Brady 2."

"Loved everything about this book. A gripping plot with unexpected twists and turns. Believable characters that you feel you really know by the last page. I could smell the sea air in Whitby..."

THE RIVER RUNS DEEP (MICHAEL BRADY: BOOK 2)

Good people do bad things

Bad people do good things

Sometimes it's hard to tell the difference...

Gina Foster's body has floated down the River Esk.

It looks like an accident. But Michael Brady has his doubts.

It's a year since his wife died. He's back in the police force, trying to prove himself to a new boss. And be a good dad to his teenage daughter.

Is it murder? Or does Brady need it to be murder?

Brady's convinced the answer lies in Gina's past. But his boss is doing everything he can to stop Brady finding out what that past was.

The River Runs Deep is the second book in the Michael Brady series. Again, it's available on Amazon as an e-book, paperback and audiobook.

"Really love this crime series. Believable characters and good pace to the storylines."

"Another fabulous book. The characters are really developing, the story is well told and there are enough twists and turns and dead ends to keep you on your toes. Great new series to follow."

"The depth of the characters is so good I couldn't stop thinking about the story for weeks after I'd finished it."

THE ECHO OF BONES (MICHAEL BRADY: BOOK 3)

"Find her for me, Mr Brady. I know she's dead. I know I'll never see her again. But find her. Give me a place to go on her birthday. Christmas Day. Somewhere I can take her teddy bear. Lay flowers. Find Alice for me, Mr Brady. Please..."

It's 20 years since Alice went missing.

There's never been any trace.

Until now.

Until some bones are found in a shallow grave on the cold, bleak North York Moors.

But is it Alice?

Or Becky? The other girl – who disappeared a month earlier...

Two local girls: two families that have finally learned to live with their grief.

But now Michael Brady must tell one family their daughter has been found.

And break the bad news to the other family.

No-one was ever convicted. Everyone's convinced the killer is in jail.

Everyone except Brady.

Brady has to re-open the old wounds. He has to find the real killer. And he has to stop seeing the similarities between his daughter and one of the murdered girls.

With the local families waiting for the 'killer' to come out of jail, with a boss determined to stop him discovering the truth – and without Frankie Thomson to help him – this is a case that affects Michael Brady like no other.

"Mike Brady is such a likeable character you want to become his friend, go for a drink with him or give him a hug when he obviously needs one. I've read all three Brady books within a week."

"Another Brady book I simply could not put down. Excellent story, brilliant dialogue. Had me hooked straight-away. And a real feeling of loss when it ended..."

You can buy *The Echo of Bones* on Amazon.

CHOKE BACK THE TEARS (MICHAEL BRADY: BOOK 4)

Michael Brady looked at Sandra Garrity's face. Grey skin. Bloodshot eyes open. Blue lips, her tongue protruding.

"Did you watch your husband die, Sandra? Or did he watch you die?"

"Brilliant. Brady is fast becoming the Yorkshire Rebus."

Billy and Sandra were childhood sweethearts.

Writing their names on a lovelock. Fastening it to the end of Whitby pier. Throwing the key into the sea.

A lifetime together. A happy retirement in a peaceful hamlet on the North Yorkshire Moors.

Until the day they were brutally murdered.

"Whoever did this – he didn't do it quickly. And he enjoyed it..."

Billy was a fisherman, making a living in the cold, cruel North Sea. One night his boat went down. Two crewmen drowned. Billy survived.

Are the families looking for revenge? It's the obvious conclusion.

But why have they waited so long?

Why have they killed Billy *and* Sandra?

And why kill them in such a barbaric way? 'This isn't a murder, Mike. It's an execution. A medieval execution.'

Choke Back the Tears is the fourth book in the Michael Brady series.

Kershaw's away, Brady's in charge. The bucks stops on his desk. But at least Frankie Thomson is back to help him. For now...

There are no clues. No motives. It's a perfect crime scene.

All Brady has is his experience and his intuition. And his small team is getting smaller by the day...

Meanwhile he's battling problems in his personal life. His daughter Ash wants to know the truth about her mother's death. Brady can't put off telling her any longer.

He's having doubts about everything.

Even the memory of his dead wife...

You can buy *Choke Back the Tears* on Amazon. It's available for the Kindle and as a paperback.

JOIN THE TEAM

If you enjoy my writing, and you would like to be more actively involved, I have a Reader Group on Facebook. The people in this group act as my advance readers, giving me feedback and constructive criticism. Sometimes you need someone to say, 'that part of the story just doesn't work' or 'you need to develop that character more.'

In return for helping, the members of the group receive previews, updates and exclusive content and the chance to take part in the occasional competitions I run for them. If you'd like to help in that way, then search for 'Mark Richards: Writer' on Facebook and ask to join.

ACKNOWLEDGMENTS

As always I'd like to thank my Reader Group on Facebook for their support, encouragement and help with the proof-reading.

But my biggest thanks, not for the first time, go to my wife, Beverley, for her advice, insight, plot suggestions and – most importantly – patience. I especially need to thank her for the conversation about local legend that led to Magic Pockets – as she'll remind me...

Mark Richards

March 2023

Printed in Great Britain
by Amazon